KISS OF THE DAY

Sometime during the morning hours Daniel had taken off his flannel shirt, leaving him clad only in a navy blue T-shirt that clung to his chest. Gwen eyed that chest with a great deal of appreciation.

Daniel's gaze settled on her mouth. "Do you have any idea how tempting your mouth is?"

Anticipation rushed through Gewn's body. "Is this when you finally kiss me?"

A small smile tugged at the corner of Daniel's mouth. "Yeah, I believe it's time, don't you?"

Daniel's hand came up and softly cupped her cheek. The pad of his thumb slid across her lower lip. "You've been driving me crazy, do you know that?"

"No, but it's nice to know."

"I've never kissed a person who was signing my paychecks before."

"I'll stop signing them if it will make you kiss me."

Daniel chuckled and slowly shook his head. "I don't think one kiss is going to be enough."

Gwen reached up and cupped the back of Daniel's head. Soft silky hair slid through her fingers. She definitely wanted more than one kiss from Daniel, but she couldn't think of a more perfect place to start. . . .

BOOK YOUR PLACE ON OUR WEBSITE AND MAKE THE READING CONNECTION!

We've created a customized website just for our very special readers, where you can get the inside scoop on everything that's going on with Zebra, Pinnacle and Kensington books.

When you come online, you'll have the exciting opportunity to:

- View covers of upcoming books
- Read sample chapters
- Learn about our future publishing schedule (listed by publication month *and author*)
- Find out when your favorite authors will be visiting a city near you
- Search for and order backlist books from our online catalog
- Check out author bios and background information
- Send e-mail to your favorite authors
- Meet the Kensington staff online
- Join us in weekly chats with authors, readers and other guests
- Get writing guidelines
- AND MUCH MORE!

**Visit our website at
http://www.kensingtonbooks.com**

CATCH OF
THE DAY

Marcia Evanick

ZEBRA BOOKS
KENSINGTON PUBLISHING CORP.

http://www.kensingtonbooks.com

ZEBRA BOOKS are published by

Kensington Publishing Corp.
850 Third Avenue
New York, NY 10022

All Kensington titles, imprints and distributed lines are available at special quantity discounts for bulk purchases for sales promotion, premiums, fund-raising, educational or institutional use.

Special book excerpts or customized printings can also be created to fit specific needs. For details, write or phone the office of the Kensington Special Sales Manager: Kensington Publishing Corp., 850 Third Avenue, New York, NY 10022. Attn. Special Sales Department. Phone: 1-800-221-2647.

Zebra and the Z logo Reg. U.S. Pat. & TM Off.

First Printing: February 2002
10 9 8 7 6 5 4 3 2 1

Printed in the United States of America

To my husband, Michael
You're my very own "Catch of the Day,"
who I caught over twenty-four years ago.
I'm never throwing you back in.

Prologue

Millicent Wyndham looked away from the computer screen to stare out the huge bay window that overlooked the harbor of her beloved Maine town, Misty Harbor. Not a soul braved the cold winter's day and the fierce gusts of arctic winds battering the weathered docks. Spring would be coming soon. February only seemed like the longest month after so many months of winter. She had to wonder if there would be any souls left in Misty Harbor to enjoy the warmer weather once it finally arrived. Her town was losing residents faster than a politician lost votes after a sex scandal. If her late husband, Jefferson, were still alive, he would know what to do. Jefferson Wyndham would have moved heaven and earth to save his town.

The Wyndham family fortune had been made long before Jefferson had even been born. The Wyndham Shipyard had produced the finest clipper ships in the country, in their time. The shipyard was long gone, but not the pride or the harbor from which those glorious ships had sailed. The Wyndham family line had ended with Jefferson, and it had been all her fault. She had offered Jefferson a divorce when she learned, after years of trying, that she couldn't conceive a child. It had been the only time in their forty-six years of marriage that Jefferson had lost his temper. Jefferson hadn't swept her off her feet in Boston when she had been only eighteen, and married her within six months, for children. Theirs had been one of those truly remarkable society marriages. They had married for love. Misty Harbor had become their child.

Now it was dying.

Money alone couldn't solve the problem. She'd learned that over the past eight years, since Jefferson's death. What Misty Harbor needed was an influx of females. Unattached, single, marriageable women. The young women of the town who left for college either met their sweethearts there and got married or went on to get an education and moved to a bigger city to use it. The girls who didn't go to college moved to bigger cities looking for adventure, better-paying jobs, and the freedom those metropolises offered. The young men of Misty Harbor were following the women. She couldn't blame them. Why have dreams of getting married and raising a family when there weren't any women within easy reach?

A chime from the computer pulled Millicent from her depressing thoughts. This afternoon she had logged onto her favorite cooking chat room because the topic, ''Lobster'' was one she knew an awful lot about, and she had been bored. At seventy-two years of age, daytime television held no appeal to her. So far she hadn't learned anything new about cooking lobster, had contributed her favorite recipe for lobster Newburg, and had reacquainted herself with an Internet friend, Gwen Fletcher. Gwen was a chef in a very prestigious Philadelphia restaurant and had visited this same chat room many times. Their last discussion had turned into a two-hour debate on the merits of marinating fish. Gwen was a wonderful, intelligent woman who obviously enjoyed all aspects of cooking. Gwen was also young and single.

She read Gwen's message for the third time and then stared thoughtfully out the bay window. The corner of the empty restaurant down at the harbor was barely visible from where she sat. The red-and-white FOR SALE sign seemed to glow in the pale afternoon light. A slow smile curved her lips, and if she hadn't known better, she would have sworn Jefferson had a hand in giving her the idea.

She barely noticed the twinge of arthritis in her hands as her fingers flew over the keyboard.

> *Gwen,*
> *I can't even begin to imagine what a restaurant in Philadelphia would cost. Have you ever considered buying one, say on the coast of Maine? The ocean, with all its delicious bounty, will be right outside your door. Lobster, cod, flounder, tuna, mackerel, striped bass, and clams, to name only a few. Picture colorful bobbing boats, fresh fish every day, and contented customers opening up their wallets and coming back for more.*
> *Millicent Wyndham*

A moment later the computer beeped with Gwen's response.

> *Millicent,*
> *Sounds like heaven to me. Owning my own restaurant has been a dream of mine for years. Been saving*

*just as long too, but I really don't see that dream
turning into a reality anytime soon. The sad truth
is, cooking is the easy part of owning your own
restaurant. Do you have any idea on what a set of
pots cost? It's mind-boggling.*

Gwen

Millicent smiled and took the "sounds like
heaven to me" as a definite sign from Jefferson.

Gwen,
*What about a fully equipped, reasonably priced res-
taurant? Maybe not the top of the line pots, but
good, solid quality. Loyal local patrons all year
round and a tourist season that lasts for months.*
Millicent

She held her breath and waited only a few heartbeats. Technology was a wonderful thing. Jefferson
would have loved the Internet.

Millicent,
*When you find such a dream, you let me be the first
to know.*

Gwen

Millicent's laughter startled Bangkok, her Sia-
mese cat, from his afternoon nap in front of the
fireplace. Bangkok gave her an indignant glare,
circled twice, and then laid back down to continue
his nap in front of the dancing flames. Lord, this
was too perfect to pass up.

Gwen,
Now that you mention it . . .

Chapter One

Gwen Fletcher stood in the middle of the restaurant and felt a sense of pride, awe, and, deep down inside, a touch of fear. That fear wanted to raise its ugly head and scream at her, "What have you done? Are you insane?" She refused to listen to that voice and instead concentrated on the positive things, as her grandmother always told her to do.

She was positively insane.

At twenty-six years of age, she was now the proud owner of a little restaurant overlooking a picturesque harbor on the coast of Maine. The amazing part was, she had nearly bought the place over the Internet. When her cyberfriend, Millicent Wyndham, told her about the small restaurant, she had been intrigued enough to ask for more information. Within a day, she had downloaded a half dozen pictures, a complete inventory list, and the asking price from Misty Harbor Real Estate. The real estate agent had felt that the current owners would definitely come down on the price. They had, and within two weeks she had found herself driving up Interstate 95 heading for Maine. One walk through the restaurant and she had known she would have signed over her soul to own it. Luckily her soul wasn't required, just the small inheritance her grandmother had left her, her life's savings, and payments for the next ten years.

Her Grandmother Augusta would have been proud of her for reaching for her own dream.

She poured herself another cup of coffee and glanced around at her dream. As dreams went, it wasn't anything to write home about. Yet. The previous owner either had had an eye condition that reacted to the sun's brightness, or he had been a vampire. The walls of what had been Ahab's were all darkly paneled, and navy blue café-style curtains covered the huge bay windows that overlooked the quaint harbor and side courtyard, where customers could enjoy their meals once the weather warmed up. Two entire windowless walls were lined with darkly stained wooden booths that were so tiny that only small children would be comfortable squeezing into them, and that was debatable. She had tried out one of the booths and within minutes made the decision that they had to go. A person couldn't enjoy a meal while being crammed into a sardine can. The threadbare, dingy brown carpeting would also have to be replaced, and the two dozen red plastic lobsters would definitely have to come down off the walls. Their beady black eyes were creeping her out, and the plastic bibs tied around their necks and the silverware hot-glued into their claws had to be someone's idea of humor. It wasn't hers.

There was a lot of work to be done, and she only had six weeks to do it. She wanted to be open for business by late April. That would give her a couple of weeks of mostly local customers before the official start of the tourist season. If she could please the locals, the tourists should be a snap. What she needed was an additional ten hours to every day and the undying devotion of an ambitious carpenter. She also needed a competent staff and some time to put her rented cottage into some semblance of order. She had arrived in Misty Harbor on Friday with her car loaded with essentials. By five o'clock the restaurant was hers, and so was the small rental cottage on Conrad Street, two blocks from the harbor. The moving van, filled with all her earthly possessions, had arrived six hours behind schedule on Saturday. So far she had only managed to unpack a grand total of eight boxes. Her furniture was at least in the proper rooms, and so were the neatly labeled stacks of boxes. It would have to do for now.

Gwen knew she couldn't do anything about the hours in the day, but the carpenter had been handled. At least she was hoping it had been handled. The real estate agent had highly recommended Daniel Creighton, a local. Mr. Creighton had returned her call on Saturday and had agreed to meet her this morning at the restaurant. Gwen glanced at her watch. Mr. Creighton wasn't late; she was just anxious to get started. Every day that went by was one less day 'til the opening. She couldn't afford to waste any of them. She had hated to waste Sunday, but she had put it to good use. The Internet was a wonderful thing. She had already ordered tables and chairs to replace the booths and some additional pots and pans for the kitchen. Linens and curtains were next on her list, but she wanted to confer with the carpenter to make sure what she was visualizing could, in reality, be accomplished.

The front door to the restaurant opened and

Gwen quickly turned to greet the carpenter, who was ten minutes early. The enthusiasm she had been feeling since Saturday's phone call slowly faded. This was Daniel Creighton? On the phone Saturday, she had gotten the impression of a younger man, say forty or maybe fifty years younger. The man standing in her restaurant smiling at her as if he had just won the lottery had to be at least seventy years old, and a weathered, sea-hardened seventy at that.

"Hello, may I help you?" She crossed her fingers and stuck her hand behind her back, praying this wasn't Mr. Creighton. Hopefully he was some local just dropping by to introduce himself or a lobster fisherman wanting to sell his daily catch.

"They said you were beautiful." The old man respectfully took off his baseball cap and ran his fingers through his gray wavy hair. "I owe Clarence a lunch now because I didn't believe him."

Gwen didn't consider herself beautiful. When she looked into a mirror the words *ordinary* or even *wholesome* described what she saw. Never beautiful. Her sisters were *beautiful.* Her brown eyes were too big and her lips too full. Her nose could only be described as pert, and her straight brown hair had the tendency to turn red whenever it saw too much sunlight. She was used to people complimenting her on her cooking, but never her looks. A flush threatened to sweep up her cheeks at the compliment. "Thank you. Whatever you're selling, I might be buying." She smiled at the man standing in front of her. She had no idea who the sweet-talking Clarence might be. She hadn't met very many people in town yet. She would have remembered a Clarence. "Who's Clarence?"

"He's the old cuss who owns the bait shop next to the pier." A wide, dazzling grin showed a set of dentures that must have cost the equivalent of a nice mid-size car. "Don't even think about Clarence; he's too old for you." The grin widened and a spark of mischief gleamed in eyes the color of a storm-tossed sea. "I'm closer to your age, and besides, I still have my driver's license. The state took Clarence's away when he drove down the boat loading ramp and into Cutter's Cove thinking it was a parking lot." A rough chuckle filled the room as he held out his hand.

Gwen placed her cup of coffee on one of the empty tables and shook his hand. She could feel the hardened calluses across his palm, but his grip was nice and firm. Carpenter hands. "Gwen Fletcher."

"Jonah Creighton, and I'm not selling a thing, little lady." Jonah's fingers gave her a light, flirtatious squeeze before he released her hand. "Heard you can cook."

She glanced around the dimly lit room and tried not to laugh. "Well, I am opening a restaurant, so I guess you heard right." He was Jonah Creighton, not Daniel Creighton.

"What are you planning on serving?" Jonah looked around the room, as if he expected to see a smorgasbord spread out before him. Jonah seemed disappointed by the half-filled coffeepot and the stack of clean cups beside it.

The answer to Jonah's question seemed obvious to her. What dockside restaurant, in a quaint coastal town in Maine, wouldn't specialize in lobster? She had a feeling Jonah Creighton could handle a joke. "Lunch and dinner."

"Beauty and wit is a rare combination in a woman." A gleam of amusement danced in Jonah's gray eyes. "I was meaning, what kind of food are you planning on serving?"

"I know you were, and since this *is Maine* . . ."

"Please don't say lobster." Jonah visibly shuddered as he interrupted her words.

"What's wrong with lobster?" She glanced out the window to the tiny boats bobbing in the harbor. There was a rocky shoreline on the other side of the inlet. It sure looked like Maine to her. If someone dressed Jonah in period clothes, he would pass for a sea captain on a whaling ship. Having Jonah shudder at the thought of lobster would be the equivalent to a Texas cowboy turning his nose up at a thick, juicy steak. It was just darn unpatriotic. "You don't like lobster?"

"Of course I like lobster; it's in the blood." Jonah banged his baseball cap against his leg and sprinkled the dismal carpeting with a few shattered snowflakes. Technically it was spring, but winter hadn't released its icy grip on Maine yet. "It's just that a man can only eat so much lobster without growing claws and antennae. Heck, I'm even developing a phobia toward pots of boiling water."

"Oh." She was at a loss for words. Visions of lobster Newburg, steamed lobster, boiled lobster, lobster bouillabaisse, and lobster chowder were quickly deflating from her crustacean-filled mind.

"Every restaurant within fifty miles of this place serves lobster. Heck, even the McDonalds three towns over serves a lobster roll value meal. Everywhere you turn someone is serving up lobster and plastic bibs."

"I didn't think of that." Gwen sat down in one of the chairs, rested her elbows on the table, and started to massage her temples with her fingertips. She was stunned. A throbbing started behind her eyes and spread toward her temples. Each pounding pulse called out another way she had been planning on serving up lobster.

"Ah, Gwennie, I didn't mean to upset you so. The tourists love lobster. You'll be cooking up so many of those ugly critters that you'd be glad to fix something else once in a while for the locals."

"You're right, Jonah. Even cowboys in Texas would get sick of steak three hundred and sixty-five days a year."

"That's why there's chili." Jonah beamed. "You can make chili, can't you?"

"Hot enough to set your tonsils on fire." The throbbing was easing slightly. Maybe all wasn't lost after all. "What else would you like to see served, besides chili?"

"I would drive twenty miles for homemade meat-loaf and real mashed potatoes, not that instant paste that comes out of the box." Jonah licked his lips in anticipation, pulled out a chair, and sat down across from her. A warm callused hand reached for hers and tenderly squeezed. "Gwennie, darling, I would get down on bended knee and ask for your hand in marriage if you can make a Yankee pot roast half as good as my beloved Margaret's was."

Gwen felt tears burning in her eyes as she tried to think of a way to tell the man sitting across from her that she had never cooked a Yankee pot roast in her life. Jonah's proposal was the sweetest thing anyone had ever said to her, and as soon as she got back to her cottage this evening she would be pouring over her cookbooks, looking for a recipe. She knew Jonah wasn't serious, but the way he had said "my beloved Margaret's was," told its own story. Jonah had lost his love, and he missed her still. Neither she nor Jonah had heard the front door open, or heard the man who had stepped inside in time to hear Jonah's proposal.

"Grandfather!"

Gwen pulled her hands out of Jonah's grasp and turned around to stare at the man standing in the dimly lit entryway holding a clipboard. Her first impression of him was big. The man had to be over six feet tall, and with a heavy winter jacket on, he looked like an enormous bear coming in from the cold. Snowflakes dusted his broad shoulders and his light brown hair.

"Go away, Daniel; can't you see I'm courting?" Jonah glared at his grandson and tried to reach for Gwen's hands again.

Gwen stood up and nervously tucked a lock of brown hair behind her ear. This was Daniel Creighton, her carpenter? The man appeared big enough for any job she might come up with, and then some. She certainly wouldn't have any second thoughts about pressuring Paul Bunyun here into hurrying the job along. With Jonah, she definitely would have had problems. Daniel Creighton appeared to be able to handle anything she could throw at him. "Jonah, I believe your grandson is here to see me."

"Well, he can just get in line." Jonah stood up and tossed his baseball cap onto the middle of the table, as if he was declaring war with his own grandson. "Two's company and three's a crowd."

Gwen rolled her eyes. "Jonah, be nice or I will have to rethink the Yankee pot roast and eliminate meatloaf from the menu altogether." She stared at Jonah's pretend look of horror and noticed the amusement dancing in his eyes. Jonah appeared to be having the time of his life. His enjoyment was either at her expense or Daniel's, she wasn't sure which. She gave Jonah a disapproving frown, just in case his silent laughter was directed at her, and took a step toward Daniel Creighton. Maybe she should clarify a few things just in case Daniel was getting the wrong idea about what he had just interrupted. After all, the man had just heard his grandfather propose marriage to a woman young enough to be his granddaughter. "Jonah was just giving me some advice on the menu, and he wasn't above bribery to get his own way on an entree or two."

"The only thing my grandfather knows about cooking is how to read the microwave directions on the back of the box or how to say 'Supersize it' when he wants a larger portion of fries. My advice to you, Ms. Fletcher, is not to believe a word he tells you." Daniel Creighton stayed in the shadowy depths of the entrance and didn't move a step forward.

She stopped halfway across the room and studied the man with the deep voice and the shadowy face. The entryway needed to be lightened up. She couldn't have her customers hiding in the shadows. Since she couldn't see Daniel's face, she concentrated on what she could detect, and that was his voice. Daniel's voice seem to rumble up from the depths of his massive body and wrap itself around her soul. For one breathtaking moment she thought she had felt something fluttering in the depths of her stomach.

Impossible. She never got flutters in her stomach unless she was in the kitchen and a soufflé was refusing to rise or some other culinary disaster was transpiring. "Jonah seems to think that I should have something on the menu besides lobster."

Daniel seemed to be staring at his grandfather, but a note of interest had crept into his voice. "Like what?"

"Meatloaf, chili, and Yankee pot roast have been mentioned." Maybe Jonah had been right. That little hitch of interest in Daniel's voice spoke volumes. "What kind of meals would you like to see served?"

"Gwen says her chili is hot enough to melt tonsils." Jonah beamed with pride as he moved closer to her and nudged her arm with his elbow. "I think I'm in love, boy."

She chuckled at Jonah's outrageous fib. The man was shameless. Adorable, but shameless.

"In today's world, Grandfather, that's called sexual harassment."

"Complimenting a woman's cooking is considered sexual harassment? No wonder the world's going to hell in a handbasket," grumbled Jonah.

"Jonah, you haven't tasted her cooking yet. How do you even know she *can* cook?"

She shot Daniel a look that should have withered his socks and all ten of his toes.

"Gwen's opening a restaurant; of course she can cook." Jonah sounded about as indignant as she felt.

"I didn't say she couldn't cook. I said you can't compliment her on her cooking without tasting it first. It smacks of bribery or something just as politically incorrect."

Her gaze narrowed on the man standing in the entry of her restaurant. Maybe Daniel didn't have ten toes nestled in his warm winter socks and thick workman's boots. Maybe he was cloven-footed.

"Bah on political correctness. They got it so that a man can't say what's on his mind anymore."

Daniel gave a heavy sigh. "Ms. Fletcher, I would like to apologize for anything my grandfather might have said that . . ."

Jonah started blustering, so she gently laid her hand on his forearm. "There's no need to apologize, Mr. Creighton. Jonah didn't offend me in the least. In fact, he helped me out tremendously in regard to the menu I'll be serving." She gave Jonah's arm a light, friendly squeeze. "His honest and politically incorrect opinions are not only welcome, but they were asked for."

"As I said before," chuckled Jonah, "smart and beautiful."

"Thank you, Jonah." She gave him a wide smile.

"Why don't you go help yourself to a cup of coffee while Daniel and I discuss some business?"

"Business?"

"It seems your grandson comes highly recommended as a carpenter, and since I'm in dire need of one ..." She let the sentence trail off. The conclusion was obvious.

"Daniel's the best in these here parts. You can't do better." Jonah turned and headed for the coffeepot. "The coffee's not that fancy-tasting stuff, is it? You know, the kind that tastes like lady's perfume?"

"No, Jonah, it's one hundred percent of Columbia's best. Regular, not decaf. Is that all right?"

Jonah gave a deep chuckle and reached for a cup. "Anytime you want to get married, you just give me a yell, and I'll contact the preacher."

"You'll be the first to know." She chuckled along with Jonah as she turned to face Daniel once again. Daniel stood two feet away from her.

She hadn't heard his footsteps as he stepped out of the shadows and crossed to where she was standing. The man was over six feet tall and moved as silently as a cat. The first thing she saw was a masculine tanned throat disappearing into layers of clothing. There was a dark brown coat, now unzipped, and a thick green-and-black plaid flannel shirt with the bright white edging of a polo shirt underneath. Daniel Creighton appeared to be nice and toasty warm. She, on the other hand, had gone past warm and was working her way to hot. Whatever possessed her to put on a turtleneck under her thick sweater this morning? Just because the weatherman had announced it was only eighteen degrees outside didn't mean the temperature wouldn't be spiking upward. She tilted her head and raised her gaze past the neatly trimmed beard and mustache to a proud, straight nose and a jagged scar that bisected his left cheek, then disappeared into a light brown beard. The breath she hadn't known she had been holding lodged in her throat when she finally encountered his eyes. Daniel Creighton's eyes were smoky gray and swirled with so many emotions she was at a lost to pick out just one.

The strange fluttering in her stomach returned with a vengeance. Daniel seemed to be studying her face for her reaction to him. The last thing she wanted was for Daniel to know just how off balance his appearance had thrown her. Instant lust was as foreign to her as T.V. dinners and instant coffee.

She took a steadying breath, prayed that Daniel hadn't noticed the fiery flush stealing up her cheeks, and held out her hand. "Gwendolyn Fletcher, proprietor and chief cook of this restaurant. Please call me Gwen."

Daniel wrapped his large hand around hers and shook. "Daniel Creighton, carpenter."

Gwen felt the heat of Daniel's hand spike its way up her arm. Incredibly, her fingers actually started to tremble at the mere touch of his callused palm and fingertips.

Daniel released her hand and quickly turned away. He removed his coat and draped it over the back of a chair.

Gwen frowned at Daniel's back and wondered what had caused his abrupt dismissal of her. Her mind quickly moved on to other things as his coat left his broad shoulders. She had been wrong. Daniel wasn't a massive bear of a man. He was tall, but his well-worn blue jeans showed slim hips, long legs, and one of the nicest-looking rears to ever fill out a pair of jeans. If she were Italian, she would have kissed the tips of her fingers and declared Daniel's derriere *"Bellissimo!"*

"Ms. Fletcher?"

She came out of her daze and realized that Daniel had asked her something. She hadn't a clue as to what he had said, besides her name. "I'm sorry, I didn't catch that. I was distracted." There was no way her face could get any redder.

"I asked if you are ready to give me a tour of the place and explain what you would like done." Daniel gave her a funny look.

Gwen glanced away from him and encountered Jonah's amused grin from across the room. The older man was leaning against a table, with a hot cup of coffee cradled between his hands. By the laughter gleaming in his eyes she knew Jonah had seen exactly what had distracted her.

She was wrong. Her face could and did get redder. A freshly boiled lobster had nothing on her blush.

Chapter Two

Daniel Creighton glanced away from Gwen Fletcher and had to wonder if the woman was sick or coming down with something. Gwen hadn't sounded sick, but her face was now beet red and she wouldn't meet his gaze. It was a strange reaction. He was used to meeting people for the first time and having them stare at the ragged scar that slashed diagonally down his cheek to disappear into his beard. People usually stared in curiosity or repulsion. Men tended to be more curious; women, especially beautiful women like Gwen, were horrified.

Here he had thought people's reaction to his scar didn't bother him any longer. He didn't like the idea that he had been lying to himself. When he had first spotted Gwen sitting there with his grandfather he had wanted to turn around and walk back out the door. He didn't want to start his day by seeing disgust, horror, or even pity in another beautiful woman's eyes. As it was, he held his ground, but it still took him a couple of minutes to move out of the shadows and into the light.

Strange thing was, Gwen's gaze had slid past his scar without even a flinch, and when he had looked into her big brown eyes there hadn't been revulsion, horror, or even pity there. There had been interest. For one blinding moment he had felt like he used to feel when confronted with an attractive woman. Until he had felt Gwen's fingers tremble within his grasp. Within that moment the spell the gorgeous restaurant owner had been weaving around him had shattered and he quickly dropped her hand.

Gwen didn't pity him; she feared him. She just hid her reaction better than most people. It was as simple as that.

His gaze skimmed the dimly lit restaurant, and he purposely ignored his grandfather, who was watching him and sadly shaking his head. Jonah had been riding him lately about finding a nice girl and settling down. Why anyone was in such an all-fired hurry to become a great-grandfather was beyond him. The last thing he needed was for Jonah to start playing matchmaker. Disney was the only one who could make the fairy tale *Beauty and the Beast* work. He glanced back over at his potential client and asked, "Do you want to start in the main room here, since this is where most of the work you told me about Saturday morning will take place?"

"That sounds good," said Gwen. "I have some stuff to show you. Ideas and things-I-like kind of stuff."

He watched as Gwen hurried over to where the coffeepot sat and picked up a manila folder sitting there. For barely hitting the five-foot-four-inch mark, the woman sure could fill out a pair of jeans. He'd like to show her some of the stuff he liked.

He cleared his throat and pulled his mind away from the gutter and his awakening hormones. "Since there seems to be a lot you want done, and not a whole bunch of time to do it in, I think we should prioritize what you have to have done before you open for business."

Gwen frowned as she glanced around the room. "Oh, I want it all done before I open. I want Catch of the Day perfect when I open the doors for business."

"Catch of the Day? Is that what you're calling the place, Gwen?" asked Jonah. "I like it. It has a nice ring to it. Better than Ahab's, which always reminded me of dead white whales."

"I don't want anyone thinking of dead whales, white or otherwise, while eating here, Jonah," answered Gwen as she handed Daniel the folder.

"Let's see the list first, before I make any promises of it being perfect on its grand opening." He opened the folder and frowned at the half-dozen ripped magazine pages and paint chip cards. "There's no list?"

"I have a master list that I've have been compiling since I decided to buy the place, but it's a list of everything, not just carpentry jobs." Gwen went back over to the coffeepot and refilled her cup. "Daniel, would you care for a cup of coffee while I walk you through the place?"

"Thanks; I take it black." The rich fragrance of freshly brewed coffee had been driving him nuts since he walked into the place. There was also the scent of something else, something like fresh bread baking, with a touch of cinnamon mingling with it.

Gwen filled another cup and handed it to him. "I think the ceiling's okay. A couple of the lightbulbs have burned out, but they should be easy to replace."

He took a sip of coffee and glanced up at the rows of white ceiling tiles with the occasional fluorescent tube lighting under a clear panel. Half the lights were out, which explained why it was so dim in the place. "I'll check them out for you, but I wouldn't be surprised if one or two fixtures were totally shot and had to be replaced." He clicked his pen and started to write on the pad of paper attached to his clipboard. "They aren't hard to replace, so it's not a major job."

"Okay." Gwen walked over to a booth and shook her head. "All the booths have to come out. I already ordered tables and chairs to replace them."

He raised his eyebrows and counted fourteen booths against two walls.

"What? You don't think they should be replaced?" Gwen frowned down at a chipped and nicked wooden tabletop. Someone had carved a huge heart with the words ANNA LOVES JASON inside. She was all for love, just not notched into her tabletops.

"I haven't been able to sit in one of those booths since junior high. I think they should have been ripped out fifteen years ago." He wrote "Remove booths" on the paper. He cast a quick glance at the base of the booth and shook his head. "It's going to ruin the carpet."

"The carpet is already ruined, in case you haven't noticed. I'm having it replaced, but not until all the carpentry work and painting is done."

"What about the walls behind the booths? When I rip them out of there, it's going to leave some mighty big holes."

"I don't know. Do you think you can spackle them?"

"That's doubtful." He glanced at the other side wall, where a single small window and door overlooked the side courtyard. "Is that where you want the two patio doors to go?"

"Yes. I want to bring as much natural light and ocean breezes as possible into the place."

"That should do it." He liked the idea of opening up that far wall. "The doors are going to cost you big time, because they have to be super-insulated because of the winters up here."

"I already considered that, but I believe they will be worth the extra cost." Gwen went over to one of the two huge bay windows facing the harbor. Dark navy blue curtains obscured the enchanting view. "I checked these out already. The windows go up and down, but I want you to look them over. See if they are usable or if they have to be replaced."

He continued to write as Gwen went on about the front door that seemed to stick a lot and the ugly dark paneling, complete with the red plastic lobsters that just had to go. The more Gwen talked, the more he had to agree with her. He could practically visualize everything she wanted done with the place. It was an added bonus when he took on a job that he appreciated and enjoyed. He was constantly amazed at some of the ugly and ridiculous things people were willing to pay a carpenter to build. When Gwen finally wound down enough to take a breath, he asked, "What about the kitchen?"

"Kitchen?" Gwen glanced at her watch and cried, "The buns!"

Amused, he watched and fully appreciated the view as she hurried from the room. Both swinging doors to the kitchen rocked in her wake. He glanced over at Jonah, who grinned and silently mouth the word *buns*. His grandfather appeared to be on the verge of drooling. He didn't blame the older man. The swinging doors were fanning in the aroma of baking cinnamon buns into the room. He felt like drooling over Gwen's buns too, and not the ones baking in the kitchen.

"Caught them just in time!" shouted Gwen from the kitchen.

Jonah rubbed his hands together and headed for the kitchen. "Need any help in there, Gwennie, my love?"

The muffled sound of Gwen's laughter rippled down his spine. He shook his head in disgust with himself and his R-rated imagination, poured himself another cup of coffee, and sat at an empty table. What he needed to do was concentrate on business, not Gwen's or anyone else's buns. He opened the folder and sorted through the torn magazine pages. He could see where Gwen had gotten some of her ideas and exactly the kind of patio doors she was looking for. He wished more of his clients would be so resourceful and thoughtful. There would be no second-guessing Gwen's wishes.

"Ah, Daniel, wait until you taste Gwen's buns," said Jonah. His grandfather joined him at the table and slid a plate containing two steaming cinnamon buns dripping with sweet white icing in front of him. "Careful; they're still hot."

He locked his back teeth together and stared down at the picture of some restaurant clutched in his fist. Just thinking about tasting Gwen's buns was causing a distinctively male reaction in his body. It was a good thing he was already sitting down. The table would hide the adverse effect. He blinked away the mist of desire and studied the glossy page. Gwen had circled the wainscoting, about chair-railing high, and the nice arrangement of paintings hung on the wall above it. Casual, comfortable, yet classy.

Just like his current client. Gwen looked casual in the red knit sweater and the white turtleneck she had on under it. Tight jeans that ought to be banned from cardiac care units of hospitals because of the effect they would have on male blood pressure, and brown boots completed her comfortable outfit. The classy part was understated, and that was his first clue that Gwen was familiar with sophisticated living. Gwen wore little jewelry, but what she wore was top of the line and classic. Not a ring graced her elegant fingers and he couldn't see a necklace, but the tiny gold beads in her ears were the real thing. It only took one glimpse of her watch to know it didn't come from any mail-order catalog, and on her right hand he had counted three different gold bracelets. One of the bracelets held pea-sized sapphires.

"Sorry to have kept you waiting. I just put on a fresh pot of coffee." Gwen slid into the chair on his right. She brought along the rest of the cinnamon buns and a small stack of colorful napkins. "I like the wainscoting. It breaks up the solid wall nicely." Gwen nodded to the picture in his hand. "Think it would look okay in here?" Gwen took a bite of a bun and scooted her chair closer to his, then reached for the folder.

"It would look great, and it will save me from worrying about the holes in the walls when I rip out the booths." He watched Gwen's hair slip from behind her ear and swing against her cheek. The straight brown strands, cut evenly with her chin, appeared silky soft. Her cheek looked like satin and her lips were full and sensual. Perfect for kissing. Not only was Gwen Fletcher gorgeous, she smelled like cinnamon and vanilla. It was a hell of a combination. He didn't know what he wanted to do more, kiss Gwen or eat her.

"I want the wainscoting left natural, but protected, so cleaning won't be a problem." Gwen handed him a paint chip card with four colors of blue on it. An unpolished and blunt-cut nail tapped the third from the left shade of blue. *Summer's Morning Blue.* "The top portion of the walls will be painted this color."

"Good choice." He pointed to the pictures hanging on the wall of the magazine page. "You plan on hanging paintings of cowboys and horses?" The photo clearly showed canvases filled with stern-faced cowboys, magnificent horses, scruffy cattle, and beautiful scenery.

Jonah snorted as he polished off his second cinnamon bun. "No cowboys in Maine, Gwen." Jonah eyed the plate of buns sitting in the middle of the table. "Did you taste Gwen's buns yet, Daniel? I swear, they are sweeter than heaven and they melt right in your mouth."

He didn't want to think about Gwen's buns melting in his mouth or even in his hands.

"I was planning on getting some paintings of Maine's coast to hang. You know the kind: surf pounding the rocks, lighthouses, bobbing boats, and maybe a puffin or two." Gwen finished her bun and then slowly licked the tips of her fingers.

Daniel could practically feel the pull of those sensual lips and the swirl of that small pink tongue against his own heated skin. The woman was dangerous just eating. How in the hell was he going to concentrate, being around her constantly for the next several weeks? "If you want good quality paintings, stop in at Wycliffe Gallery in town. Ethan only carries the best." He reached for a bun and took a big bite. Sweet heaven exploded in his mouth.

Lord save him, the woman could cook!

"Wycliffe Gallery sounds great." Gwen swiped his pen and wrote the name on a napkin. "Do either one of you know of someone looking for some temporary work? Physical, hard, and not the cleanest job. Preferably a man."

"What would he be doing?" asked Jonah after he got up and brought the coffeepot over to the table.

"Mostly scrubbing." Gwen held out her empty cup and smiled as Jonah filled it. "The kitchen is basically clean, besides some dust, but it's not good enough. I want it to shine. I want to be able to eat off the floor in there. Same with the bathrooms." Gwen glanced back at him. "Speaking of bathrooms, I think both sinks need to be replaced, and at least one of the toilets."

"I'll have a look." He reached for another bun. Gwen Fletcher was going to cause a riot in town. Not only was she gorgeous, she could cook. Every available man from nineteen to ninety was going to invade this place. His own grandfather had only been the first in what was surely going to be a very, very long line of suitors. Single females were a rare commodity in Misty Harbor.

"That's all this person has to do is clean?" Jonah had replaced the coffeepot and returned to his seat.

"Maybe some painting. Both bathrooms need a fresh coat, and so does the kitchen."

Jonah reached for the last bun. "Hunter could be your man, if he's interested."

"McCord?" Daniel hadn't thought about Hunter as a possible employee of Gwen's. It could work, if Hunter was interested, and there was no telling what interested McCord.

"What's wrong with this Hunter McCord person?" Gwen had written the name down on the napkin but was now looking at him as if something had just occurred to her.

"What makes you think something is wrong with him?"

"The way you said his name, that's all."

"Hunter is Clarence's son," Jonah said. "He grew up with my boy, Thomas, who's Daniel's father. Hunter was a fine boy, and a kind, quiet man. Won't hurt a fly, and a hell of a worker when he takes a job."

"What happened?" asked Gwen.

"The war changes some men. It changed Hunter." Jonah stared into his coffee cup. "Hunter lived for the water. That boy was either on a boat somewhere out in the ocean or was swimming. Couldn't keep that boy out of the water. He was going to follow his father into the lobster business." Jonah shook his head sadly. "He spent two years as a P.O.W. in 'Nam. Clarence says he never talks about it. Hunter doesn't talk much about anything. I haven't heard him string more than two sentences together in thirty-four years. Hunter keeps to himself and won't go near the water. If he's not doing an odd job around town, he spends his days standing on the shore staring out over the ocean."

"That's horribly sad," Gwen said.

"Could have happened to any of our boys, my Thomas included. The good Lord saw fit to return Thomas to us whole, and I thank him every day for that."

"The town's kind of protective of Hunter, but he's a hard worker once he takes a job." Daniel gathered up the magazine pages and placed them back into the folder. "Hunter turns down more jobs than he takes. There's no telling which jobs he takes, or for whom."

"How do I get in touch with him?"

"I could bring him by this afternoon," Jonah said. "That way you could show him what you need done, and he can decide for himself."

"Sounds great, but on one condition."

"What's that?"

"I need some local food testers, Jonah. Would you and Daniel consent to tasting some of my recipes? Hunter too, if he takes the job. I need to know if my chili's too hot for you New Englanders."

Daniel chuckled at his grandfather's pretend look of outrage and Gwen's too-innocent smile. The phrase "two peas in a pod" came to mind. "I think it's safe to say, if you make it, we'll eat it."

"I know you'll eat it, but will you give me an honest opinion about it?"

"Are you questioning our honesty?" This time Jonah's voice held real outrage.

"No, I'm questioning your kindness." Gwen gave Jonah a soft smile. "I don't need a 'Yes, Gwen. Everything taste delicious, Gwen.' I need you to tell me if the chili is too hot, or not hot enough. I need to know if my meat loaf is dry or the cod chowder is too salty."

Jonah flashed the dentures he was so proud of and patted his stomach. "Then I'm the man for you. Not only am I opinionated as all get-out, but not too many people in this town have been eating longer than I have."

"He's got you there, Gwen." Daniel finished off his coffee and rose. "In case you aren't aware of it, you have just created a monster: Jonah the food critic." He shook his head and headed for the bathrooms. "By the way, there was one thing wrong with the buns." He couldn't think of one thing wrong with the buns inside her jeans, but he was positive she wouldn't want to hear about his opinion on any part of her anatomy.

"What?" Gwen stood up and started to gather up the dishes.

"There weren't enough of them." He heard Jonah's laughter join Gwen's as he pushed open the door to the men's room and went back to work. Coffee break was over.

* * *

Gwen dragged a chair from the main dining room into the kitchen and set it by the small table she had hauled in earlier. There was a small office space upstairs, along with plenty of storage space and a tiny powder room, but it wouldn't suit her needs today. She needed a place to sit and gather her thoughts, as well as her lists, which were increasing by the hour. She also needed to be in the center of things and to keep an eye on the pot of chili simmering on the back burner of the stove.

She could hear Daniel banging on something in the dining room, and occasionally she could detect his faint mutterings. For hours Daniel had been measuring, inspecting, grumbling, and writing things down on his clipboard. At first she had thought his muttering to himself was cute. Then she realized the more he muttered and shook his head, the more he wrote. What Daniel was writing was his shopping list. She would have to pay for every item on that list.

As his list grew, so did her anxiety. To relieve that anxiety, she did what she always did when she got nervous. She cooked. After a trip to the local food store, she mixed up a pot of chili and baked two pans of corn bread to go along with it. The plan of action was to keep Daniel eating, so he wouldn't have time to keep adding to that list of his.

Her sisters, Jocelyn and Sydney, would die laughing if they knew she was about to feed a man until he burst just to save herself a few dollars. Fletchers didn't worry about money; they were all too busy overachieving to be bothered by something as trivial as balancing a budget. Sydney, who was three years older than Gwen, was a pediatrician at the top children's hospital back home in Baltimore.

Jocelyn, who was only a year younger than Gwen, was an assistant district attorney for the city.

Their mother was one of the top heart surgeons in the city and their father headed one of the choice cancer research facilities on the East Coast. One of their grandfathers was still the chairman on the Board of Trustees at Baltimore's biggest hospital. Her other grandfather had been Baltimore's district attorney when he had died unexpectedly. She had spent her entire life surrounded by people saving lives and fighting for justice. It had been daunting as a child, knowing she was expected to follow in their footsteps. She had tried for years to live up to everyone's expectations. Even managed to get in two years at a private college in North Carolina before admitting defeat and following her heart and her Grandmother Augusta's advice: Follow your dream, not other people's dreams.

Well, she was following her dream now, fragile as it was. She might not be out saving lives or making the streets of this country safer, but someone had to feed the doctors, the lawyers, and the Indian chiefs. It would take both Jocelyn's and Sydney's massive brain power to figure out how to bake a cake, and then it had better come in a box with explicit directions. Gwen might be the family's failure when it came to career choices, but she refused to allow her restaurant to fail. Catch of the Day was going to succeed if it took her twenty hours a day, seven days a week. She would prove to her family that she wasn't a total failure.

Gwen heard voices out in the main dining room and pulled her thoughts away from her family. Hopefully Jonah had returned with Hunter. She reached for the sheet of paper with the list of odd jobs she had just compiled. She wanted Hunter to know exactly what the job would entail. If he decided not to take the job, she would need the list when she called the nearest employment agency.

The doors to the kitchen swung open and Millicent Wyndham breezed into the room on a cloud of expensive perfume. "There you are, Gwen. Daniel told me I could find you in here." Millicent glanced around the kitchen with interest. "I hope you don't mind me dropping by."

Gwen stood up and greeted the older woman. "You're always welcome here, Millicent." She gave the woman a friendly hug. "I invited you anytime, didn't I?" Millicent was the first person she'd looked up when she arrived in Misty Harbor.

"I know, but you could have been just being nice." Millicent draped her coat over the back of Gwen's chair.

"I was being nice, but I was also telling the truth. You are always welcome." Millicent was dressed in gray wool slacks and a pink cashmere sweater that probably cost as much as four months' rent on the cottage she had just moved into. Millicent would fit in nicely with her family back in Baltimore. "If it wasn't for you, I would never have found this place."

"I take it you're still happy with your decision to move up here from Philadelphia." Millicent wandered over to the stove and lifted the lid on the simmering pot and grinned. "Chili?"

"What did you expect," Gwen laughed. "Lobster?"

Chapter Three

"Did you hear that Margaret Franklin is moving back to town?"

At seven-thirty the next morning, Gwen tried to ignore the conversation going on next to her in the frozen food aisle and glanced between the two shopping lists in her hand and the cart. One list was of cleaning supplies and the other was a half page of ingredients she needed for a couple of recipes she wanted to try. She had gotten everything on the lists, but the persistent feeling that she had forgotten something was still nagging her. She had only been in town five days and this was her fourth trip up and down every aisle in Barley's Food Store. After this trip, she could probably stock their shelves for them, or at least reorganize them. Whoever heard of putting bread crumbs in the noodle section, or stocking cat litter at the end of the produce aisle?

"Her last name is Pierce now, but I heard her husband left her and the kid."

Barley's opened at seven, and Gwen had planned on being their first customer. Quick in and out. She hadn't counted on every woman above child-bearing age to converge on the store for what appeared to be a marathon gab session. Women wearing fleece warm-up suits and L.L. Bean coats blocked just about every aisle with their shiny carts and nonstop chatter. Huge, overstuffed black or brown pocketbooks that appeared to contain everything from a complete pharmaceutical selection to road maps of every providence in Canada had replaced toddlers sitting in the cart's seat. Tuesday mornings appeared to be a tradition at Barley's. Gossip was flowing more freely than green beer on Saint Patrick's Day.

"Serves her right, she probably ran around on him too."

Gwen cringed at the nasty tone of the conversation, and the fact that the woman passing on the gossip didn't know all the facts. The "probably" said it all. Guilty until proven innocent. She was beginning to feel sorry for whoever this Margaret was without even meeting the poor woman. By the sound of it, this Margaret person wasn't going to have an easy time of it moving back here. She pushed her cart away from the sharp-tongued women and headed for the checkout counter. She needed to get to the restaurant and get everything ready before her first employee, Hunter McCord, showed up.

Yesterday afternoon Jonah had shown up with Hunter in tow just as she, Millicent, and Daniel had been sitting down to bowls of chili and freshly made corn bread. There had been plenty to go around. Jonah and Millicent had pronounced the meal delicious, and they both felt it was sure to be a huge success. Daniel thanked her, though he told her it needed more zing, but she had noticed that he managed to eat two entire bowls full of her unzinging chili. Hunter had politely and quietly thanked her and said, "It was good, ma'am."

After Millicent left and Daniel, with Jonah's help, went back to work ripping out the old booths, she had given Hunter a quick tour of the place and a detailed description of what the job would entail. Hunter had quietly followed her around and nodded his head to just about every one of her questions. He wasn't much of a talker. When she offered him the job, his reply made her laugh out loud. Hunter told her that, yes, he would take the job, because the town needed a restaurant, and he'd heard Barb Byler had just tried to poison her husband, Chris, by making his favorite meal, pork chops. Gwen had gathered from that very short statement that Barb wasn't a very good cook and that Chris was a very brave man. Poisoned pork chops aside, it meant she was almost guaranteed two very good customers.

Hunter would be showing up at eight. So would Daniel. She wanted to have the coffee on and the muffins in the oven before they both started work. She was a firm believer in caffeine being the giver of life. She didn't trust anyone before noon who didn't have at least three cups of coffee pumping through his or her system. She, herself, didn't even brush her teeth until there were at least two cups of pure caffeine running through her veins.

Baking the muffins was her way of combating the nervousness she was feeling at the prospect of spending nearly the whole day alone with Daniel. They would be heading out to one of those big home centers about forty miles away. Daniel had said he could pick up the paint and some basic hardware locally, but for the big items he needed to take a trip into Bangor. He needed her to come along so she could pick out some of the items, like toilets, bathroom sinks, and fixtures. She wasn't looking forward to being stuck in the cab of Daniel's pickup truck with him for miles. There was something about just being in the same room with that man that made her heart go all wacky and got her body all achy. The man was a walking, talking virus. Being cooped up in some tiny little space with him for more than five minutes was going to cause some serious damage to her nervous system. Baking muffins wouldn't inoculate her against him, but whipping up a batch of muffins beat popping Prozac.

"How's little Timmy adjusting to his cast?"

"He's doing real good. My grandson's a real trooper, just like his dad."

Gwen smiled to herself and pushed her cart into the line of the only register open at this time of day. The talk about little Timmy was more like the small-town gossip she had been expecting to hear. She was a big-city girl, born and raised. She was used to the anonymity of Baltimore and Philadelphia. Somewhere, deep down inside her, was a spark of something that was looking forward to living in a small, tight-knit community where one knew one's neighbors. Her foolish heart was picturing neighbors and good friends helping each other while being surrounded by white picket fences and old churches with stained-glass windows and tall steeples. She had taken one look at the white picket fence surrounding the cottage the real estate agent had shown her and agreed to the one-year lease before the key was in the front-door lock. She didn't regret her decision. The cottage was everything she thought it would be, or at least it would be once she finished unpacking all her boxes.

The cashier was a middle-aged woman wearing

an orange sweatshirt with the picture of a grinning moose on it and a name tag that was made out of brass and shaped like a lobster, proclaiming to all that her name was MURIEL. There was one woman in front of Gwen, who was busy unloading her cart onto the conveyor belt. Gloria asked the woman unloading her overflowing cart, "Did you hear that the sheriff hauled Scott Dunbar in last night for vandalism?" *Beep.* The electronic scanner picked up the price on the cereal box. *Beep.*

Gwen picked up a bottle of cleanser and wondered how good a job it was going to do on the refrigerator at the restaurant. She made a mental note to check out the cleaning supplies at the home center. They should have some industrial-strength cleansers.

"Poor Tess," sighed the woman as she loaded the black belt with packs of chicken, a couple of steaks, and a roast the size of a Christmas ham. "Like she doesn't have enough to worry about, being a widow and all." Two packs of pork chops and a whole chicken joined the pile. "I heard Scott pierced his eyebrow."

"Yes, and his tongue." The cashier scanned the meat. *Beep.* "Lord knows what else was pierced." *Beep.* "His father would roll over in his grave if he could see how Scott is turning out." *Beep.*

"Ben's not in a grave, remember. Tess had him cremated, and then his ashes were scattered from Abraham Martin's lobster boat onto the ocean."

Gwen closed her eyes and dropped the bottle of cleanser back into the cart. *I really didn't need to know that, did I? So much for my fantasy of skinny-dipping in the deep blue sea this summer with some muscle-bound fisherman.*

"God rest his soul." The cashier actually crossed herself, fleetingly glanced up at the ceiling, as if departed souls would be floating around the hanging Tide laundry detergent sign, and then scanned a gallon of milk. *Beep.* "Grace just came through my line, and she told me that Margaret is moving back in with her mother."

"I can't believe Margaret has the nerve to show her face back in this town after what she did."

Ah, we're back to Margaret and whatever sin she might have committed. Poor girl probably got a butterfly tattoo on her butt. No one seems to care that the woman's husband has left her, and that there is a child involved. Gwen watched as the cashier scanned the last item and started to bag the small mountain of groceries. So much for her rose-colored glasses where small-town living was concern. The sense of community and white picket fences came with a hefty price tag; by sundown not only would everyone within five miles know your business, they would have passed judgment on you too.

Fifty-two miles away, in Bangor, Maine, Margaret Pierce mustered up a smile as she handed her four-year-old daughter, Katie, another stuffed animal. It was either force herself to smile and act as if everything was normal or start crying. From experience Maggie knew once she started crying it would be a while before she would stop. Sometimes it seemed that for the last five years that was all she had been doing, crying. Well, no more. She was sick of crying. As the saying went, today was the first day of the rest of her life, and her new life didn't have any room for tears. The past was done, and there would be no turning back the pages of that book. Not that she wanted to. The past hadn't been that good. In fact, most of her recent past had sucked.

The only good thing to come from the past five years was Katherine Leigh Pierce, her daughter.

Katie was the reason she got out of bed every morning. Katie was the love of her life, and for that reason alone, she refused to regret some of the mistakes she had made in the past. Katie was also the reason she had taken nearly five years of Jeremy Pierce's crap. Every little girl needed a daddy, or so she had thought. Life was once again proving her wrong. Little girls were better off with no daddy than having a bad father. Jeremy was not only a terrible husband, he also failed miserably at fatherhood.

What kind of father didn't have time to spend with his adorable and loving little girl? One that was too busy boinking a coworker and climbing that corporate ladder. One that resented the hell out of having child support taken from his weekly paycheck for one moment of lust that happened almost five years in his past. Now, at twenty-six, Jeremy had a master's degree in one hand, the first rung of the corporate ladder in the other, and the whole world in front of him. His vision of the world didn't include a wife he didn't love or a little girl he helped create in a moment of beer-induced lust in his old dorm room. It didn't matter to Jeremy that Maggie had forfeited her own dreams by dropping out of college in her last year to wait tables to support them both and the child she carried. The only thing that mattered to Jeremy was his freedom and the blond coworker he had moved in with nine months earlier.

It was a hell of a way to end a marriage and a family, but end it had.

Yesterday the last tie had been severed. The divorce was final, and she and her daughter were moving back in with her parents. Temporarily. One year; that was all she needed to complete her college education. Then she could get a decent-paying job so she could support herself and Katie. No more waiting on tables and soaking sore feet after pulling a ten-hour shift. Her parents had told her that she and Katie could stay for as long as she needed to get her feet back under her. She loved her parents dearly, but at twenty-six years of age, it was time she stood on her own two feet. Katie was her responsibility, not her parents'.

She watched as Katie carefully kissed the pink fluffy bunny and then placed it into the large cardboard box with her other animals. "When is Grandpop coming, Mommy?"

She glanced at her watch. "About another hour or so. Your Uncle Gary is coming with him too." She reached out and playfully tugged on her daughter's ponytail. "Grandpop says he's going to need help loading all your toys into his truck." Her brother, Gary, had insisted on coming to help load what little furniture she had left. There wasn't much, but she appreciated her brother's help. Katie's bedroom set was coming with them, a portable television, and her grandmother's rocking chair that her mother had given to her the week before Katie's birth. There were also plenty of boxes. Five years of marriage and twenty-six years of living would fit in the bed of her father's pickup truck and the backseat of her own car. Everything else had been sold. There wouldn't be room at her parents', and most of it hadn't been worth the price of storage. For the past week, since she sold her used bedroom set to a neighbor downstairs, she had slept in Jeremy's old sleeping bag on the floor of her bedroom, surrounded by cardboard boxes filled with her clothes. She was actually looking forward to spending the night in her old childhood bed. Or at least her aching back was.

She wasn't looking forward to living, once again, in Misty Harbor. The small town held every one of her precious childhood memories. It also held her shame.

Katie placed a floppy-eared dog into the box. "Can I ride with Grandpop?"

"Not this trip, sweetie." She handed Katie a stuffed tiger that had been wedged between the bed and the wall. "This is the last of them."

Her daughter hugged the smiling beast and put him into the now-filled box. "Fred doesn't fit, Mommy."

"Sure he does." Why her daughter had named a jungle beast Fred was beyond her. Katie had named every one of her animals simple male names; there were only a few female animals to break the monotony. There was Joe the bunny, Sid the walrus, and Bill the cocker spaniel. When Katie threw a tea party for her animals, it always sounded like they should be playing five-card stud and downing a few beers instead of sipping imaginary tea and munching imaginary cookies.

She grabbed the roll of duct tape, pushed Fred into the box, and taped the box closed before Fred could exhale. "See, I told you so." She pulled a black marker from the back pocket of her jeans and wrote *Katie's stuffed animals* on the side of the box, and then added a goofy-looking bunny with big crooked ears and a smiling face and whiskers.

Katie giggled. "Can they ride with me to Grandmom's?"

"Sure thing, sweetie." Katie's was the last room to be packed up. Things were changing so drastically in Katie's young life, Margaret had wanted her daughter to have at least one room that was normal and stable. She was allowing Katie at least some measure of control by having her help pack up her own things. This way Katie would know nothing was left behind. "How about we do the bed now?"

Katie glanced between an empty box and the twin-size bed and giggled some more while shaking her head. Katie's red ponytail whipped back and forth like a real horse's tail shooing away flies. "It won't fit."

Maggie tilted her head and pretended to study the box and then the bed. "You don't think so?" What she was studying was the laughter in her daughter's dancing green eyes. What had she ever done to deserve such a perfect child?

"Silly Mommy," cried Katie as Maggie swung her up into the air and then carefully dropped her onto the bed. Katie looked adorable today in her jean bib overalls, lime green sweatshirt, Scooby-Doo sneakers, and more freckles scattered across her beautiful face than half of Ireland's population combined. Maggie's mother and father were going to spoil their only grandchild rotten.

Jeremy had been appalled when their daughter made her appearance with a thatch of bright red hair covering her adorable little head and a set of lungs that would have made her Irish great-grandpappy proud. Katherine Leigh Pierce was half his daughter, but she was the spitting image of her mother. In the four years since her birth, Maggie had tried countless times to find a resemblance to Jeremy in their daughter. She never could find a physical likeness, but she did notice two similarities: Jeremy and Katie both loved cream cheese on just about anything and Saturday-morning cartoons.

Jeremy's devotion to Tom and Jerry and Donald Duck spoke volumes about his maturity level.

Two of the first purchases Jeremy had made, once he landed a great-paying job downtown, was a fancy SUV and a big-screen television that had taken up half the living room wall in their small two-bedroom apartment. It hadn't surprised her when Jeremy had taken both with him when he left.

"Mommy, Mommy, Mommy, can I help put the bed into the box?" Katie bounced across the mattress and picked up her pillow.

"The bed's going into the back of Grandpop's truck, sweetie. What we need to do is take the blankets and sheets off the mattress and put them into the box so they won't get dirty." Katie was handling the move better than Maggie thought she would. Friday, Katie's last day at Little Tot's Daycare, had been rough. Katie had hugged her friends and teachers and cried all the way home, making Maggie feel like the worst mother in the world. Even a Happy Meal hadn't cheered her daughter. Katie had wanted to know why they couldn't go live with Daddy and his friend Alison. Her anger at Jeremy had only grown. What kind of sick man introduced his four-year-old daughter to his live-in lover? Katie was too young to realize what was really going on, but one day she would. Maggie wasn't looking forward to that day.

"I can do," shouted Katie as she pulled the Tweety Bird comforter off the bed and shoved it into the box. "See, I can do."

"I see, sweetie." Maggie helped her daughter by pulling one of the corners of the sheet off the mattress. "Why don't you take the sheets and the pillow and put them into the box too? I'll do the curtains."

Katie pulled and tugged and eventually managed to get the twisted, balled up sheets into the box. Neatness didn't count. Maggie knew her mother well enough to know everything in the box would be washed and dried before going back on the bed. Connie Franklin would have Katie's bedroom so clean and neat, a person could perform open-heart surgery within its walls.

Her mom was looking forward to having her only granddaughter move in with them, even if it was only temporary. Maggie couldn't blame her. Over the past four years, Maggie had only managed to take Katie to Misty Harbor twice, and both of those visits had been short, with no socializing. Her parents came out to see her, Jeremy, and Katie a couple of times a year, but the visits weren't really friendly or relaxing. Her parents didn't get along with Jeremy, and Jeremy always seemed to go out of his way to antagonize them. It made for one hell of a Thanksgiving dinner.

Maggie took the matching Tweety Bird curtains off the rod and dropped them into the box. She was making the right decision in returning to Misty Harbor. Katie needed to get to know her grandparents and other family members better. She couldn't stay in Bangor and do what needed to be done. Going back to college was one thing. Going back to school, working full time to support them both, and having time left over to be a good mother was impossible. Katie would never see Maggie, and when she did, she would be too tired to do anything with her daughter. There weren't enough hours in the day, and guilt seemed to fill every one of them.

With her parents' help and a part-time job, she could finish her college education, contribute something to their support, and still have time for Katie. Little girls needed their mommies, almost as much as their mommies needed their little girls.

Maggie felt tears burn the back of her eyes as she watched Katie count the boxes scattered around the tiny bedroom. "One, two, three, four . . ." Counting the box Katie had just jammed her pillow into, there were five boxes. "Five! There's five boxes, Mommy."

She hugged her daughter tight. So few boxes, so much love. "So I see, sweetie."

Katie wiggled out of her arms and headed for the door. "I go count more."

Maggie sat on the unmade bed and watched as Katie skipped out of the room and headed for the living room, where most of the boxes were already stacked and waiting for her father and brother to haul them down the flight of stairs and into the truck. The nine-by-eleven-foot room seemed empty and dull without Katie in it. Just like her life would be. She impatiently wiped at her eyes, drying any tears before they had a chance to tumble free. Katie would always be in her life. She didn't fear Jeremy going to court and trying to win custody, as some single mothers' ex-husbands did. Jeremy hadn't wanted Katie since the day he learned he was going to become a father. Nothing had changed since her birth. Maggie didn't know why she was being so emotional. She knew this move had been coming for months. She had planned it for months.

Deep down inside, Maggie knew Misty Harbor was a wonderful town in which to raise a child. After all, it was her hometown and her own childhood had been wonderful, especially the summers. Nothing beat the coast of Maine during the summer months. Katie was going to love the bobbing boats in the harbor, the smell of the fresh ocean breezes, and the secret swimming cove the locals never told the tourists about. There would be lobster bakes on the beach, rides in Uncle Gary's boat, and lots of whale and puffin sightings. Katie would be so busy being spoiled, she wouldn't have time to wonder why her daddy never came to visit her, or why the whole town seemed to shun her mommy.

Five years was a long time to hold a grudge. Maybe the town had forgotten what she had done. It was doubtful, but she could dream, couldn't she?

Wasn't it Walt Disney who had said dreams really do come true? Well, she was brought up in the Disney age. She believed in Mickey Mouse, and no one had clapped harder than she had to bring Tinker Bell back to life while watching *Peter Pan*. She was a true believer.

Just as she believed this was a good move, the right choice for her daughter and herself.

If she kept telling herself that, over and over again, she might start believing it.

Chapter Four

Gwen picked one of the balls of dough out of
the bowl, smacked it down onto the granite countertop, and proceeded to flatten it with a rolling pin.
She hadn't planned on baking an apple pie today,
but she needed something to cool her frazzled
nerves after spending the entire morning and part
of the afternoon in Daniel's company. The man
was lethal in close quarters, and the cab of his
pickup truck definitely was classified as close. She
didn't know what frustrated her more, the treacherous reaction her own body had to Daniel's nearness, or the fact that he seemed totally unaware of
his effect on the surrounding female population.
Either way, the man should be locked up for his
own good.

The ride back from the nearest home-and-
garden center had turned into a fifty-six-minute
and thirty-two-second adolescent nightmare. Who
would have thought that picking out bathroom

sinks, toilets, and wainscoting could be such a turn on?

She pressed the rolling pin harder and was rewarded with an ever-increasing size in the flattened dough. The last thing she had time for, in her busy schedule, was a relationship. Daniel certainly gave no indication that the attraction she felt for him was mutual. Her wacky hormones had been living too long in the fairy-tale land of Never Get Any and had been susceptible to the nearness of Daniel's killer body and the alluring fragrance of his aftershave.

In the world of designer colognes and signature fragrances, why would the scent of Old Spice drive her nuts? Grandpop Fletcher wore Old Spice, so she had recognized it right away, but her grandfather never smelled like Daniel had in that overheated truck cab. Calvin Klein and Ralph Lauren could take some lessons from that sea-faring fragrance.

With more force than necessary, Gwen lifted the rolling pin and smacked it back down to roll the dough width-wise. The flour she had sprinkled across the countertop puffed into the air. She muttered a curse that would have gotten her grounded for a week during her high school days and glared at the dough that was to become the bottom crust in her twelve-inch pie pan. The diameter of the now-demolished dough circle was a good thirty-six inches, and it was thin enough to be translucent. She'd never peel it off the countertop in one piece.

Gwen glanced up and saw that Hunter had abandoned the job of scrubbing the top of the stove to stare at her. A guilty flush swept up her cheeks as she waved the wooden rolling pin and said, "Sometimes I just don't know my own strength."

A twitch that might have been the beginning of a smile played in the corner of Hunter's mouth.

"Thin crust is good." Hunter's voice sounded rusty and stiff, as if he didn't use it a lot.

"There's thin, and then there's *thin.*" With a disgusted sigh, she started to peel the dough off the counter and roll it back into a ball. Hunter went back to cleaning the stovetop. "Is the industrial-strength cleaner working better than that spray stuff?"

She had picked up the top-of-the-line spray cleaner this morning at Barley's Food Store, and Hunter had used it on one stove while she had gone out with Daniel. Now Hunter was using the industrial cleaner she bought at the home-and-garden center on the other stove. The stuff smelled like rocket fuel mixed with pine trees. Two of the ovens were on self-clean, and the kitchen was not only on the warm side, it reeked of year-old burnt food and toxic fumes.

Hunter frowned at the area he had just scrubbed. "Don't know about better, but it takes less elbow grease."

Gwen dropped the ball of dough back into the bowl, washed her hands, and went to stand next to Hunter. "I still can't believe the difference a good scrubbing has made on these stoves. They actually shine." She reached out and lightly ran her fingertips over the stove Hunter had scrubbed and polished this morning. "You're doing a wonderful job, Hunter." She turned toward the man standing quietly beside her. "Thank you."

Hunter ducked his head, muttered, "You're welcome," and went back to scrubbing.

Gwen was positive that she had spotted a flush sweeping up his tanned, weathered cheeks before he had turned away from her. She didn't know if it was because of the compliment she had paid him or the fumes from the cleaner. Jonah and Daniel would have her head if Hunter left the kitchen high as a Boeing 747. She walked over to a window and cracked it open a few inches. The sun was shining today, but the temperature hadn't quite reached the forties. Cold fresh air rushed into the room, bringing in the scent of the sea and the distant calling of a few hardy seagulls.

Jonah was extremely protective of Hunter. When she had first met her new employee yesterday, she hadn't really understood why. Hunter was fifty-four years old, nearly six feet tall, and seemed in perfect physical condition, even though he was on the lean side. When he had politely taken off his baseball cap, she had noticed his brown hair was peppered with a lot of gray, and it was receding. His face was tanned and heavily etched with lines, while his hands were large, strong, and callused. Hunter had all the appearance of being a hard worker, and perfect for the job. But it had taken only one look into his soft brown eyes to see the wounds the war had inflicted upon his gentle soul. Hunter's eyes held the haunted look of distant nightmares and unspeakable torture.

Gwen immediately understood Daniel, Jonah, and the rest of the town when it came to protecting Hunter.

"Do you like apple pie, Hunter?" She washed and dried her hands before picking up the dough ball and the rolling pin once again. Maybe now that the edge had been taken off her frustration, she could concentrate on what needed to be done and stop being a source of amusement to her employee.

"I'm American." Hunter dried the top of the stove and polished it until it gleamed.

She took that for a yes. As she gently rolled out the bottom crust, she asked, "What about stuffed peppers?" She was planning on starting on the main dish as soon as the pie was in the oven.

"Sure." Hunter started to scrub the dull, dingy, and gray Formica wall behind the stove.

A sense of accomplishment comforted her battered nerves. Her business was starting to come together nicely.

The sound of Daniel ripping out the remaining booths and Jonah's mumbling about something could be heard coming from the dining room. Hammers pounded and nails seemed to scream as they released their hold on decades-old boards. Gwen had no problem with Jonah working for Daniel, as long as the younger man went easy on his grandfather. Jonah looked fit enough to be ripping out nails and stacking wood into a nice neat pile, to be used upstairs to make more storage shelves. The added storage area from the recycled wooden booths had been Daniel's suggestion, and she had jumped on it immediately. She could definitely use the extra shelves, but not if it would be too much for Jonah to handle. The man, after all, was in his seventies, and he should be sitting back enjoying his retirement, not helping his grandson redo a restaurant.

She carefully placed the rolled-out dough in the bottom of the pie pan and tried to listen to what Daniel and Jonah were arguing about. With the swinging doors closed she couldn't make out the words. She took the long way around the kitchen to get the peeler she needed for the apples and paused by the doors. The toe of her sneaker pushed the door a fraction of an inch, and Jonah's voice became clear.

"I'm telling you, Daniel, Hunter and I just had lunch an hour ago. I don't need a break." A board landed on another board with a loud smack. "Hunter heated up the leftover chili, like Gwen told us to. There was even some corn bread left, and plenty of sodas in the refrigerator."

Daniel gave a heavy sigh, followed by a hearty whack of his hammer. "You shouldn't be eating Gwen's food."

"I'm her tester!" Jonah tossed another board onto the growing pile.

Gwen pushed the door another inch until she could see into the room. Daniel had only two more booths to rip out. Already the improvement in the room was amazing, if she ignored the ruined carpet and the holes in the walls.

"You tested her chili yesterday."

"Yeah, well, it tasted even better reheated." Jonah picked up another board and started to rip a nail out of it.

"Are you going to tell her that?" Daniel stopped pounding on the wooden tabletop long enough to glance at his grandfather.

"Of course not; it would hurt her feelings."

Gwen smiled at the two men. Anyone looking at them would pick up on the family resemblance. Daniel obviously cared about his grandfather, and Jonah was stubbornly fighting that concern. She wondered if Daniel had inherited his grandfather's stubbornness. He sure hadn't received Jonah's sense of humor.

"Care to enlighten me as to why you're insisting on helping me out on this particular job?" asked Daniel.

"Ain't a grown man allowed to help out his own grandson?" Jonah braced the board he was holding and ripped out another nail. "I'm not getting any younger, Daniel. There's no telling how much time I have left on this good earth. Don't you want to spend some of it with me?"

Daniel snorted. "I'm not buying it, Pops. You're up to something. You've never wanted to work with me before; why now all of a sudden?"

"You never asked for my help before." Jonah

tossed the nail-free board onto the pile with a crash and reached for the next one.

"I don't remember asking you this time." With a mighty tug and a scream of nails against aged wood, the tabletop broke free of the wall. Daniel placed it on the stack of wood Jonah was working on.

"It's important to Gwen to have this place as near to perfect as we can get it for its grand opening." Jonah flashed Daniel a blinding smile. "I wouldn't want to disappoint that gal."

Gwen slowly moved her foot and allowed the door to swing shut. Tears were trying to fill her eyes as she pulled up a stool and started to peel the apples. Jonah's comment was one of the sweetest things anyone had ever said about her. For the first time she finally felt as if she hadn't made a mistake by coming to Misty Harbor. She had made a friend, and his name was Jonah Creighton. Of course Daniel had a point; why would Jonah all of a sudden start helping out around Daniel's job site? Maybe Jonah was up to something, but for the life of her, she couldn't image what it could be.

She dropped the first peeled apple into a bowl and looked at Hunter. The man was shooting her a couple of concerned looks from under the brim of his New England Patriots ball cap. "Chili wasn't better today." Hunter dipped the soapy rag back into the bucket and wrung it out. "Tasted the same to me."

The tears rushed back up to the surface, but she valiantly fought them back down. It was the first time Hunter had initiated a conversation. Maybe she hadn't made one friend; maybe she had made two. "Thank you."

She glanced around at the gray walls of the kitchen. The previous owner had obviously slapped the coat of ugly paint on the walls before putting the restaurant on the market. The color hid the grease and dirt that had accumulated over the years but did nothing for the appeal of the room. "What do you think about painting the kitchen yellow? Bright yellow."

Hunter gave the gray-painted wall behind her a quick glance and then went back to wiping down the white with gold speckles Formica wall behind the stove. "It could use some brightening in here."

The Formica had had a gray tint to it, before Hunter got to work on it. Now the white was actually white and the stainless-steel tops of the two stoves truly sparkled. By the time Hunter was done with this room, her own mother would be able to perform triple bypass surgery within its walls. "It definitely needs some brightening, but do you think yellow is a good choice?"

"Yellow's fine."

"What color would you choose, if this was your kitchen and you were planning on spending ten hours a day in it?" Eye-numbing yellow at ten o'clock at night, after spending the entire day on her feet cooking for other people, was beginning to lose its appeal. Maybe a soothing blue, though the dining room was going to be painted blue, and she wanted something different in here to break the monotony.

Hunter stared at the far wall for a long time before quietly saying, "Green."

"Green? You mean a dark green or a light green?" Green might work; it was a soothing, calming color.

"A soft green." Hunter picked up a towel and started to buff the wall. "The color of leaves on the trees when they first come out in the spring, before the summer sun hardens them and the chill of the fall changes them forever."

Gwen sat there and watched the thin strip of

peel get longer and longer as she peeled the apple in one continuous motion. To most men, green was green. There might be a difference between a light green and a dark green, but that was about it. Hunter had known the difference between a soft green and a hard one. The man might be the town's handyman, but his soul was that of a poet. A wounded poet.

"I think you might be right, Hunter. A soft green with white trim would be more calming than sunshine yellow." The last peeled apple joined the rest and she went in search of a knife and a cutting board. "Do you think the floor will come as clean as that backsplash?" The tiled floor appeared to be in good shape, just dull, dingy, and gray. The whole room had a gray tint to it, and she wanted that gone.

"It's going to take a lot of elbow grease and more of that cleaner you bought today."

She skimmed the toe of her sneaker across a tile. It was going to take more than elbow grease and cleanser to bring it back to its whiteness. Clairol itself wouldn't be able to get the gray out of it.

"Gwen, my love," purred Jonah as he pushed open the swinging doors and stared at the half-made pie sitting on the flour-dusted counter in front of her, "tell me you're baking an apple pie."

"I'm baking an apple pie." Gwen smiled when she heard what sounded suspiciously like a chuckle coming from Hunter.

Jonah gave a start of surprise but didn't comment on Hunter's rusty cackle. The older man rubbed his hands together. "Do we get to taste-test the pie today?"

"After dinner. I wasn't here to try one of my recipes for lunch, so if it's all right with you guys, I'd like you to stay for dinner. I want to see what you think of my stuffed peppers."

"Count me in." Jonah swiped a slice of apple out of the pie. "Can Clarence come too?"

Clarence was Jonah's friend, and Hunter's father. "Sure. There'll be plenty to go around."

Three and a half hours later the aroma of stuffed peppers and freshly baked apple pie filled the kitchen, causing Daniel's stomach to rumble with anticipation. The fast-food burger and fries that Gwen and he had stopped for after shopping the morning away at Home Depot was long gone and forgotten. He couldn't say the same thing for the blueberry muffins that Gwen had pulled out of the oven just as he and Jonah had arrived for work that morning. Gwen's warm, butter-smeared muffins would never be forgotten. If possible, they were better than yesterday morning's buns.

Gwen's buns had been at the center of a very erotic dream of his last night. He wondered what Freud would have said about erotic dreams centering around the kitchen. Probably that the dreamer had a sick and twisted mind, or that he was tired of his own cooking.

Daniel carried the last chair into the kitchen. Gwen wanted to eat in the kitchen, since the dining room was being torn apart and dust was everywhere. Jonah and Clarence were in the men's bathroom washing up and arguing as usual, about something trivial that probably happened fifty years in the past. Both older men had earned their dinner by carrying upstairs the wood from the booths. A pile of trash wood was neatly stacked in the far corner of the room, waiting until a Dumpster arrived on Thursday. With Jonah's help doing the less physical aspects of the job, Gwen just might get her wish list completed before the grand opening.

His grandfather was definitely up to something; Daniel just hadn't figured out what yet. Gwen's cooking was good enough to have Jonah hanging around the restaurant on its own account, but there was a certain look in his grandfather's gray eyes that had nothing to do with blueberry muffins and stuffed peppers.

"Are Jonah and Clarence coming?" Gwen carried over a baking dish filled with about twenty stuffed peppers and placed it in the center of the table. Tomato sauce bubbled around the green shells, and mozzarella cheese was melted across the top of every pepper.

The aroma alone caused his salivary glands to drool. "They're washing up."

Hunter brought over a pitcher of iced tea and filled a glass at each place setting. A freshly tossed salad sat on the table, along with two different kinds of dressing and a basket overflowing with warm, crusty bread. It was truly amazing that Gwen had pulled all this together, complete with apple pie for dessert, in such a short amount of time. If someone gave the woman a week and a Cuisinart, she could probably solve world hunger.

Daniel watched Gwen as she bustled about the kitchen, gathering up salt and pepper shakers and a small bowl holding lemon slices for the iced tea. "Is there anything I can help with?"

"Nope, everything is ready." Gwen set the items down and surveyed the table. "All we need now are Clarence and Jonah."

Deep muffled voices came from the dining room. "Here they come now," Daniel said as he positioned himself behind a chair that would have the scarred side of his face facing the wall. Gwen didn't need to be looking at that while she ate her meal.

A grinning Jonah pushed his way into the kitchen. "You've got company, Gwen." Clarence and another man, holding a large bouquet of brightly colored flowers, followed Jonah into the kitchen. The bouquet looked expensive and overpowering.

In his best host voice, Jonah said, "Gwendolyn Fletcher, I would like to introduce you to Wendell Kirby." Jonah flashed Wendell his sparkling dentures. "Wendell Kirby, I would like to introduce you to Gwendolyn Fletcher, the best cook on the eastern shore and the proprietor of this here fine establishment."

Daniel rolled his eyes at his grandfather's nonsense. What in the world was Jonah up to now? Everyone knew that Wendell was as slick as a used-car salesman and as slippery as a harbor seal. He was also forty-three years old, going bald, and carrying an extra thirty pounds or so, all of which were hanging over his belt, and was divorced twice for good reason. Jonah should have shown Hairplug Kirby the backside of the front door.

Wendell handed Gwen the obnoxious arrangement of flowers. "These are for you, Ms. Fletcher."

Gwen appeared a little confused but managed to smile and graciously accept the flowers. "They're beautiful, Mr. Kirby, thank you."

"They're just a small token to welcome you to our fair village." Wendell preened and stuck out his chest, which only increased the size of his waist. "I hope I didn't interrupt anything." His glance slid from Gwen to the dinner table.

"Wendell's the head of the Misty Harbor Chamber of Commerce, Gwen." Jonah took the flowers from Gwen. "I'll go find something to put these in before they start to wilt."

"Thank you," Gwen said as she watched Jonah carry the bouquet to the other side of the kitchen. "I'm afraid I don't have any vases here, but there's an empty mayonnaise jar in the cabinet above the sink." Gwen turned an apologetic look on Wendell. "Would you care to join us for dinner, Mr. Kirby?"

"I'd be delighted, but please call me Wendell." With a polished move, he held out a chair for Gwen. "All my friends call me Wendell."

Hunter rolled his eyes at Daniel and went out into the dining room to grab another chair. Clarence went to one of the cabinets and pulled down another plate and glass. Daniel was positive he did it more because he was anxious to dig into Gwen's cooking than for manners' sake. Clarence had been commenting on the aroma coming from the kitchen since he arrived, over an hour earlier.

"Hey, Kirby," called Jonah as he shoved the flowers into the water-filled jar, "if you're eating with us, you have to tell Gwen your honest opinion of the food. We're taste-testing for her."

Wendell planted his roomy backside in the chair next to Gwen's and grinned like the idiot he was. "I can tell just by looking at everything that it's going to be as delicious as the cook is beautiful."

Clarence muttered something under his breath as he took the seat across from Gwen. Hunter made an inexcusable amount of noise as he dragged a chair across the tiled floor to the table, and Jonah chuckled at some private joke. Daniel found himself grinding his back teeth together as he took his seat. Wendell Kirby was a horse's ass.

Jonah and Hunter finally took their seats and Gwen graciously started to serve the stuffed peppers while the men passed the salad. "So, Wendell, what do you do?"

"I own and operate the Misty Harbor Motor Inn out on East Main Street. I'm sure you must have seen it when you toured the town. We are only open for business during the tourist season, but we have eighteen clean and affordable rooms."

"Do you have a restaurant in the inn?" Gwen frowned as she helped herself to the tossed salad.

Daniel hid his smile as he poured dressing over his salad. Gwen obviously wasn't fooled for a moment by Wendell's smooth-talking act. He should have known Kirby would be the first unattached male to slide out from under a rock to come courting Gwen. The flowers were a nice touch, even though a tad on the expensive side. Gwen didn't appear to be the kind of woman who would be swayed by flowers.

"Yes, there is a small restaurant, but we only serve breakfast." Wendell gave her a charming smile. "It's only open from six A.M. 'til ten. We find that most of our guests are too busy either in town or out on the boats all day to warrant keeping it open later."

Gwen returned Wendell's smile with one of her own. "So we aren't in competition with one another?"

"Never, my dear." Wendell tasted his first bite of Gwen's stuffed peppers and groaned out loud. "How could I possibly compete with something this delicious? I am definitely going to have to recommend your restaurant to every one of my patrons."

Clarence gave a loud grunt and then enlightened Gwen. "Don't listen to him, Ms. Fletcher. This is the only restaurant in town and his *patrons* will be mighty happy to be eating here, with or without his recommendation."

Daniel could have kissed Clarence.

Wendell started to choke on a mouthful of iced tea. When he caught his breath, he sputtered, "Well, I never. . . ."

"Gentlemen, please." Gwen gave a gracious smile, but to Daniel it looked a little strained. "I will welcome Mr. Kirby's recommendation, even if

Catch of the Day *is* the only restaurant in town.'' Gwen speared a cherry tomato with her fork. "Did I tell you that Hunter helped me choose the color I'm going to paint this room?''

Daniel's fork stopped halfway to his mouth. Hunter was picking out paint colors? He noticed that everyone else's fork was poised in midair too, except for Hunter's. The quiet man, who probably hadn't said more than a dozen words to Daniel all year long, was eating his meal as if he hadn't a care in the world.

Clarence was the first to break the awkward silence. "What color did he choose?''

Gwen, who seemed oblivious to the fact that she had just dropped a bombshell, said, "I wanted to go with a bright, sunny yellow to brighten up the place.''

All the men nodded, as if that made perfect sense to them. Yellow was a "woman's" color.

"Then I started to think about spending ten hours or so a day, every day, in a bright yellow room. It occurred to me that I should go with something a bit more calming. Hunter suggested a soft green, and I have to agree with him.''

All the men stared at Hunter in amazement. Hunter shrugged and went on eating his meal.

Wendell, who obviously didn't like having the conversation veer away from him, changed the subject. "Gwen, do you know about all the special festivals and events the town is planning?''

"What kind of events?''

"Oh, Kirby's a great one for throwing all kinds of festivals.'' Jonah lowered his silverware to his now empty plate. "It's the Chamber of Commerce's job to help bring in tourists, and Kirby does a bang-up job.''

"Thank you, Jonah,'' said Wendell. "Of course, with you owning the only restaurant in town, your participation is required. The previous owner tried to coordinate the menu to fit with the theme of each event."

"What kind of themes?"

"Well, let's see." Wendell held up a hand and started to count off on his fingers. "The first big event is the Harbor Jazz Weekend that takes place in the middle of June. Then there's the annual Fourth of July celebration and the Lobster Festival in the end of July. Then in August there's the Nautical Weekend, the Arts and Crafts Festival, and the Wild Blueberry Festival. September has Windjammer Days, and the Tall Ships will be coming into the harbor for a day. October is the Fall Foliage Festival, and then we do a bang-up Christmas Boat Parade, where all the boats string lights all over them and sail into the harbor."

Gwen stared in horror as all ten of Wendell's fingers were up in the air. "Hold on a second and let me grab a piece of paper and a pencil. I'll never remember all of this." Gwen stood up and rushed over to her pile of lists.

Daniel couldn't allow the panic to continue to grow in Gwen's big brown eyes. Kirby had purposely made it sound like a really big deal. "Don't worry, Gwen, it's not that much more work. Tourist season is usually pretty good around here, and the special events do manage to pull in a few more customers, but it's not anything overwhelming. Catch of the Day and you will be able to handle them all just fine."

Gwen turned her grateful gaze in his direction as she walked back to her seat. "Really?"

"Really." He gave her an encouraging smile. "It's part of Kirby's job to make each and every event sound like a big deal. It draws in more tourists that way."

"I'll have you know, each and every year that

I've been the president of the Chamber of Commerce we have increased the number of tourists that visit our little village.''

"That's why you're still president.'' Daniel didn't add that no one else wanted the job. "But it doesn't give you the right to scare one of the new proprietors in town.''

Clarence stood up and started to gather the dishes. "Looks like dinner is over. It was great, Gwen, but I'm sure you're anxious to close up for the night and go home. I heard there's a storm coming.''

A rough chuckle escaped Hunter's throat as he carried over his empty plate and glass and started to fill one of the sinks with hot soapy water.

Gwen stood in amazement as the table was cleared and Wendell was shown on his way. Hunter was washing the dishes. Clarence was drying them and putting them away. Daniel's grandfather started a fresh pot of coffee, then gently led Gwen to a vacant stool and handed her the list she had started about the events. "Why don't we tell you about the festivals while we clean up, and then we can have pie?'' Gwen looked as if she could use a diversion.

"So you guys didn't forget the pie?''

Clarence, who looked like an older version of his son, Hunter, shook his head and grinned. "Nope. We just didn't feel like sharing with Kirby.''

Half an hour later the list of events and all the activities the guys could think of was four pages long and the kitchen was spotless. Gwen walked out into the dining room with everyone and reached for her coat. "Thanks again for cleaning up.''

"Thank you for dinner, Gwen,'' Clarence said. "It was wonderful.''

"It was great,'' echoed Jonah.

Hunter mumbled something about liking the cheese on top the best.

Daniel opened the door as Gwen shut off the lights. Darkness had fallen on the town and with it the temperature had dropped and the wind had kicked up. Clarence and Hunter climbed in the cab of Jonas's pickup and headed off into the night. Daniel walked Gwen to her S.U.V., parked in the back of the restaurant, next to his truck.

He glanced up at the light fixture on the outside of the building. He could tell there was a bulb in it, but it wasn't working. "I need to replace that bulb for you."

"I'll add it to my list."

He hid his smile. He had never known anyone with as many lists as Gwen. "You do that." A wicked gust of wind nearly yanked the vehicle door out of Gwen's hand. He held the door while she climbed behind the wheel. "Be careful tonight. There's a nor'easter coming up the coast. We shouldn't get much snow out of it, but they're predicting gale-force winds."

Gwen snuggled deeper into her coat as she pulled on a pair of leather gloves. "When exactly does spring hit this part of Maine?"

He had to chuckle. Today had nearly hit the forty-degree mark. "This *is* spring." He closed the door on her grumbling and headed for his pickup.

Chapter Five

Daniel frowned at the colonial blue front door of Gwen's cottage, raised a fist, and pounded a series of thumps that was guaranteed to raise the dead—or at least vibrate a picture or two on the walls inside. He had already rung the doorbell twice and had gotten no response. His next move was to break into the small cottage or notify the sheriff.

Gwen was missing.

Technically, she wasn't missing. She just hadn't shown up at the restaurant this morning. Jonah was ready to call in the National Guard or the F.B.I., and even Hunter kept coming out of the kitchen to check the dining room to see if she had arrived yet. By eight-thirty Daniel couldn't stand it any longer.

Chances were she had just overslept this morning, and he was going to look like a fool pounding on her door like some overzealous Jehovah's Witness ready to show someone the "light." Jonah had offered to come to Gwen's house to check on her, but the more Daniel thought about it, the more uneasy he became. Gwen didn't strike him as the type of woman not to show up at her own restaurant. Something wasn't right, but hopefully it was a faulty alarm clock. Maybe she had lost electricity last night during the storm. Just because he hadn't at his house didn't mean that a line hadn't gone down in this part of town.

He glanced around the tiny picket-fence enclosed front yard. Besides a few dead branches littering the property, he didn't see any damage. Gwen's S.U.V. was parked on the crushed-shell driveway, directly in front of his truck.

With a rattle of a chain and a click of a lock, the front door opened and a vision that was guaranteed to stay with him for the rest of his life filled the doorway. He had to bite the inside of his cheek to keep from laughing.

Gwen's hair was tossed and tangled and sexy as all hell. Her big brown eyes held confusion and were puffy from sleep. Pillow marks creased her right check. She had wrapped an afghan around her shoulders, he guessed for propriety's sake, but he hadn't the faintest notion as to why. There was nothing scandalous about the light blue flannel pajamas she wore. Even the smiling and dancing penguins printed all over them looked chaste. The only skin he could see was her face, throat, and the knuckles on her one hand holding the afghan in place.

Even dressed in that ridiculous outfit, she was sexy, and his body hardened painfully. The single male residents of Misty Harbor were going to riot. Erik and Gunnar, the massive Norwegian twin fishermen who looked like Viking gods, were going to take up plundering and pillaging, sacking the village to lay their booty at this goddess's door.

Erik made no secret that he was on the prowl for a wife. Gunnar was usually only one step behind his muscle-bound twin.

Gwen didn't stand a chance of remaining single for long in this female-deprived town. Some guy would catch her eye and she would be hustled down the aisle and into bed faster than he could unstick a window.

It was a depressing thought, one that gave his stomach a sudden twist.

His gaze slid down to the thick white socks covering her feet before climbing slowly back up to her sleepy eyes and her jaw-popping yawn. He wanted to do some hustling of his own, straight back upstairs to her bed to show her what a proper Down Eastener slept in . . . nothing but skin and a satisfied smile. He didn't think Gwen would appreciate that particular lesson, so he'd keep it light and friendly. "You give new meaning to the song *'Angel of the Morning.'* "

Gwen squinted against the dull morning light and muttered, "Stuff it, Daniel," before turning her back and stumbling away.

Since Gwen hadn't slammed the door in his face, he took it as an invitation. He stepped over the threshold and closed the door against the cold air. The living room was furnished, but it was hard to tell what kind of furniture Gwen owned. Most of it was buried beneath boxes, the majority of which seemed to be full and still taped shut, though a lot were empty. Crumpled newspaper was everywhere. It looked as if she had been trying to paper-train a wildebeest.

He suppressed a smile as he followed Gwen to the back of the house, where he knew the kitchen would be. The white clapboard cottage with blue trim was a simple design. Living room, kitchen, and a small dining room downstairs; two bedrooms and a bathroom would be nestled under the dormers upstairs.

The kitchen was an improvement over the living room. Gwen had obviously spent some time in it putting away her belongings. Or at least trying to. She seemed to have run out of cabinet space. Cooking gadgets cluttered every surface, including a dining room table that would comfortably sit four. At least he thought the shining, gleaming items were all cooking contraptions. Some looked as if they were props in either a *Star Trek* movie or a Julia Childs infomercial.

He propped his shoulder against the doorjamb and studied Gwen as she filled a space-age silver-and-black coffeepot. No simple Mr. Coffee machine for the chef extraordinaire. As soon as the brewed coffee started to drip into the pot, Gwen turned away and squinted at the clock on the microwave. Neon green letters that spelled out the word *set* blinked back at her.

"What time is it?" Gwen looked out of the window above the sink.

Daniel didn't think Gwen could tell time by the sun's position. Besides, the storm that had blown through town last night had left behind a cloudy, damp, dreary, cold morning. Gwen would have to be standing in Rhode Island to actually see the sun. He glanced at his watch. "It's eight-forty."

Gwen cringed. "My alarm clock must be broken." With a smooth, practiced move, she swiped the pot out from under the machine and replaced it with an empty coffee mug. Brown liquid dripped into the cup.

He hid his chuckle behind a cough. Gwen obviously had pulled that move more than once in her life. With the ease with which she had done the switch, he had to wonder if it was a daily occurrence. Not one drop had splattered against the warming plate beneath the pot. "The storm must have knocked out the electricity during the night."

"My clock has a backup battery." In one fluid motion, Gwen switched the cup for the pot.

"Most battery backups are only good for about fifteen minutes. They aren't made to keep time forever." He watched in amazement as Gwen started to drink the hot liquid. She must have cast-iron tonsils and a throat made out of lead. "Around here you need a manual windup clock, especially when a storm's predicted."

"I'll put one on my shopping list." Gwen finished the cup of coffee and impatiently eyed the dripping machine. "Thanks for waking me up."

"Jonah was worried that something might have happened to you. I told him that nothing ever happens in Misty Harbor, but he wouldn't listen to reason. Claimed he heard about some woman electrocuting herself with a wafflemaker last year."

Gwen chuckled as she got down another mug from the cabinet above the coffeemaker. "Coffee?"

"Sure." He had had a cup of coffee at home, but breakfast had only been a bowl of Cheerios, minus his usual banana. After working only two days for Gwen he was spoiled. He had been looking forward to whatever mouth-watering delight she would be pulling out of the oven. It was going to be a long time between that lone bowl of cereal and lunch.

Gwen filled his cup, and then refilled hers. This time when she brought the mug up to her mouth, she sipped instead of gulping. "Did Hunter make it to the restaurant okay?"

"Jonah picked him up on his way in." Daniel carefully tested the coffee and found it not as steaming hot as he thought it would be. Maybe Gwen's throat wasn't made out of lead after all, just a nice sturdy cooper. "He was scrubbing the refrigeration unit when I left."

"He's a great employee, so far. Hardworking and not afraid to speak his mind." Gwen's smile brightened the kitchen. "Thank you for recommending him."

"Jonah thought of him first; I just seconded the opinion."

Gwen reached into a chrome bread box and pulled out a loaf of raisin bread. She placed it on the counter, along with a knife and some butter, and motioned toward a stool. "Did you know he knew the ingredients to make sour cream dill sauce for poached salmon off the top of his head?"

"Hunter's a man with many talents." It didn't surprise him. Hunter's mother had been a fantastic cook and, per Clarence, had taught her son everything she had known. He was just startled to learn that Hunter had volunteered to tell Gwen what he knew. Then again, after discovering yesterday that Hunter thought the kitchen would look best painted "soft" green, nothing should surprise him about the usually quiet man.

Maybe, after all these years, Hunter was finally going to come out of his self-imposed exile. Or maybe Gwen was a magician, because she sure was causing Daniel to feel things he was better off not feeling. Lust was a horrible emotion to have before lunch. Especially one-sided lust.

He swabbed butter across a slice of the bread with a little more force than necessary, and took a big bite. The taste of cinnamon and raisins exploded in his mouth. "You just baked this, didn't you?"

"Last night while I was trying to straighten out this room." Gwen helped herself to a slice of bread and another cup of coffee. "It's no use. I have eighty pounds of accessories and only enough room for twenty pounds." She gave a weary sigh and a dainty bite. "I ran out of cabinet space."

He chuckled as he glanced around at some of the gadgets. Some looked as if they would make great torture devices. Stephen King could write an entire novel that would take place in this room alone, and every teenager in America would stand hours in a movie line to see it. Donna Reed meets the Marquis de Sade. He gave the small device, with rollers and a hand crank, sitting on the dining room table a thoughtful glance. "Is all this necessary to cook?"

"It all depends on one's view of cooking. Some people consider throwing a frozen dinner into the microwave and pushing a few buttons cooking. I don't."

"Hey, I can cook, and I usually only use my microwave for reheating." He looked at an electric wok sitting next to the roller contraption and shook his head. "I don't think I know anyone who actually owns a wok."

"You do now." Gwen eyed the wok for a moment. "Maybe I can do an international night at the restaurant once in a while, for a change of pace. The Chinese use a lot of fish in their meals. I also know a great recipe for Cajun swordfish. We could do a New Orleans night."

He watched as she reached for a pad of paper and a pen sitting on the counter, and started to scribble. She had to flip over three pages full of lists before finding a clean sheet. "Another list?" This woman collected lists like most accumulated shoes.

"Just some ideas, while they're still fresh in my mind." Gwen glanced up and asked, "Do you think the locals would like lobster fettuccine alfredo?"

"I think the locals will be eating everything you

set down in front of them, Gwen. In case you haven't realized it, you're a fantastic cook."

A blush stained her cheeks, but Gwen's smile was wide. "Thank you, but it's nothing."

One of his eyebrows arched high in disbelief. "Nothing?" From what he had seen so far, the woman could make pig slop into a five-course gourmet meal. Why would Gwen think her talent was nothing?

"Cooking was a hobby of mine that just kind of grew into a career."

"When you were little, didn't you want to be a chef or a restauranteur? Didn't Santa bring you one of those plastic play kitchens or an Easy Bake Oven?" From the time he had pounded in his first nail at the tender age of six, Daniel had known he would become a carpenter.

"Yes, I got an Easy Bake Oven, but I also got a microscope, a telescope, and a Doctor Barbie. I was expected to be a doctor, or at least a lawyer."

"Those are some heavy expectations."

"My father's the head of a cancer research institute at Johns Hopkins, and Mom's a cardiologist. My older sister, Sydney, is a pediatrician, and my younger sister, Jocelyn, is an assistant district attorney in Baltimore."

Whoa, talk about a family of overachievers! "And you're a restauranteur."

"Cooking is not the same thing as saving someone's life, finding the cure for a horrible disease, or fighting for justice."

"No, but someone has to feed the doctors and the lawyers of the world. It's an honest profession that requires a lot of talent if you're going to make a career of it." He could tell this was an extremely touchy subject to Gwen. "How come your younger sister broke tradition and went into law instead of medicine?"

"Jocelyn didn't break tradition; she's following it. Our grandfather was the district attorney in Baltimore when he suffered a fatal heart attack at his desk late one night."

He was almost afraid to ask, but the curiosity was killing him. "What did your grandmother do?"

"She was a stay-at-home mom who raised four children, along with volunteering for every bleeding-heart cause that came along." A dreamy smile curved Gwen's lips and softened her brown eyes. "She baked the best chocolate chip cookies, and I still can't get my meringue to come out as good as hers."

"So you *are* following tradition after all."

Gwen looked shocked for a moment, and then thoughtful. "It's not the same."

"Why? Just because Granny didn't charge you for those cookies didn't mean that she didn't put her heart and soul into baking them."

"Of course she put her heart into every batch of cookies; that's what made them so good. But it wasn't a career for her, it was an act of love."

"So what you are telling me is, Grandmom wasn't as important as DA Grandpop or Bypass Surgery Mom?"

"You're not understanding the dynamics of it, Daniel. Didn't your parents want you to be something besides a carpenter?"

"Nope." He finished off his second slice of raisin bread as he studied the woman sitting across from him. After three cups of coffee, Gwen was finally awake. Not making a lot of sense, but awake.

"What does your father do for a living? What did Jonah do before he retired?"

"Jonah was a lobster fisherman until about four years ago, and Dad's an architect. Mostly residential, but he does the occasional small business. My mother's a landscape designer, specializing in coastal properties, and I have an older sister, Rebecca, who is currently putting her career as a teacher on hold to be a stay-at-home mom to her two daughters."

"Didn't your parents want you to follow in their footsteps?"

"No, they wanted me to be happy. Being a carpenter makes me happy." He couldn't imagine what his life would have been like if his father had insisted he go to college and study architecture instead of attending trade school for two years. "Did your parents give you a hard time when you told them you wanted to be a chef?"

"Not really. Though I think they were disappointed that I traded in a full scholarship at Duke University to attend a culinary institute."

"You had a full scholarship to Duke?" They didn't award scholarships on beauty, so that meant that Gwen was not only gorgeous, she was smart too. Damn smart. And he thought she kept lists because she was a little absentminded. Instead, they were the result of a highly organized mind. Didn't the woman have a flaw, besides needing coffee first thing in the morning?

"You sound like Sydney. She only had a partial scholarship, and she's still complaining about the student loans she has to pay back."

"Didn't your parents help out with the cost?" Gwen's family was such a bunch of overachievers, surely they had the money that went along with that characteristic. His own parents paid for his trade school education and his sister's college.

"They paid the room-and-board costs; everything else was our responsibility."

"If they didn't pay for culinary school, how could they object?"

"I didn't say they objected to my career choice; they just don't understand it, that's all." Gwen busied herself with cleaning up the counter. "Thanks again for waking me up."

"You're welcome." He knew a change of subject when one hit him on the head. "I'm sure Jonah and Hunter will be relieved that a wafflemaker hasn't done you in. The worry had those two going all morning." He stood up and carried his empty cup over to the sink.

His arm brushed Gwen's flannel pajama sleeve as she was reaching for the butter to put it away. The dancing penguins were beginning to get to him. So was the enticing fragrance Gwen wore. She smelled like warm sheets, hot dreams, and fabric softener. A dangerous combination for a man who had spent a frustrating night tossing and turning in his lonely bed thinking about big brown eyes and sweet buns. He had a terrible feeling that tonight's torment would include penguins and Downy Fabric Softener.

"Tell them I'll make it up to them with a special lunch. After I shower and dress I'll stop at Barley's and see what they have that looks good. I'm thinking veal, lamb, or duck." Gwen walked with him to the front door. "Any preference?"

"One of each would be nice." By the time he was finished renovating Gwen's restaurant he would either be going out and buying all new pants in a larger size, or he'd have to take up jogging and stomach crunches.

Maggie Pierce checked her makeup one last time in the rearview mirror. Dark mascara highlighted her green eyes, while a good foundation covered most of her freckles. She had applied blush with a light hand—just enough to put some color into her winter-pale face—and she had chosen a natural shade of lipstick. Nothing too bright or glaring.

She was applying for a part-time position in an insurance office, not trying out for the role of Lolita in summer stock.

She really needed this job. The hours were perfect, and fit around the two summer courses she was already registered for at a nearby college. The pay wasn't great, but it was decent, and more importantly she would be using some of the knowledge she had picked up during the three years she had attended college. For the first time in five years she would be sharpening her computer skills and using her brain.

Not that she didn't use her brain when waiting tables. Whoever thought waitressing was a no-brainer had never done the job. It wasn't easy memorizing specials, remembering who ordered what entree, and what everyone was drinking. Then you had to listen to the customer complain if there was too much gravy, or not enough rolls. Some customers were so finicky that the only thing she hadn't done for them was cut their meat in bite-size portions. All the wonders of aching feet and ignoring lewd suggestions while getting paid less than minimum wage and questionable tips was history.

She wouldn't be the least bit sorry never to wait on another disagreeable customer again. She had a brain, and by hell, it was time she started using it.

She had to get this job.

Besides, Katie had given her her lucky green plastic charm that she had gotten from a cereal box last week. The leprechaun that was engraved into the plastic was supposed to lead the bearer to his pot of gold. Maggie wasn't interested in a pot of gold, only a chance.

A chance wasn't much to ask for, was it? Katie deserved to be raised by a self-supporting, happily adjusted mother. The happily adjusted part might take a while, but she was on her way to becoming self-supporting. All it would take was a smile, a handshake, and the simple question, "When can I start?"

The adjusting part was a lot trickier. When she looked into a mirror she didn't see a divorced woman who was raising a four-year-old daughter. Most of the time a scared little girl stared out from a pair of woman's eyes. The divorce was final, and deep down inside Maggie knew it was for the best. Jeremy and she were never really in love; they had just played house. After a couple of cans of beer they had been in lust and had paid for that one moment of stupidity for five years. If Jeremy hadn't been as scared as she was when she had found out she was pregnant, he probably never would have married her.

She had to give Jeremy credit for standing up and doing the right thing at the time. It was all the time after that, that made their marriage so hard. No marriage was better than a bad marriage, and theirs had gone from hard and shaky to downright nasty in the past two years. Marriages have a tendency to fail when the husband comes home and announces he's in love with another woman.

Of course, the other woman had a master's degree in computers, a twenty-six-inch waist, a thirty-eight-inch chest, and D-size cups that surely overflowed whatever bra she wore. If Alison the home wrecker ever wore a Wonder Bra, it would take a crowbar to separate the two colliding mountains. Alison also had a high-pitched laugh that was guaranteed to have a normal man shuddering in his shoes or downing beers to drown out the noise. Jeremy was very good at guzzling beer. You could take the boy out of the frat party, but you couldn't take the frat party out of the boy.

Maggie pulled her thoughts away from the negative and concentrated on something positive. She was positively going to walk into that building and dazzle them with her brilliance. They would have no recourse but to hire her overqualified butt.

Tonight she would take Katie out to Krup's General Store to celebrate. Krup's had an ice cream counter in the back of the store where they still served real cherry Cokes and the best root beer floats this side of Bangor.

Maggie opened the car door, stepped out into the brisk morning air, and walked to the door. A cold gust of wind blew her skirt against her legs and froze her ankles. She wished spring would hurry up and make its appearance. Just because the calendar said it was spring didn't make it so.

The heat of the office slammed into her as she closed the door behind her and took off her winter coat. Pale mauve walls and gray carpeting gave the reception area a contemporary look. A huge treelike plant took up the front window. Maggie smiled at the miniature white lights someone had strung throughout the plant. She could definitely work in a place like this.

With a smile firmly and confidently in place, she approached the receptionist. But one look at the woman and Maggie's hopes of landing the job died a very slow and humiliating death. The middle-aged woman behind the desk gave her a look filled with hatred and condemnation. With a raised eyebrow and a sniff of disapproval, the woman asked, "May I help you?"

She should have known better than to try to get a job in town. The people of Misty Harbor had long memories, and five years wasn't long enough for them to forget that she had hurt one of their own. It didn't matter that she had been born and raised in the same town. She had been the one at fault.

"Good morning, Mrs. Wietzel. I have an appointment with Mr. Pennell in regard to a part-time position." Maggie had known Olivia Wietzel all of her life; she'd even graduated high school with her oldest daughter, Claire. She had spent more than one night at Claire's house, painting each other's nails, talking about boys, and pretending to study for math tests.

"I believe that position might have already been filled." Mrs. Wietzel looked up at her as if she hadn't a clue as to her identity.

Maggie felt her heart pound in her chest and her hands start to sweat, but she refused to allow this woman to see the effect she was having on her. If she backed down now, she might as well go back to her parents and pack up all of Katie's and her belongings and move back to Bangor or any other city where her past sins could stay in the past. She wasn't about to do that. For better or worse, Misty Harbor was going to be her daughter's and her home for the next year or so. She refused to cower and hide from the "good" citizens. Yes, she had made a mistake, and she had paid dearly for it— more than this town would ever know. It was about time the residents put the past where it belonged.

Lord knew she wanted to.

"That's okay, Mrs. Wietzel. I would appreciate it if you would just inform Mr. Pennell that I'm here. Maybe there's another position available."

Chapter Six

Gwen tossed the last of the boxes into the huge red Dumpster near the back door of the restaurant. The cool spring breeze felt wonderful against her heated skin. She was filthy and exhausted, her sweatshirt had a rip in it from being caught on a nail, her jeans were dirty and dusty, and she probably had cobwebs in her hair. Yet the sense of physically accomplishing something brightened her outlook.

The storage area that Jonah had discovered upstairs under the eaves was now completely empty. The previous owners were pack rats and had jammed every available inch with junk. There was absolutely no reason that she was aware of why a sane person would save dented, rusted pots and chipped glasses. Boxes of dry-rotted linen and faded plastic flowers had taken up over half the area. There hadn't been one thing worth saving, besides an old menu that appeared to be from the fifties, when the restaurant had been called Ralph's by the Sea.

Judging by the items on the menu, Gwen had the feeling that Ralph's hadn't been in business long. Lobster burgers and crab sausages didn't sound very appealing to her, and she considered herself pretty liberal when it came to creative endeavors in the kitchen.

It had taken her three hours to empty the storage area and cart everything downstairs and out back to the Dumpster. Her back was sore from stooping over, she was grimy and in need of a shower, and she hadn't even thought about what to make for lunch. Jonah and Clarence had offered to help, but she didn't want either man hauling boxes down a flight of stairs. Besides, she had been curious whether there would be anything worthwhile in the storage area. As treasure hunts went, it had been a total bust.

In the week since Gwen had hired Daniel and Hunter, a lot had been accomplished, and she was on schedule for the opening. Hunter had scrubbed the cooking area of the kitchen 'til it gleamed. Even the floor had cleaned up better than she had thought it would. The dishwashing area was next on her list, but in the meanwhile Hunter was priming the "women's" bathroom, getting it ready for the first coat of peach-colored paint. Daniel had already replaced both toilets and sinks. The men's room had been next, but a welcome warm front had moved up the coast, and Daniel was taking advantage of the fifty-degree days to knock out half the northern wall and put in the pair of patio doors leading to the side courtyard.

Every time she walked through the dining room she was amazed at the amount of light pouring in from both the six-foot openings and the two uncurtained front bay windows. It was just as she'd envisioned it. Catch of the Day was coming together.

Her dream was coming alive before her eyes.

With a weary sigh, Gwen stretched her arms above her head and tried to work the kinks out of her back. She failed more than she succeeded. As dreams went, she figured as she walked back into the kitchen, a few aches and pains were well worth the price.

The kitchen was empty, so she headed for the sound of hammering. She found Daniel, with Hunter's help, nailing the first patio door into the opening. It was a tight, perfect fit; barely any daylight showed between the wall and the frame of the doors. Once again, Daniel proved he was a talented carpenter and could do anything with his hands. She knew absolutely zip about what it would take to put in a pair of patio doors, but she realized it wasn't as simple as Daniel made it appear.

Gwen leaned against the back wall and watched Daniel perform some intricate dance using his hammer, nails, shims, and a four-foot-long level. Hunter held the doors in place and occasionally applied more pressure or less, depending on Daniel's instructions.

Over the past week Gwen had learned that Daniel was a fascinating man to watch. She especially liked to look at his hands as they moved across a board or gripped a hammer. The man had the most incredibly sexy hands. They were broad across the palm and long in the fingers. His nails were cut short and he kept them extremely clean. His left thumbnail was discolored from where he had smacked it with a hammer last Friday. That had been her fault.

She never should have come up behind him while he was working to tell him that lunch was ready. She hadn't been thinking properly. The enticing view of his jean-clad bottom had short-circuited all her brain cells. Daniel's backside could give his hands lessons on sexiness. After apologizing to him for two minutes straight, she silently had thanked her lucky stars that the man hadn't been handling a power tool.

Daniel had been avoiding her ever since the incident.

Not that he had been overfriendly since she hired him. The closest they had come to a personal conversation had been in her kitchen five days ago, when he had awakened her because the storm had knocked out her electricity. Even then he had said it was Jonah and Hunter who had been concerned for her safety and had sent him to check on her.

She had gone over that scene a thousand times, and each time she came out the loser. Images of her answering the door in the flannel pajamas Sydney had given her as a going-away present still caused her to flinch. She was just thankful she was still half asleep and hadn't thought about putting on the moose slippers that had come with them. Sydney thought bunny slippers with big floppy ears and cute pink noses wouldn't go with the atmosphere of Maine. Sadly, Sydney had explained, the store had been out of the big red lobster slippers, and Gwen would just have to make do with antlers and wiggle eyes instead of claws.

Her sisters had thrown a surprise going-away party during her last visit to her parents' home in Baltimore. Gwen had felt uncomfortable through the whole party. For some reason she felt as if she was letting everyone down. But then again, that was her usual feeling around her family. Somehow she just never quite measured up to her sisters.

Gwen really did love her overachieving sisters. Jocelyn was the easy one to understand. Everyone loved Jocelyn for her sweetness and sense of justice.

Jocelyn never met a stranger, and she had never known an enemy. If Gwen was ever in a fix, Jocelyn would be the first person she'd call. Jocelyn had wished her well and given her an apron with a lobster printed on it, along with a bottle of very expensive wine. Jocelyn's gifts were always practical and useful.

To a stranger, Sydney would seem to be the stand-offish sister. Underneath the hard professional shell, she had a soft marshmallow heart and a wicked sense of humor. Gwen liked to refer to it as the "Richard factor." Richard Wainbright was the doctor Sydney had been living with for years. Saying Richard was a stuffed shirt would be an insult to stuffed shirts everywhere. Richard was vain, arrogant, had no sense of humor at all, and was suffering from the biggest God complex Gwen had ever seen in a person. And having been brought up in her parents' circle of friends and acquaintances, she would have to say she had seen some colossal God complexes. What Sydney saw in that man was beyond her, but to each his own.

Gwen turned her thoughts away from Needle-ass Richard and concentrated on the man standing fifteen feet away. Her first impression of Daniel had leaned toward the standoffish side, but something was telling her that wasn't the case. She wouldn't class him as shy, and he seemed to get along with everyone in town. The way he treated Jonah and Clarence was sweet, yet he considered them both reliable and able men even though they were obviously in their seventies. Daniel didn't talk down to the two elderly men, and he seemed to get along well with Hunter.

It was the scar that made Daniel a little hesitant around her, or at least that was what Gwen thought. She noticed how he always positioned himself so she wasn't looking at the left side of his face. It was a real shame he was so conscious of the mark around her. The scar didn't seem to bother him when he was with the men. She was curious to see if he acted the same way around other women. For the hundredth time she wondered how he had gotten it.

"That's it, Hunter, hold her steady." Daniel whammed a nail home. "Perfect." A moment later another nail was pounded into the framework.

Gwen watched Daniel's hands as he neatly and accurately pounded in nails, securing the door frame into the supporting studs. The hammer didn't miss its mark once. If Daniel's hands were that talented with wood and nails, she could just imagine what they would do with a woman's body. She'd heard that men who worked with their hands to make their living made fantastic lovers. They had a heightened sense of touch, or so the saying went. She wondered how sharpened Daniel's sense of touch had grown over the years. That particular question had been plaguing her for days and nights. Especially the nights.

The front door of the restaurant opened, pulling her away from her erotic thoughts of Daniel's hands. She turned her head and nearly swallowed her tongue as a Viking god wearing tight jeans and a navy windbreaker stepped into the dining room. The man was at least a couple of inches taller than Daniel's six-foot, one-inch height and had naturally blond hair, neatly combed and pulled back into a ponytail. And a square, firm jaw, light blue eyes, and a set of biceps that suggested that the man could bench press a minivan. She would have to be dead not to appreciate such male beauty and strength. The man belonged in some Hollywood action-adventure flick, not in a small Maine fishing village.

Gwen blinked twice and then looked over at

Hunter and Daniel to see if they had noticed the man—or had she breathed in too many dust bunnies from the storage space and was now hallucinating romance-novel cover models.

Hunter obviously saw him because he nodded to the man. She thought she heard Daniel groan before saying, "Morning, Erik. What brings you here?"

"I heard Misty Harbor has a new resident." The Viking flashed her a smile that appeared dazzling white against his tanned skin. "I came to welcome her to our humble village."

Daniel gave the frame of the door one last look before walking away and joining her. "Gwen, I'd like you to meet Erik Olsen. He's one of the local fishermen." Daniel glanced at the man blocking half the light coming in from the patio doors. "Erik, I'd like you to meet Gwen Fletcher, owner of this soon-to-be-open restaurant."

Erik reached for her hand and brought her knuckles up to his lips. "As they say in this country, enchanted." He brushed a kiss across her knuckles.

Gwen forced herself not to giggle as Daniel rolled his eyes and Hunter covered up his laugh with a cough. The look in Erik's sky-blue eyes was serious and measuring. She'd never had anyone kiss her hand before and was unsure how to respond to such a gesture. "Thank you" was the best she could come up with as she gently tugged her hand out of his grasp. "You have an interesting accent; where are you from originally?"

"I am Norwegian by birth, but now I'm American." Erik seemed immensely proud of that fact. "My brother and I came three years ago to find our grandfather. We decided to stay."

"Did you find your grandfather?" Erik appeared to be in his late twenties or early thirties, and he was more imposing up close and personal. The navy blue T-shirt he wore beneath the unzipped windbreaker was molded to his well-developed chest. Erik had muscles on his muscles. What did the man do in his spare time, toss tractor trailers around for the fun of it?

"Yes, Grandfather lives here in Misty Harbor." Erik picked up the beige bucket he had set down to take her hand. "I've brought you a welcoming present." He handed her the bucket. "Freshly caught this morning."

Gwen looked into the bucket and was surprised to see about a dozen Acadian redfish. They were all dead and packed with chipped ice. It was the strangest welcoming present she had ever received. Recipes danced through her mind until she selected one she knew she had the ingredients for, blackened redfish. Served with rice and some vegtables, they would be perfect. "Thank you, Erik, they're wonderful."

Erik beamed while Daniel frowned at the dead fish. "Do you know how to cook them?" Daniel asked.

"Yes, I do." Gwen eagerly glanced into the bucket. This would be the first time she would be cooking fish for the men. She was anxious to see how her fish dishes measured up to the rest of Maine's cooking. "I was just wondering what to make for lunch. I believe you just solved my problem, Erik. If I cook them up, would you care to join us?"

"Only if you allow me to clean them for you." Erik took back the heavy bucket.

"I could help him, Gwen," Hunter said as he glanced into the bucket.

Gwen didn't think anyone actually liked to gut and clean fish, so her money was on Hunter being hungry. Apparently the oatmeal raisin muffins she'd made this morning weren't enough to tide

the men over. Even Daniel was staring at the fish
with a gleam of appreciation in his gray eyes. "Deal;
you guys clean them and I'll cook them." She
tugged on her filthy sweatshirt and cringed. So
much for impressing the neighbors. "Hunter, you
know where everything is in the kitchen, right?"
At Hunter's nod, she added, "I think I'll go clean
up before I start any cooking."

Erik seemed ready to argue with her, but he took
another look at her sweatshirt and politely kept his
mouth shut. Daniel gave her a funny glance, turned
on his heels, and went back to pounding in nails.

Half an hour later Daniel entered the kitchen
and frowned at Leif Eriksson and the Galloping
Gourmet. Gwen and Erik seemed to be hitting it
off rather well. For some reason he'd rather not
dwell on, seeing them side by side frying up fish
disturbed him on a primitive male level. He wanted
to walk over there and bodily remove Erik from
Gwen's side. Hell, he wanted to toss the hulking
Viking out of the restaurant on his Norwegian ass.
It was a strange reaction to have concerning one's
boss.

And he'd better not forget that Gwen was,
indeed, his boss. She was the one paying his salary.
It didn't matter if he was suffering from some pretty
un-employeelike fantasies about the enticing cook.
Gwendolyn Fletcher was off limits.

Besides, he wasn't in the market for a relationship. Every other available male over the age of
twenty in Misty Harbor was looking for a wife, but
he wasn't. Erik Olsen was no exception. Erik had
let everyone within shouting distance know he was
shopping for a wife and the future mother of his
children.

Daniel joined Gwen, looking over her shoulder

at the quick-frying fish. The thick, heavy smoke was being sucked upward. The exhaust from the stove was turned on high, so he had to shout above the noise. "So, Erik, any luck yet finding the mother of your children?"

Gwen gave a sudden start, but Daniel couldn't tell whether he had startled her by his appearance directly behind her or by his question.

Erik smiled and looked squarely at Gwen. "No, but the prospects just got better."

Little furrows appeared on Gwen's forehead. Daniel tried not to laugh or grin. It would be totally unsportsmanlike. "You did say you wanted at least six, or was it eight, Erik?"

"Wives?" Gwen squeaked.

"No, one wife, six children," Erik said with a smile. "A man can't have enough sons." Seeing Gwen's frown, Erik quickly added, "Or daughters."

Gwen took a tentative step toward Daniel but kept her gaze on Erik. "That sounds like you're planning a lovely, *large* family." She turned back to the stove, removed the two blackened fillets from the frying pan, and put in the last two. "Lunch is just about ready. Daniel, will you set the table, please, and Erik, would you run upstairs and tell Jonah and Clarence lunch is ready?"

"What about Hunter?" Erik asked.

"I'm already here," Hunter answered as he walked into the kitchen carrying the used paint tray, roller, and brush. Hunter's dark green plaid shirt was sporting a couple of sprinkles of white paint. So were his hands, and he had a smear of white on his jaw.

Daniel reached for a stack of plates and started to set the table as Erik left the room. He was pleased that Gwen had chosen to send Erik from the room, not him. He wondered if it had been the mention of six kids that had made the choice. It wasn't really fair of him to blurt out that Erik was wife- and uterus-hunting like that, but Gwen needed to know the truth.

There were a lot more Eriks in this town, and eventually each and every one of them would come knocking on Gwen's door. Probably all of them would be bearing flowers and heart-shaped boxes of candy. He had to grudgingly admit that Erik's bucket of freshly caught fish was both original and appreciated. The way Gwen's face had lit up at the sight of those dead fish, one would think someone had just given her jewels. He speculated about Norwegian courting customs as he set out the silverware.

"Gwennie, my love," shouted Jonah as he pushed open both swinging doors and stepped into the room, along with Erik. "Something sure does smell delicious in here."

Clarence seconded Jonah's opinion. "Gwendolyn, for one of your meals, I will surely continue to build you shelves, clear up to heaven if need be."

Gwen's sparkling gaze met his before she rolled her eyes and placed the platter of fish in the center of the table. He had already carried over the rice and vegetables. "That's laying it on kind of thick, don't you think, Clarence? Especially since I know Hunter definitely knows his way around the kitchen. Your son isn't about to let you starve."

"True, but he's not as easy on the eyes," Clarence replied with smug satisfaction as he made his way to the sink to wash up.

Jonah laughed as he dried his hands on a paper towel. Gwen blushed at the compliment, and Erik grunted his approval. Daniel wholeheartedly agreed. There was no comparison between Gwen's luscious, compact body and Hunter's. Gwen could snuggle up to his stove anytime she wanted to.

Erik held out Gwen's chair and politely sat her as if she were the queen of England. A becoming blush stained her cheeks as she thanked him.

Clarence, Hunter, and Jonah all glared at Daniel, as if somehow having another guest for lunch was his fault. Daniel ignored the men and sat in his usual seat. Erik, naturally, took the seat next to Gwen.

"Do you cook lunch every day?" Erik asked as he helped himself to the rice and then passed it to Gwen.

"Yes." Gwen placed some rice on her plate and passed the bowl on. "I'm trying out recipes and fine-tuning the menu."

"We're her food critics!" Jonah said as he passed the platter of blackened redfish. "If you eat, you have to tell Gwen your honest opinion of each dish. Even if you don't like it, you still have to tell her."

Erik studied the food on his plate. "I'm sure it's all delicious, and I can't imagine anyone not liking a thing. Gwen's an excellent cook; I watched her make lunch myself."

"He's not going to give you an honest answer, Gwendolyn," Clarence said as he scooped a pile of petite green beans and almonds onto his plate. "He's going to tell you everything was great."

"I will not," Erik replied in a rather loud voice.

"You're not going to tell Gwen that her cooking is delicious?" Jonah asked with just the right hint of concern in his voice.

Daniel hid his smile at Erik's outraged expression and took his first bite of fish. It was scrumptious, both the fish and the conversation. Clarence and Jonah were overprotective of the town's newest resident, and not above yanking Erik's chain. He should have felt sorry for Erik, but he couldn't bring himself to do it. Vikings should have thick skin, to go along with their thick skulls.

Erik sputtered, and his Scandinavian accent became more pronounced. "I said no such thing."

"Jonah and Clarence, knock it off," Gwen said. She turned to Erik and lightly patted his hand. "They're teasing you. Just yesterday Clarence told me the rack of lamb was missing something, and Jonah turned his nose up at my brussels sprouts."

"Oh, Gwennie, my love," Jonah moaned. "You can't hold that against me forever. I've hated those horrible things since I was a small boy and my mother forced me to eat them." Jonah sadly shook his head. "Even for you, I can't bring myself to try them again."

"I like vegetables." Erik took a forkful of green beans and put it in his mouth to prove his words. He smiled at Gwen the whole time he chewed.

Gwen started to smile back before she glanced around the table. Her smile slipped into a frown. Every man there was eating his green beans and grinning. Including Daniel.

A moment later, Gwen's laughter filled the room. "You guys are impossible."

Jonah and Clarence beamed proudly. Hunter politely nodded his head. Erik seemed a bit confused by the conversation but smiled anyway. Daniel was too busy watching the laughter in Gwen's eyes to give a response. She was breathtakingly beautiful when she laughed. A man could count himself lucky to have such a woman in his life. Gwen wasn't only attractive on the outside, she was also beautiful on the inside, where it mattered most.

He quietly ate his meal and watched as Gwen put Erik at ease and made him feel welcome without being overly friendly or flirtatious. She had done the same with Wendell Kirby the other day.

Gwen also pulled Hunter into the conversation while mostly ignoring Jonah's and Clarence's out-rageous compliments. Topics ranged from how to cook striped bass to the Harbor Jazz Weekend com-ing up in June.

Daniel sat there and watched the way Gwen inter-acted with Jonah and Clarence. She listened to their every word, laughed at their jokes, and was interested in their outlandish fishing stories. A lot could be said about a person by how he or she treated children and the elderly. There weren't any children around the restaurant, but Gwen passed the senior-citizen test with flying colors. She honestly liked both older men, and it showed.

After everyone but Gwen had seconds, Hunter was the first to stand up and start clearing off the table. Hunter had an obsession with keeping the kitchen in tiptop shape. Daniel didn't feel like mov-ing. After every one of Gwen's meals he felt like taking a nap. The Mexicans had the right idea about siestas. Of course, it didn't help matters that he wasn't getting his usual amount of sleep at night. He was restless throughout the night, but that didn't seem to stop him from being wide awake every morning to greet the dawn.

"Daniel, do you want to come upstairs and check out the job we're doing?" Clarence asked as he carried his plate and glass to the sink.

"He doesn't need to check on us, Clarence." Jonah frowned at his lifelong friend. "I think we can manage to build some simple shelves on our own."

"I'm sure you can." Daniel didn't really need to check on the work. Jonah and Clarence were both good with their hands. He was more concerned with them overdoing it, and hurting themselves, than the actual construction of the storage shelves they were building upstairs out of the recycled booths. Gwen needed the shelves, and it kept Jonah from insisting on helping him with the heavy patio doors. "I do need to check out what kind of paint would work best on them, though. I'll be up later, okay?"

"Sure, but you better not say one word about how we're building them," Jonah said. "We were both building shelves before you were even born."

Erik and Gwen chuckled as Clarence and Jonah left the kitchen to head back upstairs. A surprisingly similar sound was coming from Hunter. It was nice to know he could bring some happiness into their lives. "When you have a minute, Gwen, I need your opinion on the outside trim of the patio doors."

"Sure, I'll be right there." Gwen put the remaining fillets in a plastic container and placed it in the refrigerator.

"I'd better be going too," Erik said as he handed Hunter the last of the dirty dishes.

Gwen walked with Erik out of the kitchen and toward the front door of the restaurant. Daniel slowly followed and headed for his toolbox, then started to rummage through it looking for a screwdriver. He found six of them, but none was the one he wanted.

"Thanks for the fish, Erik. That was really sweet of you."

"Your cooking did them justice." Erik stopped with his hand on the knob and gazed at Gwen. "Catch of the Day is going to be a huge success and I can't wait until it opens. My cooking is passable at best, but my brother Gunnar's is horrible. Most of the time it's inedible."

"Thank you, and make sure to mention the restaurant to Gunnar."

"Will do." Erik's next words made Daniel freeze.

"Would you like to go out to a movie or dinner sometime?"

Daniel frowned at the three screwdrivers in his hand and was amazed to see that the plastic handles weren't cracking from his grip. He knew the men of the village would be hounding Gwen. He just hadn't expected them to do it right in front of him. To watch Gwen accept a date with Lief Eriksson and his rippling biceps would be pure torture. Hearing her accept was going to be bad enough.

"Thank you for asking, Erik, but I can't. There's so much that needs to be done here before the grand opening, and I still haven't unpacked all the moving boxes at home."

"After you get settled in, I could show you around the area. Or maybe take you out on my boat for the day and teach you how to catch striped bass or cod."

"Clarence and Jonah have already promised me fishing lessons, Erik." Gwen's voice was low, sincere, and just a tad apologetic. "I'm sorry, but I really don't have time to form any relationships beyond friendship."

"Then friendship it will be, Gwen."

Daniel heard the door close behind Erik but didn't turn around to look at Gwen. She wouldn't appreciate the silly grin spreading across his face. Amazingly, Gwen had turned down the Norwegian hunk flat. If he hadn't heard it himself he would never have believed it.

He took the steps two at a time as he went upstairs to check on what kind of paint would be best for the shelves.

Chapter Seven

Maggie tilted her face up toward the sun and felt its warmth caress her skin. Heaven would be close to the sun. She closed her eyes and listened to the sounds that surrounded her. Familiar sounds. The joyful noise of life going on all around her. The cry of soaring seagulls gave her peace, and the sound of children's laughter lightened her heart. Among the shouts and giggles, she could pick out her daughter's laughter. Katie's laugh rang true and clear and went straight to her heart.

Katie was adjusting very well to living in Misty Harbor. It was more than she could say about herself.

She opened her eyes and searched through the bright jackets and heavy sweatshirts until she spotted her daughter sliding down a yellow plastic sliding board. Katie's dazzling orange zip-up sweatshirt with a picture of the Little Mermaid and Flounder printed on its front and her bright red hair were easy to pick out of the crowd. It seemed every mother and grandmother had had the same idea of taking the kids to the park. Today was the first nice, warm day of the year. Fifty-six degrees felt like a virtual heat wave after a harsh Maine winter. Her own mother had practically kicked her and Katie out of the house this afternoon.

Maggie knew what her mother was trying to do, and getting Katie some fresh spring air wasn't all of it. Her mother wanted her to get out, meet people, and get reacquainted with everyone. Well, she and Katie had walked the couple of blocks to the park, but so far she hadn't reacquainted herself with anyone. She already knew that every woman who was sitting in the park was talking about her, though avoiding direct eye contact.

Being the center of everyone's attention was about as appealing as walking naked down Main Street during the Fourth of July parade. Life in Misty Harbor was one big fishbowl. Everyone knew everyone else's business, and Lord help those who didn't conform to the town's standards.

She watched as Katie held another little girl's hand and dashed back up the gangplank of the miniature pirate ship the men's group at the local Lutheran church had built last year. Maggie's father and brother both had contributed many a Saturday to the project. Her mom had mailed her the article and picture the local newspaper had printed when the pirate ship had been completed. For a town as beautiful as Misty Harbor, it had a pitifully small number of children, growing smaller every year.

She smiled as first Katie and then the other little girl slid down the board, only to run back up the gangplank again. A cargo net, for climbing, was attached to the ship on the opposite end from the gangplank. A wiggling heap of arms, legs, and laughter was slowly making its way up the six-foot-wide net.

Maggie's mouth curved into an easy smile at the boys' antics. If things had been different, she would have loved to give Katie a little brother. Jeremy hadn't wanted to hear one word about having another baby, even after he received his master's degree. It had broken her heart at the time, but now she realized why he hadn't wanted any more children. He hadn't been planning to stay married for too much longer. In a way she should be thankful to him for not giving in to her tears at the time. She couldn't imagine how she would have managed with Katie and a newborn when Jeremy walked out the door without a backward glance.

She never could have asked her mother to watch two kids while she went to college and worked. Guilt was eating her alive for depending on her mother and father to help with Katie for the next year. Her mother had worked hard raising her own two children on a fisherman's pay. Now it was her mother's time to enjoy some of life's simpler pleasures, like the quilting circle she joined every Tuesday morning, and the Women's Guild meetings on Thursdays. Come September, Katie would be starting in a half-day nursery school program, but that still left the summer to get through.

The way things were going, her mom wouldn't be stuck baby-sitting all the time. So far, Maggie's schedule was only filled on Monday and Wednesday, when she took the two college courses starting in June. Employment opportunities in Misty Harbor were worse than she had expected. She was even coming up dry on prospects in the surrounding towns and villages.

Oh, there were a couple of possibilities. She had gone on three job interviews since moving in with her parents over a week earlier. She had been qualified, if not overqualified, for every one of those positions. But every interview had been a bust, and she had known it even before she had a chance to sit down with whomever was hiring. Her shame had preceded her.

She had hurt one of the finest men in Misty Harbor, and no one was about to let her forget it. She didn't owe the town an apology, and there was no way to compensate for her past sin. The townspeople had to look into their own hearts and forgive her. That would be a neat trick, since she hadn't learned to forgive herself yet. She needed Daniel Creighton's forgiveness, but she could never ask for that. She didn't deserve his leniency.

"Mommy, Mommy, Mommy," cried Katie as she ran over to her, tugging a little girl behind her. "This is my new friend, 'Lizabeth. She's four too!"

Maggie smiled at the dark-haired girl standing next to Katie. "Hello, Elizabeth. I'm Katie's mom, Maggie Pierce."

"I'm 'Lizabeth Claire Burton."

"I would have known you anywhere. You're the spitting image of your mother, Carol Ann." She glanced over to a bench where three young women sat talking. Carol Ann Burton was gently rocking a baby stroller with a sleeping baby inside it and watching her daughter. Maggie nodded in greeting, and Carol Ann slowly nodded back but didn't make any move to come join in the conversation. "I went to school with your mother years ago, and if my memory is correct, you have an older brother named Samuel."

"Sam says I'm a sissy girl." Elizabeth rolled her big brown eyes and sighed dramatically. Maggie could see an actress in the making and tried not to grin. "I've got a new baby brother named Devin," continued Elizabeth, "but he cries all the time."

"Babies do that a lot. I'm sure he'll outgrow it

soon." Maggie couldn't help but give the child some hope.

"That's what my mom says, but Daddy says it's hopeless." Elizabeth tugged on Katie's hand. "Where's your baby brother?"

"I don't have one." Katie gave her mother a look, as if to say that it was all her fault. "Maybe I can get one for Christmas this year."

It was a good thing the only objects in Maggie's mouth were her own teeth and her tongue or she would have choked to death. Somehow she didn't think any of the women sitting around the park would have rushed over to administer the Heimlich maneuver.

"I want a bicycle for Christmas," Elizabeth said. "The kind with two wheels."

"Me too!" cried Katie. "Grandpop can get me a bicycle and Mommy can get me a brother."

Maggie slowly shook her head at her daughter. A bicycle was doable; a baby was an impossibility, no matter how good her daughter was for the remainder of the year.

A baby's cry split the air, and Elizabeth groaned. "That's Devin," Elizabeth said without even turning around to see which baby was the one crying.

Maggie looked over at Carol Ann and the rest of the bench filled with sleep-deprived mothers. Every woman there had a stroller in front of her being gently rocked. A colorful bundle of blankets lay in each one. It must have been one wild Jazz weekend in Misty Harbor last June; all of the bundles appeared to be the same size. Sure enough, it was Carol Ann who lifted her bundle out of the stroller. "How did you know that was Devin crying, Elizabeth?"

The small girl gave her a resigned look and rolled her eyes. "It's always Devin crying." Elizabeth turned and tugged Katie's hand again. "Come on, Katie. Let's go climb the monkey bars."

Maggie watched her daughter and Elizabeth run across the play area and start to climb the metal bars of a giant spaceship. Someone had painted the bars an incandescent yellow that not only matched the swing set, but stood out nicely against the dark mulch covering the area. The town took great pride in Wyndham Park and kept it clean and in good repair for its residents and the occasional tourist who ventured away from the docks.

Millicent Wyndham had donated everything the park needed, including the large gazebo at the other end, where summer concerts were held nearly every Saturday night. Millicent was the town's benefactor, and one of the nicest ladies Maggie knew. The other day, while she had been in Krup's General Store, Millicent had gone out of her way to welcome her back, and to buy Katie an ice cream cone. For a whole ten minutes, Maggie had actually felt welcome in her hometown.

Now she felt like a leper. The women of the town were giving her the cold shoulder, but at least they weren't taking out their hostilities on Katie. No one had stopped her child from playing with Maggie's daughter. The hearts of Misty Harbor might be a tad slow to forgive, but they didn't hold a grudge against an innocent child. For that she was eternally grateful.

Devin's cries woke one of the other babies, whose cries woke the third. In a matter of fifty seconds all three babies were screaming their heads off and scaring away the seagulls. Three harried mothers frantically looked for bottles or pacifiers. Two of the mothers, all younger than Maggie, glared at Carol Ann the entire time they bounced a baby in one arm and with the other hand rooted through diaper bags the size of luggage that would definitely have to be checked at the airline counter.

Maggie almost felt sorry for Carol Ann. Almost.

She glanced down at the thick book sitting on her lap. She hadn't gotten very far in it. *Computer Language Concepts* had been one of her textbooks five years ago. She had passed the course with a B+, but it seemed like a lifetime ago. The book was probably hopelessly out of date by now, but it might keep her from looking like a complete idiot when she walked back into a classroom come June. She didn't have any extra money to spend on a refresher course.

If she didn't get a job real soon, she might not have the money to pay for the courses she needed to take to finally get her degree.

"Elizabeth," shouted Carol Ann over the bawling of the baby in her arms. "We have to go home now. Devin isn't cooperating."

Maggie watched as Elizabeth and Katie conferred for a moment; then the other girl headed for her mother and screaming brother. Katie slowly made her way back over to her mom and sat down on the bench beside her with a dejected sigh.

Katie's gaze followed her new friend as she walked beside her mother and the stroller heading out of the park. Devin's cries could still be heard, but they were growing fainter as the distance increased. Every few steps, Elizabeth turned around and waved. Katie waved back. When they finally disappeared from sight Katie looked directly at Maggie and said, "I only want a bicycle for Christmas."

Gwen felt a headache coming on as she looked at the five women sitting in her restaurant kitchen and forced herself to keep on smiling. They were all potential customers, or so she kept telling herself. Every one of them looked as if she could hold her own in a bake-off. "Would anyone care for another cup of coffee?"

She couldn't offer them another muffin, because the women had managed to eat not only the eight blueberry ones she had on hand, but also a dozen and a half oatmeal raisin cookies. Jonah and Clarence were going to be very upset when they came downstairs for their afternoon snack only to find the cupboard bare. The men would have to make do with reheated redfish and rice, which they'd had for lunch.

"Maybe half a cup." A birdlike woman who couldn't weigh more than a hundred pounds soaking wet and holding a sack of potatoes pushed her cup forward. Gwen couldn't remember her name—it was Nora or Norma, or something like that—but she remembered the skinny woman had polished off at least two of the muffins and a handful of cookies. Then she'd had the gall to suggest that Gwen add a pinch more cinnamon to the next batch of cookies.

"Yes, please," another woman said as she held up her cup for Gwen to refill. "My doctor said I'm allowed coffee."

Gwen remembered the woman's name. She had never met a Priscilla before, but somewhere in her mind an image of Elvis's beautiful and slim wife had been conjured up. This Priscilla could have made three of Mrs. Presley. The woman kept blabbering about doctors' orders and how she was only allowed to pick at her food. Gwen had counted her picking at three different muffins and a half dozen cookies.

The other three women, who made up the welcoming committee of the Women's Guild at the Misty Harbor Lutheran Church, seemed nice and sympathetic to Gwen's dwindling food supply. They hadn't invaded her kitchen to find another member for their church, nor did they have a religious agenda. They had stopped by to welcome her to town, and to give her a copy of a cookbook they had published at Christmastime, to help raise funds for a new organ. Every recipe in the book had been donated by a local resident and came highly recommended. Most had been handed down through the generations, or so she had been told.

Gwen refilled the last of the cups and sat back down in her seat. The Women's Guild didn't seem to have anyplace they would rather be at the moment. She resigned herself to another half hour of cooking advice from some of the town's matrons.

The third time Nora, or Norma, mentioned her grandmother's lobster chowder secret recipe that hadn't been included in the book, Gwen had had enough. While she appreciated the ladies' guidance, she had a million things that needed to be done. But there was something the Guild could help her with. "Ladies, the other day Wendell Kirby stopped by to welcome me to town."

"Watch it, Gwen," advised Connie. "He's looking for wife number three."

"That would explain the flowers," Gwen muttered to herself. It also explained the phone call she had received the next night, asking her out to the movies. Wendell had been on the make.

"Heck, he was test-driving wife number two while still married to number one. The man's a hound dog," Grace, the minister's wife, declared. "You can do much better than him, Gwen."

"I have a nephew who's still single," Priscilla said. "Gregory would make some lucky woman a wonderful husband. He's into computers, you know."

Grace shot her an amused look and shook her

head slightly. Gregory obviously wasn't as wonderful as Auntie was making him out to be.

"My husband's younger brother, Ted, would be a much better match for Gwen," Ruth, the quietest woman, finally spoke up. "Ted simply loves food."

Gwen cringed as someone—she thought Nora-Norma—muttered something about it showing too. The last thing she needed was the Women's Guild fixing her up with every available man in Misty Harbor. That thought alone was enough to give her nightmares. She needed to straighten out the women, and fast.

"Well, I'm not looking for a husband, or even a boyfriend. The restaurant will be requiring all my time. I won't have the energy for a relationship for quite some time." Gwen gave them all an apologetic smile and hoped that would be the end of it. By the calculating gleam in one or two ladies' eyes, she didn't think the old gals were buying it. "Mr. Kirby mentioned a whole list of special events and weekend activities that Misty Harbor puts on every year. He's expecting the restaurant to gear its menu and its hours to each event. I've got to admit I'm stumped on how to do it." Gwen got up and found the list and dates of the upcoming events and a pencil.

She read the first item on the list. "In June there's a Harbor Jazz Weekend. What in the world does he expect the restaurant to do? So far I figured I could play some classical jazz CDs on the sound system."

"That's a good start," Grace said.

"How are your menus printed?" Connie asked.

"The lunch menus will be the same just about every day, but the dinner menus will change constantly, depending on the catch of the day and the availability of certain items. I'm planning on doing the menu on a daily basis on my computer. Print it out on fancy paper and slip it into a clear plastic holder.''

"Wonderful.'' Connie beamed. "For the special events you can simply change the names of the entrees. Like the Duke Ellington special or the Louis Armstrong burger. It would be the same food, just different names.''

"That's great, Connie.'' Gwen liked the idea very much, but she couldn't imagine her own mother eating the Dizzy Gillespie baked salmon or the Miles Davis lobster tail special.

"Oh, I get it,'' cried Grace. "For the Fourth of July you can serve George Washington cherry pie and John Hancock prime rib.''

The more she thought about it, the more Gwen liked the idea. It wouldn't take hardly any effort on her part to think up different names and retype the menu. The waiting and kitchen staff might get a bit confused, but that could be handled. "Ladies, I do believe you are all geniuses. Not only did you help me with the Jazz Weekend, but your idea will work for all the events.'' If she had a bottle of chilled wine and another six dozen cookies, she could have thrown a party.

Maybe tonight she would go through their "local'' cookbook with a more discerning eye. Some of these ladies seemed to have a lot on the ball.

"Well, since you helped me out with that problem, I have another one for you.'' Might as well use the local grapevine. It could save her weeks of headaches and advertising money.

The ladies all leaned forward, eager to help. "Does anyone know of anyone looking for a job? I'm going to need waitresses, busers, dishwashers, an assistant cook, and a hostess. Most of the jobs will be part time and perfect for high-school students looking for summer jobs or maybe weekend work during the school year.''

Names started flying fast and furious. Gwen chuckled and held up her hand. ''Okay, here's what I want you to do. Spread the word and have whoever is interested stop by after Monday to fill out an application.''

''What if we know someone who would be perfect for the job?'' Priscilla asked.

''Tell them to fill out the application.'' She looked at Priscilla as if she were missing a couple of crayons from her box. Hadn't she just said that?

''No, I mean like a relative or a very close friend of the family.'' Priscilla looked around the table for support. A couple of gray heads nodded in understanding. ''Since we're friends and all, how would you know that we highly recommend this person for the job?''

''Ah, now I get it.'' Unbeknownst to her, Gwen had somehow magically forged a lifelong bond with the Women's Guild over muffins and cookies. Now it was going to be expected that she hire Uncle Bernie who had a habit of drinking a bottle of Jack Daniels a day and whose family has been hiding the sharp knives from him for the past decade. Great. Talk about backing yourself into a corner. ''Tell just the very special ones to put your name at the bottom of the application. That way I know they come highly recommended.''

Visions of someone's bald daughter who was into black leather and whips, snake tattoos, and eyebrow piercings seating her dinner clientele made her stomach burn and her palms break out in a sweat. Catch of the Day was going to be raided by the police before its grand opening.

* * *

Gwen pressed the phone between her ear and her shoulder as she finished unloading the dishwasher. It was after nine at night, and her sister Jocelyn had just gotten home from work. "You're working too hard, Joc."

"Look who's talking," came the reply. "Aren't you the one starting her own restaurant?"

"Yeah, but I've been home for hours." Gwen glanced at the clock. Two constituted a plural. By the time she had gotten rid of the Women's Guild she had been so far behind schedule, she hadn't known where to start. So she did what any great cook did when facing indecision—she went food shopping. By the time she unloaded her cart at the checkout counter, the cashier, who had teal hair and seven silver rings in one ear and one whopper of a barbell through her tongue, had asked her how much the buser jobs were paying and could she have weekends off? The Women's Guild had wasted no time in spreading the word.

"How's that gorgeous carpenter you're always talking about doing?" Jocelyn gave a weary sigh. "Why is it that I'm fantasizing about the man in your life?"

"Daniel's not in my life; he's in my restaurant." She never should have told her baby sister about Daniel. For some reason, he was personal. She didn't want Jocelyn or any other woman fantasizing about him.

"To you, it's the same thing."

"I did get asked on a date today." Time for a subject change. "And no, it wasn't by Daniel."

"Who?"

"A six-foot-three Viking named Erik."

"You're kidding!" Jocelyn squeaked. "They have Vikings in Maine?"

"No, he's Norwegian, with long blond hair, sky blue eyes, and a chest that is so magnificent that even Mom wouldn't cut it open to save his life." She gave a dramatic pause while her sister mulled over the description. "His idea of a welcome-to-town gift was a dozen of the most delicious redfish I have ever tasted. The man does know how to treat a woman."

"He brought you cooked fish?"

"No, he brought me dead fish, which he was nice enough to gut and clean for me. I cooked them."

Jocelyn's laughter was so loud, she had to hold the phone away from her ear for a moment. When she thought it was safe, she replaced it against her ear. She heard her sister say, "He brought you dead fish?"

"Yes, he did. An entire bucket filled and packed in chipped ice. He caught them himself too."

"I can't wait to hear where you two are going on your first date. He's probably taking you hunting or something equally revolting and manly. Maybe you can skin a polar bear together. Poor animals."

Gwen frowned at the empty dishwasher. Where did Jocelyn think the salmon she loved so much came from? A salmon tree? "There aren't any polar bears in Maine, and if there were I think they would be a little too 'gamey' for most people's taste." Just to irk her sister, Gwen added, "Now moose might be another story."

Jocelyn didn't bite. "So where is Viking man taking you?"

"He's not taking me anywhere, Joc." She didn't want her sister laughing about Erik. He had seemed very nice and sweet. Any women would count herself fortunate to go out with such an incredible hunk. Of course, the man would have to wear a bib because his date would be drooling all over his chest. "I turned him down." She definitely didn't want to examine the reasons behind that decision.

What she had told Erik and the Women's Guild was true: she didn't have time for dates or relationships. But that hadn't been the main reason behind refusing Erik. The main reason had been standing ten feet away at the time, and going through his tool box.

"Tell me you're kidding?"

"No can do." Gwen turned the tables on her little sister. "So, Joc, how's your love life?"

"The last man who showed me any interest was the night janitor. He's about seventy, has an entire photo album of pictures of his grandkids in his back pocket, and will show them to you without any provocation. Walter seems to think I work too many hours."

Gwen smiled. "Walter sounds like he knows what he's talking about."

"Could you send the Viking down this way?" Jocelyn's wistful sigh carried across the miles. "Baltimore's a little short on them right now."

"You wouldn't have time for him anyway, Joc."

"I'm usually free on Sundays."

"Erik's the kind of man you would want to spend more than one day a week with, trust me." She gave her sister a wicked chuckle just to let her know what she was missing. "You'd be calling in sick to work every day. You'd lose your job, then your apartment and your Volvo. Next thing you know, you're living on his boat, doing such manly things as fishing for a living, and raising six sons who'd want to go out raiding and pillaging with their father till all hours of the night."

"Oh, damn," Jocelyn said.

"What?"

"I don't have vacation time till July."

Gwen laughed. Jocelyn, who was even shorter than her own five-foot-four-inch height, always had a thing for big, strapping men. The bigger they were, the faster she wrapped them around her petite little finger and eventually broke off with them. Jocelyn went through men like some women went through panty hose—here one day, gone the next. Privately she thought Jocelyn was looking for a man who wouldn't cave in to her every whim. Instinct told her Erik would crumble within a week.

"This is the part of the conversation when you invite me up for a week," Jocelyn complained.

"You already know you're invited to come up anytime you want. Just give me a week's notice so I can go out and buy a guest-room bed. If not, you're sleeping on the couch. Last time I slept with you, you were six, and you stole all the covers. Let me tell you, having someone steal your covers while sleeping in Maine is the last thing you want."

This time it was Jocelyn's turn to laugh. "Who said anything about sleeping at your place, especially if Lief Eriksson is still beating his chest looking for a mate."

Gwen laughed with her sister. She knew Jocelyn well enough to realize she was all talk and no action. Erik Olsen would be one frustrated Viking by the time Jocelyn headed back to Baltimore. "I don't think Misty Harbor is ready for you yet, sister dear."

"Hmmm . . . maybe I'll bring Sydney up there with me. She needs to loosen up some, and a wild Viking sounds like just the ticket."

"She'd be fine if she just didn't give in to Richard all the time—and I didn't say Erik was wild. He seems like a very nice man."

"Oh, come on. Can you honestly compare this fantasy god to Needle Ass Richard?"

"Nope." Laughter caused her voice to crack. "There's no comparison. But Sydney's a big girl. She knows what she wants, and she obviously wants Richard." There was no accounting for some people's taste. "She seems to love him."

"I think 'seems to' are the keywords here. Syd's been with Richard since college. Hell, he was probably her first and only lover. What does she know?"

"She's got a whole lot of fancy initials after her name. I don't think she became a pediatrician on her good looks, charm, and standing in the community."

"Okay, she's a wiz at ear infections and boo-boos, but she doesn't know jack shit about men. Look who she's living with, for cripe's sake, Richard Wainbright, who is a total pompous ass and his own special gift to the medical field."

Gwen had to agree with everything her sister was saying. Richard was a pompous ass, and Syd did defer nearly every decision to him, including the all-important wedding date commitment. Richard didn't want to set a date, yet they had been living together for four years. No one could call Syd a doormat, but whenever Richard was around, she was a different person. A person Gwen didn't know, or even like very much. If that was what love did to a woman, she'd rather forego the emotion, thank you very much.

"We can't just drag her away from Richard and toss her into the arms of a Viking."

"Hey, I get first dibs on Mr. Gorgeous Chest."

"Maybe he has a brother." Gwen couldn't imagine two Eriks walking around Misty Harbor unattached.

"Lord, two of them. Are you having the same erotic fantasy I am?" Jocelyn's voice rose an octave.

"No, my mind tends to stay out of the gutter, Joc." Gwen shook her head as she took inventory of her pantry, trying to decide what to make for dinner.

"That's because you're thinking about your carpenter."

"How's Mom, Joc?" Gwen closed the pantry door. She wasn't really hungry after all.

"Changing the subject is a sure sign that I hit a nerve or two. Admit it, Gwen, and I won't mention his name for the rest of this phone call. Admit that you are kind of sweet on Daniel."

Jocelyn could be a real pain in the ass when she set her mind to it. Obviously, tonight her mind was set on it. "I will admit there's something special about him, but that's all I'm admitting to."

"Fair enough. Mom's fine. I talked to her last night. She wanted me to go to some spring charity concert with her and Dad, but I bailed. Too much happening at work this time of year. It seems after a long cold winter all the nutcases come out from their hiding holes and go crazy on the population of Baltimore."

"How's Dad? I haven't talked to him in almost a week." She didn't envy her sister her job. Being an Assistant District Attorney in a major city sounded frustrating to her.

"He's all excited. Something about a new discovery in the lab a couple of days ago. You know Dad; once he gets on the subject and gets all technical, my eyes glaze over and I don't understand a word he says. By his smile, I would have to say whatever they discovered was good news. Give him enough time and he just might find the cure for cancer."

"We can only hope."

"How's the restaurant coming along?"

"The patio doors are in, and the kitchen is just about ready for some paint. It's coming along better than even I would had dreamed. It's going to be perfect."

"When's the grand opening?"

"Less than four weeks away. I'm still working on the menu and talking to food distributors."

"How's the house?"

"It's not a house, it's a cottage." Gwen glanced into the dining area and nearly groaned out loud. Kitchen gadgets and appliances still covered the table. She had moved the ones that had been littering the counter to the floor and chairs. "It's a little crammed right now, especially the kitchen, but I finally managed to get all of the boxes unpacked. I can actually find my bathrobe now."

"I can imagine. I've never seen a person with more kitchen stuff than you."

"Spoken like a woman who has a serving of dishes for four, two frying pans, and three whole pots."

"Yes, but I have a fantastic microwave, real crystal wineglasses, and the phone numbers of some of the best caterers in town."

Gwen groaned. "The caterer numbers were a low blow, Joc."

"I know, but you're the one who moved clear up to Maine. How am I suppose to impress my dates now that you aren't within easy traveling distance?"

"Tell them to take you out to eat."

"Grandmom Augusta always told us the fastest way to a man's heart is through his stomach."

"Then you should have spent more time in the kitchen learning to cook instead of reading all those mystery novels and taking ballet lessons."

"Hey, I'm graceful."

"That's a quality most men are looking for in a woman. It's right after 'shaves her legs and pits.' "

"You're just being cruel because you had a Viking panting after you already up there."

"He was the second male to ask me out since I moved here."

"Who was the first, a pirate?"

"No, the local motel owner. He's the president of the Chamber of Commerce, and I've heard it through the grapevine that he's looking for wife number three. He came visiting the restaurant at dinnertime the other day."

"Did he bring you dead fish too?"

"Nope, flowers." Gwen grinned at her sister's huff. "He called me the next night, wanting to know if I wanted to catch a movie."

"I'm gathering you turned him down too?"

"Sure did." Gwen started to pull the ingredients for a salad out of the refrigerator. She was hungry after all. "I've come to the conclusion that there are not very many single females in town. There are a lot of single men, but I think unmarried women are a rarity."

"You're kidding."

"Afraid not. The Women's Guild stopped by to welcome me to town, and the next thing I knew they were trying to match me up with this one's nephew or that one's brother. Let me tell you, Joc, it was freaky."

"Gwen?"

"Yes?"

"I'm going to see if I can take both my weeks of vacation in July."

Chapter Eight

The men's bathroom had to be the most unromantic place in the entire restaurant. It was the reason Gwen decided to confront Daniel there. She needed his expert opinion and help, and she didn't want it to seem as if she was *coming on* to him. Tomorrow was Saturday, and she wanted to go visit Anna's Antiques, about twenty miles away.

She had it on good authority that Anna's carried dozens of antique wooden cupboards and cabinets. Grace, the minister's wife, had assured her that she was bound to find a cabinet for her dining room that would hold all her cooking gadgets. The only problem was, Anna didn't deliver or hold items. Anna's operated on a first-come-it's-yours basis. If she found her perfect cabinet, she needed to take it with her. The size she was looking for would never fit into the back of her S.U.V.

She needed Daniel's truck and hopefully his opinion on the condition of the cabinet. A carpenter would know if she was getting a good deal or not. It wouldn't be a date, it would be a business arrangement. She would gladly pay Daniel for his time. Simple. So why were her palms sweating and her heart picking up an extra beat or two?

Because the entire town of Misty Harbor had some strange notions of courtship, and she had no idea how Daniel would take her request. As far as she knew, in this town if a single female asked an available male to use his pickup truck, it might be considered a proposal to bear his children. It was only eleven o'clock in the morning, and so far she had been asked out twice: once by the mailman and once by Lawrence Blake, who operated the whale-watching tour boat. Both men seemed to take her refusal in stride. Lawrence had been sweet enough to bring her a box of chocolates and four discount coupons for his boat tour. Jonah and Clarence had already attacked the candy, and she was saving the coupons just in case Jocelyn had been serious about visiting this summer.

So far Misty Harbor was proving to be one very interesting if not strange town. A girl would never go lonely on a Saturday night if she didn't want to. Gwen had to admit she was slightly curious as to why there seemed to be a shortage of young women around town. Maybe something had polluted the drinking water about thirty years ago and killed off all the X chromosomes.

The men had fared a lot better. They might be a tad on the lonely side, but they all seemed well adjusted and most were cute, if you discounted Erik the Viking. There were a lot of adjectives that could describe that man, but cute wasn't one of them. From what she had seen so far, some of the men of Misty Harbor would make wonderful catches.

Gwen pushed open the door and spotted Daniel's jeans-clad legs stretched across the tiled floor. She would like a week to explore every inch of those long legs. The rest of his body was crammed under the countertop; he appeared to be hooking up the sinks.

Speaking of wonderful catches—handy and gorgeous. Couldn't get much better than that, unless you added rich to the mix. Daniel didn't appear to be rich, but that didn't diminish his appeal. His smile alone would make up for whatever he had lacking in the bank.

"Hunter, hand me that wrench." Daniel stuck out one hand from under the sink and pointed in the general direction of some scattered tools.

With a shrug she picked up the only wrench she could see and placed it in his upturned palm. She noticed two of his knuckles were bruised and covered with traces of dried blood. Daniel must have whacked them good earlier in the morning. His hands had been perfectly fine when he had been eating one of the ham-and-cheese omelets she had made this morning for the men to try. The idea of serving brunch on Sundays had come to her around two o'clock that morning, when she should have been sleeping. Instead, she had been lying in bed compiling a list of brunch food for the menu and trying not to think about one very interesting carpenter.

Jonah and Clarence had thought brunch would be a wonderful idea and had immediately volunteered to taste-test every dish. Hunter had politely suggested waffles, covered in strawberries or blueberries, topped with whipped cream. In between mouthfuls, Daniel's input consisted of French toast. The real thick kind sprinkled with powdered sugar and dripping with genuine maple syrup. The men of Misty Harbor obviously had a sweet tooth.

Daniel grunted, "Thanks," as he did some major

contortion that left her with an impressive view of one well-defined hip and buttocks.

She grinned and said, "You're welcome." The sound of Daniel's head hitting the bottom of the sink echoed throughout the small room. She cringed and said, "Ouch." The urge to rub her own head was overwhelming. That must have hurt like the dickens.

"What are you ouching about?" Daniel groused. "I'm the one who hit his head."

"So I heard." Gwen squatted down to get a better look at him. "Are you okay?" The sound that had echoed through the room had seemed hollow to her. She wondered if it had been the sink that made the impression, or Daniel's head.

"Peachy." Daniel slouched down and tried rubbing the top of his head. He whacked his elbow on the wall instead and muttered a word she was glad she hadn't caught all the way.

"I didn't mean to startle you." She wasn't starting this conversation on the right foot if she intended to ask Daniel for a favor. Especially after the long week he had put in. The way Daniel was working, Catch of the Day would be ready before its grand opening.

"I thought you were Hunter." Daniel stopped rubbing his elbow and gave a pipe a twist with the wrench.

"So I gathered." She plopped her butt down next to the toolbox and glanced around the small room. Daniel had replaced both toilets yesterday, and this morning he had installed the midnight blue countertop and the two white porcelain sinks. Hunter had already primed the room a flat white that had covered up the graffiti on the stalls. She glanced around at the floor. Sitting on the tile gave her an up-close and personal view of the excellent job Hunter had done at scrubbing it clean. Even the corners gleamed. She really must consider giving Hunter a sizeable bonus when his job here was done. The man could clean better than Heloise and Mr. Clean combined.

Hunter also knew his way around a kitchen.

"Is there something I can help you with? I'm sure you didn't come in here for the ambience." Daniel took one end of one of the PVC pipes, swabbed it with a toxic-smelling cleaner, and then with a liquid cement. A second later he stuck it into another section of pipe and held it still for a moment.

The cleaner and cement stuff stank to high heaven. Gwen wiggled her nose and wondered if a person could get high from the fumes. "I need to ask you a favor."

Daniel raised a brow and finally gave her all of his attention. "Favor?"

She couldn't tell if the vapors had done something to Daniel's voice or not, but he had almost sounded seductive. "More like a business proposition."

"Business?"

Was that disappointment she heard in his voice, or were the noxious fumes affecting her hearing? "I need to go out to Anna's Antiques tomorrow and look for some type of cabinet or cupboard to hold all the cooking gadgets that impressed you the other day."

"Anna only sells what I would consider 'primitive' furniture. She doesn't get in a lot of fancy cherry or mahogany pieces, and she doesn't deal in modern stuff at all."

"I know. I'm looking for something old, something that would go with the cottage and the kitchen." She had been thinking about either a big hutch, with plenty of storage space, or possibly a corner cabinet and a matching sideboard for storage.

"It would clash with your dining set," Daniel said.

"My glass-and-chrome dining set clashes with the cottage, Daniel. It was perfect and elegant in my apartment in Philadelphia, but here on the coast of Maine, it just doesn't work. I'll worry about that later; right now I need someplace to store all my stuff so I can at least eat at the table instead of the counter."

Daniel seemed to consider this for a long moment. "That's true. My advice is to measure the room before you buy anything, and to double-check on whatever you're buying. Anna's a nice lady, but she's a shrewd businesswoman first and foremost. Lots of people, especially the tourists, think they're getting a great deal, when in reality what they're getting is old dry-rotted wood with some shoddy repair work."

"That's where you come in."

"The shoddy repair work?" Amusement played in Daniel's voice and in his eyes.

Gwen smiled back. It was a good thing she was already sitting on the floor. The way she had just gone weak in the knees, she would have melted at Daniel's feet if she had been standing, and embarrassed herself right out of the state of Maine. Lord, Daniel was one incredibly sexy and handsome man when he teased. "No, I need you to check out whatever I plan on buying so I'm not taken in by a shrewd Maine businesswoman."

"Oh, so you need my expertise?"

"No, I need your pickup truck, but your expertise will also come in handy."

"You want me for my truck?" He sounded outraged.

Oh, that was dangerous ground if she had ever

treaded on any. Any woman would be a fool to want Daniel for his truck. She could name at least a dozen attributes of his that could steal a woman's heart. His smoky gray eyes would top the list, along with the seductive fullness of his lower lip, which looked so darn kissable. The silkiness of his light brown hair begged for someone to run her fingers through it, and his beard looked soft and touchable. She had never been kissed by a man with a beard before. She wondered how the short, neatly trimmed bristles would feel against her cheek. Her breasts. Her thighs.

"Gwen, are you all right?" Daniel's concern snapped her from her erotic daydream faster than a screeching fire alarm. When he started to maneuver himself out from under the sinks, she quickly pushed herself up off the floor and stood. Both of Daniel's knees cracked in protest as he stood up and joined her.

She glanced at the door as the white walls seemed to close in around her. It had to be the horrible-smelling liquid cement or cleaner making it incredibly hard to breathe all of a sudden. Why hadn't she noticed before how small the men's bathroom was? A person could barely turn around in there without tripping over something. Right now the only thing she could trip over was a toolbox or Daniel. She needed to get out of here and fast. "I've got to go start lunch."

"Gwen?" Daniel stepped in front of her and blocked the only exit.

She kept her gaze locked on his Adam's apple. His enticing, tanned Adam's apple. She had to lick her lips before she could speak. "Yes?"

"What time do you want me to pick you up tomorrow?"

Was it her imagination, or had Daniel moved closer? "I don't know, nine or ten, I guess." Sud-

denly being in Daniel's company all day, and away
from the restaurant, didn't seem like a good idea.
What if she did something stupid, like run her
tongue down his incredibly sexy throat? She forced
her gaze back to the wooden door and made herself
think of business, not pleasure. The liquid cement
fumes must have addled her brain. She raised her
gaze, and encountered his hungry stare. "I'll pay
you for your time."

"Considering the amount of food you have been
feeding me and my *crew*, I think it should be me
paying you."

"You guys are the ones doing me the favors."
She didn't know what she would have done without
the men helping her by critiquing her cooking.
Thoughts of the grand opening would have given
her ulcers and nightmares without some feedback.
At least this way she knew what the men in town
liked. And so far they had liked just about everything she had set in front of them.

"My truck and I will be by your place around
nine-thirty." Daniel's gaze dropped to her mouth.
"If you mention paying me again, the deal is off."

Her gaze shot to his incredibly sexy lower lip
nestled in the middle of his beard. She had
dreamed about caressing his beard with the tips
of her fingers. She wanted to gently bite that full
lower lip before sealing her own mouth across it.
The heat in the small room was making it impossible to breathe. Daniel's *nearness* made it purely
impossible.

"Deal," she whispered. She wasn't about to start
arguing about money now. Gwen slid around him
and headed for the door and fresh, clean air to
clear her head. A low thudding noise sounded
behind her, but she didn't look back.

If she had turned around as the door swung shut
behind her, she would have seen Daniel banging

his head against the freshly primed wall. She might even have felt better.

Five minutes later, Gwen was in the dining room staring at the courtyard from one of the new patio doors. She had cracked the door open an inch or so to get some fresh air into the room. She'd heard toxic fumes could be lethal, and she needed to clear her head and concentrate on the restaurant. Catch of the Day was the reason she was in Maine. It was the *only* reason. She couldn't fail. The restaurant couldn't fail; it had been her dream for so many years.

With everything coming along so nicely on the interior, she needed to give some thought to the exterior. The cedar-shake siding was in excellent repair. So was the roof. The trim needed a fresh coat of paint, and so did the picket fence that surrounded the courtyard. The slate patio appeared to be in good shape, and she'd already picked out the tables and chairs she wanted for outdoor use from an Internet supplier who guaranteed delivery in two weeks.

It was the garden that surrounded the patio on three sides that was currently causing her frown. By the patches of brown clumps, rocks, and withered sticks poking up here and there she would have to say the garden was a wash. It needed some serious help, and what she knew about gardening could be written in big letters with a thick crayon on a single cocktail napkin.

Daniel's mother was the obvious choice. He had told her that his mother did landscaping and garden designs. Granted, the garden was only about two feet wide, but it was probably close to a hundred feet in length. There was room for one heck of a lot of flowers, and she did want flowers. Lots of big, colorful flowers.

The front door of the restaurant opened, and

Erik, in all his long-flaxen-hair and bulging-biceps glory, stepped into the dining room. This time the god from the Land of the Midnight Sun brought lobsters. Very much alive, claw-waving, mad-as-hell lobsters. Not only was the Viking persistent, he had excellent taste in seafood.

"Erik, you shouldn't have." She closed the patio door, turned her back on the dead garden, and hurried over to get a better look at the lobsters trapped in the wooden crate. She counted six crustaceans and grinned. It was the perfect number for lunch.

Daniel came out of the men's room, but she didn't turn to face him. She was still a bit embarrassed about how she had just run from him. Daniel probably thought she had more than one screw loose, and at this point she would be tempted to agree with him.

She forced her smile wider as she looked at Erik. Today he had left his golden hair loose and long, but his light blue eyes were sparkling and his smile was just as dazzling. Her body appreciated his pure male beauty, but her heart was left untouched. No sweaty palms, no extra heartbeats. No physical response, besides the hunger churning in her gut now that she saw the lobsters and knew what was on the menu for lunch.

"You probably want a repeat of the other day. You catch, I cook." She looked at the wooden crate and wondered if this was Erik's way of persuading her to go out with him: drown her in freshly caught seafood and she'd agree to anything. If that was his plan, Erik was in for some disappointment. "At least with lobsters you don't have to gut and clean them," she said brightly as she reached out and tried to take the crate from the silently laughing man. "I absolutely adore lobster, but this isn't going to change my mind about going out with you. I meant it when I said I don't have time for a relationship, Erik.''

Daniel cleared his throat and said, "Ah, Gwen?"

"What?" She gave the crate another tug, but Erik wasn't releasing it. She tugged harder, and Erik didn't even have to tighten his hold on the box to keep it away from her. Strong, masculine fingers held the wooden slats securely and easily.

"That's not Erik." The laughter in Daniel's voice caused her to look at him first, then Erik.

Both men seemed to think something was extremely funny. "Of course it's Erik. I think I would remember him, considering it's only been two days." Maybe playing practical jokes was another Misty Harbor tradition, along with courting women with dead fish and discount sightseeing tickets. Lay a mackerel at the woman's feet and she'd be yours for life. Maybe all the young women of Misty Harbor hadn't casually left town over the years; maybe they had fled into the night.

"That's Gunnar Olsen, Erik's twin brother." Daniel laughed as he added, "His identical twin brother."

Gwen released the crate so fast she nearly fell on her ass. "There's two of them?" Good grief! If word of this ever got out, there would be a stampede of women to the small Maine town. California might have its Beach Boys and "Baywatch" studs, but Maine had the Olsen twins.

"Afraid so." Daniel seemed to be enjoying himself at her expense.

She glared at him and then had to wonder how he got the red mark in the center of his forehead. It hadn't been there five minutes earlier.

"How did you tell them apart?" She studied Gunnar from the top of his flowing blond hair, past his rugged square jaw, and down his impressive chest to the tips of his Nike sneakers. She would have bet her secret white clam sauce recipe that it was Erik standing in front of her. Gunnar seemed to be taking her scrutiny in stride.

"Erik has a scar from where they had to take his appendix out when he was twelve." Gunnar's voice held the same charming accent as his brother's. "I have a scar from eight stitches I received from falling out of a tree when I was six."

"Where's the scar?" she asked curiously.

"In a very private place." Gunnar appeared slightly embarrassed by that admission.

Now *that* definitely would raise a woman's curiosity.

Daniel frowned at both of them. "Gunnar's the shy one, while Erik tends to talk a lot."

"That's the only difference?" She didn't want to contemplate the scars that only a lover—or their mother—had seen.

"Not really," Daniel answered. "Gunnar tends to wear his hair loose, while Erik usually has his tied back."

Gunnar nodded in acknowledgment. "I prefer to catch lobsters, while my brother usually goes for fish."

"This is going to get confusing." Jocelyn was never going to believe her when she told her there were two Vikings prowling the rocky Maine coastline. Two identical Norsemen.

Hunter continued to chop cabbage for coleslaw as he listened to Gwen and Gunnar discuss lobster recipes. Gunnar obviously knew what he was talking about, but Gwen was the expert. The one thing he had learned during the time he had been working for Gwen was that the little lady sure did know how to cook. She was almost, but not quite, as good as his own mother had been.

No one could cook as well as Edith McCord had cooked. He remembered one day, as a small boy, asking his mother why his friend Thomas's mom's chowder wasn't as good as hers. His mother had smiled, given him a big hug and a kiss, and told him it was all in the secret ingredient. It had taken him days of pestering to get his mother to name that secret ingredient. Edith McCord had told him the secret was to add a pinch of love.

At the age of fifty-four, he still believed she had been right all those years ago. His mother had spent the last twenty-five years of her life teaching him everything she knew about cooking. Yet, no matter what he made and how closely he followed her directions, it just didn't taste the same. The love had been missing. Edith McCord had loved cooking, cleaning, and taking care of her husband and son, and it had shown in everything she had done.

It hadn't mattered to his mother that her only child had returned from Vietnam a shell of a man, afraid to face the world. Afraid of what the next day would bring. Afraid to do what he had been born to do, which was to follow his father into the lobster business and eventually take over that business. When he had returned from the horrors of a P.O.W. camp in 'Nam, he had been terrified of the crashing, churning waves of the Atlantic Ocean and equally petrified of the smooth, calm surface of the hidden swimming cove just north of town. Both places had been his home-away-from-home when he had been growing up in Misty Harbor. As a youth, he had been in the water so much that his friends, and then his own father, had christened him with the nickname Tuna Head.

He hadn't set foot on a boat or in the water in thirty-one years.

At the age of twenty-three Hunter had hidden

within the walls of his childhood home, where it had been safe. He had been surrounded by the love of his parents and a dozen prescription bottles, courtesy of Uncle Sam. For days on end he had refused to even go outside for some fresh air because it seemed everywhere he went, there was water. He learned that Misty Harbor had been the worst place to live for a person suffering hydrophobia, a dreadful, panic-inducing fear of water. His parents' home had become his new prison. This time, the prison had been of his own making.

For five years he had bathed himself from the bathroom sink, too afraid to even sit in a tub filled with five inches of water. It took years, but he finally managed the tub and eventually graduated to the shower; as long as his face didn't go under the spray he was fine. Washing his hair was his greatest challenge, but he forced himself to wash it nearly every day. Just to prove to himself that he could do it.

Maybe all that constant hair washing was the reason it was now more gray than brown and was receding more with each passing year. He now owned an impressive number of baseball caps and wore one constantly.

Through it all, his mother's love for him never wavered. The times the sadness had crept into her eyes and the tears clogged her throat, she would hug him extra hard and say a prayer of thanks to the Lord for bringing him home. It had been his mother's and father's unconditional love through those years that had kept him sane. That, and his enjoyment of cooking.

He had learned to cook everything his mother knew how to make and had enjoyed experimenting on new recipes with her. Yet he had never cooked an entire meal on his own until her death. His mother, who had never been sick a day in her life, had suffered a massive heart attack while hanging sheets on the back line six years ago.

Two weeks after the funeral, when all the frozen casseroles neighbors had brought were gone, he had found his father in the kitchen crying over an unopened can of soup. Clarence McCord had never cooked a meal in his life. Microwaving leftovers was the extent of his knowledge. Hunter had gently taken the can out of his father's shaking hands, and from that moment on he did all the cooking for them both. Clarence helped with the cleaning, but Hunter cooked everything from the first pot of coffee in the morning to the apple pie his father loved for dessert.

Sometimes, when a pie or a roast was cooking in the oven, and he closed his eyes real tight, Hunter could almost feel his mother's presence in the kitchen with him. It was a comforting feeling, one he cherished.

Gwen's kitchen, here at the restaurant, had a different feeling, but it too felt comfortable. He felt as if he was surrounded by friends when they all sat down at the table to eat whatever Gwen had fixed for lunch. He even liked the thought of arriving first thing in the morning and trying to guess what Gwen would have baking in the oven. This morning's omelet had been a surprise. A delicious surprise. Gwen was going to make money hand over fist with the restaurant.

He enjoyed working for Gwen. He didn't mind the scrubbing or the painting; it was hard, honest work that tired the body and soothed the mind. But he especially liked it when she asked for his help preparing one dish or another. Gwen understood about cooking. Most of the time they were on the same wavelength and he knew what she needed before she even asked for it. Gwen was the kind of person who would understand about his mother's secret ingredient.

He had heard Gwen tell the Women's Guild that she would be hiring for a bunch of positions. One of those positions had been an assistant cook. He liked the idea of cooking all day and getting paid to do it. He liked Gwen and her ideas on where she saw the restaurant heading. He even liked the idea of working every day and accomplishing something. It seemed something a "normal" man would do. Gwen treated him like he was normal. Maybe that was why he liked her so much. Gwen either didn't know or didn't care about his past. She talked directly to him, and he found himself answering her questions and giving his opinion. He even thought he had impressed her a time or two with his knowledge in the kitchen. Gwen didn't look like she would be impressed easily, especially in the kitchen.

The town of Misty Harbor had sheltered and protected Hunter from the outside world for years. Maybe he didn't need the sheltering or the protecting any longer. Maybe it was time to stand on his own two feet and face the world. He might be knocked on his ass a time or two, but he could handle that.

Monday morning, he'd be the first in line to apply for the assistant-cook position. He might never have held a full-time job before, but he could cook. He had been trained by the best cook in the county.

Hunter finished grating the entire head of cabbage and started to mix up the dressing his mother had taught him to make in another small bowl. He didn't need to disturb Gwen for the recipe. He knew how to make a bowl of coleslaw. What he didn't know how to make was a huge bucket of coleslaw. The amount Gwen would have to make

once the restaurant was open to the public. His
mother might have been the best cook in the
county, but she'd never handled what Gwen was
attempting to do. Dinner for three was one thing;
dinner for two hundred, with over a dozen different entrees to choose from, was an entirely different ball game. Edith McCord could never have
handled the stress. Gwen Fletcher seemed to thrive
on it.

He had to wonder how he would handle cooking
for hundreds, instead of just two, if Gwen did hire
him for the job as her assistant.

He beat the ingredients together and watched
Gwen, who was busy writing down Gunnar's version
of an old-fashioned clam bake and how to go about
steaming the lobster, clams, onion, and corn on
the cob in seaweed and ocean water. He'd never
met a person with so many lists. Gwen had a list
for everything. Soon she would need a list of all
the men who had asked her out and had been
turned down, just to keep track of them all. Gunnar
seemed to be suffering from the same ailment Erik
had had the other day. Both men seemed to have
a hard time keeping their eyes off Gwen. Instinct
told him Gunnar's name would be added to the
list, right below his brother's. Gwen seemed more
interested in the recipe than the man.

He couldn't blame Gunnar or any of the others
who had stopped by on the pretense of welcoming
Gwen to Misty Harbor. If he had been twenty or
thirty years younger, he'd be bringing the beautiful
chef lobsters by the boatload. Of course, that was
if his heart hadn't already been taken. Which it
was. His heart hadn't been his own since he had
been sixteen and had fallen in love with the pretti-
est fifteen-year-old to ever grace the locker-lined
hallways of Hancock County High School.

Theresa Newton had been the love of his life,

up until his return from 'Nam. He had been the one to refuse to see her, to talk to her. His sweet, innocent Tess deserved someone better than what he had become, and he was the one to break her heart and shatter the dreams they had built together. Tess had deserved a whole man, and he was sane enough to know he wasn't that man.

It had taken Tess three years before finally giving up on him and getting on with her life. She married Ben Dunbar, a good, decent man, and had three beautiful children. He used to watch her children roam the docks, play in the park, and just be happy, well-adjusted kids. He had spent a lot of time, back in those days, wondering what it might have been like if the helicopter that had been coming to rescue him, and the pitiful number of men that made up the rest of his platoon, had made it through the enemy's fire. What if he had never been captured and taken prisoner? What if the Vietcong had never tortured him and taught him how to fear? What if he had returned unafraid of something so simple yet so necessary as water?

Would Tess have become his wife and the mother of his children like they had dreamed and planned before his senior class trip to some far-off country called 'Nam? Years of unanswered questions that didn't matter a hill of beans anymore. The past was done and over with; life moved on. Tess had moved on, as he had wanted her to. As he had forced her to.

His sweet, innocent Tess was now a grandmother to two adorable little boys who lived in town. She worked full time at the sheriff's office, answering phones and typing. She shopped for her groceries every Friday night, drove an eight-year-old Jeep that was held together by prayers, and still went to church every Sunday. She was putting her son, Jason, through college down in Rhode Island. Her daughter, Marie, who looked remarkably like Tess at that age, was a stay-at-home mom, raising the boys.

It was Tess's youngest son, Scott, who was causing more than one headache in town, and he was sure in Tess too. Scott, at seventeen, was rebelling and looking for his own way in life. Scott's way was obviously different from everyone else's.

Thinking about Tess brought back all the what-if questions that had no answers. It brought back all the hurt and heartache he had caused her thirty-one years ago. It also brought back one very important fact. A fact he had been trying to ignore for the past five years.

Tess was a widow now.

Chapter Nine

Daniel tried to inspect the wooden hutch with a critical eye. It was proving impossible. Gwen was standing right behind him, looking over his shoulder and begging sweetly. There wasn't a man alive who could think clearly with an enticing female pressing against his back.

"Please tell me it's okay, Daniel." Her hand gripped his shoulder as she leaned in closer to get a better look at the interior shelf on the bottom half. "Please."

He felt like shouting for her to go away. Gwen was driving him crazy with her sweet pleas and herbal shampoo. It had been bad enough driving the twenty miles with her locked in the cab of his truck and him breathing in her scent. Now, with her practically climbing on his back, he was ready to go insane or kiss her. One or the other. Kissing Gwen would be heaven; but then again, insanity had a nice ring to it.

"Gwen, go away until I'm done." He glanced over his shoulder and tried not to be persuaded by the sexy pout of Gwen's lower lip. What he wanted to do to that lower lip had to be illegal. "This is what you brought me for, remember, my expertise?"

"But it's perfect." The tips of Gwen's fingers brushed across the worn smoothness of the aged wood.

"Perfect, no, but so far it's okay." He watched those graceful fingers dance across the surface of the cupboard and could almost feel them across his own heated skin. Gwen would make a sensual lover. She loved to touch everything with her hands. He felt his body shudder at the thought, and immediately poked his head back into the storage area of the hutch. "I'll give you my opinion after I inspect every piece, and not a moment before."

Leave it to Gwen to pick out the most expensive dining room set in Anna's Antiques. Not only was there a six-foot-long hutch with some nice storage area in the lower half and three shelves in the upper half for displaying dishes, but there was a matching corner cabinet and a table with four chairs. Gwen had excellent taste, and obviously some deep pockets. She never even batted one of her silk brown eyelashes at the price tag. Anna was going to love her.

All three pieces would fit perfectly in the cottage's dining room. He knew that for certain, because he had measured the room himself this morning while taste-testing one of Gwen's apple cinnamon muffins. Now that the weather was finally turning nicer, he was considering taking up jogging. It was either that or buy pants with a bigger waist size. Gwen's cooking was just too delicious to ignore, and his waist was beginning to tell the tale.

He needed a good workout, and by the size of this dining room set, he was about to get one.

Oak. The entire set was made of solid oak and had an aged patina that you couldn't get out of a bottle. He was going to pull a hernia trying to get it into his truck, then out of his truck and into Gwen's house. With a heavy sigh, he closed the hutch door and stood up. He needed to check out the back, and then he would move on to the table and chairs. ·

He noticed a young couple making their way through the barn barely eyeing the dining room sets as they went. The woman seemed to have her gaze directly on the set he was examining. They were heading right for him. He glanced over at Gwen, who had also spotted the approaching couple.

Gwen's eyes narrowed as she crossed her arms and took a strategic position directly in front of the table and chairs. The little general had made the first move. The woman answered with a tight smile and a tug on her handbag strap, to give it better positioning on her shoulder.

In the center of Anna's, war was being declared, and no one had heard the opening fire but he and the man accompanying the other woman. He glanced around the old barn and spotted Anna sinking into an old rocking chair that had a perfect view of the upcoming battle. Anna's smile was a testament to how well business was doing. Two years ago, she barely had five teeth left in her mouth. Today, thanks to the miracle of modern dentistry and tourists with deep pockets, she had a set of dentures that probably rivaled his own grandfather's.

Anna was the shrewdest businesswoman in Hancock County, but she was also extremely fair. There was no way Anna would allow the other woman to buy the set right out from under Gwen's nose. But she was just cantankerous enough to sit back and watch the fireworks for a while.

The approaching woman, who was a walking advertisement for L.L. Bean, walked right up to the corner cabinet and opened the door to look inside. Someone had obviously shopped at Freeport, home to L.L. Bean, and about a hundred other outlets, before continuing her tour of Maine. This couple was either a pair of tourists from New York City or recent transplants to Bangor's growing business community. Money was on being transplants. It was too early in the season for tourists.

"Excuse me," Gwen said politely with just a trace of sarcasm in her voice. "I'm afraid that this set is already sold."

The woman glanced around at all three pieces. "I don't see a SOLD tag."

"Anna doesn't use SOLD tags." Gwen moved in between the table and the hutch, effectively blocking the woman's way to the largest piece.

"Then you've paid for the set already?"

Daniel glanced back at Gwen to see what her next volley would be. It was a good thing he had just finished dissolving the tic tac that had been in his mouth. Gwen's next words would have made him choke on it.

"My husband was just doing the final inspection." Gwen kept her gaze on the woman. "Isn't that right, *dear*?"

"That's right, *honey cakes*." He forced himself to smile at the other woman while his fists clenched with the desire to strangle Gwen. Anna had probably laughed so hard, she had fallen off the rocker by now. Anna was going to be the hit of the senior citizen's bingo night with this story, on the last Friday night of the month. He heard a distant cackle, and figured if Anna had broken her hip in the fall, she wouldn't be laughing. Anna's arthritic bones were just fine. It was Gwen's neck that had reason to be concerned.

In one short morning he had gone from being her expert on cabinets and delivery service to her husband. He had to wonder if he had just been promoted or demoted. Wondering if he should throttle her or play along, he had to go with tormenting the little witch, and the bigger witch, Anna, who was back to cackling. He draped his arm across Gwen's shoulder and gave her a little squeeze. "A person can't be too careful, especially when you're paying top dollar for someone else's throwaways."

Anna laughed louder. Gwen stiffened beneath his arm, but her gaze never wandered from her opponent. "But this is the one I want."

He cringed as Gwen's foot came down, none too gently, on top of his toes. "I haven't finished with my inspection yet, *twinkle toes.*" He lowered his arm and moved his feet away from her size-six hiking boots. For such a tiny little thing, she sure did weigh a lot. He picked up one of the chairs and turned it over to inspect the bottom.

"Then this set isn't sold yet." The other woman crowed with delight and headed for the hutch.

"Anna's policy is, *First come, it's yours.*'" Gwen stepped in front of the charging woman, who had a good six inches and about twenty pounds on her. But that didn't stop her. "I was here *first.*"

"Yeah, well, Bob Vila here"—the woman nodded at Daniel—"is still inspecting it. You haven't bought it yet, so that means it's still for sale."

Gwen turned around and asked, "Who's Bob Vila?"

He rolled his eyes. So much for them having anything in common. Gwen didn't even know the name of the father of home improvement. Hell, she probably didn't even know who Tim "The Tool Man" Taylor was. "Bob's an actor. Does commercials for Craftsman tools, and a handsome devil if I do say so myself."

Gwen smiled softly. "I can definitely see the resemblance."

The chair he had been lowering hit the wooden floor with a loud thud. Anna's applause echoed from the wooden rafters. He continued to stare at Gwen, waiting to see when she would start laughing at her own joke. She didn't. Gwen was serious. What was she, blind? Didn't she notice the scar running down the side of his face? Hadn't she ever noticed that his smile was crooked? That one side of his mouth never curved upward to match the other side, no matter how many times he had done the exercises the physical therapist had given to him?

"I'm buying this set." The other woman opened her pocketbook and pulled out her wallet. Her husband started to protest, but she snapped, "Not now, Roger."

Roger obviously decided to keep his head and closed his mouth. Considering the look in the other woman's eye, Daniel figured Roger had made a smart move.

Gwen's soft expression hardened as she turned back to the woman, who was pulling out a gold credit card. "I think not."

Daniel had had enough but was thankful that the look Gwen was leveling at let's-get-on-the-cover-of-*Country-Living*-magazine wasn't directed at him. He much preferred the soft expression she had worn when she'd said he was handsome. "Anna, get off your A.A.R.P. tush and settle this before there's blood."

Anna gave a loud groan as she pushed herself out of the rocking chair and walked toward them, chuckling all the way. "Daniel, you know I can't be retired and run this place at the same time."

"You were retired for two whole years." Daniel gave Anna a friendly hug. He had known Anna all his life. She was some distant cousin, three times removed, or some such nonsense to Jonah. It didn't matter how many times someone tried to remove her from the family tree, she was still family.

"Most boring two years of my life, boy." Anna eyed Gwen with a great deal of interest. "Ah, I see you brought the little woman today."

Gwen's face turned the exact shade of red of the lobster he had eaten for lunch yesterday. He couldn't pass up such a golden opportunity; after all, she was the one who'd started it. "Honey cakes, you remember Auntie Anna, don't you? She was the one leading the conga line at our wedding."

"How could I forget?" Gwen reached out and gave the woman a quick hug and him a lengthy glare. "Your wedding present was divine. Thank you."

"You really liked that statue?" Anna beamed with pleasure.

"Oh my, yes." Gwen looked helplessly at him, but he pointedly looked at the other couple anxiously waiting to break into the conversation and buy the dining set. "We decided to put it in the living room." Gwen gave Anna a smile and a nod. "Right in the middle of the coffee table, for all to see."

"That wouldn't have been my first choice, but hey, you young people do things a little differently than my generation ever did." Anna shook her head sadly.

Daniel bit the inside of his cheek to keep from laughing. Anna was notorious for her wild stories, and Gwen had just given her carte blanche to either shock her or embarrass her. "I like it in the living room, Anna," he said. "It's a great conversation piece."

"Well, I imagine it is." Anna looked at the other couple and continued to shake her head. "I found it at an estate sale and thought it would be perfect for the newlyweds. It's one of those Japanese statues. I think it's called erotica. You know the kind. Has that cute, tubby Japanese guy in his robe laying on the ground with some nimble little woman on top."

Gwen gasped, and he groaned and bowed his head in shame for letting it get this far out of control. The last time Anna had started one of her "stories," the police had raided the bingo hall and confiscated all the punch, believing it was spiked with illegal hooch.

The other couple was now slowly backing away and staring at them as if they were female slave traffickers.

"I just couldn't pass it up," continued Anna happily. "That little tubby guy had the most wondrous smile on his face." Anna chuckled. "I guess you would too if you had . . ."

"Auntie Anna," Gwen cried desperately, "I want this dining room set."

"It's a nice one, hon." Anna pounded on the table just to prove it wasn't going to fall apart and come crashing to the ground. "What about you?" Anna turned her attention to the other woman, who was now busily putting away her credit card and wallet.

"No, thank you," said the woman as she absently wiped her hands on her pants. "I've changed my mind." She turned on her heel and headed for the exit. "Roger, come."

Anna watched the couple disappear down the crowded aisle and then smiled at the sound of bells ringing as the door closed behind them. "Was that a man or a Labrador?"

"I think you just lost two customers, Anna." He glanced at Gwen to see how she was holding up. She appeared to be in shock.

"They weren't customers."

"They weren't?" Gwen asked in confusion.

"Nope. They were driving some little sporty two-seater. The only thing that would have fit into the trunk was an antique basket, or maybe a piece of pottery."

Gwen smiled. "So we didn't cost you a sale?"

"Well, that all depends."

"On what?" Gwen asked.

"If you're buying this set or not." Anna looked directly at Daniel, as if he was the one holding up the sale.

"I'm not finished inspecting it, Anna." Women; they were always in such a hurry.

"I'll go write up the sale." Anna turned and started to walk away. "You won't find a thing wrong with it, Daniel."

Daniel didn't bother looking at Gwen. He picked up the next chair and turned it over. He grunted as a hard elbow jabbed him in the side.

"Why didn't you tell me she was your aunt?" Gwen hissed, and then jabbed him again for good measure.

This time he was expecting it and tightened his abs. Now Gwen was the one to grunt. He smiled as he turned the chair back over and sat down on it. No wobble. "You didn't ask."

"What am I supposed to do, ask you if every person living in Maine is related to you?" Gwen walked over to the corner cupboard and once again opened the bottom, then the top doors. "I made a fool of myself with that woman. Granted she was rude, but still, your aunt wouldn't have sold it to her over me, would she?" Gwen sat down in the chair he had just vacated and continued her questions. "Do you think we can take the whole set in one load, or two? It looks awful heavy, doesn't it?"

"Gwen?" His ears were ringing with her incessant chatter and questions. Either she shut her mouth or he was going to do something to keep that mouth of hers very busy.

"What?"

"Shut up. I'm beginning to feel married."

Daniel headed into town and glanced at the Burton brothers, Tom and Paul, sharing the cab of his truck with him. So much for having the pleasure of spending Saturday alone with Gwen. The six-foot-long hutch and a maple bureau were securely tied down in the back of his truck. This was his second load from Anna's. The first had consisted of the corner cabinet, table, four chairs, and a four-poster bed frame Gwen just had to have for her guest bedroom.

By the time he and Gwen had made it back to her cottage with the first load, there had been a man standing on her doorstep holding a bouquet of flowers and looking lost. But then, Gregory Patterson would have looked lost in his own house. Thankfully, Gwen had seemed just as startled to see the man standing there as he had been. After some hasty introductions, Gregory, whose only reason for being there that he could deduce was that he was Priscilla's nephew, offered to help unload the furniture. Gwen accepted Gregory's offer and his appearance as if she had strange men standing at her front door every day of the week.

Before they had two chairs off the truck, Tom Burton, who lived across the street, had come over to help. Daniel had considered it real neighborly of him, because Tom was married and the father of three kids, and wasn't doing it just to impress Gwen. Before the table made it into the house, Tom's unmarried brother, Paul, had shown up to lend a hand. Daniel didn't believe in divine intervention or coincidences.

"So, Daniel," Paul asked, "how well do you know Gwen?"

"She's my employer." He didn't want to discuss Gwen with Paul, or any other men, for that matter.

"Yeah, but today's Saturday. You usually don't work on the weekends."

"She asked if I would do her this favor. I said yes."

"That's it?"

"That's it." He wanted to tell Paul to go take a long walk off a very short pier, but he didn't have the right. Gwen was free to date whomever she wanted. Just because so far she hadn't wanted anyone who asked her didn't mean a thing. Maybe she was just waiting for the right man to come along. Though he had to wonder who Gwen would consider the right man.

"I heard she can cook," Tom said.

"She's opening a restaurant; what do you think?" Daniel shook his head as he made a left turn onto Conrad Street. Paul Burton had seaweed for brains. Was cooking the only quality Paul was looking for in a wife? Okay, there was the obvious one, but besides that, he hadn't heard a single question about Gwen that didn't concern cooking. Didn't these men realize that there was a lot more to Gwen than her talent in the kitchen and being nice on the eyes?

"Holy hell, look at this place," Tom said as he stared up the street. Gwen's cottage looked like a used-car parking lot. Gwen's S.U.V was parked in the crushed-shell driveway and Gregory's Toyota was parked in front of the house. Behind Gregory's was Lawrence Blake's beat-up old pickup truck. On the other side of the street Daniel recognized Paul's truck and Wendell Kirby's fancy, if aged, midnight blue Cadillac. Parked diagonally, with its rear bumper sticking out into the street, was Abraham Martin's tug boat of an old Ford pickup. Daniel would recognize that truck anywhere; the lobster buoy hanging from the antenna and the fuzzy stuffed lobster dangling from the rearview mirror were each one of a kind. The bed of the truck was filled with nets, ropes, and about a dozen lobster pots that probably hadn't seen ocean water in this decade. Dried seaweed was hanging from the rear bumper and a seagull was perched on the rusted roof of the cab.

What in the world had Gwen done? Hung out a plaque advertising for single men?

Daniel shivered at the thought of Gwen entertaining Abraham, Lawrence, Gregory, and Wendell while he had been gone. The two men with salt-water running through their veins didn't mix very well with the two businessmen. Abraham was probably trying to sell her some lobsters, and Lawrence could be handing out more discount coupons for his whale watching tour. Wendell was no doubt putting together a merger of his motel and Gwen's restaurant, and Gregory was probably designing a web page for the Catch of the Day.

All that was missing was Erik and Gunnar showing up and hoisting the hutch out of the bed of the truck and into her dining room without breaking a sweat or using both hands. As Saturdays went, this one had just hit rock bottom.

Daniel slowly backed the truck into her driveway, leaving plenty of room to maneuver the furniture. Before he had a chance to get out of the truck, the four men came piling out of Gwen's cottage, followed more slowly by Gwen. Daniel slammed the truck door and studied her face. She seemed a little pale, and there was a glazed look in her eye. He couldn't blame her. Knowing Abraham, he had probably come right from the docks and hadn't bothered to clean up first. Abraham and freshly cut bait usually had the same aroma.

Gwen stood beside him as the men opened the tailgate and started to untie the furniture. "You did fit them both in."

"Told you I would." He watched as Gregory got in his car and drove away. *One down, half a dozen to go.* "What did you do to scare poor Gregory off?"

"Oh, he's not leaving; he's running to the store for me." Gwen looked a bit flustered. "I believe I'm cooking dinner for the gang."

"How in the hell did that happen?" He couldn't contain the anger in his voice. He was mad. The woman cooked every day and was planning on cooking a lot more once the restaurant opened. She didn't need to be cooking for these barbarians on her day off. He had been planning on taking her over to Sullivan for some pizza. Nothing fancy, because it wasn't a date, but he thought Gwen might enjoy not cooking for once, and to see some of the sights. Sullivan not only had a decent pizza parlor, but a McDonald's too.

"I'm not sure. One minute I was directing Wendell and Lawrence in moving my old table and chairs out of the dining room and the next they were passing around a hat, collecting money for the supplies I needed to make dinner."

"What are you making?"

"Something simple and fast." Gwen glanced at her watch. "I didn't have a lot of time, so I suggested spaghetti with meat sauce."

"So you're stuck with making dinner for what,

six men?" Maybe he should start smacking some heads together. Didn't these Neanderthals know how to treat a lady? No wonder they were all single and lonely.

"I'm not stuck, Daniel. I did agree to do it. Besides, I'm not doing it all. Carol Ann, Tom's wife, is bringing the salad and their kids, and Mrs. Ruffles from next door came over to introduce herself. She just pulled a chocolate cake from the oven, so she's supplying dessert."

"Daniel, do you want to tell this idiot not to just yank the hutch from the truck?" Tom shouted from behind them. "It's an antique, for cripes sake, Abraham. It's older than you. Don't pull on it like that."

Daniel groaned, gave Gwen one last look, and then walked over to where all the men were standing around arguing with each other on the best way to remove the hutch. All the Sunday-afternoon quarterbacks were in a huddle, and no one had any idea who had the ball. "Okay, guys, since Gwen originally asked me to help her with this, I'm going to tell you how it's going to be done."

When three loud protests quickly echoed, he added, "That way if something does goes wrong, she'll know whom to blame—me." All the men nodded their heads. Everyone wanted to impress the little lady, but no one wanted to be blamed if her hutch ended up as firewood. "I'm telling you right now, not only is this sucker heavy, it's awkward. If you don't believe me, ask Paul and Tom; they helped me load it, along with Anna's nephew."

"What about the bureau?" Abraham asked.

"Two men should be able to handle that and get it upstairs." Daniel jumped into the bed of the truck. "We'll do the bureau first, then the hutch."

* * *

Three hours later Daniel stood in Gwen's dining room and accepted a piece of chocolate cake from Evelyn Ruffles with a polite thank-you. There was barely enough room to move in Gwen's over-crowded cottage, but no one seemed to mind. Everyone was having a great time. Even Gwen seemed to be enjoying herself.

Gwen's cooking had been superb, as usual. Abraham had proposed to her over his second helping. She had graciously declined and passed him the basket overflowing with garlic bread. Red wine had been brought out for the meal, but every man in the house accepted one of the beers Tom had brought over, along with four folding chairs. Tom and Carol Ann's kids were great. Samuel, who was six, never left his Uncle Paul's side, much to Paul's annoyance, since he had been trying to corner Gwen in the kitchen all evening. Their four-year-old daughter, Elizabeth, talked Lawrence's ear off about whales and puffins. Devin, their newborn son, had cried just about the whole time, until Carol Ann had thrust him into Gwen's unsuspecting arms.

Everyone in the cottage, including himself, gave a sigh of relief as silence finally reigned. How a ten-pound, three-ounce baby could cause such a commotion was beyond him. After listening to Devin cry for the first half hour straight, he had been ready to leave Gwen to her suitors. With his blessings.

By the expression of horror on Gwen's face, he had gotten the impression she wasn't used to han-dling babies. When Devin had immediately shut up and begun to coo, her smile had been radiant and filled with wonder. Daniel was afraid he would be dreaming about that smile tonight. Ten minutes later Devin had been asleep, and the women had quickly made a makeshift bed on the couch for the infant, barricading him in with the coffee table and enough pillows to cushion a trapeze artist's fall. After that the only sound Devin had made was a couple of grunts and a bunch of sucking noises as he tried to jam his tiny fist into his tinier mouth.

Wendell stepped on Daniel's toe, as he tried to squeeze by. "Sorry."

"No problem." He lifted his plate of cake out of the man's way. Wendell appeared to be on a mission. Curious, Daniel watched the motel owner approach Gwen, who was in the corner of the kitchen, putting on another pot of coffee. She seemed to be having the time of her life, even though Daniel couldn't remember her sitting for more than twenty minutes during the meal. At Wendell's approach, Gwen's expression became more guarded, less open.

Interesting.

Daniel stepped around Paul and Samuel and got a couple of feet closer to Gwen and Wendell. His money was on Wendell asking her out. Wendell's first words confirmed his suspicions. Gwen's very polite yet firm refusal came next. The men in the room were batting zero tonight.

If he counted Abraham's marriage proposal, Gwen had been asked out four times and had turned every one of them down flat. In his opinion the men were making fools of themselves. Gregory had asked her to some concert in Bangor at the end of the month. Abraham wanted marriage and a home-cooked meal for the rest of his life. Wendell wanted dinner and dancing, and Lawrence had been maneuvering for a private boat tour of some of the islands off the coast. Gwen hadn't been buying any of it.

Paul would be making his move as soon as he

could shake his nephew. Daniel had a feeling he would be meeting with the same results. Gwen didn't seem to be interested in a relationship, and the men were just wasting their time pestering her.

Daniel was smart enough to know that in this day and age there were some women who just didn't like men. Gwen wasn't one of them. He had seen the female appreciation spark in her eyes when Erik or Gunnar came around, yet she had rejected dates with both of them. In the men's room yesterday morning he had been positive that Gwen had been as aware of him as he had been of her. Her gaze had dropped to his mouth, and a flash of hunger had leaped into her big brown eyes. That hunger had nearly driven him to his knees.

If Gwen hadn't run from the bathroom when she did, he would have kissed her. There had been no other choice—it was either kiss her or go insane. Instead, she had been the one to run, and he was positive she had run. He didn't understand why she had left the way she did, but he had given up thinking about it because it had only made his aching head hurt worse. Banging it against the men's room wall hadn't been the smartest thing he had ever done.

At least he wasn't making a fool of himself by asking Gwen out. He wouldn't be making that mistake. He had been a fool once in the eyes of every resident of Misty Harbor. He wasn't going to do that again. Never again.

No matter how much he wanted to, there was no way he would ask Gwen out only to get the same rejection and pat reply she gave to every other man in town. She was too busy and didn't have time for dating or a relationship. So far the men seemed to be taking her rebuff in stride, with no hurt feelings. That was probably due to the fact that she was declining everyone. Gwen was an equal-opportunity rejecter.

"Daniel, have you seen Muffy?" Evelyn Ruffles asked as she peered under the table.

Muffy was a black Scottish terrier and the love of Mrs. Ruffles's life since her husband passed away four months earlier. "He's in the living room beside the couch. I think he's guarding Devin while he's sleeping."

"How that precious angel is sleeping through all this racket, I'll never know." Evelyn brushed a gray curl off her cheek. "Have you ever seen such a party? It was so sweet of all you nice, strong men to help Gwen move that furniture."

"I think it's more of a gathering than a party." He glanced around the crowded kitchen and dining room and was amused by the variety of men who were trying to court Gwen. Everything from lobster fishermen to computer geeks. "Your cake was delicious, Evelyn. It was very nice of you to bring it over."

"It was the least I could do. That poor girl has enough on her hands with opening a business, unpacking, and trying to get this place in order. I've come over here twice before, but Gwen's never home. She seems to live at the restaurant."

"That she does." He glanced over at Gwen, only to find her in the opposite corner of the kitchen with Paul. Tom was in the dining room, holding a squirming Samuel by the back of his shirt. From Gwen's polite smile, Daniel could tell Paul was getting shot down.

Men's batting average for the night, zero!

The doorbell rang, Muffy started to bark, and Devin woke up with a howl. The front door opened and Lawrence yelled, "Bob and Sally are here." Carol Ann was making cooing noises, but Devin wasn't in the mood to listen. The more the baby cried, the more Muffy howled.

"Were invitations to this mailed out, or what?" What in the world were Bob and Sally doing here? The newly engaged couple were making quite a few of the town's folk uncomfortable, with all their smiles and happiness. Daniel thought it was cute that they were so obviously in love, but they were both too young for marriage. Bob and Sally would only be graduating from high school in two months.

Evelyn chuckled. "No, Daniel. While you were out getting the second load of furniture, Carol Ann called her baby sister and asked her if Bobby and she would be interested in Gwen's old table and chairs. Sally likes modern stuff, and Bobby likes whatever Sally likes."

"That explains why Gwen had it moved into the living room and was spraying the glass top with Windex a moment ago." Lawrence had made himself useful by wiping down the chairs. The information pipeline had been busy tonight. Misty Harbor hadn't seen this much excitement on a Saturday night since the Christmas boat parade last December and the Women's Guild opened up the Fellowship Hall of the Lutheran Church afterward for hot chocolate, cookies, and caroling.

A smiling Bob and a radiant Sally walked into the kitchen, still holding hands. "It's perfect Ms. Fletcher. We'll take it."

Gwen stepped around Paul, looking relieved by the interruption. "Great. Would you care for some coffee and cake? Evelyn brought the most delicious chocolate cake, and I know for a fact it didn't come from any box."

Daniel didn't think either of the eighteen-year-olds looked old enough to drink coffee. Evelyn beamed with pride at Gwen's compliment. "Isn't

Gwen wonderful? She's going to fit right in in Misty Harbor.'' Evelyn tapped her chin and glanced around the room. ''Do you know what she needs?''

''No, what?'' He could think of a couple of things he would like to give Gwen. None of which he could tell Evelyn, or anyone else in the room.

''A husband.''

Chapter Ten

Daniel helped himself to another handful of chips and looked at his mother. "Will you stop by and see it for yourself?" He had stopped over to ask his mother if she would design Gwen's garden.

"You know how busy my schedule is, Daniel." Mary Creighton was putting their lunch dishes into the dishwasher. His father had already disappeared into the den to watch a basketball game. "It must be important to you if you're asking me to do it."

"I'm in charge of renovating the restaurant for her, Mom. I don't want to have everything perfect and then have some idiot come in and plant three dozen lupines just because people expect to see them while in Maine."

"True, but lupines are a good choice."

"Okay, I'll have Hunter turn the soil and plant lupines around the whole patio."

Mary's eyes narrowed dangerously. "You wouldn't dare."

"It would be better than having Gwen waste hundreds of dollars on expert advice, only to end up with nothing but lupines anyway." He knew how to manipulate his mother when he needed to. He hadn't been her son for twenty-nine years without learning a thing or two. Mary Creighton couldn't stand to see a garden not live up to its full potential. "The restaurant is high class for Misty Harbor, and I'll guarantee you, once you've tasted Gwen's cooking you and Dad will be eating there quite regularly." He munched on a few more chips and then added, "I'm sure you'll appreciate the beauty of the lupines on your *every* visit."

Mary shuddered. "You're being cruel, Daniel."

"No, I'm not. Just stating the truth. Gwen wants the best, and I told her you're the best."

"Thank you." Mary swiped the biggest chip out of his hand. "Just tell me, how am I supposed to work another whole garden into my schedule? Your father is already complaining I'm putting in too many hours and ignoring him."

"Think about all the hours of food shopping, cooking, and clean-up time you'll be saving once the restaurant opens."

"True." Mary tapped the counter with the tip of one of her fingers. Her nails were broken and in need of a manicure, but they were clean. Daniel knew his mother well enough to realize that as soon as it hit the fifties, she had been out in the gardens, turning and mulching and getting them ready for spring. "You did say it wasn't a very big garden."

"It's not really a garden at all, Mom. More like an edge or a border. It's only about two-feet wide, and it circles the outdoor eating patio on three sides."

"There's a picket fence around it, if I'm not mistaken."

His mom's gaze got that faraway look in it, as if she was already seeing the garden in her mind. He knew he had her hooked, but just to make sure, he added his bonus shot. "You won't even have to do the work. You design it on paper, and between Hunter, Jonah, and me, we'll do the planting. I worked for you enough every high-school summer to know how to plant a few plants."

"This is that important to you?" His mother's gaze didn't look faraway now. It looked too darn close for his peace of mind. He didn't need his well-meaning mom to dig too deeply into his growing feelings for Gwen.

"The work I've done on the restaurant is very important to me. I don't want some weekend gardener with a trowel and six bags of mulch to detract from that."

"Well, Jonah seems to think the world of this wonder chef. Gwen Fletcher is all he talked about last night when he came to dinner. Your grandfather also critiqued my pot roast, which didn't endear him to me. I think for his birthday I'll get him socks. Jonah hates getting socks for presents. About as much as I hate to have someone tell me my pot roast needs more onions, or that the gravy is lumpy."

"Gwen has Jonah and Clarence critique her every meal. That way she knows if she's satisfying Maine taste buds." He gave him mother a winning smile. His mother didn't like to spend hours away from her gardens just to cook a meal. The last thing she would appreciate was a play-by-play description as to how she didn't match up to the town's new chef. "I wouldn't take it personally, Mom. Gwen's a fantastic chef, but her chili doesn't have the same zing as yours." He was smart enough to offer his mom some praise, or he would be opening boxes of socks next Christmas.

"A mother appreciates compliments from her son. Thank you." Mary gave her son a considering look. "I tried calling you yesterday afternoon to invite you to dinner, but you weren't home."

"I was out." His mom didn't need to know that he had been at Gwen's until well after nine. He had made sure he was the last to leave by disappearing upstairs to the guest bedroom and putting together the bed frame he had hauled home from Anna's.

"Did you do anything interesting?"

"Just helped a friend move some stuff, that's all." Daniel knew enough to change the subject. "So, will you help Gwen out or not?"

"To save myself from facing dozens of lupines over my poached salmon with sour cream dill sauce, I'll make room on my schedule and stop by this week."

"Great." He leaned forward and brushed her cheek with a kiss. "Thanks."

"Hmmmm." His mom cupped her cheek where the kiss had landed. "Now that we have a moment to ourselves, there's something I need to discuss with you."

"What's that?" Daniel didn't like the look in her eyes. She looked worried about something.

"Maggie Franklin is back in town." Mary studied his face as the words left her lips.

He prayed his mom couldn't detect what that news had just done to him. He always knew that one day she would return, if only to visit with her parents. "It's Pierce now, I believe."

"It's still Pierce, but she's divorced now." His mother toyed with the edge of the bag of chips. "She's moved back in with her parents until she can finish her college education and get back on her feet."

He nodded and kept his face perfectly blank as a barrage of emotions assaulted him. Betrayal, anger, and humiliation were the main ones. Every one of those emotions was connected to Maggie and what she had put him through. "Sounds like a smart idea. I hope she succeeds."

"Katie's with her."

"Why wouldn't she be, Mom? Maggie is her mother." He hadn't seen Maggie in five years. The last he had spoken to her, she had been round with the child. He had heard Katie was the spitting image of her mother, but he'd never set eyes on the child. All that was about to change, he guessed. Misty Harbor was too small a town for them not to bump into each other occasionally. It was amazing that he hadn't already run into mother and daughter, but then again, he had been very busy at the restaurant.

"I just didn't want you accidentally running into them without being prepared."

"Mom, it's okay, honest." Even to his own ears, his words didn't sound honest. "It all happened a long time ago."

"I know it did, son. But I don't think you've ever gotten over it." Mary Creighton reached out and covered her son's clenched fist. "Don't you think it's time to put it behind you?"

"I don't know what you're talking about. I put Maggie behind me when she left me five years ago, Mom."

"Oh, Daniel." Tears threatened to clog his mother's throat and spill from her eyes. "What about the baby? Have you put the baby behind you too?"

By eleven o'clock Monday morning, Gwen was ready to pull her hair out or hit the bottle of Tylenol. Six people had filled out job applications. And every one of them had the name of one of the Women's Guild members on the bottom. None of the applicants seemed qualified to sweep the floor, let alone wait tables. She hadn't really been expecting so many applications this early in the morning. She had figured the high school crowd would hit her in the afternoon.

Gwen rubbed the back of her neck, where the tension was building, and watched as Daniel nailed up another piece of wainscoting. The top portion of the walls was smooth and primed, ready for the final blue coat of paint. The bottom portion, where Daniel had ripped out the booths and all the dark paneling, was now patched and smooth enough for the wainscoting to go over it. The dining room was barely recognizable from her first visit to the restaurant. Thank goodness.

She had set up one of the tables as a desk for herself, and another table for the applicants to use to fill out the paperwork if they wanted to. Daniel's hammering didn't distract her. In fact, the sound was almost comforting. Work was being done on her restaurant. Her dream.

She could hear Jonah and Clarence upstairs, ripping up the old carpeting and arguing about something every foot of the way. The two men weren't really Daniel's employees. Jonah had just happened to be there that first morning when Daniel had walked in, and the rest, as they said, was history. It was awfully sweet of Daniel to make both of them feel needed and wanted, giving them some of the easier, but no less important jobs. With the men doing most of the lighter jobs, Daniel was free to accomplish a lot more around the restaurant. By all the noise the two men were making, she wasn't sure how "light" a job carpet removal should be considered. It sounded as if they were removing the walls along with the threadbare carpet.

The way things were going, not only would the dining room and bathrooms be ready for the grand opening, but so would the office area upstairs, and maybe even some of the exterior work.

Hunter was in the kitchen, painting the ceiling, so that area was off-bounds today. She had stopped at the store on the way in and picked up lunch meat and bread. The men would have to settle for plain fare today. She didn't think they would mind too much. They seemed to enjoy whatever she made, and she'd even overheard Jonah tell Daniel to slow the job down. Gwen wasn't paying him by the hour, so the longer Daniel could drag the job out, the more meals they got. Jonah and Clarence had both voiced their appreciation for the "little lady's" cooking. She had taken that as high praise, until Daniel told them that, once the job was done and Gwen opened the restaurant, they could still stop in and get two meals a day of her fantastic cooking. Plus they wouldn't have to break a sweat or rub Ben-Gay onto sore muscles every night to get it either.

The highest praise imaginable was Daniel thinking her cooking was "fantastic."

The walls of the kitchen would be painted their soft green as soon as Hunter finished scrubbing and shining the dish washing area. Then all that would be left was the white trim and the shelves that held the dishes and such.

The restaurant was coming together nicely. So why wasn't she celebrating? She glanced through the six applications again, wondering if she'd missed something. Anything. Three of the applicants had never held a job longer than two weeks, and she didn't want to speculate as to why. One had actually smelled like a brewery, and it hadn't even been ten o'clock in the morning.

Maybe getting customers in every night wasn't going to be the hard part—finding reliable help would be. Gwen already knew that the cooking was going to be the most enjoyable part of running Catch of the Day. Maybe she should have stayed a chef in that upscale Philadelphia restaurant. That way she would be doing what she loved—cooking—not being bothered with the thousand and one details of running the place.

Not!

"My mom always said never to make faces like that; they just might freeze that way." Daniel stopped by her chair and nodded to the applications in her hands. "Problem?"

"I was hoping for better odds."

"Odds on what?" Daniel leaned against another table and faced her.

"One out of six applicants would have been better odds than this. None of these are qualified to do any of the jobs I'm hiring for." She placed the applications into a folder and sighed. "I was looking forward to hiring my first employee today."

"I thought Hunter was your first employee."

"Hunter was hired on a temporary basis. Once all the cleaning and painting are done, he's done. I'm really going to miss him, though."

"He's pretty handy in the kitchen." Daniel gave the swinging door at the other end of the room a thoughtful look. "Did I actually hear Hunter laughing in the kitchen this morning?"

"Yeah. I wasn't paying attention to what I was doing and ended up spraying water all over my face and sweatshirt. Hunter thought it was hysterical." He also had been sweet enough to hand her a clean towel after he had stopped laughing.

"Hunter never laughs, Gwen."

"Of course he does." She could remember at least two other times Hunter had laughed, or at least chuckled. "He also has a very witty, if not dry sense of humor."

"Hunter?" Daniel shook his head and glanced

back at the doors. "I know we told you a little bit about Hunter before you offered him the job."

"Excellent advice, best thing I ever did." Gwen smiled at Daniel, who was all serious and concerned. "Hunter's a hard worker, and I never have to worry about getting my hourly wage from him. I'm planning on giving him a nice bonus when he's done."

"Hunter's changed, Gwen." Daniel ran his fingers through his hair, making Gwen's fingers itch to follow the same path. "He's not the same man you hired. Even Clarence and Jonah have noticed it."

"Changed, how?" She hated to admit that she was totally confused. Hunter might have been quieter when he first started working for her, but some people just took longer to warm up to strangers. Why was Daniel making it sound so amazing?

"He laughs now, Gwen." Daniel continued to watch the swinging doors. "He's friendlier and even joins in the occasional conversation. Clarence said he's sleeping better at night. Doesn't get up at all hours of the night to wander the house or to sit out on the back porch. I don't know, Hunter just seems happier, more content."

"Okay, I'll take your word on it. Hunter's changing. From what you've been telling me, the change seems to be for the better. So, what does it have to do with me? I haven't done or said anything different to Hunter than I would have to any other person."

"Maybe that's the reason." Daniel pulled out a chair and sat down directly across from her. "You didn't treat him differently."

"I'm not getting your point." As far as she could tell, Hunter was the same as everyone else, just a little more quiet. Hunter was definitely a follower, not a leader. Now, Daniel was a leader.

"We all know Hunter, and something of what he must have been through. Hunter never talks about 'Nam, or the time before he went over. My dad knows some of the history, but not all of it. They were in different divisions. Everyone in town treats Hunter differently."

"You mean like he's 'special.' "

"Yeah, special."

"Do you mean kid-glove special or special like he's slow in the thinking department?" There was absolutely nothing slow about Hunter, and she was prepared to argue with Daniel about that until she was blue in the face.

"I mean like walking-on-eggshells special." Daniel gave a frustrated sigh. "No one thinks Hunter is 'slow,' Gwen. I used to worry that one day he just wouldn't bother going home. Disappear and never be heard from again. I know my dad used to think the same thing; maybe that's where I got my fear. But year after year Hunter always returned home."

"And now?"

"Now I know he'll always be there for Clarence. I watch them at breakfast and lunch here, and I see how Hunter takes care of his father."

"I think he's always done that, Daniel." She also noticed the way Clarence had intergrated himself into the restaurant and working for Daniel. She didn't think Clarence had done it to become closer to Jonah or Daniel. The father had done it to watch over his son. Everyone seemed to watch over Hunter. Maybe that was where the problem was. With so many people watching his every move, Hunter could no longer escape the "special" box in which his friends had placed him. "That has nothing to do with me or the restaurant."

"I think Hunter likes working here." Daniel gave her a considering look. "I think it's good for him."

"There's only so much cleaning and painting to be done. I don't see Hunter as a night janitor, do you?"

"No, but can you see him as your assistant chef?"

The question took her by surprise. Not that she hadn't thought about Hunter as her assistant, but because Daniel had also spotted the man's talent. Interesting. Maybe she wasn't so far off the mark after all. "Hunter's never held down a full-time job—if you don't count his military time, that is."

"I think a man's military time should count for something."

Gwen smiled. "So do I." She thought Hunter's time should count for a hell of a lot more than just *something*. "I'm not sure Hunter would want to work full time."

"He's working for you full time now, and it doesn't seem to affect him any."

"True, but I really haven't seen him cook anything besides a dish of coleslaw, some vegetables, or rice. I know he makes a mean pitcher of iced tea and can peel potatoes like a whiz, but there's more to cooking in a restaurant than peeling and chopping."

"Clarence tells me that Hunter can outcook you." Daniel gave her a smug smile and leaned back in his chair.

"That's a father's love speaking." She had to give Daniel credit; the man knew exactly which buttons to press. Hunter might be a maestro in his kitchen at home, whipping up a meal for dear old dad and himself, but there was a big difference between cooking for two and cooking for two hundred.

"You can stop trying to sell me on Hunter, Daniel. I've been thinking of asking him if he would be interested in the job for the past couple of days. Hunter already has the skills, talent, and ambition to do the job. The bad news is, he's never worked in the kitchen of a restaurant, so he doesn't know the pressure he'd be under. The good news is, since he's never done it before, I can train him to do things the right way."

"Your way?"

"Of course my way; it's my restaurant, after all." The more she thought about it, the more she liked the idea of training Hunter. Catch of the Day would be open for four or six weeks before the tourist season started. Plenty of time to fine-tune the menu, and for training Hunter to make potato salad and coleslaw by the bucket instead of the bowlful.

Daniel chuckled along with her. "So you'd give him the job?"

"He's got to want it first, Daniel. Hunter's a little on the shy side, so maybe he won't come right out and ask for an application." Gwen frowned at the folder of useless applications. "I think I know of a way, though. Don't worry, Daniel, if Hunter wants the job, it's his."

Gwen parked behind the restaurant, feeling guilty as hell. She had just pulled a horrible trick on Hunter, and now she was praying it wouldn't backfire on him. Ever since she'd talked to Daniel about hiring Hunter yesterday she'd been thinking out this plan, and it had seemed like a darn fine one until about ten minutes ago. Then her well-intended plan had turned into an appalling trick against a very sweet man.

At ten-thirty that morning she'd stood on the pier, watching Erik dock his fishing boat, *The Maelstrom*. She ignored the look of male appreciation in Erik's eyes, and bought some of his catch of the day, four very fine-looking winter flounders. Erik had personally delivered them to the restaurant, while she'd picked up Millicent Wyndham and they'd gone shopping.

"Problem, Gwen?" Millicent looked at her with a touch of concern. "Your mind seemed to be wandering while we were in the gallery, but I must say, you did pick out some wonderful paintings for the restaurant."

"There were too many painting to choose from. Daniel and Jonah were right; Wycliffe Gallery had just the kind of paintings I was looking for to hang in the dining room." She was thrilled with her purchases, but right now Gwen couldn't appreciate their beauty. She had a sinking feeling in the pit of her stomach.

"So what's the problem?"

"Hunter cooked lunch." She looked at the back of the restaurant with a critical eye. Having a corner lot made the back more visible to the strolling tourist and the town residents. And as backs of restaurants went, it wasn't bad. In fact, it was pretty good. Some new paint on the trim and door, and maybe a fresh coat of asphalt sealer, and it would be good to go as soon as Daniel's huge construction Dumpster was removed and a new regular Dumpster was placed in the far corner.

"What's wrong with Hunter cooking lunch? Clarence told me that boy can cook."

"Hunter's not a boy, and it's a test of sorts."

"What kind of test?" Millicent turned in her chair to face her, placed her leather handbag directly in the center of her lap, and folded her hands precisely on top. Millicent looked like a prim teacher getting ready to lecture one of her students on manners and ladylike behavior. The finishing school Millicent must have attended over fifty years earlier was showing.

"I had Erik drop off some winter flounders while

I was picking you up to go shopping. Hunter had no idea I wouldn't be around to cook lunch until I called him. I told him that you and I would be back around twelve-thirty and suggested he invite Erik if he seemed hungry." She glanced at the clock in the dashboard. It was twelve twenty-eight.

"Why are you testing Hunter?"

"I'd like him to apply for the assistant chef position, but I think he might be too shy to ask. With this test I was hoping to give him enough confidence to see that he can do it, if that's what he wants."

"I see, but why are you worried?"

"What if he didn't pull it all together, Millicent? What if cooking a meal for seven is too much for him?"

Millicent laughed delightfully. "Oh, Gwen, you really are new to Maine aren't you?" Millicent shook her head and opened the car door. "Come on, I'm hungry. Hunter did fine."

"How do you know?" Gwen opened her door and joined Millicent at the back door of the restaurant.

"People who live in Maine are made of stronger stuff than that, Gwen. We don't fall apart at the thought of cooking a simple meal."

Gwen had to admit that maybe Millicent was right. On the phone, Hunter hadn't seemed to fall apart. In fact, he'd said it was "no problem." Gwen's sisters were the only people she knew who would fall apart at the thought of cooking a meal for seven people with only an hour's notice. Neither Jocelyn nor Sydney would know what to do with a couple of pounds of flounder. They might actually know which end was what, but together they wouldn't be able to gut and clean it and figure out which was the edible part. Of course, the winter flounder was a right-sided flounder, meaning its eyes were located on its right side. That ought to throw the doctor and the lawyer off center for a while.

Gwen prayed Millicent was right, and that she hadn't set Hunter up for a fall, and opened the back door. Delicious aromas were the first hint that Hunter had passed the test; the second was the sight of the perfectly set table and the men busily washing up at one of the sinks. "Hi, we're back."

"Heard you pull up." Jonah hurried forward and took Millicent's coat. "Didn't know you would be joining us, Milly, or I would have dressed for the occasion."

Erik gallantly took Gwen's coat and hung it next to Millicent's. "Hunter invited me to stay."

"I told him if you looked hungry to ask. After all, it was your catch." Gwen glanced around the room and was delighted to see that Hunter had cooked exactly what she told him to. Hunter had followed her directions in regard to the food, but she hadn't left any recipes, and the stack of books she had brought to the restaurant and placed on a shelf didn't appear to have been rifled through. So far he was passing with flying colors.

"But you paid for the fish, no?" Erik questioned.

"Yes, I paid for it, and if it tastes as good as it smells, I'll be paying for many, many more just like it."

Erik beamed his dazzling white smile. "You will be buying many more. Hunter knows how to cook fish."

Clarence and Daniel placed bowls of tiny boiled red potatoes and baby peas on the table. Hunter carried a platter of cooked fish and a gravy boat filled with lemon sauce. Gwen and Millicent hurried to wash their hands; they didn't want to keep the men waiting. By the time they made it to the table, everything had been brought over.

"This looks wonderful, Hunter." Gwen allowed Erik to seat her and tried to ignore the look Daniel was giving her. What was she supposed to do, decline Erik's polite gesture? It wasn't like anyone else was offering to get her chair. Jonah and Clarence were fighting over who got to seat Millicent. Clarence won only because Millicent settled the matter for them. Jonah had taken her coat, and Clarence could get her chair.

Everyone made appropriate sounds while the dishes were being passed. Gwen inspected each dish carefully and couldn't find fault with any. Once everyone dug into their meal, the polite muttering went to full-blown appreciation with each mouthful. The lemon cream sauce enhanced the fillets to perfection.

By her second forkful Gwen was convinced she had found her assistant chef. Now to convince Hunter. "This is delicious, Hunter."

"Thank you." He seemed a bit embarrassed by the praise.

She glanced over at Daniel, who was enjoying his meal. He looked up and gave her a small encouraging smile. It was clear he knew what she had been doing and approved.

"Hunter," Millicent said as she passed Jonah the basket filled with warm biscuits, "are you planning on staying on to help Gwen cook once the restaurant is open?"

Everyone seemed to hold his or her breath, waiting for Hunter's answer. Hunter continued to look at his plate and pick at his fish. "I haven't thought about it."

"Well, you should, young man. This piece of fish is some of the best I've ever tasted, and believe me, I've tasted a lot of fish in my time."

Everyone chuckled and dug back into the food. Gwen chewed a piece of red potato and liked the buttery garlic taste of it. "Well, Hunter, if you do give it some thought and decide you'd like to work here full time, just let me know. There's an opening."

Clarence looked ready to protest, but then he gave a sudden jerk, as if someone had kicked him under the table, and glared at Jonah.

"What will the job entail, Gwen? Maybe I know someone who would be interested," Millicent said innocently when Hunter didn't jump at the opportunity.

Gwen saw right through Millicent. "The assistant cook wouldn't just be cooking, but that will be the main part of the job. I need someone responsible in the kitchen to keep an eye on the kitchen staff. The busers to some extent, but mainly the dishwashers. I'll be handling the dining room staff and making sure things are running smoothly, and doing a lot of the cooking."

"Doesn't sound that difficult," Jonah said before turning to Daniel and asking, "Pass the peas, please."

"Difficult, no, but on really busy nights, it can get a bit stressful." Gwen tasted the flounder again and redoubled her efforts to recruit Hunter. "The job also includes filling in for me when I take an occasional night off. The restaurant will be open seven nights a week during tourist season, but I won't be working every night, nor will I expect the assistant chef to work that kind of schedule."

"What about the rest of the year?" Jonah looked upset at the thought of the restaurant not being open year-round.

"Oh, don't worry, Jonah. I wasn't planning on closing down totally. Maybe only closing on Mondays and Tuesdays, if business is slow, and only doing brunch on Sundays. Most families like to have dinner at home on Sundays."

"True," Millicent said. "But can two of you handle it all? And what about the nights when one of you is off? That would leave one person cooking everything."

Clarence shook his head. "Can't be done."

"I was planning on hiring some part-time help in the kitchen. College or high-school students who need the extra money. They wouldn't have to be great cooks or anything. Mostly it would be grating, peeling, and chopping kind of stuff. Prep cooking."

"My neighbor has a kid looking for part-time work," Erik said. "After school and weekend hours. He wanted to know if I needed any help on the boat."

"You got Crazy Simon working for you," Jonah said.

"Simon's not crazy; he's just a little strange," Erik clarified. "Just because he talks to seagulls and the fish doesn't mean he's not the best fisherman I've ever worked with."

"Simon talks to everything, Erik, including telephone poles and rocks."

"Ya, and I'll start worrying about it when they start talking back." Erik's accent got thicker the angrier he got.

Gwen held up her hands. "Okay, guys, that's enough about Simon. Erik, what about your neighbor? Could you mention to him that I'll be hiring soon?"

"I'll do it this afternoon when he comes home from school."

"Great." Gwen frowned at her plate. Throughout the entire conversation, Hunter had never asked a question. She knew he had been listening closely, but she couldn't tell from his expression whether he was really interested in the position.

She had been worrying about the test backfiring

on Hunter, when she should have been worrying about it ricocheting right back in her face. Hunter had cooked an exquisite meal that not only tasted great but had been artfully arranged on the platters, with sprigs of parsley and lemon slices. Presentation was just as important as taste, and Hunter had known that instinctively. Hunter might have gotten a boost to his self-confidence, but who said he even wanted the job? Meanwhile she had gotten a taste for something she wanted and now might not be able to get. She couldn't force Hunter to work for her. Blackmailing seemed a little extreme.

She looked at Daniel for help. He shrugged and went back to cleaning every morsel of food off his plate. So much for Daniel's leadership skills.

Chapter Eleven

"No, Mom, I'm fine, honest." Gwen glanced across the kitchen to Hunter, who gave her a small smile of understanding. Moms across the world were the same.

"You sound tired. Are you getting enough sleep?" Gloria Fletcher's voice held nothing but concern for her middle daughter.

"I'm not tired, and yes, I'm getting enough sleep." Gwen grinned at Hunter's amused expression. "And before you ask, yes, I'm warm enough. They do have heat way up here in Maine, you know." The kitchen at the restaurant wasn't the place to hold a private phone conversation, but that was okay; her mother and she didn't have "private" conversations.

Her mom chuckled. "You always were my difficult child."

"So you tell me." Gwen knew her mother didn't

really mean anything by that comment, yet it still hurt. She wasn't being difficult, she was being different, that's all. "How's Dad?"

"Fine, busy as ever. Between both of our schedules we barely see each other anymore."

Gwen heard the wistfulness in her mother's voice. Her parents had one of those unusual relationships in today's society; they loved each other. It seemed the older they got, the busier they got. They both had taken time for the family when she and her sisters were younger, but the less the kids needed them, the more they concentrated on their careers. Both her mother and father had hit their strides in their forties. Now, in their upper fifties, they were at the top of their professions, and home plate still wasn't in sight. Gwen was afraid they would both spend the rest of their lives running the bases and never really enjoying the game. "Far be it for me to offer you advice, Mom, but maybe you and Dad should be making the time."

"If you dare to follow that line with 'You're not getting any younger,' I will personally cancel the next surgery on my schedule and come up there and paddle you, Gwendolyn Augusta Fletcher."

"Those words will never leave my lips." Gwen chuckled. "Tell me, Mom, when was the last time you and Dad went out on a date?"

"A date? We've been married for thirty-two years. Why would we go on a date?"

"I don't know, maybe for the fun of it. Go see a movie, or just walk on the beach at night holding hands. You can listen to the waves pound the sand and the cries of the gulls circling overhead. The shore's not that far away from Baltimore."

"You've been giving this dating stuff a lot of thought, haven't you?"

"What do you mean?" Gwen didn't like the tone in which her mother asked that question. Gloria Fletcher, M.D., could read her daughters faster than a patient's electrocardiogram.

"Jocelyn's been telling me some really strange stories lately. Something about Vikings and a 'hunky' carpenter you have working for you."

Gwen turned her back so Hunter wouldn't see the flush sweeping up her cheeks. She had the white cord stretched as far as it would go, and still she felt as if she were wedged into Hunter's back pocket. Where was her shopping list? As soon as she went to the store she was buying a cordless phone for inside the kitchen. "What's that got to do with you spending some time with Dad?"

"I don't know, but your voice got all dreamy and sweet when you mentioned walking in the moonlight on the beach."

"It must be a lousy connection." No way was she mentioning Daniel's name.

"Ah, now I see it's change-the-subject time." Her mom laughed, and then asked, "How's the restaurant coming along?"

"Fine. The carpeting is being installed next Monday, so all the painting and carpentry work has to be done by then. I think we're even ahead of schedule, so everything is going really well. I bought some artwork this morning to hang in the dining room. Every painting was done by an artist living in Maine."

"Sounds wonderful, and charming." There was a slight pause, then her mother asked, "So when is the grand opening of Catch of the Day?"

"In about three weeks or so." Gwen knew the exact date, of course; it was circled in red on every calendar she owned. Saturday night, April 20. Reservations were being taken for seating beginning at four and ending at nine. She wanted to invite her parents and sisters to the grand opening, but something held her back. Why would they take time from their busy schedules to drive or fly all the way up to Maine, just to eat a meal and share a glass of champagne? She never bothered her mother, father, or sisters when they were at work.

Catch of the Day was her dream, but in reality it was just a restaurant. America had thousands upon thousands of restaurants. Her family wouldn't be impressed because they wouldn't understand what had gone into its opening. They had more important things on their minds than making the perfect cream sauce—like saving someone's life, finding the cure for cancer, or putting criminals behind bars. She had put her parents in awkward situations all her life, like when she'd given up a full scholarship to Duke University's pre-med program to attend a culinary institute. She was positive that her parents had a hard time explaining that one to their colleagues. She wasn't about to put them in another uncomfortable spot in which they had to come up with excuses as to why they couldn't make it up to Maine in a couple of weeks.

"I ordered the sign, and it should be here in about two more weeks." Gwen grabbed a piece of paper and wrote, *Champagne for opening.*

"You let me know how much it is. Your father and I wanted to help you out, but since you're being stubborn about money, I guess the sign will have to do."

"The sign's a wonderful gift, Mom, thanks. It's carved wood about three feet by six feet long. The background will be painted white, the letters are blue, and there's a ship's steering wheel in brown."

"It's a helm, dear."

"I stayed away from having them carve sea creatures all over the sign." A huge six-foot plywood whale that had been painted white, with AHAB's in lobster-red letters had been hanging out front until she made Daniel take it down and deposit it in the Dumpster.

"Smart move. No one wants to look at one's dinner grinning down at you while you eat it."

Gwen refrained from filling her mother in on the plastic lobsters with bibs and silverware that had been nailed up around the dining room. A high-pitched beep sounded on the other end of the phone. Gwen knew that sound; her mother was being paged.

"I've got to go, Gwen."

"I heard." Gwen smiled as she pictured her mother pulling herself together to go face whatever challenge awaited her. "I love you, Mom. Tell Dad I love him too."

"Will do, bye, I love you too, and be safe. Oh, Gwen?"

"What?"

"Are there really Vikings up there?"

She grinned. "Yes, but there are only two."

Her mother's laugh sounded young and carefree. "I would think that would be plenty."

Gwen was still chuckling as she hung up the phone. Jonah and Clarence walked in the back door. They were arguing about who Millicent liked better. Jonah was positive Milly had been making eyes at him all through lunch. Clarence swore the woman had been playing footsie with him in the cab of Jonah's pickup when they had driven her home.

Both men barely nodded at her and Hunter as they stormed their way through the kitchen and

out into the dining room. Gwen could still hear
them arguing as they stomped their feet up the
stairs to what would soon be her office and storage
area.

Gwen turned to Hunter to see what he thought
of the men's behavior. Hunter was chuckling as
he pulled the tray of clean dishes from the dishwasher. So much for Daniel's assumption that
Hunter never laughed. "Have they always argued
like that?"

"Ever since I can remember." Hunter inspected
the steaming-hot dishes. "Dishwasher is working
much better now that it's clean. The tracks could
use some lubricant, but that's no big deal."

"Great. I don't know what I would do without
you, Hunter." The dishwashing area was just about
as spotless as the cooking area. "Do you think one
dishwasher could handle the job on his own?"

"Guess that would depend on the crowd, and
the kid."

Gwen contemplated that for a moment, then had
to agree. There were too many variables. "True."
She started to scrub the pans soaking in the deep
sink while Hunter put away the dishes. "No one
came in to fill out an application while I was out,
did they?"

"Nope. Daniel would have told me if someone
came in."

"I was hoping for a couple of high school kids
to come in yesterday afternoon, but none showed."
She knew it was too soon to panic, but she was
beginning to worry. "I think I should place an ad
in the local paper."

"Couldn't hurt. Kids are funny." Hunter carefully lined up the glasses on the shelf. "Every one
of them will be looking for summer work, but
they'll all wait until the day before school lets out
to go looking."

"You seem to know a lot about kids." She rinsed two pots and started to scrub the pan Hunter had used to fry the fish. From what Daniel had told her, Hunter had practically been a hermit. How would a hermit know the idiosyncrasies of a teenage mind?

"Years of observing them, that's all." Hunter picked up a clean towel and started to dry the pots. "It happens every summer."

Gwen nodded as she rinsed the heavy pan. "Maybe the school will allow me to put up a sign on their bulletin board."

"Couldn't hurt to ask." Hunter took the pan from her.

"Gwen, you've got company!" Daniel's voice carried from the dining room.

She smiled and used the end of the towel Hunter was holding to dry her hands. It was too early in the afternoon for the high school crowd to be pounding its way to her door. But it didn't mean someone else who was qualified hadn't shown up. "Hopefully that's an applicant I can hire." *And not some slick-hair Romeo bringing me roses and a picture of his tuna boat.*

She and Hunter both glanced at the swinging doors as they forcefully swung open and nearly as forcefully knocked the visitor on her butt. Or was it *their* butts? Three women barged into the kitchen as if they were the health inspectors and someone had reported a fly in their soup.

Hunter leaned down and whispered, "You're on your own. I'm ripping up carpet."

Gwen watched Hunter nearly sprint from the room and knew she was in trouble. The man had received a Purple Heart for being shot while serving in 'Nam. The word *coward* and Hunter didn't even belong on the same page. The second hint that trouble was brewing was the fact that Priscilla, who was under doctor's orders only to pick at her food, was leading the other two women.

Gwen forced herself to smile and greet her visitors. "Priscilla, it's so nice to see you again." She nodded pleasantly. "Are you ladies from the Women's Guild too?"

"No, we're members of the Citizens for a Better Tomorrow Club." The petite fake-blonde had obviously been a cheerleader back in the sixties, and she wasn't going to let anyone forget it. All she was missing was her pom-poms. One dainty, well-manicured hand reached out. "Hello, I'm Sandi, with an *i*, Humphrey."

"Gwen Fletcher. Nice to meet you Sandi, with an *i*." Cyclops Sandi didn't seem to have a clue that she was a little too old to be introducing herself with only one *i*. Sandi gave her a smile so perfect that her parents must have had to remortgage the house to afford the orthodontist bill. What was with the Maine population and their teeth? Sandi's eyes sparkled with periwinkle blue contacts, but Gwen didn't see any sign of intelligence behind that twinkle. It was either all that bleached-blond hair dye had finally destroying what few brain cells she had been born with or Sandi had spent way too much time in tanning booths.

Gwen reached out to shake the other woman's hand. "Gwen Fletcher."

"Janet Pennell. My husband is Ray; you bought your fire insurance from him."

"Small world."

"Smaller town." Janet and Sandi glanced around the kitchen with curiosity. Priscilla had already seen the place. "I hadn't realized how big the kitchen was in this place," Janet said.

"It's a nice size." She had to wonder if the ladies

had stopped in to give her some cooking advice. It seemed that every woman in town couldn't keep herself from offering a suggestion or two. Some had gone so far as to write down family recipes for her. "I was just about to put on a pot of coffee; would you ladies care for a cup?"

"That would be lovely," Priscilla said as she led the group over to the table and chairs.

Gwen tried not to sigh out loud as she walked over to the coffeemaker and started a fresh pot.

What she had been planning on doing was to put on the pot of coffee and spend the next couple of hours on the phone. She needed to haggle over prices with one of the food distributors who was going to be supplying the restaurant. She needed to contact Gunnar Olsen to see if he could provide her all the lobsters she would be needing. Clarence had given her the name of a clam digger who would be willing to sell her fresh-caught clams every day. She had to check on the dinner dishes she had ordered last week, and then there were the linens to check on, and a washer and dryer to buy. The to-do list was endless, and growing longer every day.

And here she was, frittering away the afternoon, serving tea and biscuits to the town's pep club. Okay, it was going to be coffee and banana-nut muffins, but she could still think of a hundred different things she'd rather be doing than watching Priscilla pick her way through her snack. She could only hope that the Citizens for a Better Tomorrow Club wouldn't want her or the restaurant to do anything special. She had more than enough on her plate already.

The aroma of freshly brewed coffee filled the kitchen. "So, ladies, what does your club do?" She set a plate of muffins in the center of the table, along with a stack of napkins.

"We strive to make sure Misty Harbor has a better future," Sandi said as she eyed the muffins with a hungry look, though she didn't take one.

Priscilla cut a muffin in half and smeared butter on both pieces, then started to pick. "We keep an eye on everything and make sure it's improving our community, not detracting from it."

Gwen stared at the three women in confusion as an eerie shudder slid down her spine. "Who decides if it's improving or detracting?"

"We do, of course." Janet helped herself to a muffin.

"I see." Gwen got the now-filled coffeepot and brought it over to the table. She couldn't believe it; she was entertaining a band of SS men in her kitchen. Hitler would have been proud, knowing some of his policies lived on.

Curiosity overran caution. She had to ask, "What is Catch of the Day, an improvement or a detraction?"

All three ladies giggled. Janet was the first to recover. "A definite improvement. Our little town needed a fine dining establishment."

"It needed any kind of restaurant," Priscilla said before jamming the rest of the muffin into her mouth.

"Yes, well, having a fine establishment such as this will be a feather in our caps." Sandi looked immensely pleased. "Sullivan will be green with jealousy."

"Who's Sullivan?" Gwen asked.

"Sullivan's a town, not a who." Priscilla started to unwrap the paper baking cup from another muffin. "They have a pizza shop and a McDonald's."

"Now I see." Hopefully she'd be pulling in some customers and tourists from Sullivan and the surrounding area. "So you guys are happy I'm opening this restaurant?"

"Of course, Gwen," Sandi said. Priscilla, who had a mouthful of muffin, nodded her head in agreement.

"We only have one small favor to ask you." Janet sipped her coffee and smiled.

"What's that?" She didn't like the feeling she was getting.

"We heard you're going to be hiring high-school students for summer help," Sandi said.

"Yes, that's right." Gwen gave them all a pleasant smile. Maybe they were here to recommend some kids. "It'll be after school and weekends until tourist season starts; then I'll be able to give them more hours. The positions are mainly for dishwashers, busboys, and waiters, if they have experience."

"So we heard correctly." Janet nodded.

"So what's the favor? Got a kid in high school needing a job?" Priscilla looked kind of old to have a high schooler at home, but Sandi and Janet seemed about the right age.

"Sandi's the only one who still has them young enough to be in school," Priscilla said.

"My daughter Mandi is in the eleventh grade, but she's not looking for summer employment. Her father and I believe Mandi needs time just to be a kid and enjoy her teenage years." Sandi's fingers toyed with one of three gold bracelets on her wrist.

"There are some, let's say 'undesirables' in our local high school, Gwen," Janet clarified. "They reflect badly on the community, and we want to make sure that the tourists, who this town depends on for its livelihood, aren't offended."

"I thought this town depended on its fishing industry for its livelihood." As far as Gwen was concerned, there were definitely a couple of fishermen just stepping off the boats who could give a new meaning to the word *offend*.

"It does, but tourism is our second leading industry," Sandi said.

"What kind of kids are 'undesirable'?" She could think of three ladies who were becoming more undesirable by the minute.

"You know the kind, Gwen. They have earrings in their noses, eyebrows, and tongues," Janet said. "Some even have tattoos."

"The girls all dye their hair black and the boys are bald," Sandi added. "The school system can't seem to control them. What we need are uniforms and a moral code of conduct in our school. These freaks need to conform to the rules of society."

Priscilla, not to be outdone, said, "Some even wear thumb rings!"

"I see." Gwen didn't know if she wanted to laugh or bodily throw these bigots out of her restaurant. She had to repeat, over and over again, to herself that these ladies, their husbands and families, and all their relatives and friends were potential customers. It would be career suicide. "If these kids are as bad as you say they are, I'm sure none of them will be looking for summer jobs." She looked directly at Sandi. "Employment means responsibility, and I'm sure none of these kids would have such a quality."

Sandi with an *i* never blinked. The snide remark went right over her head. Big surprise there. Someone should tell Sandi to stay out of the sun; the ultraviolet rays were wrinkling her perfectly tanned skin. She was beginning to get the appearance of a stick of beef jerky with a dazzling white smile.

Priscilla wouldn't know what to do with a clue unless someone sautéed it in onions and served it up on a sesame-seed roll. Priscilla appeared to be in this charming little club for the food. It was probably the same reason she joined the Women's Guild.

Janet was the obvious choice for ringleader. "So, Janet, do you have any children?"

"No. Wendell didn't want any."

"Wendell? I thought you were married to Ray."

"Janet was married to Wendell Kirby for ten years before she married Ray about two years ago," Sandi said.

"She was married to Abraham Martin before Wendell too, but we aren't allowed to discuss that." Priscilla looked awfully proud of sharing that little secret.

"Priscilla, you weren't supposed to tell anyone that! You're not supposed to go around telling strangers intimate details of my life. I don't care if you are my cousin." Janet looked ready to shove the rest of the muffins down Priscilla's throat.

Gwen stared at the primly dressed Janet and couldn't imagine her being married to the same Abraham Martin who had been at her house on Saturday night. As for hearing any intimate details of that reunion, she would rather get a bikini wax. Janet was on her third husband and she wasn't even forty yet. Oh, yeah, the youth in the high school needed a moral code.

Priscilla looked upset and hurt by Janet's reprimand. "Gwen's not a stranger."

"Excuse me, ladies." Daniel, still clutching his hammer, walked into the kitchen and glanced around the table. "I hate to break this up, but I really need Gwen."

Sandi giggled at Daniel's choice of words.

If Sandi thought that was amusing, wait until Gwen stood up and kissed Daniel for rescuing her from the clutches of the SS men. "Sorry, ladies, business is calling." She stood up and started to gather the cups and dirty napkins.

Daniel plucked the ladies' coats off the rack and bundled the Citizens for a Better Tomorrow Club into them and out the swinging doors with a minimum of fuss and good-byes. Gwen wasn't even sure if they all had on the right coats before leaving. And she really didn't care one way or the other. She was just thrilled to see their backsides disappearing through those doors.

A moment later Daniel returned to the kitchen. "Are you all right?"

"Sure. Why shouldn't I be?" She loaded the dirty dishes into a tray and wiped down the table.

"I heard yelling in here." Daniel slowly slid his hammer into the loop on his tool belt.

Gwen watched the movement and chuckled. It reminded her of old westerns where the "good guy" reholstered his gun after the threat of danger had passed. Come to think of it, Daniel had come charging into the kitchen with his hammer drawn. Lord, what a hero.

"What's so funny?" Daniel helped himself to a cup of coffee.

"Nothing." Gwen leaned against the counter and studied the way Daniel cradled the cup between his hands. Big hands. Tender hands. "You should have warned me about the Citizens for a Better Tomorrow Club."

"Yeah, well, most of the town just ignores them,

or hopes they'll just go away." Daniel glanced at her over the rim of his cup. "What did they want?"

"They were advising me not to hire any freaky high school students. It would be bad for business and tourism."

"Are you going to take their advice?"

Two weeks ago she had been worried about leather-wearing, spiked-pink-haired hostesses seating her customers. Now she just might hire the first freak to walk in and fill out an application, just for spite. "I'll take their advice when they start paying my bills."

Daniel chuckled and saluted her with the cup. "Don't pass judgment on the town because of a few rotten apples. Priscilla's not too bad; she's lonely now that all her children have left the nest. She's joined every club and organization in town. Sandi's just window dressing. She stands in the background waving her pom-poms and cheering 'Go Team Go.'"

Gwen dumped her now-cold coffee down the drain and refilled her cup. "Glad to see I had them pegged." She leaned against the counter. Her thigh was about eight inches away from Daniel's, but his height put him a good nine inches above her. The kitchen got suddenly more intimate and warm. "What's Janet's story?"

"She's making a career out of marrying up." Daniel shrugged. "I guess she believes her own propaganda about creating a better tomorrow."

"Nice." She shook her head.

"I like what you did for Hunter this morning, but I don't think he lacks confidence in his cooking abilities."

"You also think he doesn't laugh." She placed her cup on the counter behind her and turned to face Daniel. Damn, why did he always have to look so darn good at everything he did? Daniel looked like an advertisement selling coffee, or toothpaste, or even blue jeans. Whatever he was selling, she was surely buying. Life was truly unfair.

Daniel placed his empty cup next to hers. "He never used to laugh."

"Maybe he's happier now. More contented."

"What are you doing that's so different from the rest of the town?" Daniel seemed to move closer.

"I'm not doing anything different. Hunter wasn't laughing at anything I said or did. He was chuckling over Jonah and Clarence arguing about who Millicent likes more." Sometime during the morning hours Daniel had taken off his flannel shirt, leaving him clad only in a navy blue T-shirt that clung to his chest. She eyed that chest with a great deal of appreciation. Her tongue felt like it was sticking to the roof of her mouth.

"Clarence told me this morning that Hunter was whistling as he made their dinner last night."

She grinned. "Hunter must like to cook."

Daniel's gaze settled on her mouth. "Do you have any idea how tempting your mouth is?"

Her smile faded and her breath got lodged in her throat. It was the first time Daniel had given any hint that he was feeling the same attraction she had been experiencing since he walked into her dining room over two weeks ago. Anticipation rushed through her body. "Is this when you finally kiss me?"

A small smile tugged at the corner of Daniel's mouth. "Yeah, I believe it's time, don't you?"

She licked her lower lip and moved closer. The tips of her breasts brushed against Daniel's chest, and she tilted her head back and stared up into his smoky-gray eyes. "Way past time."

Daniel's hand came up and softly cupped her cheek. The pad of his thumb slid across her lower lip, following the moist trail her tongue had left behind. "You've been driving me crazy, do you know that?"

She smiled against his thumb. "No, but it's nice to know." She could feel the rapid pounding of her heart against her rib cage and wondered if her mother would be able to fix that medical defect before it became serious.

One of Daniel's light brown eyebrows rose in response, and he seemed to hesitate for a moment. His thumb lightly pressed against the seam of her lips. "I've never kissed a person who was signing my paychecks before."

Gwen slowly opened her mouth and nipped at Daniel's thumb. "I'll stop signing them if it will make you kiss me."

Daniel chuckled and slowly shook his head. "I don't think one kiss is going to be enough."

She reached up and cupped the back of Daniel's head. Soft silky hair slid through her fingers. She definitely wanted more than one kiss from Daniel, but she couldn't think of a more perfect place to start. The sound of Jonah and Clarence stomping down the stairs caused her stomach to drop, and Daniel glanced over his shoulder toward the swinging doors. *No, not now!*

She pulled Daniel's head down and planted a fleeting kiss on his surprised mouth. "Next time don't be so darn slow about it." She took a swift step back just as the doors swung open.

The kiss had been so quick that she felt absolutely nothing but frustration and a bit of satisfaction at the astonished look on Daniel's face.

Daniel ignored Clarence and Jonah as they came barging into the kitchen, arguing about who had been the better swimmer in their youth. Daniel leaned in closer and whispered, "Some things, Gwen, are meant to be done so slowly and thoroughly that a person could savor them for a life-time." Daniel's gaze held heat and hunger as it stared at her mouth. "One day soon I'm going to have to show you what a real kiss feels like."

Gwen felt her knees go weak with the thought.

"What are you two yammering about?" Jonah asked as he headed for the coffeepot.

"We're discussing whether it's better to hurry through a job, or to take your time and do it right," Daniel replied without taking his eyes off her face.

"Take your time," Clarence said.

"Any job worth doing is worth doing right," Jonah said.

She nodded slowly. "I stand corrected."

"Gwen," shouted Hunter from the other room, "you've got company."

Daniel muttered something under his breath, gave her a look that promised that one long, slow kiss, and stormed out of the room. Clarence and Jonah glanced at each other, shrugged, and followed Daniel.

She stood there for the count of ten and tried to get her heartbeat back under control. She wanted that kiss Daniel had promised. She would kill for that kiss. Whoever had come to call had better be filling out an application and be related to Julia Child. With a deep breath, she followed the men into the dining room.

A man she had never seen before was standing in the center of the room. He was clutching a bouquet of carnations and daisies and appeared to be very nervous. She couldn't blame him. He was surrounded by four glaring men—her bodyguards.

Gwen shook her head at the insanity of it all. Where were all these men coming from, and didn't they have something better to do with their time? She forced herself to smile at the gentleman caller. "Hello. Are you looking for me?"

"You're Gwen Fletcher?"

"Who else would she be?" grunted Jonah.

She gave Jonah a small nudge with her elbow and whispered, "Be nice."

"Yes, I am, and who would you be?"

"He's Ted Busby," snapped Daniel, glaring at the flowers.

"I'm Ruth Busby's brother-in-law. I was told she mentioned me to you the other day when the Women's Guild paid you a visit." Ted held the flowers out to her. "These are for you."

"Thank you, Ted, they're lovely." She took the bouquet because it would have been rude not to. "Yes, Ruth did mention you." One of the other ladies had mentioned Ted's enjoyment of eating. One look at Ted and anyone would have been able to figure it out on their own.

"She can put them in the kitchen with the other three bouquets," Clarence said.

Hunter grunted. "Heard she's got some at her house too."

"The chocolate candies Lawrence brought were good. You should have brought a box of candy, Ted." Jonah wiggled his nose at the flowers.

"Don't forget the lobsters from Gunnar," Clarence added.

"And the redfish from Erik," Jonah said.

"Who brought her the bucket of clams?" Hunter asked.

"Will you guys stop it? You're making Ted uncomfortable." She wanted to stamp her foot. Ted was sweating profusely and appeared ready to bolt toward the door without the least bit of provocation.

"Ted's always uncomfortable when he's getting ready to ask a woman out," Jonah said.

She had already figured that one out for herself,

but she would have preferred not to have an audience when she turned him down. "Jonah, please."

"She's not going." Daniel's voice was loud and firm, practically daring anyone to argue with him.

Everyone turned and stared at Daniel. Jonah and Clarence both had huge knowing grins on their faces. Hunter's mouth looked suspiciously like it was ready to break into a smile. Ted turned whiter than that stupid whale the previous owner had had swinging out front. Lord help them if Ted fainted. They'd never be able to move him. Then again, there was nowhere to move him to.

She wasn't amused or delighted by Daniel's uncharacteristic outburst. The man obviously needed some lessons in decorum. "Daniel?" Rumors would surely start to fly around town if word got out that Daniel was scaring off her potential dates.

"Gwen's busy, Ted. She's a very busy businesswoman, trying to get a restaurant remodeled and ready to open in a couple of weeks. She can't keep entertaining people and serving coffee and muffins to every person, organization, or lonely man in town." Daniel took a deep breath. "It's a wonder the men of Misty Harbor haven't scared her right back to Philadelphia. All she's trying to do is be nice and open her restaurant. Can't everyone just leave her alone? I don't know how she's doing it, because I can barely get any work done around here without tripping over all kinds of people."

"Oh, my," said a female voice. "Maybe I've come at a bad time."

Gwen quickly turned and stared at the woman standing in the opening of one of the patio doors. She had been so caught up in Daniel's ranting that she hadn't even felt the cold air rushing into the dining room. The woman appeared deeply amused by the situation. She looked familiar, but Gwen didn't remember having met her before. Great; just what she needed at the moment—another guest.

The woman stared right at Daniel and raised one brow as if she was waiting for something.

A long moment passed before Daniel reluctantly said, "Hello, Mom. You're early."

Chapter Twelve

Daniel stared at his mother and wondered what in the world she had been doing outside on Gwen's patio by herself. The picket fence surrounding the garden didn't have a gate, so how had his mother gotten in there?

"I was coming to tell Gwen that Mrs. Creighton was here when Ted arrived," Hunter said.

That explained it. Anxious to get her first ideas, his mother would immediately head for the garden. He was surprised she wasn't still out there, measuring and planning away.

"Hey, Mary," Jonah said. "Heard you were going to be doing Gwen's garden."

"Well, I'm going to be suggesting a couple of ideas, and if Gwen likes them, I'll work them up into a plan for you guys to follow." Mary stepped into the dining room and closed the patio door.

Gwen stepped forward and held out her hand.

"Gwen Fletcher, and thank you for making time in your busy schedule to bail me out."

"How could I refuse when Daniel asked so nicely?" His mother gave him an amused look, as if she knew something he didn't. He hated that look. "My son even volunteered himself, Jonah, and Hunter to put in the plants, so all I have to do is design which plants go where."

"Isn't it too cold to be planting now?" Gwen looked out the patio doors and frowned.

"The ground can be turned, and I heard the weather might be warming later this week. If it hits as high as they're predicting, you might want to get the picket fence repaired and painted." Mary looked at her son.

"No problem; we're almost done inside, other than the painting."

"I think I'd better be going," Ted said as he started to slowly make his way to the front door.

Gwen gave Ted a friendly, polite smile. "I'll walk you out, Ted."

Daniel watched as Gwen and Ted disappeared. He stood there and called himself a fool for going off on Ted like that. Gwen must think he was either unbalanced or a Neanderthal. Ted and every other guy in town had the right to bring Gwen flowers, spout poetry, and lay dead fish at her feet. Gwen was single and free, and he was a fool for thinking otherwise. It had been pure sexual frustration that had him yelling at Ted like some jealous lover. He had wanted to kiss Gwen so damn bad, he had practically tasted it. That quick peck she had brushed against his mouth hadn't even whet his appetite.

And Gwen had had the gall to tell him he had been too darn slow, and he had nearly lost it in front of his grandfather and Clarence. Finally tasting one's fantasy shouldn't be hurried or timed like a sporting event. No one would be handing out medals for the fastest kisser. When he finally got around to kissing Gwen he wanted all the time in the world and one hell of a lot of privacy.

He heard Jonah and Clarence say something to his mother and then go stomping up the stairs. Hunter disappeared back into the kitchen, but he was more interested in what was happening in front of the restaurant rather than inside.

Through one of the big picture windows he saw Ted talking and Gwen slowly shaking her head. The wind was blowing Gwen's hair around her face, and the flowers she was still holding were flapping back and forth. Gwen looked cold, while Ted looked disappointed. Ted was obviously getting shot down, just like every other man in town. The same thing would have happened if he had only kept his mouth shut instead of acting like some jealous idiot. Gwen wasn't interested in dating any of the men from town.

So why had she pressed her breasts against his chest and turned her face upward for his kiss back in the kitchen? Gwen could be kissing any guy in town, yet she had chosen him. Why? Had she been serious, or was Gwen playing some sick game?

"Gwen's very pretty," his mother said. "No wonder the men in town are going crazy over her."

He gave a slight start at his mother's voice. He had forgotten she was still in the room. A quick glance showed his mother standing right beside him, staring at the same view. Mary Creighton had a mother's habit of seeing too much and putting her own interpretations on what she saw. "The men of this town are already crazy; they didn't need Gwen to help them along in that direction."

"They aren't crazy, Daniel. They're lonely; there's a difference."

"Well, stalking the new restaurant owner isn't

the way to endear our town to the world's population of females." Daniel turned away from the window as Ted walked away. Gwen had a look of
sadness about her, as if she were upset for hurting
Ted's feelings. It was the same look she had worn
when she'd turned down Erik, Gunnar, Wendell,
and every other man in town. He had to wonder,
if he asked her out, would she be wearing the same
somber expression?

"No one's stalking Gwen."

"Could have fooled me. The poor woman
doesn't get a minute alone. They are even showing
up on her doorstep. Cripes, some idiot even went
as far as to write a poem to her and have it printed
in the local paper." Forty-eight lines of the worst
poetry imaginable had made it to page three of
the local weekly newspaper. Two lines had burned
their way into his memory forever: *While you cook
and serve the lobsters, I will protect you from the mobsters.*
As far as he knew, there weren't any mobsters in
Maine. Nor was Gwen running from any unsavory
characters. Someone had obviously been watching
one too many episodes of *The Sopranos.*

"Oh, you read it too." His mother smiled as
Gwen came back in. "I especially liked how the
author rhymed a brown-haired Gwendolyn with a
fretted-neck mandolin."

Gwen groaned at his mother's words. "Please
don't remind me. The paper's due out tomorrow
and I don't think my heart can take it if there's
another poem in it." Gwen smiled at his mother.
"Of course, being compared to a mandolin was
better than one of my least favorite childhood
taunts, 'Gwen, Gwen, the big fat hen!' "

"I can't imagine you fat," Mary said with a laugh.

Daniel ran his gaze down Gwen's luscious body
and wisely kept his mouth shut. There was no way
Gwen would be considered fat in any man's eyes,

but he was smart enough to know that any conversation concerning a woman's weight was a time bomb ready to explode. It was a no-win situation.

"I wasn't obese, but I did tend to carry a bunch of baby fat when I was a lot younger. Food has always been my passion, in one form or another." Gwen nodded to the bouquet of flowers she still held in her hand. "Let me go put these in some water and then we can discuss the garden, okay?"

"Take your time," Mary said. "Daniel will keep me company."

He watched the enticing sway of Gwen's hips as she hurried into the kitchen. "Since when do you need someone to keep you company?" He knew his mother well enough to know she preferred to be surrounded by trees, flowers, and freshly turned soil than people. Heck, his mother had been known to turn down shopping trips into Bangor just to turn manure into a newly dug garden.

"You're my son; of course I'll always want your company." His mother seemed to study his face for a long moment before saying, "I like your Gwen."

"She's not my Gwen."

His mother's knowing smile held a dreamy quality. "We'll see about that one."

He refrained from commenting because Gwen came back out of the kitchen, carrying her coat. "I only have one or two suggestions, Mrs. Creighton, and the rest will be up to you."

"Call me Mary, please." Mary looked at him. "I want you to come with us, Daniel. You'll be the one doing all the actual work."

So much for him getting a break to go hide for awhile. Gwen hadn't even looked at him since she'd walked Ted outside. He had definitely stepped into a pile of manure this time. He followed the ladies out onto the slate patio without bothering to put on his coat. The cold air would clear his head and hopefully kill whatever frustration he was still feeling in Gwen's presence. Her mouth looked even more tempting now than it had in the kitchen.

The small edge of a garden that bordered the courtyard looked dead. A few clumps of brown, which at one time must have been plants, a dead rhododendron broken down to its roots, and a couple of sticklike things poked their way out of the dirt. He already knew his mother would have to start from scratch. She would prefer it that way. Mary Creighton didn't like to finish someone else's vision.

"Along this back fence, I think we should put in something that will grow big and tall to block the view." Gwen walked over to the back fence and pointed to the parking lot and Dumpster.

"Definitely," Mary agreed. "No one wants to eat their meal staring at beat-up pickup trucks and smelly trash containers. I'm thinking one or two smaller pines, maybe some lilac bushes and rhododendrons for color and fragrance. They'll have to be trimmed annually so they won't get too big, but that shouldn't be a problem."

"Great." Gwen seemed relieved that his mother had agreed with her. "The other idea I had wasn't really about what to plant. I was thinking about possibly stringing miniature white lights up around the fence. Give it a more festive, romantic feel for the diners who'll eat out here on warm nights."

"I like that idea." Mary tapped her pencil against her pursed lips as she stared around the courtyard. "Daniel, can you get electricity out here?"

"What are you talking? One or two outlets to plug in the strings of lights?"

"If Gwen is planning on serving meals out here during the evening hours, she'll need some type of lighting."

Gwen glanced around the harbor. Her gaze

seemed to land on the lamppost, about ten feet away from the picket fence. "I didn't even think about that."

"It's no problem if Daniel can get electricity out here," Mary said.

"Can you?" Gwen finally turned around to face him.

The way she was looking at him, he would have promised her a nuclear power plant in her back parking lot. "Sure. You tell me how much and where."

Gwen gave him a smile that was guaranteed to jump-start every ember of sexual frustration that had been just about killed by the forty-degree temperature. "Thank you."

He pulled his gaze away from Gwen's mouth and looked at his mother. "What are you thinking?"

"Well, I think low lighting would be best. You don't want floodlights pointed at the diners and having them squint through their meal. I'm picturing a big concrete pot with a miniature maple tree between the two patio doors. You can wrap the tree in lights."

"I like." Gwen smiled at his mother, and then at him.

"The view across the front fence is fantastic the way it is. Everyone likes to look at the harbor, and at night it's especially pretty with all the lights on the boats reflecting off the water. You wouldn't want anything to block that view, so I suggest we put in a bunch of different flowers, but none that would grow too high. There are columbines, poppies, irises; even morning glories can use the fence as a trellis. You need to please the lunch crowd as well as the late-night diners."

"Sounds wonderful to me." Gwen nodded at the stretch of fence that bordered a main walkway that led down from the parking lot. "What about this section?"

"This is where it might get expensive, so don't worry, I won't get upset if you'd rather not." Mary tapped her pencil against her clipboard. "There's a place outside of Camden that sells the most wonderful statues for gardens. Some are obviously too big for the garden you have here, but I've seen some that would be perfect. Mermaids, seahorses, even dolphins that are fountains. You can keep with the ocean theme and use spotlights to highlight the statues, while giving your waitresses enough light to work by. I would think two should do it, and maybe a smaller one for the front fence. You wouldn't want to overdo it."

"It sounds wonderful. Do you have the time to come with me to this statue place?" Gwen asked.

"I'm afraid not, but Daniel knows where it is. I'm sure he'll take you, won't you, dear?"

Daniel looked at his mother, wondering what the chances were that he had been adopted. Either way his mother would definitely be receiving socks for her birthday next month. "It will have to be on Saturday or sometime next week. I can't lose a day if I'm to have the inside ready for the carpet layers on Monday."

"Saturday sounds wonderful, doesn't it, Gwen?" His mother handed him her measuring tape but didn't give Gwen time enough to answer her question. "Be a dear and help me measure the length of these gardens."

Gwen muttered something about Saturday being fine, but her mind was obviously elsewhere. She stood in the center of the patio and stared around her with a faraway look in her eyes. He figured she was seeing the courtyard full of diners eating grilled lobster Rosarita and mussels marinara and linguine. Miniature white lights would be twinkling all around them, boats would be bobbing gently in the harbor, and a candle would be glowing at each linen-covered table.

Romantic dining would finally arrive in Misty Harbor.

Hunter refused both Jonah's and Daniel's offer of a ride home. The exercise would do him good, and besides, it was only two miles. He needed the time alone to think things through, and he always thought best when walking. Besides, he needed the fresh clean air to clear the paint fumes from his brain.

He never used to mind the scrubbing, cleaning, and general handyman work he did to pull in a few extra bucks. Money had never been important to him or his family. They got by comfortably, but then again, they didn't do anything that cost a lot of money. The last vacation he could remember taking was when he had been fourteen and his parents had taken him down to Boston to see the sights. Forty years was a hell of a long time to go without a vacation. His senior-class trip had been to 'Nam, but no one could consider that a vacation. Vietnam back in '67 was what hell's idea of Disneyland would be.

He absently rubbed his left arm, where he had been shot, waiting for that helicopter to rescue him and the rest of his platoon. He caught himself rubbing his arm and forced himself to stop. The old wound never really bothered him unless it was about to rain; then it was more accurate than the Weather Channel. It wouldn't be raining in the next twenty-four hours.

Hunter saw Abraham Martin's pickup truck come flying around the bend and jumped off the side of the road and onto the grass. Everyone knew

Abraham's eyesight wasn't as keen as it once was. The lobster buoy swung wildly from the antenna, and aged lobster pots bounced around in the bed of the rusty truck, threatening to either fall into the road or apart; it was hard to tell which. He chuckled at two seagulls dive-bombing for whatever had been in the back of Abraham's truck. By the odor trailing in the wake of the rusty Ford, whatever it had been, it was dead now.

He stepped back out onto the side of the road and thought about getting his driver's license again. He hadn't driven on American soil since he shipped out to 'Nam. Everything in his life had changed that summer. His innocence had been shredded, his faith tested and failed. Humanity had failed, yet he had been too much of a coward to end his own life. Every time he had seen the love in his mother's eyes or the quiet understanding in this father's, he knew he couldn't do that to them. He had stayed alive for his parents, yet 'Nam still controlled his life. 'Nam had beaten him, and after thirty-one years, it was still beating him every day.

For the first time in his life, Hunter was beginning to feel strong enough to fight back. He liked waking up in the morning, knowing he had to go to work. To accomplish something, even if it was only scrubbing ten years of grime off the kitchen floor or painting the women's bathroom a pale peach. It still felt good to work. It felt better to cook.

Gwen had trusted him to cook up the winter flounder with the lemon cream sauce. He had a feeling it had been some kind of test, and that he had passed it. His mother would have rolled over in her grave if he couldn't prepare a simple sole with lemon cream dish. He had been cooking that meal for at least twenty years. It was one of his father's favorites. His father had sat across from him during lunch and given him an occasional wink and, once, a thumbs-up sign. By everyone's compliments, especially Gwen's, he figured they liked it.

But did they like it enough, or were they just being nice to him? *Pity the poor vet.* Every resident of the town usually went out of his or her way to be nice to him. In the beginning, when he first noticed it, he had thought it was nice, even respectful. For the past couple of years he'd started resenting their niceness. He hadn't done anything to deserve it, besides staying alive long enough in some rat-infested POW camp to be rescued. The men who had risked their own lives to save him, and a handful of other men, were the true heroes.

He didn't trust the town to tell him the truth. Not because they were liars, but because they were too nice to give him the truth if they thought it would hurt his feelings. He did trust Gwen, though. For some reason, probably because she didn't know all of his back history, Gwen treated him as an equal. She expected a good day's work for a good day's pay. She didn't watch every word that came out of her mouth, just in case she should say something to upset the poor POW. Gwen treated him like an ordinary person, like a friend. She treated everyone like a friend. Maybe that was why he liked working for her so much.

When he came to the road that led to his home, he turned in the opposite direction and headed for the small private scenic overlook. He had spent many an hour quietly sitting on an old log, contemplating the power and beauty of the magnificent ocean. He might never find the courage to frolic in its waves, like he had done as a young boy. But the pounding of each wave against the rocky shore matched the beating of his heart. He had been born with the ocean in his blood. 'Nam had put the terror in his mind.

He followed the footpath through the pines and climbed the small incline to one of his favorite spots. The scent of pine and salt air washed away the remnants of paint fumes clouding his mind. He lowered himself to a log and studied the ocean and the night sky. With the approaching night, the sea was dark and turbulent. The white foam of the curling waves looked gray and angry. Soon the sea and the sky would meet, and it would be hard to tell one from the other. Here, perched high about the pounding surf surrounded by towering pines, a person could think clearly.

It was time to resume his life. Way past time, if he were going to be honest with himself.

He knew it had been coming for years; he just hadn't known how to go about it. A year ago he had gotten up the nerve to approach George Barley about working behind the fish counter in his store. Waiting on people all day long hadn't really appealed to him, but no one knew fish better than he. He thought it might have been a good match. George would have hired him on the spot, but for all the wrong reasons. He didn't want a job out of pity. He wanted a job because he was good at it, because he deserved to have that job.

Gwen had come right out and offered him the assistant chef's job. She hadn't done it out of pity. She had made the offer because she knew he could cook. Pity employment would have been a dishwasher or busboy position. Gwen Fletcher wouldn't allow someone who didn't know what he was doing to stand in front of one of her stoves. Not as long as her name was listed as proprietor of the restaurant.

Gwen had paid him the highest compliment imaginable. Now the question was, was he going to accept it? Taking that job would mean a complete change in his and his father's lifestyles. His father wasn't getting any younger, and it was about time Hunter started taking care of the old man instead of the other way around.

A smile softened the hard lines etched into his face as the sea and sky merged as one and darkness fell on this tiny slice of the world. He was going to accept Gwen's offer and pray that he wouldn't let her, or his father, down.

"No, Sydney, Jocelyn wasn't lying, there really are Vikings up here." Gwen chuckled at her older sister's groan. Sydney had thought to catch the baby of the family, Jocelyn in a fib. "To be honest, they aren't really Vikings, they're Norwegians."

"I knew it!" cried Sydney. "She owes me five bucks."

"Vikings were Scandinavians, Syd, and if you saw these two you would swear they had just stepped off some wooden boat with massive sails and a curved dragon's head as its figurehead."

"Really?"

"Really. I'm talking long blond hair, sky-blue eyes, and more muscles than the membership of the World Wrestling Federation combined. Erik's going to be supplying my restaurant with a good portion of its fish, and his identical twin brother, Gunnar, will be supplying the lobsters. They are both fishermen."

"Something must be wrong with them if they're still single and walking around without a woman clinging to each ankle being dragged everywhere they go."

"Nothing's wrong with them that I can see." Gwen frowned at the bowl of salad sitting on the counter. Dinner was consisting of rabbit food because her pants were starting to get too darn tight. Either she was gaining weight or Maine water had a shrinking agent in it. "There just aren't a lot of females around. Young females, that is. I see a lot of older women around town, and even some kids who are girls. But for some reason the eighteen-to-thirty-five-year-old group is pretty sparse. There are some younger married women, or there wouldn't be the kids, but it seems out of proportion to me."

"That's strange."

"I asked Millicent about it, and she said most of the girls who graduate from high school either go off to college, meet their sweethearts there, and get married and go live somewhere else, or they move to the big cities for higher-paying jobs." Gwen opened the refrigerator and took out a bottle of Ranch dressing. She was too tired to make up her own tonight.

"Sounds reasonable. So what, the men don't go off to college or big towns?"

"Some do, but a lot of them stay in Misty Harbor and follow their fathers and grandfathers into the fishing business. I guess the sea's in their blood or some such thing, but it makes for a lonely existence if there are no women. Any single female is fair game in this town."

"That would explain the two marriage proposals Jocelyn told me about." Sydney's laugh sounded a bit strained.

Gwen knew marriage proposals were a touchy subject for her older sister. Sydney had been living with Richard Wainbright, M.D., since med school four years ago. So far Needle Ass Richard hadn't popped the million-dollar question. At twenty-nine, and a Pediatrician who loved babies, Sydney was feeling the old biological clock starting to tick away. Sydney wanted a ring on her finger and a baby in the nursery. "Both of the proposals came from men over the age of sixty, Syd. Don't worry; the Norwegian gods haven't popped the question yet, or I might have to say yes just to get to Valhalla with a very satisfied smile on my face."

"Strange, you would marry one of them, but not date him." Syd clucked her tongue. "Joc told me you turned them both down when they asked you out."

"They weren't my type." Joc had a big mouth.

"I can't wait to meet this carpenter Joc told me about."

"Why do you want to meet Daniel?" Gwen was sending Jocelyn a box filled with dead bait first thing in the morning. "I'm not dating him either." Technically that was true. The only reason she wasn't dating him was because the stubborn man hadn't asked her out. Daniel could melt every bone in her body with one heated look. He promised her slow, long kisses that would be remembered for the rest of her life. Yet he couldn't form such simple words as "Hey, let's go out on Friday night." Every other man in town had come up with some variation of those words, yet Daniel remained mute.

"Oh, I thought you'd be dating him by now." Syd sounded disappointed. It was pretty bad when your own sister was dissatisfied by your love life.

"Afraid not. I don't have time for dates and romantic evenings cuddled up in front of the burning fire. I'm spending all my time trying to get a business up and running."

"How is the restaurant coming along?"

"Great. I hired my first employee this afternoon. She's a housewife looking to wait tables during the lunch shift so she'll be back home when the kids get home from school. She had some experience before she got married, so I think she'll work out."

"My sister the boss."

"Hey, you have employees. There are all those nurses, receptionists, billing clerks."

"They are not mine, they're the firm's." Syd was in a practice with four other pediatricians. She was the youngest doctor, and the only female, and not even a partner in the firm yet. But Sydney knew what she was doing. Two of the older doctors were approaching retirement age and looking for doctors to buy out their share of the business. "The only employee I have is the woman who comes in three times a week to clean the apartment and fix some meals."

"Sounds like a tough life to me." Gwen made a face at the pile of dishes sitting in her sink. "We lesser mortals have to scrub our own toilets, you know."

"I don't have time to keep the place as clean as Richard likes it." Syd sounded defensive—something she had been doing more and more lately. Gwen had a feeling that all was not well in la-la Richard land, but Sydney wasn't saying and Gwen didn't feel she had the right to demand answers. When Sydney wanted to talk, she would.

"Speaking of Needle Ass, how is he?"

"I wish you wouldn't call him that." Syd sounded resigned that her wish was never going to be granted.

"Sorry." Gwen wasn't sorry in the least, and Sydney knew it. Richard Wainbright, M.D., had been a thorn in her side since the day she had met him six years ago. She might have been only twenty years old at the time, but she knew an asshole when she met one. Richard had taken one look at the Fletcher estate, their parents' success in their chosen fields and social circle, and a family tree that could be traced back to the roots of Baltimore, and had hitched his sorry-ass star to Sydney's coattails. "How is Richard, the magnificent? Better?"

"Hardly, but since I miss you I'll be civil. He's been extremely busy lately. We barely get a night to ourselves anymore. He's been invited to sit on the surgical board at the hospital."

Gwen was dying to make a comment about needle asses and wooden boards, but since Sydney admitted to missing her, she couldn't bring herself to say it. For whatever reason, still unexplained by the laws of physics, Sydney loved Richard. Gwen could only pray that when Cupid shot her with that famous old arrow, he would be kinder and not match her up with someone like Richard. Because if he did, one of them would be dead within a week. Her money would be on Richard being found with a kabob skewer jammed in a very embarrassing place.

"That's nice." Their grandfather had probably arranged for that little perk. Richard was always expecting perks like that from Sydney's family, yet he didn't have the gumption to marry her and start a family of his own. "Do you think you two will have time to come visit me this summer? Jocelyn has already claimed the use of my guest room for two weeks in July. If you want to come up with her, she can bunk in with me, and you and Richard can have the guest room."

"I did mention something about visiting you this summer to Richard, but he wants to go to Hilton Head and get in some golf and tennis."

"No problem." There was a big problem, but Sydney didn't sound like she was in the mood to hear her sister's opinion on what it was. She would start off by mentioning that Sydney didn't play golf or tennis. Some vacation that was going to be for her sister. "Maybe you can manage a few days by yourself to visit. If you fly into Bangor, I could pick you up."

"I just might do that. I always wanted to see the coast of Maine."

"Hey, I even got discount tickets for the whale watching boat tour."

"Vikings and a boat tour; how could I pass it up?"

Chapter Thirteen

Gwen set the two grocery bags down on the counter and glanced around the freshly painted kitchen with a sense of pride. Her kitchen looked fantastic. Not quite ready for a full house of diners, but fantastic nevertheless. Hunter had been absolutely correct in suggesting the soft green paint instead of yellow. The crisp white trim and shelves popped right out at you, and the floor actually sparkled under the high-voltage lights. Hunter had done an amazing job at polishing all of the stainless steel and the rest of the appliances.

Catch of the Day would be ready for its grand opening.

She gave the room one last nod of approval before hurrying to her car to retrieve the other two bags of food she had just bought. Barley's Food Store was going to start missing her usual morning business in two weeks. This morning she was planning on making the best French toast on the entire eastern seaboard.

French toast had been Daniel's request to serve at Sunday brunch.

Daniel had been avoiding her; there was no other explanation for his behavior lately. Ever since that near kiss in the kitchen the other day, he had been going out of his way never to be alone in the same room with her. The quick peck she had brushed against his unsuspecting mouth couldn't be counted as a kiss. She wouldn't even consider it a buzz. She didn't know why he had been avoiding her. He had seemed to want the kiss just as much as she had. So why the sudden change of heart? It didn't make any sense, to her way of thinking.

And then there had been Daniel's totally uncharacteristic behavior when he had yelled at Ted Busby and practically thrown the man out of her restaurant. What in the world had he been thinking? She knew what the town had thought. By dinner that evening rumors had spread from one end of town to the other: Daniel and the new restaurant owner were an item.

She had just parked her S.U.V in front of the cottage that night when a harried-looking Carol Ann and her screaming Devin came calling. Carol Ann was disappointed that Gwen hadn't chosen her brother-in-law, Paul, but had assured her that Daniel was a réally nice guy. Gwen had handed Carol Ann the big canvas tote filled with all her lists and other paperwork and the key to the cottage front door. Carol Ann handed her the crying infant. A moment later, Devin had quieted. Ten minutes after that, Gwen had passed Carol Ann her sleeping son and had learned that in the eyes of Misty Harbor, Daniel was a candidate for sainthood.

If she had thought Carol Ann's assumption that

she and Daniel were now a couple had been strange, it was nothing compared to the drastic change in the male population of town. She hadn't received flowers or brightly wrapped boxes of candy in days. Erik still brought her some of his catch, but he was polite, distant, and never stayed for lunch. Even the postman had stopped hitting on her.

It was great. It was also disquieting, because the man she was supposed to be so close to hadn't spoken more than ten words to her since his mother's visit to the outdoor patio. Gwen liked being linked to Daniel, and not just because she thought he was gorgeous, sexy, and so darn yummy she could eat him with a spoon. Having a boyfriend, even if it wasn't true, had gotten the other guys to back off and give her some room. Some breathing space. She had accomplished more work in the past few days, with Daniel as her imaginary boyfriend, than she had in the previous two weeks combined.

Now if only the guilt would go away. In a way, Gwen was using Daniel. She hadn't come right out and lied to anyone and said they actually were dating. But she hadn't denied it, either. Guilt by omission deserved French toast, cut extra thick and with powdered sugar sprinkled on top. Just the way Daniel had suggested it.

Gwen started to unpack the bags when she heard the front door open and the men come in. She was running behind because Priscilla had cornered her in the frozen food aisle and preached for ten minutes about Daniel's wonderful character, adding that Gregory was quite brokenhearted but was expected to make a full recovery.

"Morning, love," Clarence said as he walked into the kitchen and hung up his coat.

"Lord, Gwen, you get more beautiful with each

new sunrise. How is that possible?'' Jonah gave her a flirtatious wink and hung his coat.

Gwen shared an amused look with Hunter, who had followed the men in and immediately gone to the coffeemaker to start a pot. "If you talked to Millicent like that, you just might convince her to go to those islands with you yet."

"He's too old for all that sun and late-night partying," Clarence said. "Besides, he's got knobby knees and would look like hell in a swimsuit."

Jonah looked down at the legs of his pants and frowned. "My knees aren't knobby."

"Hell, man, last time I saw them, they looked like two doorknobs glued onto matchsticks."

"Dad, leave Jonah's knees alone. You don't have any room to talk. I've seen your chicken legs sticking out from your boxers." Hunter carefully measured the coffee grounds and started the machine.

"Your mother loved my legs!" Clarence seemed insulted, but there was a gleam of amusement in his eyes.

"Mom loved your hooked nose and your big ears too. Didn't say much for her eyesight."

Jonah howled with delight as he wrapped his arm around Clarence's shoulders. "Come on, old friend. We'll go upstairs to make sure everything is ready for painting after breakfast. We'll let these two do what they do best, cook." With that the two older men waltzed out of the kitchen.

Gwen wasn't positive, but she thought she heard Clarence tell Jonah his nose wasn't hooked, it was a proud nose. Edith had called it an eagle's nose.

"What can I help you with?" Hunter asked.

"We're going to do French toast this morning." She glanced at the swinging doors. She could hear Daniel moving a ladder around out in the dining room, but he hadn't stopped in to say hello. Great, another day of being avoided. She wondered if he had also heard the latest rumors, and if that was the reason he had been sidestepping her every chance he got. Daniel probably figured that if he didn't talk, or even look at her, the rumors would die. Maybe she should tell Daniel his strategy wasn't working.

Without asking, Hunter pulled out two large frying pans and started to get the stove ready. "Has anyone applied for the assistant chef's job yet?"

Gwen froze with a carton of eggs in one hand and a loaf of bread in the other. "Please tell me you're interested." Hunter was perfect for the job.

"I'm interested."

"Really?" She lowered the carton to the counter and studied the man before her. Hunter was six feet tall and on the lean side. Time and pain had etched many lines deep in his face, and harsh winters and the burning sun of summer had finished the job. His receding hairline was mostly gray and his brown eyes held a touch of sadness, even when he was laughing and teasing his father. Hunter McCord had haunting eyes. This morning he looked nervous. She gave him a reassuring smile.

"Really." Hunter gave her a brief smile in return. "I'll fill out an application after breakfast, if that's okay with you."

"You don't have to apply for the job, Hunter, it's yours." She pulled up a stool and sat. "You know it's a full-time position, and you'll be working late every night. It's going to be over forty hours a week, but I'll try to keep you to just five days. Summers will be the busiest, and the weekends the worst." She needed to know that Hunter understood the hours and the responsibilities. "You'll also be in charge of the kitchen staff, and you'll have to handle everything when I'm not working."

"I know."

"You're going to have to give up some of your wild nights."

Hunter gave her a small smile. "I think I'll manage to survive."

"I think you will too." She stood up and shook his hand. She was so happy and excited, she didn't know what to do first. "Welcome aboard, Mr. McCord."

Maggie cradled the cup of hot coffee between her hands and stared out into the distance. From her parents' backyard a person had a pretty decent view of the harbor below. April in Maine wasn't the best, weatherwise, but it beat January. The days were getting warmer and the ground was actually defrosting and showing some signs of life. It was a real shame her hands and legs were going to take until June to feel warm again. Wearing panty hose and dresses in this type of weather was ridiculous but necessary. Prospective employers liked to see a lady look like a lady.

This morning she had frozen her butt off trying to impress a prospective employer, all for nothing. Daniel's high-school buddy had taken one look at her and the application she had neatly filled out and said she was overqualified for the job. While it was true—she *was* overqualified—and it should have been a compliment, it hadn't been. Daniel's buddy hadn't hired her because of what she had done to Daniel.

She felt tears pool in her eyes and took another sip of coffee. How long did one stupid mistake follow a person through life? Okay, it was a whopper, but she couldn't really classify it as a mistake. She had gotten Katie out of that moment of impropriety. *No regrets!* Maggie forced herself to blink back the tears and concentrate on her daughter.

Katie needed her, now more than ever. She couldn't keep failing her daughter.

The patio door opened, and her mom came outside carrying a mug of cocoa for Katie and a cup of coffee for herself. Katie was right on her grandmother's heels, carefully balancing a plate of cookies.

"I helped Grandmom make the cookies, Mommy." Katie placed the plate on the picnic table and handed her a large misshaped cookie. "They're made out of peanut butter."

"So I see." Maggie gave her mother a warm smile of thanks for allowing her daughter to mutilate the cookies. Katie had taken the tines of a fork and flattened each beyond recognition. She took a big bite and grinned while she chewed. "Delicious." They might look questionable, but they tasted the same as her mother always made them.

Connie Franklin took the seat next to her daughter, tilted her face upward, and closed her eyes. "The sun feels good."

Maggie watched her daughter go running across the yard after a bird, a cookie clutched in each hand. Lunch was only a half an hour away. "You're spoiling her, Mom." There wasn't any heat to her words. Katie was such an easy child to spoil. Her parents had missed out on a lot of Katie's young life. That, in a way, had been Maggie's fault too. She should have gone against Jeremy's wishes and visited her parents more often. What would it have mattered in the long run? Jeremy hadn't cared if she was a good, obedient wife. It wouldn't had made her husband love her after all.

Then again, had she really been in love with her own husband?

"She needs the extra attention right now." Connie watched her granddaughter give up on the bird and stand there on the edge of the property to watch the harbor below. "Katie sure does love the boats."

"Gary promised her a ride on his lobster boat as soon as the weather turns nicer." Her brother was stopping by more frequently now that Katie was living in the house. Katie thought the sun rose and set on her Uncle Gary. By the amount of attention he was giving his niece, the feeling had to be mutual. Who would have thought cynical and disillusioned Gary would have the heart of a marshmallow when it came to kids?

Last night Gary had stopped by after dinner just to give Katie her own personal kid-size life preserver. It had taken Maggie twenty minutes to talk Katie out of wearing the bright orange jacket to bed over her pajamas. They had compromised: Fred the tiger had worn the jacket instead.

Katie had inherited Gary's old bedroom that faced the back of the house and had a commanding view of the harbor. Maggie remembered that her eyes had filled with tears when she had first seen the room. Her parents, with Gary's help, had painted it a soft yellow for Katie's arrival. Gary had bought and put together a shelving unit so Katie would have a special place for all her stuffed animals and books. Her mother had bought an overstuffed light green chair and a colorful braided rug at the church rummage sale. Kate's room was now her castle, and she loved it.

"Katie likes to sit in her chair and look out the bedroom window at all the boats. She tries to spot Gary's blue-and-white one. She can spend hours just counting all the boats coming and going." Maggie was afraid her daughter had been born with the sea in her blood, just like her grandpop and uncle.

"She likes to count everything, doesn't she?" Connie chuckled. "Yesterday when I took her food shopping with me, she counted the curlers in Sadie's hair."

Maggie had to laugh along with her mother. "Sadie's still wearing curlers?" In twenty-six years, she could only remember seeing Sadie's hair without curlers twice. Once had been at her own daughter's wedding, the other during a Christmas Eve church service.

"Everywhere she goes. Her daughter sent her some fancy hair net things that go over the curlers and all. They're from California. One's a leopard print, the other zebra. Sadie wears them in the summer months with bright red sunglasses and lipstick. No one in town has the heart to tell her she looks like a fool. The tourists think she's eccentric, selling her blueberries and vegetables at her roadside stand and wearing those men's overalls with plastic flip-flops."

"Sadie's definitely unique, Mom. You can't argue that one." Maggie's mouth watered at the memory of biting into her mother's warm blueberry cobbler made from Sadie's berries. "She grows the best blueberries around." It would be months before she would be able to taste that cobbler again.

"True. The Annual Maine Wild Blueberry Festival wouldn't be the same without her. Last year three of her grandkids dressed up like blueberry muffins, pulled wagons filled with blueberries, and sold them by the quart to the tourists. Sadie made enough money in that one day to put a down payment on a big old pink convertible." Connie shook her head and chuckled. "That woman is a menace behind the wheel, so watch out for her. Take my word for it, one of these days they'll be pulling her and her pink convertible out of the harbor."

"I hope you're wrong on that one, but knowing Sadie, she'll come out spitting and sputtering with a lobster clutched in each hand and cussing that her hair was ruined."

"True." Connie looked at her daughter. "I take it the interview didn't go well."

"What interview? Pete took one look at me and told me I was overqualified for the job."

"Pete's been looking for someone to fill that part-time position since Christmas."

"Yeah, well, it isn't going to be me." Maggie tried desperately to push down the anger she was feeling at the unfairness of it all. "I told him I really needed the job." She couldn't tell her mother that she had practically begged Pete for the job. It was humiliating enough that Pete had witnessed her desperation.

"What did he say to that?"

"Said by the time he trained me, I'd leave him for a better job."

"Hmmmm." Connie kept her gaze on Katie, who was now using her fingers to count the boats. "I thought he was smarter than that."

"Yeah, well . . ." Maggie knew why Pete hadn't hired her. So did her mother, but she was too nice to say it out loud. By now she had hoped to be employed and bringing in some money to help with their support. "I don't know how much I can give you this week, Mom."

"Margaret Franklin Pierce, there will no more talk like that." Connie turned her attention away from her granddaughter to her daughter. "We told you not to fret about money. It will be a sad day in Misty Harbor when money becomes more important than love. Your father and I love you and Katie dearly. We love having you both here."

"I'm twenty-six, Mom. I should be supporting myself and my daughter." Why couldn't her parents see that? It was so clear to her, yet they stubbornly refused to discuss money.

" 'Pride goeth before destruction, and a haughty spirit before a fall.' Proverbs, Sixteen. Your father and I will take care of you and Katie until you get your feet back under you. We don't care if you contribute one blasted dime to the kitty. We know you're trying, Maggie, and we have complete faith that you'll get those feet back under you, faster than we would like."

Maggie knew she was in trouble the moment her mother started quoting from the Bible. She had lost the battle before it had even begun. Her mother had God and the Good Book on her side. With her mother beside them, she and Katie just might make it through the coming year.

Maggie looked at her mother and saw nothing but love. Unconditional love. The same love she felt for her daughter. If Katie ever needed her, she would be there for her, no matter how old she had grown. How could she expect her own mother to do differently? Connie Franklin was a proud woman and would never accept a humble thank-you from her daughter. But she would accept laughter. " 'There's no place like home. There's no place like home.' Dorothy, *The Wizard of Oz.* "

Her mother's laughter filled the backyard and brought Katie running to see what was so funny.

Daniel used the men's bathroom to wash up for lunch. His hands were splattered with "Summer's Morning Blue" paint. As usual, Gwen's taste had been right on the mark. The dining room was looking fantastic. By the time he packed it all up tonight, the dining room, stairs, and upstairs office would be ready for the carpet layers first thing Monday morning. Gwen's restaurant would definitely be ready for the grand opening. If he pushed it, he might be able to have the outside in shape too. Maybe not all the plants, because of the weather, but the row of bushes was possible, even probable.

No one would be dining outside this early, but the lighting and statues would be up and lit. It would make for a nicer view out the patio doors. It would also make Gwen extremely happy, and for some perverse reason he had yet to fathom, Gwen's happiness had become very important to him.

Why else would he be willing to subject himself to spending another entire Saturday in her company? It wasn't just because his own mother had volunteered his services to take Gwen statue shopping. He wanted to spend his day with her, without his grandfather, Clarence, and Hunter around. He might actually get that long-awaited kiss.

For the past several nights, he had gone to bed thinking about that kiss and where it might lead. Each and every morning he had awakened flushed, frustrated, and in dire need of a cold shower.

He didn't have to worry about other suitors any longer, now that the rumor that he and Gwen were dating had spread across town. The men of Misty Harbor had an unspoken rule: single females were fair game, but once one was spoken for, she was off limits. Amazingly, Gwen was not officially off limits, but the town didn't seem to know that.

Ted Busby hadn't wasted any time in spreading the news that Daniel had been acting like some love-sick fool. Ted also had inaccurately jumped to the conclusion that Gwen and Daniel were a couple. Interestingly enough, Gwen wasn't denying the rumors.

He dried his hands and wondered what the chances were that Gwen would accept an honest-to-goodness date with him, when she had turned down every other guy in town. No fighting over dining room sets. No garden statue shopping. No

stumbling over six other men in her kitchen. Just
the two of them, and maybe a movie up in Brewer.
Possibly a romantic dinner, but that seemed like
an impossibility. How would he ever find a restaurant that would impress Gwen? Better to stick to
movies and maybe a moonlit walk around the cove.
That scenario sounded better than what Bob Newman had offered Gwen—a midnight cruise around
the harbor in his tuna boat.

Daniel left the men's room and headed for the
kitchen and the delicious aroma of meat loaf. Lord,
he was going to miss this job. Bologna sandwiches
and a pack of Ring-Dings were never going to measure up to Gwen's cooking.

"Daniel, good you're here," Jonah said as he
entered the room. "We need you to settle an argu-
ment for us."

"About what?" His gaze went immediately to
Gwen. She was stirring a saucepan of what looked
like gravy. Her cheeks were all pink and glowing
from the heat. Her hair was pulled back and up
with some monster-size clip, but a lock or two had
escaped the beast and were clinging to her flushed
face. She looked sexy enough to kiss. Hell, she
looked sexy enough to toss in his bed and not be
let up for a month or two. Beauty, brains, and a
cooking ability to make Julia Child weep in defeat.

It was a powerful combination, all in one pint-
size package.

"I say Gwen should contact Jimmy Ray's Market
over in Sullivan for her blueberries. Clarence and
Hunter say Sadie has the best. Where do you think
she should go first, Jimmy Ray's or Sadie?" Jonah
asked.

"I have to agree with Clarence and Hunter on
that one. Sadie grows the best blueberries. I don't
know what she uses out there for fertilizer, and
she won't tell, but whatever it is, it works." Daniel

handed Jonah two glasses and reached for three more. Helping in the kitchen had become a routine over the past several weeks. Everyone pitched in, everyone ate.

Clarence grabbed a pitcher of iced tea from the refrigerator and some napkins. Someone had already set the plates and silverware out on the table.

Hunter finished whipping the potatoes and set the bowl on the table, along with the salt and pepper shakers. "She uses dead fish carcasses."

Gwen stopped pouring the gravy into a server and looked at Hunter in surprise. "Pardon?"

"I said Sadie uses dead fish as her fertilizer," Hunter said as he took a bowl of steaming green beans out of the microwave.

"How would you know?" Jonah asked as he took his seat.

Gwen put the gravy boat on the table and went to the oven for the main dish. "Yeah, how would you know that?"

"All you have to do is walk within a mile or so of her place in October. The smell will knock you over." Hunter took his seat. "She rototills under most of what's left come spring."

Gwen sat the platter of meat loaf in the center of the table. "I tried a little something different this time with the meat loaf. See if you guys like it better this way, or the way I made it the other week."

Jonah and Clarence dug into the meal as if Gwen would be giving a final exam before dessert. Hunter chuckled.

Daniel filled his plate while secretly studying Hunter. The man had changed, there was no doubt about it. He had a sinking feeling that he had looked like a large mouth bass this morning during breakfast when Gwen broke the news that Hunter was staying on full time as her assistant chef. Who would have thought that after all these years, Hunter would be rejoining the human race?

He originally thought that Gwen had pulled off a blooming miracle. But the more he thought about it and studied Hunter, the more he realized that maybe it had just been time.

Clarence and Jonah had both obviously known of Hunter's decision before Gwen had made the announcement and proposed a toast with orange juice. Both men had seemed pleased as punch but not surprised. He had been the only one caught with his mouth hanging open, trawling for flies.

He looked at Jonah and Clarence. "You guys about done upstairs?"

"Yes." Jonah passed Clarence the green beans. "All we have to do is a little cleaning up after lunch, and everything will be ready for the carpet on Monday."

"Good. I have another job for you two this afternoon."

"What's that?"

"I have two tarps in the back of the truck. We need to move all the dining room tables outside onto the patio and then cover them for the weekend. The chairs we can stack in the bathrooms and kitchen. Everything has to be out of here for them to lay the carpet."

"What about that desk upstairs?" Clarence asked. "The chair can be stored in the bathroom up there, but that desk isn't going to fit."

Daniel groaned silently. He didn't want to carry that old battleship of a desk down a flight of stairs, only to carry it right back up Monday afternoon. The desk looked like the previous owner had purchased it at some army surplus store. It was gray metal and weighed a couple hundred pounds. A nuclear blast could hit in Misty Harbor and that desk would be the last thing standing. He could feel a hernia coming on. There was no way he was allowing Jonah or Clarence to touch the beast.

"Would it fit in the laundry closet up there?" Gwen asked. "There's no washer, and the broken dryer has to be taken out of there anyway."

Daniel pictured the long closet with its huge bifold doors. "It might." It looked like he would be able to father children after all. "I'll measure it right after lunch. Bringing down the dryer will be easier than the desk."

Gwen seemed to be pushing her food around her plate instead of eating it. He frowned at her lunch. "Something wrong with your meat loaf?"

The three other men stopped eating and stared at her, and then her plate. Gwen blushed a becoming scarlet. "No, there's nothing wrong with my meat loaf. I was just thinking about tomorrow." Gwen stabbed a piece of meat and placed it in her mouth.

"What's tomorrow?" Clarence asked as he went back to eating his lunch, now that he knew there wasn't anything wrong with it.

Daniel had a feeling he could tell Clarence there was rat poison in the meat loaf and the man still would have eaten it. "We don't have to go statue shopping if you have other plans." Maybe Gwen had a hot-and-heavy date planned. Someone in town must have finally broken through her no-date barrier.

"Oh, no. It's nothing like that."

He felt the lump of dread dislodge itself from his throat. Gwen wasn't going out with anyone. So why was she worrying about tomorrow? Could Gwen be suffering a cash flow problem? It took more than pocket change to open a restaurant. From what he had been seeing over the past couple of weeks, Gwen had been laying out some serious cash.

He had heard her arguing about delivery dates with a bunch of different suppliers. He also knew she had ordered new dishes and stemware for the dinner crowd. Lunch would be served using the plain, sturdy white dishes that had come with the restaurant. The dinner set was lighter, fancier, and he was sure it came with a hefty price tag. Yesterday afternoon he had come into the kitchen for something to drink, and she and Hunter had been gushing over cooking catalogs and drooling over stockpots.

Gwen was pouring more than just her heart and soul into the restaurant. She was dumping in an impressive amount of cash. Maybe she had taken a look at the bottom line, and the statues would have to wait until she recouped some of her investment.

"It might be better to wait a couple of months before buying any statues." He wanted to offer her an easy out; after all, the garden displays had been his mother's idea, not hers. "They can be awfully expensive, and I'm sure there are other things you need more than hunks of concrete or wood."

"I love the idea of having the statues out there, Daniel." Gwen toyed with her fork. "It's not the money."

"So what has you so worried?" Jonah asked as he looked at her full plate.

Gwen blushed to the roots of her hair. "It's kind of embarrassing."

All the men stopped eating and waited for her to continue.

Gwen took a deep breath and blurted out what had been on her mind. "If Daniel and I take off for the day, it will just feed the rumors some more."

"Ah, the rumors that Daniel and you are an item." Jonah gave her a knowing wink.

"Item, hell." Clarence chuckled. "I heard they were hot for each other."

Daniel glanced at Gwen. She looked ready to crawl under the table. He couldn't blame her. "Knock it off. Can't you see you're embarrassing Gwen?" He shook his head at his grandfather and Clarence. "Gwen, us not going shopping isn't going to stop the rumors. People will talk no matter what."

"I know." Gwen took a sip of iced tea, but averted her gaze.

"Ever since you and Daniel have become an item, I noticed a decline in the flower supply throughout the kitchen," Jonah offered. "My allergies are much better now that there are only three vases of flowers in here."

"I'm not tripping over every single man in town trying to get the painting done," Hunter said.

"I miss the candy." Clarence sighed. "Especially the cream-center ones. The nut ones mess up my dentures too much."

Gwen smiled slowly. "Then you should be thanking Daniel for not denying the rumor."

"You haven't denied it either." He had to point out the obvious.

"True," agreed Gwen, "but I didn't deny it so I could get some peace and quiet."

"I didn't deny it so I could get some work done around here. One would have thought it was mating season on the savanna, the way those tomcats came prowling around every five minutes."

Hunter, Jonah, and Clarence were attentively following the conversation.

"Then it benefits us both to be considered a couple?" Gwen questioned in a hard tone.

"Exactly."

"Good," Gwen snapped. She stabbed at a green bean, popped it into her mouth, and chewed.

"Good," he snapped right back. He glared at the three older men and was amazed they hadn't suffered whiplash, the way their heads had been going back and forth.

He concentrated on his meal, with no idea what had just transpired. Gwen seemed upset about something, but for the life of him, he didn't know what. *Women! Who in the hell could possibly understand them?* Did she or did she not want her name associated with his? Who needed all these problems anyway? He hadn't even gotten to kiss her yet, and already they were fighting.

Relationships—even imaginary ones it seemed— were a minefield just ready to explode.

The meal continued in silence, but Daniel could feel everyone's gaze on him. For once, he wasn't enjoying Gwen's cooking. He wanted to apologize to her, but he didn't know what to apologize for. Not denying the rumor? Hell, she hadn't denied it either. Maybe the tomcat remark was a little harsh. Gwen never encouraged any of the guys who came calling. He frowned at his plate.

"Well, since we're a couple"—Gwen's voice was hesitant and low—"shouldn't we be seen together outside of the restaurant?"

One of the vertebra in his neck actually gave a cracking sound as his head shot up at her words. He wanted to shout "Hell yes," but he was afraid that if he opened his mouth, somehow his size-twelve boot was going to end up in it.

"Maybe you should come to dinner at my place Saturday night?" Gwen suggested softly. By the warm gentle glow in her eyes, he knew she was serious. Gwen was asking him out on a date.

Daniel was positive that the kitchen had gone so quiet he could hear the butter melting on top of his green beans. Gwen was inviting him to dinner! It took him a full minute to get his rapidly pounding heart under control. "I think you've cooked me enough meals, Gwen." He saw the first gleam of rejection in her big brown eyes and quickly added, "It's about time I returned the favor. How about if you come out to my place and I throw some steaks on the grill?"

Chapter Fourteen

Gwen parked her S.U.V. in front of Daniel's garage and stared at his house. Daniel's name was on the mailbox, so she knew she must be at the right house, but she was still having a hard time believing it. If this was the home of a simple carpenter, she was in the wrong line of work. She picked up her purse and the chilled bottle of wine and slowly climbed out of her car. She wasn't sure what impressed her the most—the view or the house.

Daniel's house was a newly constructed log home wrapped in porches, decks, and balconies. Huge glass windows dominated the eastern portion of the house, giving the occupant the same awe-inspiring view she was now seeing. Daniel's property ended with the pounding waves of the Atlantic Ocean. The house wasn't situated on a sandy beachfront property, like those she was used to in Maryland. Daniel's place was perched high on a bluff above the rocky shoreline. A towering pine forest was behind the house, but nothing obstructed the view of the battering surf.

Even in the approaching darkness, it was magnificent. She would love to see the view and the house in the dazzling light of day. The ocean breeze tossed her hair around her face and blew gusty cold air beneath the collar of her coat. She stood there in the twilight, breathing in the scent of pine and sea while listening to the endless sound of the waves crashing against the rocks below. How in the world did Daniel leave this place every morning to go to work?

"You're right on time." His voice came from behind her. She had been so caught up in the view, she hadn't even heard his approach.

Gwen gave a slight nod, to acknowledge his presence, but she felt herself being drawn forward. To the sea. She walked the path that led to the edge of the cliff. A split-rail fence made out of the same logs as the house bordered the dangerous dropoff. From what she could see, she would guess it was a good thirty-foot drop to the foam-covered rocks below. "Why didn't you tell me?"

"Tell you what?" Daniel stood beside her and followed her gaze to the wet, dark rocks below.

"That you live on the edge of the world." She slowly turned to face him. Daniel hadn't bothered to put on a coat to meet her. He was dressed in a light gray sweater and dark gray Dockers. The wind tugged charmingly at his hair. He looked solid and dependable against the elements. Daniel Creighton looked like he belonged right where he stood.

Daniel flashed her a smile. "Not quite, but sometimes in the dead of winter, when a nor'easter pounds the coast, it sure does seem like it."

"I would love to see the view in the daylight." Darkness had fallen and only the stars and the house's outside lighting lit their way back to the house.

"Consider yourself invited anytime." Daniel gently cupped her elbow as they traveled the uneven path. "Watch your step out here. I haven't had time to level the path out, now that spring has arrived."

"I can't imagine why." She chuckled as their feet met the even stone path that led to the porch, which ran the entire length of the front of the house. Daniel and his crew had been putting in some extra-long hours at the restaurant. Last Saturday he had spent the day helping her pick out and deliver furniture. Then he had gotten upset when she mentioned paying him for his time and gas. Today they had spent all morning and a good portion of the afternoon on the outskirts of Camden, looking at statues.

Daniel's truck had been loaded down with three crated statues when they arrived back at the restaurant. It had taken Daniel, Gunnar, and two other fishermen an hour to unload the artwork. No one would take cash from her, so she handed out dinner I.O.U.s instead.

Nestled in the biggest and heaviest crate was a curved wooden mermaid. She was a wonderfully painted and nearly life-size creature, captured in a giant wave and holding a clear sphere in her outstretched hands. A wire went through the statue, and the globe actually lit up from below. Different-colored lightbulbs would make the sphere glow in different shades.

The other two pieces weren't really statues; they were more like works of art for the outdoors. One was of two steel dolphins, each about three feet long, frolicking under the sun. The other was a small, whimsical piece of six seahorses that moved with the wind and reflected different colors as they twisted and turned under the light of the sun. A carefully aimed spotlight would have the same effect on them at night.

She couldn't wait for warm summer nights when diners would enjoy the evening eating under the stars and admiring her recent purchases. "I have to do something especially nice for your mother for suggesting the statues. I not only love them, but I think they add a whole other dimension to the patio dining area." She also had to do something for Daniel, but she didn't know what. The stubborn man had refused gas money and even an I.O.U. for a free dinner. "Any idea of what she might like?"

"My mom just appreciates a beautiful garden." Daniel removed his hand from her elbow as they stepped up onto the porch. "She's excited about the mermaid. She's seen the other two pieces before, but not the mermaid."

"You told her already?"

"I called her when I got home. She wanted me to give her measurements as soon as you knew what you were putting in there." Daniel opened the front door and allowed her to enter first. "I wouldn't be surprised if she had the whole garden drawn and planned out by Monday morning and will be looking over my shoulder as I uncrate the mermaid."

Gwen stepped into Daniel's house and froze. She felt him gently push her farther into the entryway so he could close the door behind them. "My God, it's like living in a tree house." Wood seemed to be everywhere. Gleaming, shining, beautiful golden brown wood.

"Not quite." Daniel chuckled as he took the bottle of wine out of her hand. "The interior walls are plastered."

She released the bottle and started to unbutton

her coat. The floors were random pine, and every exterior wall was made up of beautifully cut, sanded, and varnished golden logs, just like the outside. Splashes of color came from throw rugs and the painted interior walls. The wooden staircase was curved and seemed to soar to the second floor without any visible means of support. The large foyer ceiling was two stories above her head. She blindly handed Daniel her coat and purse and then absently ran her fingers through her wind-tossed hair. "This is wonderful, Daniel. Who designed it?"

"I did." Daniel hung up her coat and purse on the coat tree next to the door.

Gwen glanced away from the room to her left. The only thing in it was a light hanging from the center of the log-beam ceiling. A dining room, perhaps? "You designed this house?"

"Why so shocked, Gwen? It's what I do."

"I thought you were a carpenter." Gwen studied his beautiful gray eyes. They matched his sweater perfectly.

"I am." Daniel's voice was proud and strong. "I also have been reading and understanding blueprints since I was about ten." He swept his arm to the opening to their right. "Come on, I'll give you the nickel tour. You don't have to worry about the house collapsing in on top of you. I had my dad, a 'real' architect, look over the plans before I built."

"I wasn't worried about it collapsing." She gave him a flirtatious smile. Tonight she was planning on finally tasting one of Daniel's long, slow kisses. "I was wondering how much property along the coast cost, and if I'd ever be able to afford paying you to build me a house just like this one."

Daniel chuckled. "You better start franchising out."

Gwen shuddered at the thought of multiple

Catch of the Day restaurants up and down the coast, where people stood in lines and ordered things like value meals or extra fries. There would be drive-through windows and teenagers dressed in red lobster suits waving in the customers. "Forget it. I'll stay with the cottage on Conrad Street."

"Smart move." Daniel led the way into the kitchen.

Gwen followed and felt her heart leap at her surroundings. The kitchen and eating area were open to the living room, where Daniel had a crackling fire roaring. Three French patio doors opened to a massive deck and the ocean beyond. This was the soul of the house, and for some inexplicable reason it called to her. Tantalized her.

The spacious kitchen had wooden cabinets, granite countertops, and a small table would seat four comfortably. The room had all the modern conveniences but none of the frills. It was a man's kitchen, and it matched the informal living room, with its stone fireplace and massive beige couch. A worn leather recliner was positioned so it could view the big-screen television along with the ocean. The only thing missing to make it a total man's paradise were antlers mounted on the walls and empty beer cans littering the coffee table.

Daniel obviously had some redeeming qualities. "It's lovely." She crossed the kitchen and headed for a bookshelf that held a dozen or so paperbacks and two healthy-looking philodendrons. It wasn't the books or the plants that had caught her attention. A dozen wooden animals, all exquisitely carved, lined the shelves. The smallest was a crab, no more than two inches across; the largest was an eight-inch moose, with massive antlers and a proud stance. She picked up a small fox and examined every detail, from his pointy nose to his bushy tail.

"These are wonderful, Daniel. Wherever did you get them?"

"Thank you, and I carved them myself." Daniel picked up a seagull, frowned, and sat it back down next to a stack of paperbacks. "I never could get his wings exactly the same. It bugs me every time I see him."

The bird looked delicate and perfectly in proportion to her. She carefully placed the fox back on the shelf. "You're a man of many talents." Her opinion of Daniel's talents was growing by leaps and bounds, and she hadn't even been here for fifteen minutes. This was no simple carpenter before her. Daniel was a craftsman.

"If it's wood, I'm there." Daniel led her from the room, back out into the hallway. The top couple of stairs leading to the second floor were above their heads. Daniel motioned to two doors on their right. "Laundry room and powder room." Ahead of him was another door, partially open. Daniel pushed it all the way open and turned on the light. "The den."

Gwen stepped into the room and grinned. A computer sat on the desk, along with a couple of rolled-up blueprints. A smaller version of the fireplace that was in the living room was against the far wall, and another set of patio doors led to the outside. An entire wall of bookshelves held books, seashells, more rolled-up blueprints, and what appeared to be another two dozen hand-carved animals. "I never knew carpenters kept offices with high-tech computers. I always thought you guys worked out of the back of your truck or something."

"Welcome to the twenty-first century." Daniel shook his head as he ushered her back out of the room and turned off the light. "As Bob Dylan said, 'The times, they are a changin'.' "

"True." She flashed him a smile. "Did you build the fireplaces?"

"Every stone was placed by my hands."

"What about spindles on the staircase? Did you carve them too?" She was curious as to everything Daniel could do with his hands.

"I have a lathe in the garage. They are 'turned,' not carved." Daniel raised a brow and waited patiently for her next question.

"You can't tell me you built this house with your bare hands. One man wouldn't be able to lift one of those logs by himself." She nodded to the exterior wall.

"I have a couple of men I employ when the job calls for it, and there's something called a crane. A very handy piece of machinery, if I do say so myself."

"There's no way Jonah and Clarence helped you lift those logs."

Daniel chuckled and shook his head. "Ned and Quin both have strong backs and talented hands, and they follow directions without questioning my every word, unlike some people we know. They also don't bicker from sunup to sundown. I hadn't been planning on employing anyone for the work you needed done at the restaurant. My grandfather and Clarence showed up one day and just happened not to leave. I didn't have the heart to kick them off the job."

She wished Daniel's heart wasn't so darn good and pure. It was one of the things she found most attractive about him. That, and his hands. His big, tender, talented hands. If his fingers managed to carve those tiny pincers on the end of the crab's claw, imagine what they could do to a woman's body. She nearly melted at the thought.

They walked back down the hallway, toward the front door. Daniel stopped by the entranceway to the empty room. "This will be the dining room, eventually."

"What, you used up your quota of trees this year?" she teased. It was either tease him or collect on that slow, long kiss. "Can't cut down another oak or two to carve up a table and whittle up eight matching chairs with silk-padded seats in your spare time?" Calling Daniel a carpenter would be like calling her sister a candy striper.

"Eight? I was thinking six chairs would do it." Daniel looked at the empty room as if he really was considering the difference between six chairs and eight. "Don't you think it would be too crowded with eight? Where would I put the china cabinet and buffet sideboard I just finished chiseling out of a pine tree lightning had struck last week?"

"Does your mother know you have a smart mouth?" Mary Creighton had seemed like a very nice woman.

"Who do you think taught me everything I know?" Daniel nodded toward the staircase before leading her back into the kitchen. "Three bedrooms and two baths."

Gwen stared at the upstairs banister for a moment before following Daniel into the kitchen. A man on the make would have offered to show her his etchings, or something as lame. She was curious to see where Daniel slept. The master bedroom was probably all massive wood furniture and depressingly dark plaid linens. Hopefully there would be dirty clothes everywhere, an unmade bed, and a master bathroom that would take an army of scrubbing bubbles on a suicide mission to clean. Daniel needed a serious flaw to knock him off the perfect pedestal her mind was setting him up on. So far she had discovered two imperfections, and neither were fatal. Daniel drove a Chevy, while she preferred a Ford, and he was too darn slow to kiss her. The truck was forgivable, but the timing of the kiss needed some work.

"How do you like your steak?" Daniel pulled two steaks out of the refrigerator.

"Medium, and what can I do to help?"

"I've got everything under control." Daniel handed her a corkscrew. "You can open the wine. Glasses are in the cabinet above the dishwasher." Daniel took the steaks and headed out onto the deck.

Gwen watched for a moment while Daniel started the grill and tossed on the steaks. She had discovered over time that most men found it extremely uncomfortable to cook for her. Daniel didn't seem to have that problem, which was fine by her. It was a pure luxury to have someone else do the cooking.

Daniel stared at the woman standing before him wrapped in the afghan from the back of his couch. The wind was tugging at her hair and the blanket. Gwen was the most beautiful woman ever to grace Misty Harbor, and amazingly, she was standing in the moonlight looking out over the ocean with him. Who would have thought? Oh, he had dreamed a scene something like this, but not quite. His dream involved the upstairs balcony off the master bedroom and, considering what Gwen hadn't been wearing, definitely a warmer night.

"How come the stars in Maine seem so much closer than the stars in Baltimore?" Gwen tilted her face upward as she studied the star-studded sky.

He moved a step closer and couldn't help but wrap his arms around her waist. He needed to hold her. His chin rested on the top of her head as he followed her gaze upward. "Maine's closer to heaven." He pulled her nearer and felt her laughter against his chest. "Aren't you cold yet?" It was in the mid-forties, with some good strong gusts coming in off the water.

"No, but I'm the one with the blanket. Aren't you cold?" Gwen tilted her head and looked up at him, over her shoulder.

Lord, her mouth was so close. Kissable close. "No. To us Down Easters, this is balmy weather." If he got any hotter, the soles of his socks would be setting the deck on fire. Maybe it wasn't such a good idea to come out here and stargaze. He had thought the cold air would cool him down. Instead he was warmer now than when he had been sitting next to Gwen on the couch, enjoying the fire and the last of the wine from dinner.

Gwen seemed to snuggle deeper into his arms. "I'm beginning to feel a tad balmy myself."

He had left the outside lights off, and there was only one light lit in the living room behind him. They were both standing in the shadows. He slowly traced the gentle curve of her cheek. He couldn't read her dark eyes, but he felt her breath quicken at his touch. Desire pounded thick and heavy through his body. Lord, how he wanted this woman. "I think I might have to kiss you now."

Gwen turned her head and pressed her lips to the center of his palm. "Might?"

He tenderly turned her, cupped both her cheeks, and tilted her face upward. "Make that a definite."

Gwen's arms escaped the cocoon of the blanket and wrapped themselves around his neck. Her mouth rose to his, and he captured her next breath. Warm, soft, damp lips and the sweetest sigh met his mouth. His tongue teased the seam of her lips, and she retaliated by playfully nipping at it before teasing him right back.

A fierce growl of approval vibrated in his chest

as he ran his hands down her back and hauled her closer. A blanket and a sweet woman filled his arms as his mouth tasted and savored every inch of her mouth. Gwen stood on her toes and pressed her hips closer to his arousal. This time it was Gwen who made a soft moaning sound that nearly shattered what little control he had left.

How could one kiss get so hot, so out of control, so darn fast? He broke the kiss and trailed a string of kisses to the soft skin behind her ear. Gwen shivered in his arms. "You're cold." How could he have been so thoughtless? The only thing holding up the blanket was the pressure from being wedged in between their bodies and his hands, where he was cupping her bottom. Her enticing, sweetly curved bottom, filling his palms to perfection.

Gwen gave a broken laugh and pressed her mouth against his neck. "I would have to be dead to be cold."

He felt her tongue swirl against his neck, and the same shiver that had shook Gwen, shook him. "If we stay out here much longer, you'll catch your death." He was walking a thin line between sanity and desire. Sanity was getting Gwen inside, where it was warm and welcoming. Desire was this uncontrollable urge to take the blanket off Gwen, lay it on the deck, and make love to every inch of her luscious body under the twinkling stars. Thankfully, reason won out. He swung Gwen up into his arms and carried her into the living room. With Gwen still cradled against his chest, he closed the patio door and turned off the lamp. The only light came from the low, dancing flames in the fireplace.

In the golden glow of the fire, Daniel slowly lowered Gwen to her feet. He tossed the blanket to one side and pulled her back into his arms, where she belonged. Her rose-colored silk blouse was cool beneath his fingertips and shimmered with the flickering flames. He tenderly brushed a lock of her hair behind her ear. Deep brown eyes, filled with desire, stared up at him. Whatever he was feeling, it wasn't all one-sided. Gwen was feeling it too.

"I think I miscalculated." His thumb traced over the gleam of moisture on her lower lip. Her mouth trembled beneath his touch.

"About what?" Gwen whispered.

"Long, slow kisses." His fingertips skimmed down her soft neck and toyed with the golden necklace she wore. A sparkling pink stone rested against the base of her throat. All through dinner he had stared at that seductive spot and wondered if he kissed her there, would he be able to feel her heartbeat against his lips. "The long part isn't the problem; it's the slow I seem to be having trouble with." He felt the rapid beating of her pulse against the back of his fingers. The racing pace matched his own perfectly.

Gwen's hands found their way up under his sweater and T-shirt to caress his back. "Slow's over-rated." One warm fingertip started at the base of his neck and slowly traced over every vertebra and disk along his backbone, until his belt and pants stopped their downward motion.

He felt heat pool thick and heavy behind the zipper of his pants. Gwen was not only standing in the light of the fire, she was playing with it. His hands swept up her throat and he tilted her chin with his thumbs. Firelight enhanced the curve of her jaw and the height of her cheekbones. "Do you realize how beautiful you are?" His mouth captured the beginning of her smile.

The taste of Gwen intoxicated him. He was drunk on the taste of hot, sweet kisses, shampoo that smelled like his mother's herb garden, and just a hint of lavender. For weeks Gwen had been driving him crazy with desire. Tonight she had driven him over the line of caution, and all it had taken was one kiss in the moonlight. His tongue mated with hers as his hands slid down her back to cup her rounded behind. This time there wasn't any afghan between his fingers and the sweet, soft curves.

When Gwen pressed herself against his straining arousal, he knew that line of caution had crumbled into dust. There were a dozen reasons why he shouldn't make love to Gwen. With her pressed so intimately against him, he couldn't think of a single one. Heck, he could barely remember his own name, let alone a list of reasons.

He slowly lowered them both to the rug in front of the glowing fire. He leaned over her but kept his weight off her body. Gwen was such a petite little thing, he didn't want to hurt her or frighten her. It was one thing to be kissing one minute, but quite another to find yourself laying on the floor with a very aroused man looming over you.

Gwen looked like a goddess spread out in the golden light. Her eyes were large and luminous, and her mouth was temptingly close. She didn't look frightened. Gwen looked seductively desirable. "I feel as if I ought to be worshiping you." His fingers toyed with the first button on her blouse. "Do you have any idea how much I want you, Gwen?"

"Hopefully as much as I want you." Gwen's fingers tugged at his hair, trying to bring his mouth down to hers.

He couldn't help but smile, but he still held back. If Gwen responded to his next kiss like the last one, he feared he wouldn't be able to stop himself from loving her. "We're both adults, Gwen." He needed to make sure Gwen understood just where their kisses were leading.

"Amen to that." Gwen's fingers slipped through his hair and brushed his beard.

The first button on her blouse slipped through its hole. His fingers traveled to the next button. "How much wine did you drink?"

"It was a very small bottle, Daniel, and we shared it equally." The tip of Gwen's finger outlined his mouth. "I might be dizzy, giddy, and totally without inhibitions, but it isn't the wine's fault. It's your kisses that do that to me."

He grinned against her finger. "My kisses?"

"You kiss like you mean it."

"Of course I mean them. But they aren't just my kisses, they're *our* kisses. Kissing definitely requires a partner, a participating partner." He studied the honesty glowing in her deep brown eyes. There was no confusion or any other sign of her being intoxicated, just heat, desire, and honesty. Gwen knew exactly what she was doing, and where this was heading.

Gwen's fingers scraped his beard. "I like your beard. It's soft." She caressed the short hair with her palm. "I thought it would be hard and bristly, but it's not. I've never kissed a man with a beard before."

The next button came undone. His fingers moved lower. "I'm glad." Her blouse parted and he sucked in his breath at the sight of the pale pink bra overflowing with Gwen's perfectly proportioned breasts. Hard nipples were pressing against the lace, begging for his attention. "Lord, how can you get more beautiful?"

Gwen reached for the hem of his sweater and tugged upward. She sighed with pleasure as both his sweater and T-shirt came up and over his head. Both of her hands immediately caressed his chest. "Talk about beautiful."

Daniel felt those small, delicate hands stroke his

chest and his passion. He wasn't going to last too much longer. He leaned down and strung a line of kisses from the corner of her mouth to the deep valley between her breasts. Gwen's fingers were now in his hair, pulling him closer. Needing him as much as he needed her.

He undid the front clasp of her bra and captured one of those nipples with his lips. Gwen arched her hips off the floor, cupped his buttocks, and urged him to come closer. His hand slid down her smooth stomach and unbuttoned her slacks. He brushed his beard across the sensitive nipple and allowed his last reasonable thought to become words. "Gwen, if you want to stop, it has to be now."

Gwen's fingers undid his belt and lowered his zipper. His heart nearly pounded through his rib cage when she slowly slid her hand into his boxers and wrapped it around his penis. His hand froze in the middle of lowering her zipper. Gwen's mouth brushed his ear. "What do you think?" Her hand gently squeezed before traveling up the length of him, and then back down to the base of his straining erection.

His back teeth ground together and he tried to breathe through his nose. "Is that your final answer?"

Gwen chuckled and lightly bit his lobe. "This is my final answer." Delicate fingers increased their pace as Gwen's tongue outlined his ear.

He was dangerously close to embarrassing himself, so he grasped her wrist and pulled her hand from his pants. He captured her mouth before she could protest. While his mouth tasted and tormented, he pulled her pants and panties down in one fluid motion. Gwen kicked off her shoes and raised her hips to help him. Her nylon socks joined the pile.

As Daniel kicked off his pants and boxers, Gwen unbuttoned the cuffs of her blouse and started to tug it off. Daniel's socks landed across the room the same instant Gwen's bra alighted on the coffee table.

He smiled at her impatience.

Daniel tried to catch his breath as his gaze explored the woman before him. The word *beautiful* didn't do Gwen justice. She was breathtakingly exquisite. Her pale skin glowed golden in the firelight. Tight rose-colored nipples begged to be kissed, and the dark triangle at the junction of her thighs begged to be explored. Savored and satisfied.

He leaned forward and placed a kiss on each hard nipple. "You smell like lavender and herbs." His fingers danced across her stomach and teased the bush of tightly wound curls. "I don't know if I should kiss you or eat you."

Gwen raised her hips, and his fingers sank farther into the nest. Her hands cupped his cheeks and forced his mouth back up to hers. "Kiss me, Daniel, long and slow."

He nipped at her lower lip as his fingers found her moist center. "I'll try, sweet love, I'll try." He fastened his mouth across hers and slowly sank his fingers into her heat. Gwen's moan and the urgent movement of her hips matched the wild mating of their tongues.

Greedy hands pulled him nearer, and he found himself positioned above Gwen. Their bodies aligned perfectly as he slid a second finger into her tight, moist opening. Gwen's mouth opened wider as she deepened the kiss and wrapped her legs around his thighs.

A haze blurred his vision as he teased and tormented Gwen and himself into near madness. He was male enough to know he was never going to last long, this first time with Gwen. He was man enough to know that her pleasure and satisfaction should and must come first. There would never be another "first time," and he was determined that Gwen would remember this night not only fondly, but with a smile of pure feminine satisfaction.

"Daniel," Gwen's voice was a harsh plea coming between rapid breaths, "now."

He slid his hands to the back of her thighs and pulled her legs up higher until she was encircling his hips. The tip of his arousal nudged her opening, and he could feel the heat and the moisture surround his swollen flesh. With a slowness that caused his back teeth to mash and perspiration to bead his forehead, he inched his way in, the whole time studying Gwen's face. He was looking for a sign of discomfort or pain. Tightness, sweet and moist, engulfed him. But it was the look of wonder and hunger on Gwen's face that made him want to crow in victory.

Gwen's legs tightened in protest as he slowly pulled back, but he didn't leave her. The world could end at this precious moment and he wouldn't leave her. Couldn't leave her. He slowly sank back in, only to feel Gwen's legs tighten in reaction and her hips leave the floor. This time he went in farther, and Gwen closed her eyes while pulling him in deeper still.

The haze that had been blurring his vision turned into thick clouds of desire as his body overruled his mind. His pace quickened, and Gwen matched him thrust for thrust. Groan for moan.

He could feel his climax in the base of his shaft, screaming for release, yet he thrust on, taking Gwen higher with every plunge. His beard scraped her delicate chin and jaw as he kissed her. He could feel Gwen's heels digging into the back of his thighs, and he urged her on. Needing for her to climax first.

Their pace increased to a wild frenzy as sweat coated their bodies and their harsh breathing filled their ears.

Gwen tore her mouth away from his and nearly screamed his name, "Daniel!" as her eyes went wide.

Daniel could feel the climax that shook Gwen's body. Delicate silken muscles clutched him tighter and contracted around him, shattering the last of his strength. Her cry of release had barely faded as he shuddered and pumped his own climax into Gwen's hot, sweet body. He vaguely remembered shouting Gwen's name.

Chapter Fifteen

Gwen slowly opened her eyes and immediately closed them again when she encountered the morning sun climbing its way up over the ocean. Dawn could be a wonderful time, or a very embarrassing one. Depending on whose bed one awoke in.

Waking up in Daniel's bed was both wonderful and a bit embarrassing. She wasn't experienced enough to handle the situation with total nonchalance. She wasn't naive and innocent, but she also didn't have the habit of waking up in someone else's bed.

Gwen cracked open one eye. She was definitely in Daniel's bed. Navy cotton sheets and a thick plaid comforter were her first clue. The second, and more interesting one, was the naked arm wrapped around her waist. Her gaze followed the masculine forearm, past the thickly boned wrist to the long, strong fingers that had always fascinated her. Those fingers were lightly cupping one of her breasts.

She felt her nipple harden and bit her lower lip to keep the moan of desire from escaping. Daniel was asleep, and after the night they had shared, the man deserved his rest. Hell, the man deserved a standing ovation and roses tossed at his feet. The memory of him carrying her up the stairs and to his bed was a bit foggy. She had been so satiated and satisfied after making love with Daniel before the low-burning fire, she had no idea how long they had lain there. She thought she might have fallen asleep.

She definitely hadn't been asleep when Daniel made love to her the second time in the comfort of his king-size bed. *Long* and *slow* were given new meanings, and she had a new appreciation for soft, short beards. A blush swept up her cheeks as she remembered not only shouting Daniel's name when he had brought her to a climax with his mouth, but she had actually screamed when he pushed her over the edge one more time before reaching his own release.

Her nipple tightened more between Daniel's relaxed fingers. She felt her body melt with the memory of what Daniel could do with those talented, tender fingers. She silently groaned with disgust at her treacherous body. Who would have thought that within weeks of moving to Maine she would not only acquire a restaurant, but a lover as well? Not her.

She didn't have time for a relationship, let alone a hot-and-heavy affair. With great care, she removed Daniel's hand and pulled herself up, until her back was resting against a soft pillow and the wooden headboard. She smiled as Daniel muttered something, shifted his position slightly, and buried his face under his pillow.

Her smile slowly faded as she studied the back of his head and his naked shoulders and back. Three scratches, made by her fingernails, scored the perfection of his back. She had marked him, just as surely as his whisker burns marked her thighs and breasts. The comforter was pulled up to his waist, but she knew he wasn't wearing anything under that blanket. Neither was she. One troubling thought filtered through her mind as she clutched her fingers so she wouldn't smooth those three red lines. She was in a relationship with Daniel, and after last night there was no way she could deny it was hot and heavy. She also couldn't hide the truth from herself any longer.

She was falling in love with Daniel.

The pillow cushioned the back of her head as she closed her eyes and wondered why she wasn't panicking, or at least hauling her butt back to her cottage before Daniel woke up. Amazingly, she didn't want to run. She wanted to snuggle closer to him and spend her entire Sunday in his bed making love.

Daniel hadn't declared how he felt about her, besides needing and wanting during the height of their passion. Then again, she hadn't made any declarations herself. She had even been the one to suggest the dinner date to begin with. While nearly every other available man in town had asked her out, Daniel had kept amazingly silent. She had to wonder why, especially after the night they had just shared.

Gwen tugged the comforter up higher, and nearly managed to cover both of her breasts. Curiously, she glanced around the bedroom. Last night it had been too dark to see anything, besides the outline of furniture. In the light of dawn she studied Daniel's bedroom and couldn't find one flaw, other than a rumpled bed.

The entire eastern wall was made up of uncurtained patio doors leading to a balcony. This morning the ocean looked grayish blue, the sun glittering across its surface. The endless pounding of the waves against the rocks was a dull, low roar, and the occasional cry of a gull could be heard through the closed doors. The rising sun lit the bedroom like a thousand-watt lamp.

The north wall had an exact duplicate of the stone fireplace in front of which they had made love last night in the living room. A pile of ashes testified to its occasional use. A big, comfortable chair and ottoman was positioned to one side. A high-powered telescope, mounted on a tripod, was near one of the patio doors. The light blue wall, opposite the fireplace, held a door, which she assumed led to to the master bath and closet.

No dirty laundry littered the floor. No crumpled newspapers or half-read books were piled by the chair. Even the ashes in the fireplace looked neat and orderly. Daniel was either a saint among men or a robot. She glanced back down at him and wondered why some local girl hadn't dragged him down the aisle by now.

She looked at the door leading to the bathroom, then slowly eased herself out of Daniel's bed. Mother Nature was calling, and she wanted to at least wash off yesterday's makeup and run a comb through her hair before Daniel woke up and died of fright.

Five minutes later, wrapped in Daniel's thick terry-cloth robe, Gwen opened one of the patio doors and stepped out onto the dew-covered balcony. Her bare feet immediately protested the chill, but she ignored them and fell in love with the view. The sunrise over the Atlantic had never looked this wonderful to her before. The sea breeze tossed her recently combed hair, but she didn't care. The only thing that would make this moment more perfect was to have Daniel share it with her. But she didn't have the heart to wake him. He had looked so peaceful when she had checked on him a moment earlier.

Daniel had the most sinfully rich bathroom she had ever encountered. Who else would have thought of putting patio doors in the master bath? Daniel had, and he had positioned the huge whirlpool tub so that whoever was using it could see out the doors. Daniel didn't have to worry about nosy neighbors or Peeping Toms, only people on boats with binoculars. She had kept one eye on that deep navy tub with its brass fixtures while scrubbing her face. A very erotic image of Daniel reclining in that tub kept playing through her mind. She found a comb and a brand-new toothbrush and used them both.

The only thing missing now was Daniel, and a cup of strong coffee. She would kill for a pot of Colombia's best. Borrowing Daniel's robe and comb were one thing, but invading his kitchen without his permission was another. Kitchens to her were personal domains, and strictly off limits unless invited. If Daniel didn't wake up soon, his personal domain was going to be compromised.

The sound of one of the patio doors opening made her sigh in relief, but she didn't turn around. Strong arms wrapped around her waist and Daniel's mouth teased the back of her neck. "Your feet must be freezing."

Daniel's robe came to her ankles and her hands were swallowed by the sleeves. With the heat of Daniel's mouth caressing her neck, she forgot all about her feet. "It's so beautiful out here, I couldn't resist." She tilted her neck to one side to give him better access.

Daniel's hand slipped into the front of the robe

and gently cupped one of her breasts. "It's you I can't resist."

She noticed that he had put on another robe that must had been in his closet. She had swiped the one she wore from the back of the bathroom door. A seagull swooped down and gave a loud cry before disappearing beyond the cliff. A moment later the bird reappeared, screeching a victory call before flying off. "Do you know what I would really like right now?"

Daniel chuckled as he skimmed his mouth from the side of her neck across her shoulder. The robe was in immediate danger of slipping off her body. "I hope it's the same thing I want."

She felt him pluck at her hard nipple and knew she was losing the battle. Her voice was low and strained as she whispered, "Coffee. I want coffee."

Daniel raised his head and stared at her for a moment in disbelief. Then he laughed, a full-body laugh that softened his face and captured her heart. "How could I have forgotten?"

"Forgotten what?" She turned in his arms and smiled up at him.

"How much you like your coffee in the morning." He pressed a quick kiss to the tip of her nose. "Come on. I'll go put on a pot."

She frowned at the offending brotherly kiss. That was definitely not a morning-after kiss. In the clear light of day, she wanted Daniel to kiss her, really kiss her, like he meant it. Like he had kissed her last night in the dark. She wrapped her arms around his neck and felt the cold air blow across her breasts. Daniel's robe had a bigger gap than the Grand Canyon. She raised herself up onto her toes and brushed her mouth across his. Daniel smelled of mint toothpaste and sea mist.

"This isn't how you get coffee, Gwen." Daniel's

voice was choked as his gaze slid down her chest. He seemed to be having a hard time swallowing.

She smiled and pressed herself against him. She could feel his desire hardening and thickening beneath his robe. "I changed my mind; coffee can wait." Who needed caffeine to start the day when there was Daniel?

Daniel picked her up and sealed his mouth over hers. Gwen wrapped her legs around his waist and bit his lower lip in retaliation for making her wait so long for that kiss. Daniel moaned something that sounded like a curse; but then again, it could have been a prayer, as he stumbled backward and reached for the door handle.

They almost didn't make it to the bed.

Gwen smelled the coffee before she opened her eyes. There were other aromas mixed with the scent of coffee, but she couldn't sort them out. Her whole body was craving that caffeine. She opened one eye and stared at the tray Daniel was holding in his hands. Two plates containing fluffy scrambled eggs and lightly buttered toast made her stomach growl, but it was an entire pot of coffee that made her sit up.

Seeing the direction of Daniel's gaze, she quickly reached for the sheet and tucked it under her arms. "I need nourishment."

Daniel chuckled and set the tray on the nightstand. "That's why I'm standing here and not lying there." He nodded toward the other side of the bed. He handed her a cup already filled. "Here; I believe I promised you this a couple of hours ago."

After the last time they had made love, Daniel had sprawled beside her and promised that as soon as he could feel his feet again, he would get her

her coffee. Gwen took a big sip and stared out the patio doors. She couldn't see the sun any longer. "What time is it?" Daniel wasn't wearing his robe. He was wearing flannel pajama bottoms that rode low on his hips and caused her mind to remember how powerful those hips could be when he put his mind to it.

"After eleven." Daniel sat on the edge of the mattress. "Scoot over."

Gwen took another hasty sip and scooted over.

Daniel slid under the covers with her, picked up the tray, and carefully set it on his lap. "Sorry for the simple fare. I wasn't expecting company for breakfast."

Gwen smiled as she reached for her fork. "I take that as a compliment, and this looks delicious." The first taste of eggs had her leaning over and kissing Daniel's cheek. "These are wonderful."

"Boy, if I get a kiss for simple scrambled eggs, I can't imagine what I would have gotten for my famous blueberry waffles." Daniel dug into his breakfast like a starving man.

She chuckled at his enthusiasm and followed suit. She finished her first cup of coffee, and Daniel gave her a refill without being asked. "We're going to get crumbs all over the bed."

"I've got other sheets." Daniel finished everything on his plate and downed his glass of orange juice. He handed her the other glass. "Drink up; you're going to need your strength."

She grinned and hoisted her glass in a salute. "Here's to strenuous exercise."

Daniel placed the tray back on the nightstand and took the empty glass from her hand. He gave her a wicked smile and reached for the sheet she had tucked beneath her arms, then slowly pulled. Daniel stopped tugging the sheet as one breast came into full view. An appalled look came over his face as he reached out and gently touched her. "Did I do this?"

Gwen glanced down. A small pink whisker burn was barely visible on the side of her pale breast. She relaxed. From Daniel's expression, she was expecting to see something hideous. "I don't see anyone else around." She laughed lightly when Daniel's expression turned from appalled to distressed. "Relax, Daniel"—she reached out and caressed his soft beard—"I love your beard."

"Why?" Daniel's gaze bore into hers.

"Why what?"

"Why do you like the beard? Because it hides some of the scar?"

Now it was her turn to be appalled. "That's insulting, Daniel." She reached out, snatched the sheet, and covered herself back up. "I have never done, said, or looked at your scar in any way that would warrant that comment." She kept the sheet clutched to her chest and glared at the oaf sharing the bed. "Do you know why I know that to be a fact, Daniel?"

Daniel slowly shook his head.

"Because the scar doesn't bother me at all. You're the one with the problem about it, not me." She leaned forward and gently kissed the pale line bisecting his cheek. "I'm only sad for the pain you must have endured to receive such a wound."

She pulled back and gave him a forceful shove. Daniel ended up flat on his back with a small smile teasing his mouth. "Now that *you* have brought up the subject, it's only fair you tell me how you were hurt."

"You mean to tell me you didn't ask Jonah or Hunter?"

"Nope. I didn't want to pry into your business." She leaned back against the headboard and crossed her arms over her sheet-covered chest. "I think after last night that has changed a little bit."

Daniel grinned and wiggled his eyebrows. "I'd say."

"Good, but before you start that story I have another question for you. Why didn't you ask me out? Every single man within a ten-mile radius of the restaurant has asked me out, except you. Why?"

A big hand wrapped around her thigh and pulled her down, so that they were now laying side by side, facing each other. "I watched every man in town make a fool of himself over you and decided not to join their ranks."

"I don't remember anyone making a fool of himself, Daniel." She slid one of her legs between his flannel-covered thighs. She didn't like Daniel's disbelieving expression. "Okay, maybe the guy who published the poem in the paper came close, but at least he signed it 'Anonymous.'"

"I watched you turn guys down right and left, day after day."

"So? What did you want me to do, accept their invitations?" Daniel wasn't making any sense.

"Hell no." Daniel wrapped his arm around her and hauled her closer. "Why didn't you accept any of their offers? I saw the way you looked at Erik when he first walked into the restaurant. Your tongue nearly fell out of your mouth."

"It did not!" She gave his chest a hard thump. "I might have drooled a bit, but that was all."

Daniel growled and hauled her hips against his straining arousal.

She laughed. "Erik might be every woman's fantasy, Daniel, but he wasn't mine." Her smile slowly faded as she looked into smoky-gray eyes. "I was waiting for some stubborn carpenter, with the most incredible hands, to ask me out. Why didn't you?"

She pressed her lips against the scar again. "Was it because of this?"

"Partly." Daniel tucked her against his chest. "I was engaged once, about five years ago."

Gwen tried to raise her head, but Daniel wouldn't let her. "What happened?" Visions of Daniel and some faceless fiancée being in some fiery car accident teased her mind. The fiancée died in Daniel's loving arms after one last kiss. An old sixties song played in her mind as she hugged Daniel tighter. Was five years long enough to heal a broken heart?

"She broke it off after the accident that gave me this." Daniel's hand left her back to trace the jagged line down his cheek and into his beard.

"She left you because of the scar?" Gwen forced herself out of Daniel's arms so she could see his face. No loving fiancée had died in his arms. Daniel might have suffered a broken heart, but she had a feeling his self-confidence had taken a worse beating. Daniel hadn't asked her out because he had been afraid she would say no because of the scar. The man was certifiable.

"What in the hell kind of woman were you engaged to?" She brushed her mouth over his cheek and nuzzled his beard with her lips. "I say 'good riddance.'" Her fingers toyed with the silky, curly hair on his chest and teased lower. "What kind of accident was it?"

"It was a boating accident in the harbor, five years ago. I was down on the docks helping Jonah that afternoon. Some drunk tourists came flying into the harbor in a souped-up boat, misjudged a turn, and ended up smashing into another boat. Both tourists were killed instantly in the explosion. Ben Dunbar owned the other boat. He had been anchored only a couple of yards off the dock. He had his two-year-old grandson on board."

Daniel was silent for so long, she was afraid he

wasn't going to continue. By the look on his face, he was reliving the accident and the pain. She felt like a world-class heel. She didn't mean to hurt him, but she had.

"Nathan, the little boy, had his life vest on and was thrown away from the boat by the force of the first explosion. I dove in to get him just as a second explosion ripped apart Ben's boat. Ben died, a piece of flying debris sliced up my face, and Nathan attended second grade this year."

Gwen studied Daniel's face. There was a whole lot more to the story than what he had told her. She could see it etched into his face and the sadness that clouded his eyes. Here she had thought she might be falling in love with this man. She had been fooling herself. She was already in love.

She brushed her mouth over his and tenderly bit his lower lip before pulling it in between hers. A moan rocked his chest as he hauled her closer and deepened the kiss.

Three minutes later she came up for air and to glance into his gray eyes. The sadness was gone. It had been replaced with hunger and desire. Daniel was rock hard against her hip. She smiled wickedly and wiggled. "I think orange juice is an aphrodisiac."

Daniel rolled over, until she was laying beneath him. "I'm selling the house and we're moving to Florida."

Hunter twisted his body, aimed the gun, and gently squeezed the trigger. A steady stream of grease coated the tracks of the dishwasher, just where he wanted it. No one would be able to say he wasn't taking this job seriously, or that he was hired out of pity. He would uphold his end or

Gwen would just have to find someone else to do the job.

The way Gwen was acting today, he could probably dance around the kitchen with one of the lobster cooking pots on his head and she wouldn't notice. His boss was only noticing a certain carpenter. Daniel was noticing her right back. Something had happened with those two over the weekend, but he was too much of a gentleman to ask. Jonah had been crowing all through breakfast.

He wouldn't be surprised if Misty Harbor had a wedding in the near future.

He considered Daniel the son he'd never had, and the boy's older sister, Rebecca, a daughter. Thomas, Daniel's father, had been his best friend and constant companion before the war. They'd even attended the same boot camp but were shipped out to 'Nam in different units. Thomas had come home and picked up the pieces of his life, while he had hidden from it all. In a lot of ways he'd lived vicariously through Thomas.

Daniel deserved the love of a good woman, and from what he had seen so far, Gwen was better than a "good" woman. In his opinion she was bordering on exceptional. He had figured out weeks ago that Daniel and Gwen made a wonderful couple. He was just amazed that it had taken them this long to figure it out for themselves.

Kids; who could understand them? Then again, who could understand a lot of things in life?

He still tortured himself by playing the what-if game. What if he had returned from 'Nam a whole man? And he wasn't referring to the bullet he had taken in the arm. That wound was the least of his traumas. What if he instead of Ben Dunbar had married Tess? What if he had been on the docks five years ago when the boating accident had occurred? Would he have dived into the water to save the drowning little boy, as Daniel had? Could he have reached Ben Dunbar before that second explosion ended his life? Would he have had the courage to face his biggest fear, water, knowing that little boy was Tess's precious grandson?

On his good days, he would like to think he could have found that courage. On his bad days, he was positive he would have frozen, just like the other dozen or so people who had watched that horrible scene play out before their very eyes. Daniel had been hailed a hero.

Over the next six months, Hunter and the rest of the town had stood silently by and watched their town hero's life fall apart. Maybe now Daniel's life was on an upward swing. Sometimes, Hunter figured, God was just a little slow in rewarding his heroes.

"Hunter, I have someone you need to meet," Gwen said as she pushed her way into the kitchen. "I just hired our first dishwasher."

Hunter smiled as he backed out of the dishwashing unit and tried to work a kink out of his back. For a Monday, it had been awfully slow around the restaurant. He had helped Daniel uncrate the statues Gwen had bought on Saturday and turned over the garden outside. Daniel's mother, Mary, had been issuing orders and directions like a drill sergeant, when she hadn't been ohing and ahing over the wood mermaid statue. The rest of the day he had spent in the kitchen, doing some light maintenance and staying out of the carpet layers way.

Now it was late afternoon, and he could use a break from grease guns and oil cans. "Great."

He wiped his hands on a rag and turned to face Gwen and one of the dishwashers he would ultimately be responsible for.

"Hunter, meet Scott," Gwen said.

He looked at the teenager standing beside Gwen and felt his heart slam against his chest. Scott stood nearly six feet tall and was dressed in a pair of battered jeans, a black leather coat, and a T-shirt with what appeared to be a psychotic serial killer on the front of it. Scott's hair was nonexistent. The seventeen-year-old had shaved his head completely bald. A thick silver ring pierced his left eyebrow, and a trio of hoops decorated one of his ears. Sky-blue eyes stared warily back at him. "Hello, Scott." He reached out his hand and waited.

Scott slowly shook his extended hand. "Hi."

He tried not to flinch at the sight of a huge silver bar penetrating the boy's tongue. He didn't care what anyone said, that had to hurt like hell. "Welcome aboard."

Scott Dunbar had his mother's eyes. How in the hell was he suppose to work every night with Tess's sky-blue eyes looking at him?

Daniel pointed to the chair and said, "Sit."

Gwen frowned but sat. "I don't have time for this, Daniel."

"You don't have time to eat?" Daniel opened the pizza box, put two slices on a plate, and slid the meal into the microwave. It was one of the disadvantages of having the nearest pizza shop twenty minutes away; Pizza never arrived home hot. In the six days since they had become lovers, Gwen had gone from worrying about the restaurant to being obsessed with the grand opening. She need to relax or she was never going to make it through the next two weeks.

He was never going to make it through the next two weeks. He was going to drown in the pile of paperwork and lists Gwen compiled. He was a self-employed business owner. He understood all about the worries and the responsibilities. He also understood that if Gwen didn't *slow* down, she was going to *fall* down.

At first he thought it was cute how Gwen made lists and worried about the restaurant. It showed him not only how much she cared, but what kind of person she was. Lately that caring had turned into an obsession, and he was the one beginning to worry. Something wasn't right. Gwen seemed to be trying to prove herself to someone; the question was who?

When the buzzer sounded, he placed Gwen's dinner in front of her and put his two slices into the microwave. He opened Gwen's refrigerator and pulled out the bottle of chilled wine he had placed there earlier. Over the last six nights they had been alternating spending their nights in his king-size bed with its ocean view and her queen-size bed, nestled under the eves of the cottage roof. Either bed was fine by him, as long as Gwen was in it with him.

He filled two glasses and carried them over to the table, just as the buzzer sounded again. Daniel joined her at the table and sighed when he noticed she hadn't even taken a bite of pizza yet. Gwen was wearing what he had labeled her "distracted" look. "What's wrong now?"

"The tables should have arrived today, but they didn't."

"They'll get here in time, Gwen. Deliveries up here have been known to be a day or two late, that's all." He nodded toward her plate. "Eat, before it gets cold again."

Gwen picked up a piece and took a bite. "Thank you, Daniel. You didn't have to drive into Sullivan. I would have made us dinner."

"You've been cooking too much as it is. I wanted to give you a break, and I wanted something simple tonight." Gwen was starting to get dark circles under her beautiful brown eyes. She needed to rest, and to catch up on some much-needed sleep. He had made a promise to himself that tonight, once they were in bed, he would actually allow Gwen to sleep.

"Simple? I could have made cheeseburgers or something. You didn't have to drive nearly an hour to pick up pizza."

"It's only a forty-minute round-trip, and you didn't hear me. I didn't want you cooking tonight. Every time I cook, you somehow manage to take over for me."

"If I'm that pushy, why do you put up with me?" Gwen stuck out her lower lip in a pout.

"Because I'm in love with your French toast." He grinned at the way she was trying to hide her own smile. He had to wonder what she would say if he told her the truth—that he was falling in love with her.

"You only want me for my cooking?" Gwen batted her ridiculously long eyelashes.

He gave her a wicked leer. "Among other things." He felt his body harden at the thought of what those other things were. Mentally, he threw a pail of ice water onto his lap. What was needed was a change of subject, and fast, before all his good intentions went down the tubes and he ended up making love to Gwen on the dining-room table. "Did you call your mom?" Gwen had said she was going to call her family while he ran for pizza.

"Yeah, but she wasn't home. I talked to my dad instead."

"How is he?"

"A little distracted, as usual, but he seemed happy to hear from me. I usually miss him when I call home." Gwen grinned. "He thanked me for suggesting to my mom that she take him to the beach. They went the other day—only for a night, though—but he said they really enjoyed it. His voice got all kinds of funny, and I wasn't going to ask what they did at the beach. There are just some things kids don't need to know about their parents."

He raised his glass. "Amen to that." He watched as Gwen toasted him back. She was starting to unwind. "Did you reach either of your sisters?"

"Both, actually." Gwen frowned at her pizza, took a big bite, and chewed. "Sydney couldn't talk long; she was getting ready to go out socializing with Needle Ass."

He chuckled. "Why do you call him Needle Ass? From what you told me, the man's a gifted doctor."

"He's gifted, all right, in his own mind. Richard considers himself above most of the doctors seeing to America's health care. Needle Ass is an 'okay' doctor, but he'll never be great because he only cares about prestige and money."

"He must care about your sister. They've been living together for four years now, right?" Gwen didn't talk much about her family, but when she did, he listened. Understanding Gwen's family would be the key to understanding Gwen.

"Oh, they live together, and I guess Sydney loves him or she wouldn't be doing that, but if Richard cared anything at all for my sister, he wouldn't be forcing her to go out socializing to further his own career and standing with the hospital board." Gwen waved a piece of pizza at him. "She had a hellish day today, and it started at three in the morning when one of her little patients was admitted into the hospital with seizures. Sydney's heartbroken at the diagnosis."

"Which is?"

"Brain tumor." Gwen lowered her pizza back to her plate. "An inoperable brain tumor."

He reached for his glass and emptied it in one fluid motion. "Oh, yeah, that would make you want to go out and socialize with the country club set."

"See, even you understand. Needle Ass couldn't care less."

"You still haven't told me why you and Jocelyn christened Dr. Richard Needle Ass."

"Because when it comes to money, he has such a tight ass even a needle wouldn't fit up it. He makes Sydney pay for half of everything, including all their vacations to wherever *he* wants to go." Gwen took another sip of wine. "I swear, the only reason they got a place together was because with both their salaries combined, he could get an upscale apartment. That, and the Fletcher name is golden in most Baltimore hospitals."

"He sounds like a winner." Daniel shook his head. "What about Jocelyn?"

"She's fine. Putting in some ungodly hours but enjoying herself. We spent ten minutes bad-mouthing Needle Ass." Gwen grinned.

"That seems to be something you Fletcher girls all have in common." At first he thought Gwen was trying to prove something to her family, but the more she talked about them—and she was quite honest in her revelations—the more he dismissed that thought. Her family didn't seem to be putting her down or belittling her chosen career. As far as he could see, Gwen didn't have anything to prove to them.

"What?"

"Putting in some ungodly hours." He wondered if Gwen saw the same family trait as he did, or was she too close to the situation to make that call?

"Oh, you can't compare what I do to what Sydney and Jocelyn do all day. That would be like comparing the Baltimore Ravens to a pee-wee football team for six-year-olds."

Daniel sat there and listened to Gwen's words play over and over in his mind. Gwen wasn't trying to prove anything to her family. She was trying to prove it to herself.

Chapter Sixteen

Gwen stood in the warmth of the dining room at the patio doors and watched Hunter and Daniel try to plant the bushes they had picked up that morning. The bushes weren't the little twigs one usually bought in five-gallon bucket. They appeared nearly full-grown already. Mary Creighton had wanted that view of the back parking lot blocked, and she didn't want to wait years' worth of growing seasons to do it. Gwen had agreed, and the money had been spent on more mature bushes and trees.

Hunter and Daniel had dug the holes and were trying to position the first tree, a nice-size pine, that would fill the corner against the wall nicely. Jonah and Clarence were supervising or arguing; it was hard to tell from her position inside. She wasn't going out there and get dragged into something she knew nothing about. Heck, last Christmas she hadn't even put up an artificial Christmas tree in her apartment. What would she know about a live one?

Daniel was on one side of the tree, Hunter on the other. The tree topped both men by a good foot, and it appeared full and healthy. Jonah was supervising Daniel and directing him to turn it one way. Clarence was instructing his son, Hunter, to lean the tree one way and then another. Daniel and Hunter were tugging and pulling, and twisting and leaning. Daniel's latest tug knocked Hunter's cap off.

She tried not to laugh, but she couldn't prevent the amusement that bubbled up inside her. It looked like a comedy routine—the four stooges, instead of the usual three, go gardening. Daniel shot her an exasperated look. She smiled and waved. Daniel sent her a quick smile that stole her heart and then went back to arguing with Jonah and Clarence.

The sound of someone opening the front door pulled her away from the enticing view of Daniel in tight jeans and a flannel shirt. An older woman stepped into the restaurant and softly closed the door behind her. Gwen eyed the woman and couldn't decide if she was waitress material or a part-time cook. Either one she'd take, though she especially wanted to fill the waitressing position.

She crossed the room, put on her most welcoming smile, and stuck out her hand. "Hi, I'm Gwen Fletcher."

The woman shook her hand and smiled softly. "Tess Dunbar."

"Dunbar? Scott Dunbar's mother?" Scott was one of the dishwashers she had just hired. This was the widow of Ben Dunbar, who had been killed in the boating accident that had scarred Daniel. Tess Dunbar didn't look old enough to have a grandchild in second grade.

"That's me." A slight blush swept up her cheeks. "Some mothers might not admit to being the mother to someone who looks like Scott, but that's not me. I love my children, warts and all."

Gwen immediately liked the woman and smiled. "I didn't notice any warts, but I bet you he couldn't pass through a metal detector at an airport without setting it off."

"Yet you hired him anyway." Tess didn't seem offended by Gwen's humor, just curious.

"He was honest with me, and seemed willing to work." She nodded to one of the tables and chairs. "Let's sit." She didn't know what position Tess was applying for, and she wasn't sure about having a mother and son working at the same place, but she was short on personnel. Beggars couldn't be choosers.

Tess looked out the patio doors at the men working or arguing, depending on the moment. Her gaze seemed to linger for a long moment before she pulled it away and sat. "Thanks, but I only have a moment. I'm on my lunch break."

"You already have a job?"

"Yes, I'm the receptionist for the Sheriff's Department." Tess looked confused for a moment, but then she smiled. "I get it; you thought I was applying for a job?"

"I wish you *were* applying for a job. I still have a couple of positions to fill." Gwen tried to follow Tess's gaze, to see what was so fascinating out on the patio. She knew what interested her, but somehow she didn't think Tess was eyeing Daniel. Jonah and Clarence seemed a tad old for Tess, so that left Hunter. Interesting.

"No, I'm sorry." Tess pulled her gaze away from the patio doors. "I came here to welcome you to Misty Harbor and to thank you for giving Scott a chance. I know a lot of people and different groups and clubs have dropped by, and most seem to want something from you or the restaurant. I just want you to know, there are people living here who are just so darn happy that you're opening the restaurant back up, and we don't want anything from you except good food."

Gwen grinned. "Looks like I just got another customer." Now that they were sitting in the light coming in from the patio doors, she could see that Tess wasn't as young as she had originally thought. She placed the woman at about fifty instead of forty. "You don't have to thank me for hiring Scott. He'll have to work for his wages."

Tess nodded and quietly said, "I heard the Citizens for a Better Tomorrow Club paid you a visit."

"Ah, little perky Sandi with an *i*, and Janet with one very long list of last names." Gwen smiled. Now Tess's thanks made sense. The club hadn't wanted her to hire any of the so-called "freaks." Scott, with assorted piercings and bald head, probably made their top-ten list. "Last I heard it was a free country. I can hire whom I want, and if someone doesn't want to patronize my restaurant, they don't have to."

Tess returned her smile. "As a mother I have to love him, no matter what he looks like. I understand that by looking so different, Scott tends to put people on the offensive."

"Only small-minded people, who judge others by their appearance, not by their deeds." *Like Daniel's ex-fiancée.* Gwen couldn't imagine what it must have been like for Tess when she lost her husband five years ago. "I understand that Scott lost his father when he was twelve. I imagine any age would be rough, but I think at twelve it could be devastating." Scott had been totally honest and up front with her during his job interview. He needed a paycheck to pay damages and fines on some mischief he had caused. The local high school hadn't appreciated Scott's amateur attempts at poetry combined with his artistic abilities with a can of spray paint.

"He took it the hardest of all the kids. Scott was extremely close to his father. Marie was already married and out of the house, and Jason was sixteen at the time."

"Cars and girlfriends?" Everyone knew that to a sixteen-year-old boy, only two things mattered: cars and the opposite sex. She didn't have to be a parent to guess that one.

"Jason had both. He was at the age where he was pulling away from the family and becoming an individual. Not that he didn't grieve for his father; he did. But with Scott it was different. Ben and he were just starting to enjoy themselves and each other. They liked to go camping and hiking together, and finally Scott was old enough to match his father's stamina."

A sad longing darkened Tess's light blue eyes. Gwen remembered that Scott had the same eyes. " 'I'm sorry' seems so inadequate."

"I call it missed opportunities." Tess's gaze once again went to the patio beyond the glass doors. "Life's full of them."

Gwen turned and watched as all four men stomped and grumbled their way into the dining room. She also noticed that all the men wiped their feet before stepping onto her brand-new carpet. She closely watched Hunter's expression. The man seemed shocked to find Tess sitting there talking to her. The three other men shot quick glances at Hunter and then at Tess.

"Hi, Tess," Daniel said as he walked over to their table. "Long time no see."

"I've been around." Tess stood up and smiled at Jonah and Clarence. All of a sudden Tess seemed not to want to look at Hunter.

"Afternoon, Tess," Jonah said before he headed for the kitchen and probably a cup of coffee to warm his insides.

Gwen felt funny sitting, so she stood up and moved to Daniel's side. Daniel wrapped his arm around her waist and pulled her closer. He brought in the scent of sea mist and pine.

Clarence's smile held fondness and a touch of hope as he stared at the woman before him. "How have you been doing, Tess?"

"Just fine, Clarence, and yourself?"

"Never been better." Clarence nudged Hunter.

Hunter was staring at Tess as if she were the most precious thing in the universe, and he couldn't have her. His head slowly nodded in greeting, but he didn't say anything. Gwen resisted the urge to kick his shin.

Tess nodded back. The longing in Tess's eyes nearly broke her heart.

Gwen couldn't stand the silence any longer. There was past history here; she hadn't a clue what it involved, but whatever had happened between Hunter and Tess wasn't over. "Tess, this is Hunter. He's going to be the one taking Scott under his wing and showing him the ropes."

"That's good." Tess blinked and pulled her gaze away from Hunter. "I have to go or I'm going to be late." She picked up her purse. "Thanks, Ms. Fletcher, for everything, and again, welcome to Misty Harbor." Tess glanced pointedly at Daniel's possessive hold. "I see you're settling in quite nicely."

Gwen grinned. "It's a friendly little village, I'll give you that." Daniel gave her a hard squeeze as Tess chuckled and closed the door behind her.

Clarence headed for the kitchen. Daniel pulled her in that direction too. "I could use something hot right about now." Daniel leaned down and whispered, "Since I can't have you, I'll settle for coffee."

Gwen turned and looked back at Hunter as she entered the kitchen. The swinging doors gave her a flickering view of Hunter standing exactly where they had left him. He was still staring at the door Tess had closed behind her.

Gwen cradled the cup of hot coffee between her hands and stared out Daniel's kitchen door toward the rising sun. It looked like it was going to be another beautiful spring day in Maine. Daniel's robe warmed her on the outside, while the coffee warmed her on the inside. Daniel was still upstairs sleeping, but she had been jerked awake by a nightmare.

It was the same nightmare that had been plaguing her for weeks. The dream was always the same. Customers had been arriving at the restaurant, and nothing was ready. The tables weren't set and nothing was cooking in the kitchen. None of the employees she had hired had shown up for work, and the plumbing in one of the bathrooms was broken. Water was gushing everywhere and flooding her new carpeting. Hunter spent the entire nightmare chasing live lobsters around the waterlogged dining-room floor. This morning's dream had a new element of disaster thrown in: She had been running from kitchen to dining room to upstairs office looking for her lists. She hadn't been able to find any of them.

Daniel had told her the other night that she was going to give herself a nervous breakdown if she didn't start relaxing. He was positive the restaurant was going to be a huge success. He had assured her that even the residents of Sullivan were talking about how they couldn't wait for the opening. She should have been thrilled. Instead she was now more nervous; what would happen if she didn't live up to the customers' expectations? They wouldn't come back, and she would be out of business by July.

Her family would have proof that she was a total failure.

Gwen frowned at her empty cup and went to refill it. Maybe what she needed was a vacation. A soft chuckle escaped her as she filled the cup. Like she would have time for a week off to go sun her buns on some Caribbean island. What she really needed was a good eight hours of sleep, and maybe a couple of therapy sessions thrown in for good measure.

Deep down inside her, she knew Catch of the Day was going to be a success. It had everything going for it, including her cooking. So why was she so worried? Why hadn't she invited her family to come up for the grand opening? Why was it that every time one of her sisters mentioned the grand opening she was the one to change the subject? Both her sisters and her parents seemed interested and excited about the restaurant.

Why was she raining on her own parade instead of enjoying it? This was her dream coming true. More importantly, why wasn't she inviting the people who mattered the most in her life to the parade and to her dream?

Maybe she really did need those therapy sessions.

She gave herself a mental shake, turned off the coffeemaker, and walked out of the kitchen. Instead of feeling sorry for herself, she should be upstair snuggling up to Daniel's warm and incredible body while watching the sun slowly climb its way above the horizon. Daniel had a way of welcoming in the new day that was guaranteed to put a smile on her face.

Still cradling her coffee, she headed upstairs to Daniel and his king-size bed. At the top of the stairs she stopped to admire the way the sunlight, pouring out of his bedroom doorway, was creeping across the wooden floor. The golden glow went directly to the closed door of one of the spare bedrooms. She had never seen the inside of the bedrooms. They were probably empty, like the dining room, but curiosity compelled her to reach for the nearest brass doorknob.

Gwen opened the door, stepped into the room, and felt her heart lurch in shock. The room wasn't empty. It was completely furnished, which normally wouldn't have surprised her. What it was furnished with was the shock. Total astonishment and confusion was more like it.

She stepped farther into the room and glanced around, trying to blink the room into a clearer focus. It took her a moment, but she soon realized that the reason the room was looking fuzzy wasn't because of the shock; it was the dust. A thick layer of dust covered everything, giving the room a sad and neglected appearance.

Pale pastel wallpaper, with cute little bunnies, covered two interior walls. A wooden crib, completely made up with a bunny quilt and matching sheets, was the main focus of the room. In a daze she walked over to the crib and stared at the large, adorable pink bunny sitting in the corner of the crib. A mobile, with dancing bunnies, was attached to the far side of the crib.

She looked away from the crib and glanced at the other items in the room, hoping she could make some sense of this. What in the world was Daniel doing with a baby's nursery in his house? The antique rocker near the window couldn't answer her question. The yellow curtains, with cute bunny trim, were faded from what appeared to be years of sunlight. The oak dresser was covered in a coat of dust so thick she could not only write her name in it, but if she gathered it up she could possibly build a miniature dust castle.

The faded braided rug beneath her feet muffled her footsteps as she crossed to the window and the items that had captured her attention. In slow motion, she placed her cup on the small table that had been placed before the window. Her fingers trembled as she picked up one of the dozen or so carved animals. The giraffe was just as beautifully carved as Daniel's other animals, but it had been made for little fingers and the rough-and-tumble abuse only a child could dish out. The other giraffe was just as graceful.

Noah's ark was a good-size boat that could easily hold all the wonderful animals that Daniel had carved. Pairs of monkeys, camels, elephants, and lions were placed around the table and the ark. Two horses and a pair of bears stood on the deck of the ark. Daniel had gone to a lot of time and trouble to make such an exquisite set.

But who was it for? Daniel didn't have any children. He claimed never to have been married, only to have been engaged once. The engagement had ended when the boating accident had occurred. So why this sad, heartbreaking nursery?

She picked up the male lion and tenderly brushed the dust off his mane with the sleeve of Daniel's robe.

"What in the hell are you doing?" Daniel's angry voice boomed into the room.

She quickly turned around and stared at Daniel, who was still standing in the doorway, as if he were afraid to enter the room. Her fist clenched around the lion as she held it out to him. "I was dusting the lion."

"Put it back."

"I'm sorry, Daniel. I just wanted to see what the room looked like." She didn't think he would appreciate the fact that she had followed the sunlight. With tender care she positioned the lion in the exact spot where he had been standing, for what appeared to be years.

"You were snooping." Daniel glanced around the room as if inspecting to see what else she had touched. "This room is off limits."

She crossed her arms and glared at him. "I can see you're upset, Daniel. That doesn't give you the right to be rude and nasty." She had never seen Daniel like this before. The scar bisecting his cheek was red against his usually pale face. The flannel pajama bottoms hung low on his hips and his hair was sleep-tossed. There was a wild look about his eyes. "You never said I couldn't come into this room."

"You never asked to go into it," Daniel said. "I didn't expect you to sneak out of my bed in the middle of the night and go poking around where you don't belong."

The hurt slammed into her with more force than she could have expected. She actually took a step back from the blow. "I don't belong?" There it was: the plain, simple truth. She didn't belong in

Daniel's house. Maybe she didn't belong in Misty Harbor, or even the restaurant business. She should have been a doctor or a lawyer like the rest of the family. One thing was for certain—she didn't belong in this solemn nursery with its empty crib and years of dust.

Daniel held out a hand in apology, but he didn't cross the room to her. "Gwen, I didn't mean that."

Tears filled her eyes, but she refused to allow them to fall. Daniel looked like he wanted to come to her, but something was holding him back. For some reason, he couldn't bring himself to enter the room. "Did you have a baby, Daniel?" Could some woman have given Daniel a child, and then something happened to the child so that he or she never got to enjoy this room?

"No, women have babies, not men."

"Real funny. Did you father a child?" Daniel was avoiding looking directly at her. His gaze seemed to be studying the dust patterns across the floor.

"No woman ever carried my child, if that's what you're asking, Gwen."

"Then explain to me"—she waved her hand in the direction of the crib—"about this?"

"It was a mistake." Daniel turned and walked away.

She stood there, breathing in dust and fighting tears, as he disappeared into the master bedroom. No explanations. No excuses. A grown man, living alone, with no steady girlfriend, fiancée, or wife on the scene didn't convert one of his spare bedrooms into a bunny-filled nursery without a reason. It must have taken Daniel months to carve the animals and to build the ark. So why did he do it? There had to be a reason, a sensible reason.

Daniel was a reasonable man. He hadn't done this on a whim. Whatever his reason had been, he wasn't sharing it with her. That was what hurt the most, Daniel not sharing. Discovering a nursery behind one of Daniel's bedroom doors had been a shock, but it hadn't hurt.

Daniel walking away had hurt. It felt like he had ripped her heart out and taken it with him.

Tears rolled down her cheeks as she looked around at the room and the love that must have gone into it. For some unexplained reason, she knew it had been Daniel who had picked out the bunny print wallpaper and the rest of the furnishings. This was Daniel's life and his secret, and he refused to share it with her.

Daniel had been right: She didn't belong here.

Gwen gave the ark set one last look and then walked out of the room, making sure she closed the door behind her.

The first thing she saw as she walked through the master bedroom was Daniel standing on the deck outside. He was facing the rising sun and the choppy ocean. A good stiff breeze was ruffling his hair, but he didn't seem to notice the cold. The only thing Daniel was wearing were the pajama bottoms she'd had so much fun removing last night.

She swiped at her tears as she entered the bathroom and quickly got dressed. Within two minutes she was out the front door and driving home. She didn't look back.

Maggie stared up at the sign. Catch of the Day was sure to be a hit in Misty Harbor. Everyone was talking about it, and from what she'd heard, it was bound to be a success. Misty Harbor, and the surrounding area, could use a "fine dining" establishment. The last person to open the restaurant had thought lobsters only came boiled, and that tuna fish sandwiches were a delicacy.

She didn't want to apply for a job waitressing. She wanted to use what skills she possessed and work in an office, honing those skills and building some more. It wasn't to be. She had applied for every available and even the unavailable part-time jobs within thirty miles of her parents' home. No luck.

Hopefully this Gwen Fletcher, who was new to Misty Harbor, wouldn't have heard the stories about her. Maggie needed this job desperately. Even though her parents hadn't asked her for a cent since she moved back home weeks ago, she still felt obligated to pay them something every week. Katie was growing and would soon be needing summer clothes. Textbooks were ridiculously expensive, and she was going to be needing gas money. Then there were the fall courses she needed to graduate.

Maggie took a deep breath, put on her best friendly smile, and opened the door. Total chaos, and the ringing of a bell, greeted her. Boxes were everywhere. The entire dining room appeared to be flooded with boxes.

"Hello to whoever just came in," a pleasant female voice called from behind a stack of boxes.

"Hello back." Maggie stepped around a small mountain of boxes and smiled at the woman kneeling on the floor, inspecting a box full of glasses. Water glasses, if she wasn't mistaken. "If you're busy, I could come back."

"Depends on what you're selling."

"I'm not selling a thing." Maggie glanced around the room with approval. The stories going around town were true: Gwen Fletcher was doing a wonderful job fixing up the restaurant. Maybe it wouldn't be such a bad place to work after all. Dinner tips might be decent. "I'm here to apply for a job." She had paid particular attention to her outfit this afternoon, knowing she was applying for a waitressing position. She had worn a plain black skirt, a green blouse to match her eyes, and sensible shoes. Change her blouse to white and she would look like a waitress.

The woman stood up and grinned. "Please tell me you have experience waiting tables."

"Would you like to see the blisters?" Maggie held out her hand, prayed real hard, and blurted out her name. "Maggie Pierce, and I have over five years' experience."

"Gwen Fletcher." Gwen shook her hand. "What hours can you work?"

There had been a flare of recognition in Gwen's eyes, but the woman didn't seem put off by who was shaking her hand. "Just about anything you can give me. Starting in June I'll be attending college on Monday and Wednesday mornings. In September I'm planning on going back for at least four courses during the days, but I can still work nights and weekends."

Gwen cleared a box off a table, nodded to the opposite chair, and sat. "You're a college student?"

Maggie sat, wondering how much to tell Gwen. In a town the size of Misty Harbor, the truth was always the best bet, because eventually everyone knew everyone else's business anyway. "I only have a year to go; then I'll be graduating next May."

"Ambitious?"

"Desperate is more like it." Maggie dug through her purse and pulled out the most recent photo of Katie. It had been taken at Christmas, and Katie looked like an angel to her. "I'm a single mom, now that my divorce is final." She slid the picture across the table. "This is my daughter, and the love of my life, Katie. I need the college degree to get a good job so I can support us both. In the meanwhile we just moved in with my parents, so baby-sitting won't be a problem when it comes to my job or the hours."

Gwen picked up the photo and studied it for a moment. "She looks like you." No one looking at this woman sitting across from her and the adorable freckle-faced girl in the photo would mistake them for anything but mother and daughter. She had recognized Maggie's name from the gossipers at the grocery store several weeks ago. Maggie's husband had left her and their child for another women. The man was a fool. "When can you start?"

Maggie flashed her a smile. "Yesterday."

She chuckled. "We don't open for another week, but if you want some hours this week I could use some extra help." Gwen pointed to a stack of boxes. "It seems everything I've been ordering for weeks is arriving at the same time. The upstair storage area has recently been painted, and it's totally empty."

Clarence and Jonah had taken a couple of days off, now that the restaurant was nearly ready for its opening. They had headed for Vermont this morning, to visit an old friend. The boxes had started to arrive en masse within five minutes of their departure. Hunter was in the kitchen painting shelves and Daniel was ignoring her and installing the warming lamps above the counter. She didn't want to think of Daniel and the scene at his house yesterday morning. They had been avoiding each other ever since she had left his house.

"It's getting late today, but what do you say about a couple of hours tomorrow?" Gwen reached behind her and picked up a blank application from the other table. "Fill this out and bring it back in with you."

"What time do you want me here?" Maggie took the application and slid it and Katie's picture back into her purse.

"Anytime after nine will be fine." Gwen shook her hand. "Welcome aboard, Maggie, and wear jeans and sneakers. The next couple of days are going to make your blisters scream."

Chapter Seventeen

Gwen unlocked the back door of the restaurant and let herself in. Breakfast this morning was going to consist of the oatmeal raisin muffins she had baked at three in the morning and coffee. She had baked them because Hunter might be hungry, and she had been pacing the floors since one in the morning. She couldn't sleep. She couldn't eat. All because of one man.

One hardheaded, stubborn, and secretive man named Daniel. At three in the morning she had been furious at that stubborn man for breaking her heart. By four o'clock she had been curled up on the couch crying into a pillow. At five o'clock she had been cleaning out the refrigerator and scrubbing the kitchen floor. By six she had gone out jogging, only to end up walking along the docks and the rocky shoreline. Watching the sun rise had only made her think of Daniel and the mornings they had shared in his bed.

Now, at eight o'clock in the morning, she was so exhausted she was beginning to doubt she would make it to lunchtime without a nap. To add insult to injury, she had nearly given herself a heart attack when she had glanced in a mirror this morning. She had looked like a horror movie extra. No amount of makeup could cover the dark circles beneath her eyes. She hadn't even tried to repair the damage.

She put the bag containing the muffins on the counter and started a pot of coffee. Sitting on a rock this morning watching the sun rise, she had come to a couple of startling conclusions, the first being that the breakup with Daniel hadn't been her fault. She was so used to taking the blame for anything that went wrong in her life that she had at first assumed she had done something wrong. Like she was supposed to have psychic powers and know not to open that bedroom door. The whole episode had been Daniel's fault, and then he had compounded the situation by refusing to talk about it.

If he loved her, he would have talked.

Daniel was the one missing out on a wonderful woman. Plenty of men wanted to take her out. Hell, she had been asked out by so many men in this town she had lost count. Just because she didn't want to go out with any of them didn't mean a thing.

She was pouring her first cup of coffee as Hunter walked in the back door. "Morning, Gwen." Hunter hung up his coat next to hers, but left his baseball cap on. "It's going to be a gorgeous day today. Weatherman is predicting it might reach sixty."

"Great." She handed Hunter a cup of coffee.

"I met Daniel on the road into town, and he just dropped me off." Hunter took a sip of his coffee.

"He said to tell you he had a couple of things to do this morning, and then he's picking up the paint for the fence. We'll be painting it today, if that's okay with you."

"That's fine." Daniel was still obviously avoiding her. "With the nice weather coming, maybe you and Daniel can get the outside trim painted before the opening." She put the muffins onto a plate and slid it onto the counter. The most important thing in her life right now had to be the restaurant. It was her livelihood. Her dream.

"We'll try." Hunter picked up a muffin and gave her a concerned look. "I told you before that you don't have to supply breakfast, Gwen. I think, as your assistant, I should be able to fix my own breakfast."

"I know, but at three in the morning I got this sudden urge to bake." It was either bake something or drive to Daniel's and demand to know why he had broken her heart.

She could see the questions in Hunter's gaze. The questions had been there for two days now, ever since Daniel and she had arrived separately at the restaurant and barely spoken a word to each other. Hunter was too much of a gentleman to voice those questions.

It was a good thing Jonah and Clarence were still in Vermont visiting their friend. Neither one of them would think twice about asking her what the hell was going on between her and Daniel. The first time Daniel and she had arrived at the restaurant together, Jonah had practically welcomed her into the family. Jonah would want to know what went wrong, and the only thing she could tell him was that she'd opened a closed bedroom door.

She didn't know the answers to Hunter's unasked questions.

* * *

An hour later, Gwen found herself knee-deep in boxes, showing Maggie what needed to be done. "This stack of boxes are the tablecloths and napkins I ordered. I already checked out the colors to make sure they're what I ordered. I need you to make sure the quantity matches the packing slip, and then just check to make sure there's nothing wrong with each item. There's no room in the kitchen, so we're going to have to store them upstairs."

"Check." Maggie stood there looking well rested and raring to go.

Gwen would have hated her, except it was her restaurant she was raring to go at. A quick glance at Maggie's application had shown that they were the same age. So why wasn't she looking as fresh and perky this early in the morning? "Any boxes with computer supplies, just haul them upstairs to my office. I'll check them against the packing slips. One of these boxes has the engraved menu holders I ordered. I saw them yesterday, but I can't find them this morning. That box goes upstairs too."

Maggie looked in the box sitting on the table in front of her. "Vases?"

"They can go in the kitchen for now."

"Do you want me to check them against the packing slip?"

"Yes, everything gets checked." Gwen felt the beginning of a headache coming on. All this stuff had to be cleared out of here within the next two days, before the food started to arrive. "The biggest job will be unpacking, washing, and then putting away the new dishes I bought. The old set we're going to use serving lunch, but I wanted something better for dinner."

"Okay." Maggie pushed up the sleeves of her

baggy University of Maine sweatshirt. Her red hair was pulled back in a ponytail, and not a speck of makeup covered the freckles dusting her nose and cheeks. "You go take care of whatever you need to do, Ms. Fletcher. I can handle the unpacking, and even the dishwashing, if it comes to that." Maggie's green eyes sparkled with excitement as she picked up the first box of tablecloths. "This is like Christmas morning."

Gwen chuckled. "Call me Gwen, Maggie. If you need anything and can't find me around, just ask Hunter. He's in the kitchen tossing out the chipped dishes and washing up the ones that pass his inspection."

Maggie headed for the stairs and flashed her a smile over her shoulder. "Will do, Gwen."

She returned Maggie's gesture with her first smile in three days. Maggie's enthusiasm was contagious. With her help, they should have the dining room cleared out in no time. She might even manage to get an hour or two on the computer to try to figure out how to print out the menus.

Gwen turned and groaned as the front door opened. A stack of chairs was being wheeled in by a man wearing blue overalls.

"Hey, lady, where do you want these?" the man asked.

"Anywhere you can find the room." She glanced around the already crowded room and suppressed the urge to scream. The tables and chairs she had ordered to replace the booths had finally arrived.

The man glanced around the room and then gave her a look that had to be saying, "You've got to be kidding!" "There's a whole lot more on the truck, lady."

She started to pull tables together to give the man some room, but if he called her *lady* one more time, she wouldn't be responsible for what she might do. "You just bring them in; I'll figure out where to put them."

The man removed the stack of eight chairs from his dolly and headed back out the door. "No problem, lady."

Gwen glared at the man's back and yanked on the table she was pulling so hard, she would have landed on her butt if it hadn't been for Daniel. Strong hands came up behind her and steadied her waist as she regained her balance. She knew whose hands they were just from the jolt of awareness shooting through her body.

"Easy, Gwen," Daniel said. He held her against his body longer than necessary, and then he slowly lowered his hands over her hips. Daniel's voice sounded shaky when he asked, "What are you trying to do?"

It took her a moment to get her breath back. "I need to make room in here for eight more tables and thirty-two chairs."

"The chairs shouldn't be a problem, but the tables might." Daniel started moving tables closer together. "What's with all the boxes?"

"Most of them should be out of here today. One of the waitresses I hired is already upstairs unpacking stuff."

"Okay. How about if you just keep the tables out front until the end of the day? Hunter and I will bring them in for you once we finish painting the fence." Daniel's gaze never left her face. "The weather is perfect, and no one is going to steal them or anything."

"Fine." She studied Daniel's face. He looked as bad as she felt. Two of the walking wounded, and she hadn't even known a battle had been waged. Until Daniel was ready to open up and talk to her, there was nothing she could do. "I'll go tell Hunter you're here."

"He already knows." Daniel looked at her as if he had something else to say. Something important.

She waited anxiously.

"If the weather holds, we should have all the trim painted before the opening."

Gwen felt disappointment wash over her. "Fine." She turned away and headed for the kitchen.

Daniel reached out a hand, but he was too late. His fingers held nothing but air. Maggie Franklin Pierce's voice stopped his words before he could call Gwen back.

"Gwen, do you want me to do the dishes first, or the linens?" Maggie practically skipped down the last two steps and bounced into the dining room.

Gwen turned toward Maggie and frowned as the other woman came to a halt and stared at Daniel as if she had seen a ghost. Every freckle stood out against her pale complexion. Gwen looked at Daniel to see his reaction. He looked furious at finding Maggie in the restaurant. Neither said a word.

She looked at Maggie and saw tears fill her remarkable green eyes. What in the world was going on? "Maggie?" She would have been jealous of the beautiful redhead, but she hadn't seen desire in Daniel's gaze. Only pain and anger had filled his gray eyes.

Maggie turned and rapidly blinked her eyes. A tear rolled down her left cheek. "I'll leave," Maggie whispered and took a step toward the front door.

Gwen stepped in front of her. She didn't know what was going on between Maggie and Daniel, but one thing she did know was that she needed Maggie at the restaurant. Experienced waitresses in Misty Harbor were as rare as cowboys and rodeo clowns. "You can't leave, Maggie. I need you here." She turned and picked up a box of cloth napkins and shoved it into her arms. "Why don't you go put these away? I'll be with you in a minute."

Maggie gave her a grateful smile. "Are you sure?"

"Positive."

Gwen watched as Maggie disappeared back up the stairs. Maggie must have been Daniel's ex-fiancée. It was the only thing that made sense. She'd only just met Maggie, but the young woman didn't strike her as the kind of person who would dump a man because of a scar. Maggie had been staring at Daniel with regret, not revulsion.

"Maggie was your fiancée five years ago, wasn't she?" She turned and faced Daniel.

"Yes."

She mulled that one over and thought about the picture of Maggie's daughter, Katie. Maggie had said her daughter was four years and some months old. Their engagement had ended five years ago. Could Katie be Daniel's daughter? Katie was the spitting image of her mother from her bright red hair to her startling green eyes and her face full of freckles. It didn't seem possible. From what she knew of Daniel, there was no way he wouldn't be active in his own child's life. So who had the nursery been built for, and why was Daniel so upset by just running into Maggie?

Was it possible that Daniel still loved Maggie? Daniel had never once told her that he loved her, only that he wanted and needed her. She might be deluding herself, but she honestly didn't think Daniel was still in love with Maggie. He never would have made love to her the way he had, if he was still pining for another woman. Daniel felt something for her, but the question was, was it love or just lust?

When Daniel had looked at Maggie, there hadn't been love or lust in his gaze. Whatever his problem was, it concerned Maggie. The best way for him to work out his problem, and give them a chance of getting their relationship back on track, was to force him to confront Maggie.

"I see," Gwen lied. She didn't see anything. The only thing she knew was that Daniel and Maggie had once been engaged. Rolling the dice, and risking any chance they might have at future happiness, she said, "Maggie's now my employee. I expect you to treat her as such."

Gwen's fingers trembled as she picked up the last box of tablecloths and headed for the stairs. She held her breath and waited for Daniel to stop her. To explain. He never did.

The flight of steps that led to the upstairs office and storage area was the longest she'd ever climbed. There was silence below her, and the higher she climbed the more she picked up on the sound of weeping.

Maggie was crying, and Gwen didn't know if she had the strength to confront Daniel's ex-fiancée. Hearing him directing the deliveryman as to where to put the next stack of chairs gave her the courage to walk into her office.

Maggie was sitting at the desk with her face buried in a handful of tissues. As soon as she realized she was no longer alone, she jumped up and immediately started to apologize. "I'm sorry, Gwen. I hadn't realized that Daniel would be working here."

She waved Maggie back into the seat and pulled an old dining-room chair closer and sat down. "Daniel's doing the renovations on the restaurant." She wondered how much to tell Maggie and decided on the truth. Maggie would find out sooner or later anyway. "Daniel is a whole lot more than just a carpenter to me, though."

Maggie wiped her eyes and smiled as understanding dawned. "I'm glad he found someone like you."

Gwen shifted uncomfortably on the chair. Anyone who spent more than two minutes in the same room with Daniel and Gwen would know something was wrong. "Things are a little *tense* right now between us."

"Oh?"

She watched Maggie's eyes, but hope never leaped into them. Maggie didn't appear to be harboring any hopes and dreams of reconciling with Daniel. "I know you were once his fiancée. You broke the engagement off while he was in the hospital recuperating from an accident."

Maggie winced. "I can't deny that the timing was horrible."

Gwen raised an eyebrow at that one. "Daniel seems to think that the scar he received scared you off."

"Lord, no. I told him and told him that wasn't the reason." Tears once again started to flow. Maggie reached for more tissues.

"What was the reason, if I may ask?" Daniel should have been the one telling her this, but for some reason, Maggie and Daniel had different stories of how their engagement had ended.

"It's a long story." Maggie blew her nose and reached for more tissues.

Gwen's mouth curved up. "I'm paying you by the hour."

"You'll be firing me by the end of it." Maggie wiped her eyes again. "Don't worry, I won't take it too hard. To tell you the truth, I've been expecting to be canned as soon as you hired me."

"Did you do something illegal?"

"Illegal, no. Immoral, yes." Maggie gave a sniffle, but the waterworks seemed to have slowed to a trickle. "I can't regret what I did, and I did try to correct it and do the 'right thing,' but I only ended up hurting Daniel more."

"Can you start at the beginning?"

"In this town a girl, or a woman, has her choice of men. When I was twenty, I went after the town's catch and caught him."

"Daniel?"

"Daniel." Maggie gave her a small smile. "At twenty-four Daniel had his own business, a breath-taking piece of property on the bluff overlooking the ocean, and the beginnings of a gorgeous log house. He was everything I was taught a woman would want in a husband. He was handsome, hard-working, kind, and generous. Daniel even supported the idea of me going to college and having a career along with a family." Maggie bit her lower lip and studied the balled-up tissues clasped in her hand. "What wasn't there to love about him?"

"Did you love him?" Gwen's heart gave a sudden lurch as she waited for Maggie's answer.

"I thought I did." Maggie shrugged but wouldn't meet her gaze. "Did it really matter that fireworks never went off when we were . . . let's say intimate?" A fiery blush stained Maggie's cheeks.

Gwen closed her eyes against the vivid image of this gorgeous woman and Daniel tangled up in the sheets of his king-size bed as the sun rose above the ocean. "You were lovers?" It was a stupid question, and she regretted asking it as soon as she did. Of course they were lovers. They had been engaged, hadn't they?

"Lovers? No. We were intimate on a few occasions, but I wouldn't call us lovers. There was something missing, but I was too blinded by all the qualities a woman is supposed to look for in a man to notice."

Gwen looked at Maggie in confusion. How could Maggie sit there and not think Daniel was the most perfect lover ever to come to a woman? Not only was Daniel's body perfection, but he was so darn incredible in bed, her body practically wept every night he had been gone. Maggie was either frigid enough to sink the *Titanic,* or Daniel had been practicing one hell of a lot in the last five years. She prayed Maggie was frigid.

"Right before I came home for summer break in my junior year I went to a party in one of the dorms. I met a fellow student and fell instantly in lust. In the heat of the moment we made love without protection. A few weeks after I was home in Misty Harbor I realized I was pregnant. I told Daniel, and he naturally assumed the baby was his."

Gwen cringed but stayed silent.

"The baby's father hadn't made any commitment to me, and he was still a college student. I knew Daniel would make a wonderful husband and father. For weeks I was torn as to what to do, and Daniel kept pressuring me to move up the wedding date. He didn't want his child being born before we were married.

"The day of the boat accident in the harbor changed everything. Daniel had put his own life in jeopardy to save that little boy. He was a true hero, and he deserved the truth. I couldn't pass off another man's child as his. My mistake was telling him the truth while he was still in the hospital."

"He didn't believe you, did he?"

"No, he thought I was breaking off the engagement because of the mess his face was. I'd be the first one to admit to you that Daniel looked horrible after the accident, but I never would have left him because of that. The doctors tried to reassure me that the swelling and discoloration would go away over time, and they didn't believe me when

I told them Daniel's appearance wasn't upsetting me. I was three months pregnant, hurting the one man who didn't deserved to be hurt anymore, and was terrified of telling my family what I had done.''

"What did you do?''

"Drove back to Bangor, found Jeremy, and made him marry me to give our child a name. I dropped out of college and started waiting tables to support us while Jeremy got his degree. Daniel followed me to Bangor and wasn't real happy to find me married to another man. He insisted that the baby was his, and nothing short of a DNA test would satisfy him. Daniel didn't want me back; he wanted his child, and he was very vocal about it. The entire town of Misty Harbor knew every embarrassing detail.''

Visions of bunny wallpaper filled her mind. Daniel had spent the months waiting for his child to be born completing the nursery and carving animals for Noah's ark. Gwen felt tears fill her own eyes and rapidly blinked them away. Maggie was crying enough for the both of them.

"The initial blood test they did proved Daniel couldn't have fathered Katie.'' Maggie wiped away a small river of fresh tears. "I regret hurting Daniel that way, but I can't regret what happened in that dorm room five years ago. I conceived the best thing in my life that night, Katie.''

Gwen nodded slowly. She now understood what the nursery had meant to Daniel, and why he had closed the door. The child he had been waiting for wasn't even his. Daniel was a very private person, and to have the whole town know about Maggie cheating on him while they were engaged must have been a low blow.

Daniel had told her that the reason he never asked her out, like the rest of the men in town, was because he refused to be made a fool of. She didn't consider the other men fools, but she now understood Daniel's reasoning. If she hadn't been the one to practically ask Daniel out, they might never have gotten together. Daniel's hurt went deep.

She reached out and touched Maggie's hand. "Thank you."

Maggie raised her head and stared at her in confusion. "For what?"

"For telling me what was obviously a very painful story, and for telling Daniel the truth five years ago. You did the right thing—maybe at the wrong time, but it was the right thing to do."

"I keep reminding myself how much worse it would have been to have married Daniel and have the truth come out now, or even in the future. Jeremy might not have been the best husband or father, but he was the right one."

"Imagine how much worse it would be to find out your boss was in love with your husband."

"You're in love with Daniel?" Maggie gave her a watery grin. "Now I know I'm fired, but somehow that's okay."

"You're not fired." Gwen stood up and gently pushed Maggie toward the small powder room. "Go splash some cold water on your face; we've got boxes to unpack."

"What about Daniel?"

"What about him?"

"He's not going to be too happy with me working here." Maggie stopped in the doorway and refused to budge a step farther.

"He'll get over it. In fact, I want you to promise not to hide from him." She knew that putting Daniel and his old lover together would be taking a big chance, but she was willing to take that risk. Daniel needed to work out his problem, and to do that he needed to confront it. Having Maggie around would force him to face the problem.

"Are you sure?"

"Positive."

Daniel stared at the blue paint chips on the card in front of him. One was a shade darker than Gwen had picked out for the trim on the outside of the restaurant, the other a shade lighter. No matter which way he held the cards up to the light, they didn't match.

Just like his preconceived notion of Maggie wasn't matching up to the woman who had been in Gwen's restaurant today. When Maggie had first come down those steps he had felt as if someone had taken a two-by-four and whammed him in the head. He'd known she was back in town; he just hadn't expected that Gwen would have hired her.

All afternoon as he and Hunter had painted the fence he'd kept glancing through the patio doors. He had been hoping to catch a few glimpses of Gwen. Mostly he saw Maggie lugging boxes back and forth between the dining room and the kitchen. Amazingly, she seemed to be enjoying herself. The few times that he and Hunter had taken breaks, she had been quiet, but she hadn't run from the room or him.

Gwen, on the other hand, looked combative, as if she was expecting him to say something nasty to Maggie. He had a feeling that if he had said anything unpleasant, Gwen would have been the first one to jump down his throat. The entire situation was absurd.

The woman he loved was sticking up for the woman who had betrayed him five years ago. The day he understood women was the day he would be writing a *New York Times* best-seller and retiring a rich man. There was no use denying it any longer: He was in love with Gwen. He was fully, completely, to-death-do-us-part, happily-ever-after in love with a woman who made French toast just the way he liked it and could kiss him into a climax in under two minutes.

Gwen Fletcher also was barely talking to him, and it was all his fault. He'd take full blame for the fiasco the other morning when he climbed out of bed only to find Gwen standing in the nursery. A room he had closed the door to over four years ago. What in the world had ever possessed him to tell Gwen she didn't belong there? It was the nursery that didn't belong, not Gwen.

Lord, how he missed her. Not just in his bed, but in his life. His house was empty without her. The sun still rose every morning, but now instead of watching it with Gwen snuggled next to him, he buried his head beneath a pillow and prayed for rain.

Daniel angled the blue paint chips under the overhead lights. He wanted the trim to be perfect for Gwen's dream. He should go with the one-shade-darker blue. Paint faded easily beneath the relentless summer sun and the constant battering of sea mist.

"Hey, Daniel, how are you doing?" A young man wearing a business suit and carrying a box of lightbulbs stood next to him.

"Hey, Pete, how's life been treating you?" He and Pete Bencher had gone through high school together. They had been in some of the same classes, but their friendship had been forged on the baseball field, the year their team had won their division championship. Pete was one hell of a shortstop. Nowadays, Pete was an accountant.

"Good, and you?"

"Can't complain. Doing some work on the new

restaurant in town that will be opening Saturday night; then I've got two log houses going up this summer."

"Heard the woman who's opening that restaurant can really cook."

Daniel felt a stab of jealousy but reminded himself that Pete was a happily married man with a two-year-old son and another child on the way. "You heard right. Do yourself a favor and make some reservations. Janice will love it."

"Will do, and speaking of favors, I did you one the other day."

"You did?" He didn't remember anything special happening. "What was it?"

"Maggie Franklin came in looking for a job."

"The part-time one you've been advertising since Christmas?" Maggie sure was getting around town.

"Since Janice learned she was carrying number-two. She can handle the part-time work with just Kyle, but when the second one arrives, she wants to stay home full time."

"Can't blame her there. What's this got to do with Maggie or me?"

"I told Maggie she was overqualified." Pete smiled, as if he expected to be thanked profusely.

"Was she overqualified?" Daniel got the feeling he wasn't going to like the punch line.

"Damn straight she was." Pete chuckled. "I would have hired any other person with those qualifications and gone out celebrating."

"But not Maggie, right?" A sick burning feeling was twisting in the bottom of Daniel's stomach.

"After what she did to you, buddy, no way." Pete smacked him on the arm. "I wouldn't have hired Maggie if Janice went into labor at the office and had to hold her legs together until her replacement was hired."

"Did you know Maggie's divorced now?" Daniel asked.

"Heard her husband left her for another woman." Pete shook his head and grinned. "Janice always said what goes around, comes around."

Daniel didn't see the humor in the situation. For years he had heard rumors that Maggie's marriage hadn't been made in heaven, and that she was waiting tables to support her child and husband while he finished his education. Maggie had given up her dream of getting a degree because of her husband and child.

Pete wasn't finished yet. "Heard her husband lived off of her while he went and got his master's degree. Landed himself a big-paying job at a top corporation. Next thing you know he's shacking up with a sexy blond corporate player, leaving little old Maggie high and dry."

"He also left his daughter high and dry." Daniel might not have liked what Maggie had done to him all those years ago, but an innocent child shouldn't have to suffer because of the games adults play.

"I'm sure Maggie is socking him with some healthy child-support payments." Pete shook his head sadly. "Poor bastard."

The burning sensation in Daniel's stomach erupted into a full-blown inferno. A man leaves his wife and his daughter for another woman, and he's the "poor bastard"? "Hey, Pete, do me a favor?"

"What's that?"

Daniel dropped the paint-chip cards into the pocket of his coat. "Don't do me any more favors." He walked out of the hardware store without buying the paint or even glancing at Pete. He'd pick up the paint on the way into work tomorrow morning. For now he just needed some fresh air.

Pete hadn't hired Maggie because of him. How many other people in town had done the same thing? Maggie was trying to support not only herself, but her daughter. Maggie had come home to her parents for help. It must have taken a lot of courage to move back to Misty Harbor. Or was it desperation? How financially strapped were Maggie and her daughter? He'd always liked Maggie's parents, but they weren't what he would call comfortably well off.

When he had looked at Maggie this morning, he hadn't felt love or desire. He hadn't felt what he should have felt for a woman he'd professed to love five years before. He had been shocked and surprised, but he wasn't looking for revenge.

Maggie was qualified to do a lot of things besides wait tables, yet it was the only job she probably could get. Gwen hadn't known about the past and had inadvertently hired his ex-fiancée. Maggie was back to waiting tables to support her daughter, and it was all the fault of his well-meaning friends.

Daniel walked to his truck wondering if this was how bankers felt during the Depression when they were evicting widows and orphans from their homes. It never should have come to this.

Chapter Eighteen

Maggie pushed the grocery cart to one side of the aisle and smiled at Katie as she stared in childish delight at the choice of cereals crowding the shelves. "Remember, you can only choose one box."

Katie nodded and continued to scrutinize the brightly colored boxes.

Maggie's money was on her daughter picking the glittery blue box with the polar bear on the front and enough sugar in every bowlful to satisfy even a four-year-old's sweet tooth. Katie looked adorable today in her Winnie the Pooh sneakers and Tigger sweatshirt. Her red hair was pulled back into its usual ponytail, but this morning, Grandmom had done it with a special Tigger hair band. Katie now had a miniature Tigger's head on one side of the ponytail and his tail on the other.

Grandmom and Grandpop were clearly enjoying having Katie staying with them. She couldn't really say they were spoiling her, but they definitely allowed Katie to get her way more often than not. Maggie couldn't fault them; she tended to spoil her own daughter—up to a point. One sugar-filled box of cereal a week was enough.

After working this past week at the restaurant, she wanted to spend some time with her daughter and had volunteered to do the grocery shopping. She hadn't received a paycheck yet, but she knew one was coming at the end of next week. She felt better about Katie's and her own future.

Gwen Fletcher was not only a wonderful boss, she was a very special woman. Maggie didn't know of any other woman who wouldn't have fired her ass once they learned she was the ex-fiancée of the man they loved. Gwen had listened to her story, and instead of condemning her, she had actually thanked her for dumping Daniel. Maggie could see her logic, but it was still strange.

If Gwen had a fault, it would be that she cooked too darn well. Gwen was always in the kitchen whipping up this or sautéeing that. The bad part was, she made everyone eat. Maggie had noticed that her favorite pair of jeans had been a bit harder to button this morning, and it wasn't that time of the month. Working at Catch of the Day would definitely have a down side.

Gwen's other fault was that she seemed to be blind to the way Daniel kept looking at her. Watching Daniel watching Gwen had been a real eye-opener. Daniel's heart was in his eyes every time he looked at Gwen. The man was definitely in love, and it showed.

Five years ago, Daniel had never once looked at her that way.

Maggie's mother always said that everything happens for a reason. She hadn't believed her mother years ago, but maybe she had been right all along. That impulsive encounter with Jeremy in the dorm room had given her Katie. She could easily have passed Katie off as Daniel's child, but eventually the truth would have come out. The guilt and fear alone would have had her confessing before their first anniversary. She would have been married to a man who hated her, instead of just living in the same town with him. Daniel would insist on staying married because he'd once told her he didn't believe in divorce, that married people should work their problems out. Maybe Katie would have gotten a baby brother or sister.

Then Gwen would have moved to town and opened her restaurant.

In hindsight, Maggie was darn thankful that she had found the courage to tell Daniel the truth. She just wished she had found her backbone sooner. She'd known she was going to hurt Daniel, but to hurt him while he was in the hospital was inexcusable. Daniel hadn't deserved that, but she had been running out of time. She'd already been three months pregnant when she told him.

"Mommy, Mommy, I want this one!" Katie came running over clutching the glittery blue box with the polar bear on the front.

"Are you sure?" Maggie glanced at the box and shook her head at the picture of tiny marshmallows shaped like igloos and penguins. It looked about as appealing as eating cotton candy and pixie sticks for breakfast. Last week it had been a monkey on the box with chocolate cereal and yellow marshmallows shaped like bananas. Even her father, who had a sweet tooth the size of Rhode Island, had shuddered at that combination.

Katie nodded her head. "Yes. Grandpop said no chocolate this time."

Maggie smiled. Leave it to her father to manipulate his own granddaughter into supplying his sugar habit. "Okay, but don't let Grandpop eat it all." Her father was leaning toward the heavy side of the scale, and her mother was fretting about every extra pound taking a year off their retirement time together.

Katie dropped the box into the cart. "Grandmom said not to forget the milk."

She playfully tugged her daughter's ponytail. "Okay, short stuff."

Maggie pushed the cart two feet and nearly collided with Daniel as he maneuvered his cart around the corner. "Sorry." She wanted to take her daughter and go hide in shame, but she didn't. Maggie held her ground and looked directly at Daniel. The hatred and anger that had been burning in his eyes that first day at the restaurant had diminished to a cautious curiosity.

"My fault," Daniel said. "I wasn't paying attention." Daniel looked down at her daughter.

She tried to read his expression but couldn't. "Daniel, I would like you to meet my daughter, Katherine Leigh Pierce. Otherwise known as Katie." She looked at her daughter, who was staring at Daniel while hanging on to her coat. "Katie, this is Daniel Creighton. He's an old"—she looked at Daniel and managed a small, hesitant smile—"friend of mine."

Daniel raised an eyebrow but didn't contradict her assessment of their relationship. "Hello, Katie. You look just like your mother."

Katie glanced up at her and grinned. "Mommy's bigger."

Daniel returned Katie's smile. "That she is."

"Do you have a boat?" Katie released her coat and took a step closer to Daniel. "My Uncle Gary has a boat. It's blue and white, and he took me out on it." Katie took another step closer and whispered, "He let me steer, but I'm not supposed to tell Mommy."

Daniel managed to control his smile. "I'm afraid I don't have a boat. My grandfather had a boat just like your Uncle Gary's, but it was red and white."

Katie nodded. "My grandpop has a boat too, but it's broke. He can't take me for a ride yet."

Daniel glanced at Maggie, and she explained, "The engine's being rebuilt." Everyone who lived in a village that depended upon the sea for their livelihood knew that a disabled boat meant no income.

"I'm sure your grandpop will take you out as soon as his boat is fixed." Daniel gave Katie another small smile. "It was nice meeting you, Katie. Have fun shopping with your mommy, and remember to always wear a life vest when you go out on your Uncle Gary and Grandpop's boats, okay?" Daniel's fingertips absently rubbed at the scar on his cheek, as if he were remembering the past and another little kid out on his grandpop's boat.

"Uncle Gary says I always have to wear the vest he bought me." Katie gave Daniel a smile and a wave. "Bye-bye."

Daniel nodded, first to Katie, then to her. "Maggie."

She nodded back and quickly pushed her cart around the corner so Daniel wouldn't see the tears that had suddenly filled her eyes.

* * *

Tess Dunbar parked her car near a stand of trees
and was afraid she was going to make the biggest
fool of herself within the next several minutes. She
stared out of the window at a place she hadn't
visited in thirty-odd years. Sunset Cove hadn't
changed that much over the years. The trees
looked bigger, and the dirt road she had followed
to get to it was in better shape than she remembered. The cove was Misty Harbor's secret, and the
residents guarded it well from the tourists.

Thirty-odd years ago the cove was the "in" place
to go necking with your boyfriend. From some of
the whispers she had picked up when her own
children hadn't known she could hear, the cove
was still the "in" place. Sunset Cove was every
parent's nightmare and every teenager's fantasy.

The last time she had been here, she had been
seventeen and deeply in love, and more scared
than she had ever been in her life. It was the night
before Hunter McCord was due to report to boot
camp and an almost guaranteed trip to Vietnam
and hell. Hunter and she had spent many summer
days swimming in the cove with their friends, and
some heated summer nights necking in his daddy's
truck, steaming up the windows. But they had never
gone "all the way." Hunter had never pressured
her to do anything she wasn't comfortable with,
and back then she had some illusion about wearing
white on her wedding day and having it mean something.

That last night together, with their future looking
so uncertain, the illusion had vanished. They had
made love on an old quilt with the water gently
lapping at the shore and the stars shining down
on them. She had held on to Hunter as tight as
she could and prayed with all her heart, and still
the need of their country had yanked him out
of her arms and into hell. Her prayers had been

answered, but the man who came home hadn't been her Hunter.

Her Hunter was gone, and in his place was the shell of a man who wouldn't see her, wouldn't talk to her. She waited and prayed, but God hadn't seen fit to answer her prayers a second time. Three years after Hunter's return, she'd married another man. Ben Dunbar had been a good man, and a wonderful father. Tess had given him everything that was left of her heart. They'd had a good, solid marriage and three beautiful children.

Ben's death five years earlier had shattered Tess's life a second time. She kept going because the children needed her and it was expected of her. She'd never once thought about what she needed until last week, when Hunter came in from the patio at the restaurant and stared at her. Really looked at her for the first time in thirty years. In his soft, yet hauntingly sad brown eyes, she had seen a glimpse of the old Hunter, her Hunter, and she had run like the silly old woman she was.

Over fifty was a little too old to be having secret dreams about white wedding dresses. All week long Tess had tried to push her thoughts of Hunter back where they belonged, in the past. They wouldn't stay. Her son, Ben's son, Scott was going to be working with the man who had claimed a huge piece of her heart and never given it back. Hunter had accepted a full-time position at the restaurant. His first "real" job. The whole town was talking about how Clarence had an extra spring in his step lately. His boy was finally returning home.

That morning, when Tess stepped into church, she knew her life was at a crossroad. Hunter, for the first time since his return, had attended a service. Every time she glanced in his direction, she had encountered his gaze. She would have to have been blind not to see that Hunter had been paying more attention to her than to the sermon. The rest of the congregation wasn't blind or stupid. She had received more than her share of knowing looks when the service was over.

Tess scanned the shoreline and knew she would find the outline of a man before she had even seen him. Hunter was sitting on an old log, staring out across the water. She wondered for the thousandth time what he saw when he stared out over the water like that. Did he see a distant land? The distant past? Was he reliving his days as a P.O.W.?

With a nervous sigh she wiped her sweaty palms on a tissue and opened the car door. The worst that could happen was that Hunter would ignore her and not talk. Nothing that hadn't happened to her hundreds of times in the past. Today she had a feeling it would be different. This morning Hunter had made the first move by coming to church. His second move had been coming here, to "their" place.

She knew she would never have found the courage to walk up to his front door and knock on it. But here, she didn't have to knock. She could pretend this was just some chance encounter. A twig snapped beneath her foot, but Hunter never even flinched or turned around. He already knew she was there.

She wondered if perhaps she should have changed out of the dress she had worn to church. But what did it matter? The last time she had dressed for Hunter, she had worn bell bottom jeans and a skimpy halter top that had raised her father's blood pressure. She carefully stepped over the log and sat. The flowing blue dress fell over her knees, past her shins, and teased her ankles. Her winter dress coat was a little too heavy, now that the sun was warming up the day nicely. She left it unbuttoned and enjoyed the breeze blowing in off the water.

Hunter never took his gaze off the water.

The silence grew as she studied the swells and dips across the surface of the cove. She remembered how Hunter could swim circles around the other boys and hold his breath underwater for so long that it used to frighten her. As a young boy, before she had even fallen in love with him, Hunter had earned the nickname Tuna Head. Hunter had loved the water. Rumor had it that Hunter hadn't dipped so much as a big toe into it since his return from 'Nam.

Tears filled her eyes. How could a war kill the love of water?

Hunter's voice was low as he quietly asked, "Do you know how many ways there are to torture a man with water?"

Tess quickly glanced at him, but he was still looking out over the water. She could see his hands balled into tight fists as they rested on his knees. With trembling fingers she reached out and covered one hand.

Before she could figure out how to answer him, he continued. "How can something so peaceful and beautiful be so deadly and harsh? The Earth is mostly water, did you know that?"

She could only nod her head. Tears were clogging her throat. She now understood how Hunter's love of water had died. It had been tortured out of him. Her fingers gripped his hand harder. Amazingly, it was Hunter's hand that relaxed. He turned his palm upward and interlaced his fingers with hers.

"I owe this cove a debt of gratitude. It was during all those summers of swimming here that I learned to hold my breath for so long."

Tears slid down Hunter's face, and his jaw

clenched against the memories. One part of her wanted to shout for him to shut up. She would go insane if he told her what they had done to him. It was bad enough that she had seen the results; she didn't need the details. The other part of her heart called her a coward. If Hunter could physically survive what they had done to him, then she could damn well sit there and listen to the words.

She was so thankful that Hunter was finally talking to her, talking about what had happened, that she moved closer so that their shoulders touched. Her fingers tightened around his, but she didn't say a word. She didn't want to break whatever spell had started him talking after all these years.

"It took me years to finally find the courage to sit in a bathtub. Years more to stand under the shower. Getting my face wet was the worst, and washing my hair was a form of torture all in itself. I used to force myself to wash it every day, sometimes twice a day, just to prove to myself I could do it." Hunter gave a poor imitation of a laugh. "That's probably the reason I'm going bald today."

Tess swallowed the lump in her throat. "You have more courage than ten men, Hunter." She felt his fingers tremble around hers. "Never forget that."

"I still can't have the water from the shower hit me in the face." From his voice she could tell he thought he was a coward still for not conquering all his fear.

With her free hand, she wiped at her tears, and tried for some levity. "I still can't throw a live lobster into a pot of boiling water." Hunter used to tease her unmercifully about that when they were younger.

Hunter turned and looked at her for the first time since she'd sat down. Tears had streaked their way down his cheeks and his eyes were red, but there was a tiny spark of life in their depths. A spark that had been missing for so many years. "You're kidding, right?"

"Afraid not." She slowly reached out and caressed his jaw. Whiskers were starting to push their way to the surface after his morning shave. Her fingers trembled as that tiny spark of life flared bigger. "Why now, Hunter? Why are you finally telling me now?"

Hunter's gaze devoured her face and seemed to memorize every line and wrinkle. "Fear of water has ruled my life for so long that I thought nothing would ever top it." The tip of his finger wiped away the tear that was slowly making its way down her cheek. "I discovered a new fear these last couple of weeks."

"What?" Lord, what could be worse than what he had gone through in 'Nam?

"I'm afraid that you'll find another man, another husband, and be out of my reach forever."

Tess felt her heart swell with love and, for the first time in thirty years, hope. She wanted to throw her arms around his neck, plaster her mouth against his, and drag him to the ground. Instead she faced the water, placed her head against his shoulder, and softly said, "Welcome home, Hunter."

Daniel held the cardboard box in his arms as he glanced around the empty room. What had been the nursery was now completely bare. Even the wallpaper was gone, and the plaster walls were painted white. Plain, simple white, like a blank piece of paper ready for someone to draw a picture.

He was praying that Gwen would want to draw that picture with him.

For two days he had been working like a madman to dismantle what it had taken him months to do.

All the furniture had been taken apart, loaded in his truck, and donated to a women's shelter in Bangor. He had washed, dried, and carefully packed up all the baby paraphernalia and placed it beside the furniture. Someone, somewhere, would get some good use out of it all.

His job at the restaurant was complete, and he hadn't seen Gwen in two days. Two of the longest and busiest days of his life. He was sure Gwen felt the same way, but for different reasons. Tonight was Catch of the Day's grand opening. He had reservations for nine o'clock. One of the last reservations of the night. Tonight, if all went according to plan, he was going to be the happiest man in Maine. If not, his dinner was going to consist of a main entree of crow.

He didn't have time to worry about tonight. He still had a full day ahead of him, and the first thing he had to do was make a delivery. A very special delivery.

Ten minutes later, he parked in front of the Franklins' house. It looked the same as it had the last time he had been there, five years ago. Maybe the shade of yellow was brighter, and the bushes bigger, but that was about it. Maggie's parents weren't into change. They were comfortable with things just as they were. Daniel got out of the truck, walked around to the passenger door, and picked up the cardboard box from the seat.

He walked up to the front door, shifted the box, and rang the bell. Connie Franklin, Maggie's mom, answered the door a moment later.

"Daniel? What a surprise." Mrs. Franklin looked more confused and worried than surprised.

"Are Maggie or Katie home?" He gave her what he hoped was a reassuring smile.

"They're out back." Connie opened the door wider. "Come on in."

Daniel stepped into the house and headed for the back door. "I won't take up too much of their time. I know Maggie has to go to work soon."

Connie glanced at her watch. "She has a couple of hours yet. Take your time."

"Thanks." Daniel shifted the box again and opened the back door. Katie's laughter was the first thing that greeted him as he stepped outside. He spotted Maggie and Katie at the far corner of the property. Maggie was pushing her daughter on a swing someone had hung from a giant oak tree. He carefully set the box on the picnic table and made his way over to the pair.

Maggie looked surprised to see him. Katie gave him a grin that was guaranteed to break a few hearts in a few more years. Katie's smile was the exact replica of her mother's. There was no denying it—Maggie Franklin Pierce was a beautiful woman, and he felt absolutely nothing for her.

It was a wonderfully free feeling. For years he had thought he hated her, and that hatred had laid heavy in his heart. Watching and studying Maggie over the last week, he'd come to realize quite a few things, not only about her, but about himself as well. He had never loved Maggie.

By the time he had entered his twenties he had known what he wanted out of life. He wanted to work with his hands, own his own business, and have a family. The business and the work were the easy part. The family end of things took some thought. The first thing he required was a wife. Misty Harbor didn't have an abundance of females to choose from, and he had just broadened his search to other nearby towns when little Margaret Franklin came home from her freshman year at college. All of a sudden the three-year age difference that had been such an obstacle during their high school years didn't seem to matter.

Sparkling green eyes, silky red hair, and a killer smile had him proposing and promising the wedding could wait until after she graduated from college. Maggie had been determined to complete her education and start a career before starting a family. He had been confident that she would be carrying their first child before their first wedding anniversary.

He had been a world-class fool for not realizing the difference in their dreams. He should have heeded the warning signs, and the first major one had been their "love life," or their lack of one. Maggie had been, and still was, a very beautiful and desirable woman, yet their love life had left a lot to be desired. He couldn't say Maggie was frigid, or that he was clumsy or inept whenever they had been intimate. They just hadn't seemed to mesh. They were definitely not two halves of a whole.

He now knew what had been wrong five years earlier. He had been with the wrong woman. Maggie Franklin hadn't been Gwen Fletcher. It was as simple as that.

It had taken Maggie, and her daughter, moving back into town and into his life for him to realize that. All these years he had harbored hatred and anger for a woman he had thought betrayed his love. Maggie had never betrayed his love, because he had never loved her.

He knew what love was now. Love was Gwen.

In some sick and twisted way, he had been the one using Maggie. His dream had been for a family. Someone to come home to every night. Small bundles of joy, childish laughter, and Christmas mornings. Baseball teams, cartoons on Saturday mornings, and ballet lessons.

Daniel looked at Katie sitting on the swing and smiled back. When he had first seen her in the grocery store, he was sure his heart would break at the sight of her. The little girl who was supposed to be his. He had stood there with his heart in his throat and waited for the pain. None had come. Katie Pierce was a beautiful little girl. Just like every other little girl in town. There had been nothing more, and nothing less.

Maggie slowly stopped the swing. "Daniel? What are you doing here?"

He nodded toward the picnic table where he had left the box. "I brought something for Katie."

Katie's eyes grew wider. "Me?"

"You." Daniel helped her off the swing. "Why don't you go see if you like it?"

Katie took off across the yard and scrambled up onto one of the benches. Little fingers lifted a carved elephant from the box. "Mommy, Mommy, come see all the animals!"

Maggie glanced at Daniel and headed for her daughter.

Daniel followed Katie to the table. He reached into the box and picked up the big ark. The boat would be too heavy for Katie to lift, and he didn't want the little girl to hurt herself. "Do you know the story of Noah's ark?"

"Yes," cried Katie, and she dug back into the box for more animals. "Sunday School teached me."

"Taught you," corrected Maggie.

He sat the ark onto the table and showed Katie how to lift the latch so a ramp was lowered on one side of the boat. "The animals can go in here, or up on the deck." The joy lighting Katie's face made all the hours he had spent working on the set worthwhile.

Maggie stepped away from the table but kept her gaze on her daughter, who was now busily playing with the animals.

Daniel moved away with her.

"Why?" Maggie asked in a low voice that sounded suspiciously close to tears.

"I carved them for her years ago." He shrugged but kept his gaze on Katie. "I figured it was about time she got to play with them."

"Does this mean I'm forgiven?"

Daniel looked at the woman standing next to him. From what he had seen, Maggie was a wonderful mother to her little girl. She would probably make a fantastic wife for the right man. He wasn't the right man. He should have realized that seven years ago, before he had asked her to marry him. "There's nothing to forgive you for, Maggie. I was as much at fault for what happened, if not more than you were."

Maggie gave a very unladylike snort. "Come off it, Daniel. I was there, remember?"

"You were young, and you made a mistake. I didn't have that excuse. I was three years older and I stubbornly refused to accept the truth from you. For that I'm sorry."

"Katie's not a mistake." Maggie gave him a crooked smile. "Now her father, that's a different story."

Daniel relaxed for the first time in days. This was a Maggie he could talk to. "I'm sorry it didn't work out between you and him."

"It was kind of doomed from the beginning, but I had to keep trying for Katie's sake."

The rumors he had picked up about Maggie's rough marriage must have been correct. Maggie hadn't deserved that, and neither had Katie. "I came here for another reason besides to give Katie the animals."

"What's that?"

"I wanted to thank you."

"For what?"

"For doing the right thing and telling me the truth five years ago."

Maggie's reaction wasn't what he had expected. She laughed out loud. A joyful, carefree sound that filled the backyard. Katie looked at them both, flashed a smile, and then went right back to putting the bears inside the belly of the ark. A seagull swooped low and gave an answering cry.

"What's so funny?" He didn't see any humor in his apology.

"That's the second thank-you I've gotten in the past week for causing the biggest scandal this town has ever seen." Maggie shook her head and chuckled.

He frowned. "Who else thanked you?"

Maggie grinned. "My boss."

Gwen glanced over the counter at Hunter and grinned. She hadn't been able to stop smiling all night. The grand opening of Catch of the Day was a bigger success than she had ever dreamed. Reservations had come pouring in all week. They'd had to stop taking them for the opening night, and next week was already nearly full.

She knew Hunter had been worried all week about tonight. He hadn't been worried about whether people would show up; he already knew they were completely booked. Hunter had been anxious to see if he would be able to keep up with the orders. Tonight he had learned that his concerns had been groundless. Hunter was doing a masterful job, all the while smiling and humming. Hunter McCord was a born chef.

Maggie hurried into the kitchen, gave Hunter another order, and started to load up a tray with plates ready to be served. "When you get a moment, Gwen," Maggie said as she lifted the heavy tray as if it weighed next to nothing, "table five wants to pay their compliments to the chef." Maggie gave her a look that clearly said she knew something Gwen didn't. It was the same look Maggie had been giving her all night long, and it was driving Gwen nuts.

Gwen glanced around the kitchen and sighed. For the past couple of hours she had been running between the kitchen and the dining room, either checking on things or graciously receiving compliments. The two high-school students she had hired as busboys were feeding Scott bin after bin of dirty dishes. Scott Dunbar looked a bit overwhelmed at the amount of dishes piling up, but he was handling it like a pro. Karen, a young housewife she had hired as a prep cook for the weekends, was busy chopping onions.

It was getting close to nine o'clock. The last reservations for the evening would be arriving soon. "Hunter, would you like to go out there and speak to table five?"

Hunter looked at her as if she had lost her mind. "No way. You hired me to work in the kitchen, and that's exactly where I intend to stay."

She had to chuckle. "Fine, I'll go." She glanced at the two orders waiting to be filled. "You'll be okay for a moment?"

"We'll be fine," Hunter said as he nodded toward the swinging doors. "Go."

Gwen went, while the going was good. In a couple of minutes the last of the reservations would be arriving, and they would be swamped with orders. She stepped into the dining room and allowed the sense of accomplishment to wash over her. The restaurant was perfect, just the way she had envisioned it on the day she had bought it. Nearly every table was occupied. One of the busboys was clearing off a table while the other was busy placing a clean tablecloth on another table. Maggie and the other waitress Gwen had hired looked professional in their white blouses and black skirts as they bustled around the dining room.

The hum of conversations and low music being piped in over the sound system filled the air. Along with delicious, mouthwatering aromas. Over the past several days, a local florist had made several stops at the restaurant. It seemed everyone had had the idea of sending her plants for the opening. A huge weeping fig tree, from Millicent, took up one corner. Three palms had arrived from her family. Mary Creighton had sent her two trailing plants for the bay windows overlooking the harbor. A five-foot-tall hibiscus, in full bloom, had arrived yesterday. The card had read, *Your dream looks perfect.* There hadn't been a signature, but she had known it came from Daniel. The splash of green livened up the room.

Daniel hadn't shown up yet, but she had a feeling he would. She had glanced at the reservation book earlier and had been totally confused by the last four reservations. All four were under the name Creighton. Two of the reservations were for parties of four, one was for a party of two, and one was for a single person. She had no idea which Creighton reservation was Daniel's, but she prayed one of them was. She wanted Daniel here tonight.

She also wanted her family here. Two days ago she had called home and spoken to her mother. Gwen knew she had left it until it was too late for everyone to change their schedules to come up to Maine for the opening, but she wanted to try anyway. When she had broached the subject of the date of the opening to her mother, she had changed the subject. Both Sydney and Jocelyn hadn't returned her phone calls.

Feeling a bit dejected, Gwen had called Millicent,

the woman responsible for her buying the restaurant in the first place, to invite her to the opening as her guest. Millicent had informed her that she and her "date" already had reservations.

Gwen glanced around the dining room as she made her way to table five. Millicent still hadn't shown, but Erik and Gunnar Olsen, the Norwegian twins, had. They were both wearing suits and killer smiles, and were sitting at table five. "Erik"—she nodded at the man with the ponytail first—"Gunnar."

"You remembered." Erik flashed her a dazzling smile.

"How could I forget?" Gwen looked at the empty soup bowls in front of each man and frowned. "I thought you guys wanted to pay me a compliment on the food. You haven't even got your main course yet."

"The crab soup was delicious, Gwen," Erik said.

"The vegetable soup was better," Gunnar added absently. Gunnar's gaze was following Maggie's every move as she waited on another table.

Gwen smiled. Love was definitely in the air in Misty Harbor. "You guys let me know how you like the main course, once you've tasted it."

Gwen watched as Mary and Thomas Creighton entered the restaurant and were shown to their table. The mystery of the booking for two Creightons had been solved. She left the Olsens and stopped at Daniel's parents' table. "I'm glad you two could make it."

Mary beamed. "Wouldn't miss it for the world."

Gwen wasn't sure, but Mary seemed a bit too happy just to be going out to dinner. Thomas even looked proud about something before glancing at the door. "Look who's here!"

Gwen turned and watched as Jonah, Clarence, Millicent, and Anna, from the antique shop, walked into the restaurant. By the way Jonah was cupping Millicent's elbow, she gathered that the cagey old Creighton was her mystery date. The riddle of one of the four-person bookings under the Creighton name was now solved. "Would you two excuse me, please?"

"Go." Mary waved her away with a smile. "I want to look over the menu. If you cook as well as Daniel swears you do, I might need to try everything."

Gwen chuckled as she walked over to the table where the four new arrivals were being seated. "So, what took you guys so long? I was beginning to worry that my food critics wouldn't show up for the big night."

"Never fear, Gwennie, my love," Jonah said as he gallantly placed a kiss on the back of her hand. "I wouldn't have missed tonight for all the tea in China."

"More like the beer in Milwaukee," Clarence added with a laugh.

Millicent looked over at the front door. "Look who else is here!"

Gwen turned toward the door and felt her breath lodge in her throat. Daniel stood there wearing an incredible gray suit instead of his usual jeans and flannel shirt. He looked handsome as sin and was staring right back at her.

The hostess she had hired greeted Daniel and showed him to a table. Daniel kept his gaze on her as he took his seat alone at the table. The mystery of the one-person reservation under the Creighton name was solved. She didn't know of any other Creightons. Either Daniel had a relative she hadn't known about, or whoever had written the reservations had made a mistake. It didn't matter. The one person she wanted there, besides her family, had arrived.

Now if only she could figure out what to say to him!

The front door opened again, and the cold spring air ushered in four more people.

Gwen stood there in shock as her mother, father, Jocelyn, and Sydney entered her restaurant.

Chapter Nineteen

Gwen rushed across the room and hugged her mom. "Mom, what are you guys doing here?" Before her mother could answer, Gwen released her and threw her arms around her father. "Dad?"

Stan Fletcher chuckled and gave Gwen a good squeeze. "Just seemed right that we should see our daughter's success."

She gave her sister Sydney a hug next. "Syd, you came?"

"Of course I came." Sydney hugged her back and whispered, "I like your Daniel."

Gwen glanced over at Daniel. He was sitting there taking in the entire scene with a smile. She was smart enough to see a conspiracy when it was staring right back at her. Somehow Daniel had been the one responsible for getting her family to Maine.

Jocelyn hugged her next. "Oh my God, it's true!"

Gwen forced her gaze away from Daniel and back

to her sister. "What's true?" What in the world was Joc blabbering about?

"Vikings!" Joc's voice rose to a squeak. "Gorgeous Vikings who wear suits."

Gwen glanced over her shoulder to where Erik and Gunnar were sitting. Sure enough, the two Norwegian hunks were eyeing her sisters with a great deal of interest. She chuckled. "I would tell you not to worry, they're harmless, but I'm not too sure about that."

She smiled at her family. "Come on, let's get you out of the doorway." She glanced over to the table the hostess had just gotten ready. Everything looked perfect, and it was large enough to seat six. "I'm gathering you're the Creighton reservation for four."

"Yes. Daniel was nice enough to take care of that for us." Gloria Fletcher allowed her husband to seat her.

"Where are you guys staying?" Gwen tried to remember what her house looked like, and if she had done any laundry lately. They would need towels and sheets. "When did you get here? Did you drive up?" She lowered herself into the extra chair. Hunter could manage for another minute or two.

"We all flew into Bangor this afternoon and rented a car," her father said. "Daniel was nice enough to fax me the directions from the airport to your cottage, and then he met us there with a key a couple of hours ago. We're all settled in nicely for the night."

She glanced over to Daniel and silently mouthed the words *thank you*. Daniel picked up his water glass and toasted her while mouthing *you're welcome*. She could feel a suspicious moisture filling her eyes and blinked rapidly. He had done this for her. Daniel still cared enough about her to see that her family saw the opening of her dream. Lord, could she possibly love that man any more?

"I already claimed the guest room," Sydney said.

"I lost the coin toss and ended up with the couch," Jocelyn groused.

"You have a very nice house, Gwen." Her mother glanced around the restaurant with pride. "But *this* is truly wonderful."

Gwen felt a flush sweep up her cheeks. "Thank you, but wait until you taste the food." Hunter must be going nuts by now. "I have to get back to the kitchen."

"Can't you eat with us?" her father asked.

"Since you're the last reservation, I think I can manage." Gwen stood up. "Order anything you want; it's on the house."

Gwen slowly made her way over to Daniel's table. She had no idea what to say to him. She hadn't seen him at all in the last couple of days, and now he'd gone and done something like this. What in the world was she supposed to make of it all? She stood next to his table and eyed his tie. When he had first walked into the restaurant she had thought it was just a deep red design. Now she could see that the entire tie was a picture of lobsters, piled on top of lobsters. The corner of her mouth kicked up into a smile. "Nice tie."

"Thank you." There wasn't an answering smile in Daniel's gaze. There was desire.

She shifted her weight. "You clean up pretty good." Daniel was more than "pretty good," he was downright delicious-looking in that suit. Then again, Daniel was appetizing in just about anything he wore, and totally mouthwatering in nothing at all.

"You look sexy as hell in the chef's smock."

A blush swept up her cheeks at the look of heat that had leaped into Daniel's eyes. She didn't want to think about how her family had just overrun her house and taken every available sleeping spot. Where exactly did her parents expect her to sleep? At Daniel's? "Would you like to join my family and me for dinner?"

"I thought you might like some time alone with them."

She shook her head. "I would like you to join us." She wanted Daniel to get to know her family. They were very important to her.

"Then I will."

Twenty-five minutes later, Gwen joined her family and Daniel just as Maggie brought out the tray loaded with their dinner. "There. Hunter and Karen should be able to handle the kitchen now." The appetizers she had sent out earlier were long gone. Her father and both of her sisters had ordered the lobster. Daniel and her mother had ordered the haddock, and she had picked a veal chop with a curry cream sauce. Jonah had been right the first day she had met him: Most of the town's residents were sick of lobster.

Everyone started to eat, and Daniel chuckled as Jocelyn sighed in ecstasy. "Lord, Gwen, move back home. I miss your cooking."

She grinned. "Glad to know I'm missed for something."

Sydney popped a piece of lobster into her mouth and moaned. "You should have seen Richard's face last week when the caterers handed him the bill for the small dinner party he insisted on throwing." Sydney dug back into her lobster with relish. "After he wrote out the check he wanted to know why I couldn't cook like my sister." Sydney dipped a piece of meat into the small bowl of melted butter. "Like I could do something this fantastic."

"Amen to that one," Jocelyn added.

"Gwen inherited her grandmother's talent in

the kitchen, Daniel." Gloria Fletcher beamed at her middle daughter. "She surely didn't get it from me. I have trouble scrambling eggs and frying bacon at the same time."

Stan looked like he wanted to agree with that statement but wisely kept his mouth closed.

"I once got a boyfriend on Gwen's cooking." Jocelyn turned to Daniel. "As soon as he figured out it wasn't my cooking he ate every Friday night, he dumped me and then had the nerve to ask for my sister's phone number."

"Which I hope you didn't give him," Daniel said.

Gwen shivered at the hint of possessiveness in Daniel's voice. "We never share men, Daniel. It was one of our golden rules that kept peace in the house as we grew up."

Jocelyn glanced across the restaurant to where Erik and Gunnar were still enjoying their dessert. "Please tell me you haven't gone through the Viking population yet."

Gwen chuckled and Daniel scowled. Everyone else at the table turned to look across the restaurant. Erik's wicked gaze seemed to be settled on Sydney, and Gunnar was still tracking Maggie's every move. "Nope. They're free and clear, as far as I know." She had to wonder if Maggie was aware of the interest she was stirring at table number five.

Her father huffed and went back to his lobster. Sydney appeared flustered by Erik's gaze. Her mother gently laid down her fork and stared at her middle daughter. "Now that you have fed us, there's something important that needs to be said."

Gwen shifted nervously. She didn't like the steely look that had come into her mother's eyes. It was the same look she'd had when she discovered her favorite vase had been broken because her daughters had been playing dodge ball in the living room. That look spoke of disapproval.

"I want you to know, Gwen, how upset we all were when you didn't invite us to the opening. When Daniel called, we jumped at the chance to be here." Gloria softened her reprimand with a small smile. "Do you want to tell us why you felt you shouldn't invite us?"

"This wasn't the same as asking you up to Philadelphia to the restaurant I was working in, Mom. A trip to Maine requires airfare, or a fifteen-hour drive up ninety-five."

"Catch of the Day isn't some restaurant you're working in, it's *yours*. This has been your dream for years, Gwen. Isn't it important enough to share with your family?"

Gwen could feel tears starting to sting. "To me it's important enough to share, but you all have such busy and important lives; I didn't want to make you feel uncomfortable by having to refuse the invitation."

Daniel reached over and gently took her hand. She knew he could feel her trembling with emotion.

Her father pushed his plate away from him and stared at her. "I believe I told you once before, but obviously I wasn't clear enough. Listen carefully, Gwen. Nothing, and we do mean nothing, is more important to us than our daughters and their happiness. We are very proud of you, Gwen, and everything you have accomplished here."

"I'm seconding what your father said, dear." Gloria Fletcher gave her a winning smile. "I'm proud of all my daughters."

"Sydney's a doctor and Jocelyn's a lawyer, Mom."

"So?" Sydney said.

"So?" Jocelyn echoed.

"It's not the same thing. I wouldn't know the

difference between an ear infection and a hang-nail." She looked at Jocelyn. "The only briefs I know are the kind men wear."

Her sisters glanced at Daniel and chuckled. "Well, there are briefs, and then there are *briefs*," Jocelyn said.

"Your parents are at the table, young lady." Stan looked at Daniel for some help. "Do you have any idea what it was like living in a house with four females? The things they discussed at the dinner table used to turn my hair gray. I learned more about PMS, tampons, makeup, and push-up bras than any man has the right to know."

Daniel tried to cover his laughter with a cough. It failed miserably. "You have my sympathy, sir."

Stan nodded. "Finally some understanding and respect. You girls should take some notes."

Jocelyn stuck her tongue out at Daniel. "Suck-up."

Gwen relaxed. This was the family she knew and loved. They were teasing Daniel because they were accepting him into their close family circle. "Okay, message received. I'm sorry for not inviting you, but I'm very thankful that Daniel had the foresight to." She squeezed his hand. "You are all officially invited back anytime you want. Maine's a great vacation state."

"I already booked a week in July in Gwen's guest bedroom," Jocelyn announced. "I'm trying to make it two, but my boss hasn't given me his approval yet."

Sydney rooted through her purse and pulled out a leather-bound planner. "I'm not sure if Richard could make it, but I know I would love to come for a visit, once the weather warms up." Sydney started flipping pages and muttering to herself.

"Stan, what about a week in August?" asked her mother as she started to flip through her planner.

Stan pulled an electronic planner out of his suit jacket pocket. "What about the second week?"

"That doesn't look good," Gloria sighed as she started to chew on the cap of her pen. "What about the first week?"

Daniel turned to Gwen as her family consulted their planners and one of the busboys started to clear off the table. "It looks like you're going to be getting a lot of company this summer."

She smiled. "I don't mind." She was feeling so much better about a lot of things. Her family really did support her career. Glancing around her restaurant, she felt damn good about it too. Daniel was sitting next to her, holding her hand and acting like the past week and a half had never happened.

Today was one of the best days of her life. It was a night on which anything could happen. She leaned toward Daniel, gently brushed her lips over his, and whispered the words she had been dying to say. "I love you."

Daniel raised one brow and smiled. "Hold that thought."

Suddenly, the lights in the restaurant flickered on and off. "What the . . ."

Millicent stood up and loudly rapped her spoon against an empty glass. "May I have everyone's attention?" The restaurant quieted down. "Now for the fun part of the evening."

Gwen glanced around the dining room and for the first time noticed that the only people left were those she considered acquaintances or friends.

Through the swinging doors came Hunter, carrying a tray of glasses, all filled with what appeared to be champagne. Tess Dunbar followed Hunter into the room. She was carrying a huge cake on which someone who was extremely talented had drawn in icing an exact duplicate of the sign hanging out front. Maggie carried out a stack of plates and forks and Karen, the prep cook, brought a bucket filled with ice and three more champagne bottles.

Hunter started passing around the filled glasses. Gwen numbly took one in her hand. This was definitely a conspiracy. No one appeared shocked or surprised by this carefully planned spontaneous celebration. She had been had!

"I would like to propose a toast." Millicent raised her voice and her glass. "To Misty Harbor's newest resident, Gwendolyn Fletcher, and her restaurant. May one find happiness and the other success!"

"Here, here," was shouted by someone. The rest of the dining room seconded the toast and drank.

She stood up and raised her own glass. "Thank you all very much. You have all made me feel extremely welcome, and if tonight was any indication, I do believe Catch of the Day is already a success."

Champagne corks popped as Hunter and Jonah opened the other bottles. With Maggie's help, everyone's glass was topped off.

Daniel rose to stand beside Gwen. He took her glass and placed it on the table. "Now it's my turn."

The dining room got so quiet, Gwen could actually hear her own heart pounding. What was Daniel up to now? Gwen felt her heart skip a beat as Daniel got on bended knee and gently took her hand. She forgot to breath.

Daniel cleared his throat twice, looked directly into her eyes, and asked, "Gwendolyn Augusta Fletcher, would you do me the honor of becoming my wife?"

Gwen nodded as tears of happiness overflowed her eyes and rolled down her cheeks. Her answer was a tear-choked, but loud, "Yes."

In one fluid motion, Daniel stood up and swept her into his arms. His mouth was tender as he brushed her mouth with a kiss and whispered, "I love you."

Gwen heard her sisters sigh in dramatic unison, and the wild cheers that erupted in the dining room. Gwen cupped both of Daniel's cheeks and pulled his mouth back down to hers. She wanted a real kiss from Daniel.

The cheers in the dining room grew louder, and it was Daniel who had the sense to break the kiss before she embarrassed herself by ripping off his suit. When she got her breath back, she asked, "How did you know my middle name?"

"Your father told me, when I asked him if I could have his permission to marry you." Daniel gave her another quick hug and then sent her into her father's arms. Gloria Fletcher was wiping away tears, and Stan looked as if he was starting to get a little misty around the edges.

"You asked my father permission to marry me?" Gwen's glance shot between Daniel and her father.

"I told him if you said yes, then it was fine by me." Stan Fletcher kissed Gwen's cheek. "You girls might have driven me crazy for years, but one thing I do know is that you all know your own minds. If you love Daniel, you love him, and nothing I would have said would change your mind."

Gwen kissed her father's cheek. "Thank you, Dad."

"What about your mother? Don't I get a hug?" Gloria held her arms open for Gwen.

Daniel breathed a sigh of relief and grinned. Gwen had said yes. He had risked making the biggest fool of himself by proposing to Gwen in front of both their families and their friends. Seeing the joy and love shining in Gwen's eyes had made the risk worth it.

Daniel hugged his mother as she joined the group. He felt his father's hand land on his shoulder and smiled. "Seems you two will be getting a daughter-in-law."

Mary Creighton was using one of Gwen's new cloth napkins to wipe her tears. "We love her already." His mother hugged Gwen. "Just think, Thomas, with Gwen in the family, I won't have to worry about fixing all those holiday meals."

Everyone laughed as more people came up to the group and congratulated everyone.

Someone turned up the music to a nice slow song. Erik and Gunnar moved tables out of the center of the dining room. Daniel grabbed Gwen's hand and hauled her into the center of the clearing and into his arms. "I haven't even danced with you yet."

Gwen snuggled deeper into his arms and swayed to the beat. "There are a lot of things we haven't done together." Gwen's fingers climbed the lapel of his suit jacket and teased the side of his neck. "We've got the rest of our lives to do all kinds of things."

Daniel felt the heat of desire pool in his gut. Gwen's voice was low and seductive. He could think of about a thousand different things he would like to do with Gwen right at that moment. None were appropriate to do in front of her family or his. "Did I mention that I love you?"

"Yes, as a matter of fact you did." Gwen's lips teased his earlobe. "I can't believe you did all this."

"I didn't do it all." His fingers tightened on her nicely rounded hip. "I had help. Lots of help." He brushed his lips against her hair. "Millicent handled the cake and champagne. Hunter and Maggie handled the reservations, to make sure we were the last ones eating."

"How long has all this planning been going on?" Gwen playfully bit his ear, causing another flare of heat to spike through his body.

"The last week or so." Daniel turned her toward his grandfather, who was pounding Clarence on the back.

Jonah's voice could be heard throughout the entire room. "See, I told you everything would work out. I knew they were perfect for each other the first time I saw them together." Jonah reached for Maggie's hand and pulled her onto the makeshift dance floor. "Come on, lass, let's show these deadheads how it's done."

"Deadheads?" Daniel's father looked at Jonah as he dragged his own wife out onto the floor. "We'll show you how to dance, Dad."

Daniel chuckled and pulled Gwen closer as the dance floor suddenly became quite crowded. Gwen's parents joined in, and Clarence hauled a bewildered Jocelyn out onto the floor. "Your sisters are in for a surprise. I hope to hell you warned them about being a bit outnumbered by our male population."

"I warned them both. Jocelyn can handle herself, and Sydney could use the shake-up." Gwen glanced at her sisters.

Daniel followed her gaze. Millicent had Sydney backed into a corner, probably telling her about old Doc Jeffreys, and how the poor man wanted to retire, but there wasn't a doctor around to take over his practice. "Millicent appears to be trying to recruit Sydney as the town's doctor."

Gwen chuckled into Daniel's tie as Bob Newman cut in on Clarence and stole Jocelyn right out of the older man's arms. Jocelyn looked a bit dazed as Bob pulled out a five-by-seven color photograph of his tuna boat and showed it to her.

The music went into another slow number, and Hunter pulled a blushing Tess out onto the dance floor and into his arms. Daniel looked over at Clarence, who had tears streaming down his cheeks as he watched his son dance with his childhood sweetheart.

Scott Dunbar was in the far corner, keeping an eye on his mother and Hunter.

Abraham Martin headed for Sydney, but Erik beat him to the woman by a step. Daniel chuckled as Erik tugged a reluctant-looking Sydney out onto the dance floor and into his arms. Erik looked like he'd rather throw Sydney over his shoulder and disappear out the front door, instead of dancing with her. Daniel didn't blame the man. Sydney resembled Gwen, and he had known that primitive feeling a time or two over the past several weeks.

Gwen stopped dancing as soon as Jonah and Maggie came dancing by. With a smile, she tapped Maggie on the shoulder. "Excuse me, may I cut in and get a dance out of my soon-to-be grand-father-in-law?"

Jonah laughed with delight, released Maggie, and pulled Gwen into his arms.

Daniel looked at Maggie and smiled. "Would you care for this dance, Ms. Pierce?"

Maggie bowed graciously. "I would love to."

Daniel swept Maggie into his arms but didn't pull her close, as he had done with Gwen. He knew every gaze in the place was following them, and that, he expected, was the reason Gwen had switched partners. It was time he showed this town that all was forgiven and the past was definitely in the past. Maggie had paid enough for past mistakes. Too much, in his opinion, but he couldn't change the past, only the future.

"Katie loves the ark set, Daniel. Thank you."

"I'm glad someone is enjoying it." Daniel swept her around the floor one more time.

"Can I ask you a question?"

"What?" He smiled over Maggie's head at Gwen, who was wiggling her fingers at him.

"Who's the guy with the long blond hair who keeps staring at me?" Maggie smiled at Daniel's tie. "He's standing by himself on the far side of the room."

Daniel glanced over and encountered Gunnar's stare. "You haven't met Gunnar?" It seemed strange that Maggie didn't know the Olsen twins, but she had left town nearly five years earlier. Erik and Gunnar had arrived about three years ago, looking for their grandfather. Daniel kept a firm grip on a suddenly squirming Maggie as he danced them over to Gunnar.

"Gunnar Olsen, I would like you to meet Maggie Pierce."

Maggie's face was beet red as she glared at Daniel. "Maggie Pierce, I would like you to meet Gunnar Olsen."

Gunnar smiled and Maggie went speechless. Daniel shook his head.

"Excuse me, Gunnar and Maggie. I need to steal my fiancé for a moment," Gwen said as she wrapped her arm around Daniel's waist.

Gunnar nodded, but Maggie never blinked.

Gwen chuckled as she dragged Daniel toward the stairs that led to the upstairs office. "I need to see you in private for a moment."

Daniel pulled her closer and whispered, "If you get me somewhere private, I can guarantee that it's going to be longer than a moment." He loved the way Gwen's blush swept up her cheeks.

Anna stopped them before they made it halfway across the room. "Daniel! Gwen! Have I got a wedding present for you."

Gwen choked on her laughter, and he envisioned a Japanese piece of art they would have to hide from their children.

He looked at his distant relative and teased her

right back. "Who says you'll be invited to the wedding?"

Anna's cackling followed them across the room.

They passed his and Gwen's parents. "Hey, Mom and Dad."

"Yes?" his father and Gwen's responded in unison.

Daniel grinned. "Get out your planners and start comparing notes. The wedding's going to be sometime this summer, and the sooner the better." He heard both of their mothers' cries of surprise but kept pulling Gwen toward the stairs. His mother said something about a June wedding. Gwen's mother said that August looked better.

Daniel and Gwen had to go around Millicent and Jocelyn, who were blocking the bottom of the steps. He picked up a portion of their conversation and chuckled. Millicent was on a recruiting mission to get the town a lawyer. He tugged Gwen up the stairs, and then cursed when he realized there wasn't a door on the office. "This isn't private enough for what I want to do to you, love."

Gwen smiled and teased his lower lip with her teeth. "I just had this overwhelming urge to taste you."

"Taste me?" His brow rose with hope and despair. He had hours yet to get through before he had Gwen alone and naked in his bed. He calmed himself with the knowledge that they would have the rest of their lives together.

"Yes." Gwen's tongue traced his lower lip. "After all, you are my catch of the day."

Discover the Magic of
Romance With

Kat Martin

__The Secret
0-8217-6798-4 $6.99US/$8.99CAN

Kat Rollins moved to Montana looking to change her life, not find
another man like Chance McLain, with a sexy smile and empty
heart. Chance can't ignore the desire he feels for her—or the suspi-
cion that somebody wants her to leave Lost Peak . . .

__Dream
0-8217-6568-X $6.99US/$8.99CAN

Genny Austin is convinced that her nightmares are visions of another
life she lived long ago. Jack Brennan is having nightmares, too, but
his are real. In the shadows of dreams lurks a terrible truth, and only
by unlocking the past will Genny be free to love at last . . .

__Silent Rose
0-8217-6281-8 $6.99US/$8.50CAN

When best-selling author Devon James checks into a bed-and-breakfast
in Connecticut, she only hopes to put the spark back into her relationship with her fiancé. But what she experiences at the Stafford Inn
changes her life forever . . .

Call toll free **1-888-345-BOOK** to order by phone or use this
coupon to order by mail.

Name_____

Address_____

City _____ State_____ Zip_____

Please send me the books I have checked above.

I am enclosing $_____
Plus postage and handling* $_____
Sales tax (in New York and Tennessee only) $_____
Total amount enclosed $_____

*Add $2.50 for the first book and $.50 for each additional book.

Send check or money order (no cash or CODs) to: **Kensington Publishing
Corp., Dept. C.O., 850 Third Avenue, New York, NY 10022**

Prices and numbers subject to change without notice. All orders subject
to availability. Visit our website at **www.kensingtonbooks.com**.

Contemporary Romance by
Kasey Michaels

__Can't Take My Eyes Off of You
  0-8217-6522-1   **$6.50**US/**$8.50**CAN

East Wapaneken? Shelby Taite has never heard of it. Neither has
the rest of Philadelphia's Main Line society. Which is precisely
why the town is so appealing. No one would ever think to look
for Shelby here. Nobody but Quinn Delaney . . .

__Too Good To Be True
  0-8217-6774-7   **$6.50**US/**$8.50**CAN

To know Grady Sullivan is to love him . . . unless you're Annie
Kendall. After all, Annie is here at Peevers Manor trying to prove
she's the long-lost illegitimate great-granddaughter of a toilet paper
tycoon. How's a girl supposed to focus on charming her way into
an old man's will with Grady breathing down her neck . . .

Call toll free **1-888-345-BOOK** to order by phone or use this
coupon to order by mail.

Name_____

Address _____

City_____ State _____ Zip _____

Please send me the books I have checked above.

I am enclosing $_____

Plus postage and handling* $_____

Sales tax (in New York and Tennessee only) $_____

Total amount enclosed $_____

*Add $2.50 for the first book and $.50 for each additional book.

Send check or money order (no cash or CODs) to: **Kensington Publishing,
Dept. C.O., 850 Third Avenue, New York, NY 10022**

Prices and numbers subject to change without notice.

All orders subject to availability.

Visit our website at **www.kensingtonbooks.com**.

DO YOU HAVE THE HOHL COLLECTION?